Gang Girl

Gang Girl

DAVID WHITTET

Published 2021
by CP Books

ISBN 978-0-473-57301-0 (softcover)
ISBN 978-0-9951499-4-6 (ePub)
ISBN 978-0-9951499-5-3 (Kindle)

Printed and distributed by The Copy Press, 141 Pascoe Street, Nelson, New Zealand.
www.copypress.co.nz

Original Cover Art by Renata Curtis, 'Toi by Ren'.

Disclaimer

For Siriporn, Mark and Rebecca

Part One

Born of the Gang

Chapter One

Matara Marae, East Cape, New Zealand, 1974.

The sharpened blade of the chisel glistened in the early morning sun. Laid out beside it, the ceremonial mallet and the decorative glass jars filled with ink. Aroha watched the women arrange the brutal weapons on the flax-covered table. She heard them joke about 'instruments of torture'. How could they laugh at something so horrid?

The boys stood in line on the dais in front of the marae, their bodies shaking. Aroha shielded her eyes. She'd witnessed the savage ritual many times before. It hurt as much today as it had the first time her father, Tautaru, made her sit through the ordeal.

'Take your hands away from your eyes,' Tautaru said. 'You're the Gang president's daughter. You're ten years old. Act your age. Blood and ink! They are sacred to this Gang.'

Aroha peeked through her fingers. She groaned as the elders removed the boys' shirts and laid their half-naked bodies on an ornately woven rug. Chase, the heavily inked tattooist, chanted a karakia, his chisel hovering over each of the boys' foreheads in turn. Aroha smelt the boys' fear. Laid bare on their backs, they were utterly defenceless. She glanced at the crowd. Heads remained bowed until Chase finished singing, then everyone chorused a half-hearted 'Amen'.

The moment she dreaded had arrived. Aroha gripped her mother Ngaio's hand, waiting for the first gash. Chase was a bully like her father. Aroha saw it in his eyes as he teased the boys with the blade. She dug her fingernails into her mother's wrists when the mallet stuck the albatross bone. Another life stolen by the Gang. The boys were never the same afterwards.

Why? Aroha looked down at her feet. How could everyone just sit there and let it happen? She covered her ears, desperate to blot out the relentless beat of the hammer and the shrieks from the boys. Her father nudged her. Raising her head, the sight of gushing blood tore her apart as violently as the blade gouged the boys' flesh and the dye stained their skin.

Aroha waved her arms at the tattooist then turned to her mother. 'Make him stop. He's going to kill that boy!'

'You know I can't. Everyone's looking at us.' Ngaio pressed a finger to her lips. 'Listen, all boys have to go through it when they come of age. You know the rules. It shows their loyalty to the Gang. They don't mind the pain.'

Aroha spotted her mother blink back a tear of her own. 'Of course they do. Look at their faces!'

'Oh, Aroha! My darling! You take everything to heart.' Ngaio put her arm around her daughter. 'It's their chance to show everyone how brave they are and prove they're men. They're proud of their tā moko.'

Another cry forced Aroha's eyes back to the chiselling. Two minions held her friend Jonno down. He was such a nice lad—she'd had a childhood crush on him once. She saw the terror in his eyes—he didn't deserve this. If only she could help. Instead, she endured the crowd's jeering as the chisel struck his head and blood streamed over his face, soiling the ceremonial rug.

Aroha grabbed her mother's arm. 'Why is he so rough with Jonno? He's bleeding to death!'

'Try not to upset yourself.' Ngaio dried her daughter's eyes with a dirty old handkerchief. 'I told you, it's just a Gang tradition. You'll understand one day. When you're older.'

Aroha scowled at her mother. 'Then I hope I never grow up!'

The elders wiped the blood from Jonno's face. Aroha shied away as Chase continued carving, the grooves revealing a taiaha, a Māori spear. Such a brutal weapon branded on this gentle boy's skin. It was all wrong.

                    David Whittet

She began scratching her arms with her fingernails, mimicking the action of the chisel. As blood flowed from Jonno's forehead, blood trickled from Aroha's forearm. She overheard some gangsters scoffing behind her. 'Jonno's old man must be right out of favour with Tautaru. Your kids cop it when you upset the boss.'

Jonno lay in a pool of blood. Tautaru grinned and signalled to the boy's parents to come and carry him off the dais. Aroha hid her face. How dare her father treat her friend like that?

Tautaru thumped Chase on the back. 'No mercy on the next one either, bro. Ollie's a wimp. Just like his father. Give him hell!'

'No, Dad! Please!' Aroha sprang to her feet. 'Ollie's got a weak heart!'

'Shut it, Aroha!' Tautaru pushed her back down onto her chair. 'Gang traditions are tapu. Learn some respect!'

More blood surged. More ink deposited. Small black pigments at first, shining through the congealed blood, until the Gang's mark appeared on each of the boys' faces. Aroha hated it. The words 'Māhiti Gang' branded in bold letters across their foreheads. So ugly. Their smooth cheeks dug up and blackened. She didn't know what all the curved lines meant. Only that they were mighty scary.

Aroha had spent many sleepless nights over the past couple of weeks trying to work out how she could help the boys. Her dad was a cruel man. He'd never stop hurting those kids. Her mother wouldn't do anything about it either. That was obvious. Aroha had to think of something herself. But what?

It was after midnight when the answer came to her.

Kawakawa leaves! Aroha sat bolt upright in her bed. *Of course!*

Her Aunt Maia swore they'd heal anything. Ngaio always went on about Aunt Maia being as good as any doctor. Maybe she was. When Aroha was six, she got a nasty bee sting on her leg. Aunt Maia rubbed kawakawa leaves into the bite and the pain disappeared.

If it worked for me, it'll work for them.

Aroha couldn't get back to sleep. Before anyone else was up the next morning, she slipped out of the house to collect kawakawa twigs and leaves from the nearby bush. She snuck into the kitchen and used her mother's pestle and mortar to grind the leaves into a pulp.

❧

Once the ceremony was over, Aroha ushered Jonno, Ollie and the rest of the boys to the back of the marae. The moment they were out of sight, she thrust a jar of the kawakawa paste into their hands.

'Here, take this. Rub it in,' she urged. 'It'll help with the pain!'

'It damn well works,' Jonno said, massaging the balm into the lacerations on his forehead. 'You're a bloody legend, Aroha!' He smeared another dollop on his face and hugged her.

'Careful!' Aroha said. 'The ink's still wet. You're smudging your tattoo. My dad'll go ballistic.' She blotted his tā moko with her sleeve. 'That's better. Okay, Jonno. You're done.'

The boys crowded around her, each jostling to be next.

'Steady on! One at a time!' Aroha said. 'Come on, Ollie. Your turn.'

She glanced over her shoulder. The coast was still clear. Phew. She couldn't stop herself grinning when the boys gasped in relief as the kawakawa leaves worked their magic.

Footsteps. Panic. Brushing the sweat from her forehead, Aroha stuffed the jar of kawakawa paste into her skirt pocket.

'Scoot. All of you,' she hissed at the boys. 'Keep your heads down.'

Too late.

'Aroha! Where are you?'

Her mother's voice. A shiver ran through her body. *Damn. What am I going to do?*

      David Whittet

No time to think. Ngaio burst around the corner and glared at Aroha and the fleeing boys.

'Stop that at once!' Ngaio clutched Aroha's arm. 'Before your father catches you. God knows what he'll do to you. Will you never learn?'

'Mum! Please! Let go of me! They need me! Can't you see?'

'You'll get the belt! And so will those boys!' Ngaio said. 'Is that what you want?'

Aroha shook her head.

Ngaio's voice softened. 'Then come and help me with the hāngī.' She took Aroha's hand and led her back to the crowd. 'But promise me you'll *never* do this again.'

Aroha knew she *would* do it again at any possible opportunity. She felt a surge of pride, watching the boys reunite with their families and knowing it was her boldness that had eased their pain. Right under her father's nose. And he hadn't even noticed. Or had he?

'What the hell's going on?' Tautaru demanded when they emerged from behind the marae. 'What was Aroha doing?'

'Nothing,' Ngaio blustered. 'Aroha was just … she's … she's been admiring the boys' tattoos.'

'Don't lie to me!' Tautaru spat in Ngaio's face. 'Whakianga mai!'

Aroha could tell her father was angry when he swore in his native Māori. Had he been spying on them? Had he seen everything?

Tautaru grabbed Aroha by her ear. 'It's time you learnt about your responsibilities. You don't speak to those kids. You don't play with them. Understand?'

'Yes, Dad. Please let go!'

He pulled hard on her ear, making her wince. 'They won't learn respect for the Gang from fraternising with my daughter!'

Fraternising? Aroha had no idea what that meant. She almost fell over when her father let go. Pulling herself up, she went to help her mother and the women elders lift the hāngī out of the underground oven. He hadn't seen. She'd got away with it.

Aroha was about to tuck in—the feast was the only good thing about the ceremony—when her father's booming voice silenced the festivities.

'What the hell is that?'

Aroha's heart stood still. She watched her father pick up the jar.

He opened the lid and sniffed. 'Kawakawa leaves.'

Damn! It must have fallen out of my pocket!

Tautaru marched up to the boys and eyeballed each of them.

Oh, God! He's seen the smudges! He knows! She saw his face turn bright red and his neck veins bulge. She often thought they would burst when he was in a mood.

He spun around and slapped her face. 'Damn you! How dare you mock everything we hold sacred? You're a disgrace to the whānau.'

Another slap. Aroha fell and grazed her knee on the ground. 'Please, Dad! I only wanted to help.'

'Taurekareka! E mero! Whiti te rā!' Tautaru's voice rose an octave with each successive Māori expletive.

'Leave her alone!' Ngaio interrupted, helping Aroha out of the mud and back on her feet. 'She's just a child … she doesn't know what she's doing.'

Tautaru shoved Ngaio aside. 'I'll deal with her later.'

Aroha cringed as he dragged the boys away from their families and lined them up in front of the marae. His nostrils flared as he marched up and down the line.

'You crybabies, where are your balls? Need a nurse to look after you? Today was a test of your masculinity. And you've failed!' Tautaru ran his hands over the chiselled grooves on their foreheads. A mixture of blotched ink and kawakawa paste stuck to his fingers. 'Tā moko represents the honour of the Gang. We'll ink you again in the morning.'

Aroha gulped. *Don't take it out on them. Please. It was my fault.*

'And boy, it will hurt!' Tautaru pumped his fist. 'This is the last time you mock our formalities.' He turned to face Aroha. 'Don't you dare show your face until tomorrow. There'll be no kai for you today!'

'I'd throw up anyway,' Aroha said. 'I will *never* understand how you can be so cruel to those poor boys.'

'You need to think about your loyalties,' Tautaru hit back.

     David Whittet

He was about to land her a punch when Ngaio intervened, standing between them.

'Stop that!' Ngaio grabbed Aroha and dragged her away. 'We're going home.'

'Doesn't anyone care?' Aroha asked her mother while they walked. 'Don't you care?'

'Of course I care—we *all* do.' Ngaio stopped and hugged her daughter. 'Don't fret. The pain doesn't last forever.'

Aroha's eyes locked on her mother's. 'Belonging to the Gang *does* last forever!'

Aroha wanted to cry as she sat alone in her room, but her eyes remained stubbornly dry. Loyalties? What were they? Her father was always going on about pain as if it was a good thing. Surviving the bone chisel was supposed to show a gangster's courage. Aroha screwed up her nose. Ngaio talked rubbish too. How could she say the boys didn't mind being hacked to pieces?

Footsteps in the passageway. Was it Tautaru come to give her a thrashing? No. Her mother.

'I brought you some leftovers.' Ngaio bustled through the door with a tray of food. 'I know how much you look forward to the hāngī.'

Aroha's stomach churned at the smell of the meat and vegetables. She threw the food in the rubbish bin as soon as her mother left.

Four in the morning and Aroha's mind was still racing. *Just a few hours, then I'll have to watch them go through it all again. Jonno, Ollie, Mikie, Wally, Dan. All because of me. How can I look them in the eye?* She dug her nails into her arms, even more ferociously than before. *They'll think I got them into trouble on purpose. I have to share their pain.*

She was still awake when her mother came into her room at daybreak.

Ngaio drew back the curtains. 'Time to get ready.'

Aroha peered through the window. The sun looked as miserable as she felt.

'Hurry up,' Ngaio said. 'Breakfast's on the table.'

'I'm not hungry.' No way could Aroha face going into the kitchen. Not with her father there. He'd be gloating at her between each mouthful of black pudding.

'You have to eat something.' Ngaio glanced down at the discarded food in the bin. 'Your dad won't be happy if you faint during the ceremony.'

Aroha bit the inside of her cheek. Why should she make her father happy?

Her mother's hand felt limp as she led Aroha to the marae in silence. Aroha's legs were so weak that she was afraid of falling over. Tautaru was there already, lining the boys up on the dais. She caught Ollie's bloodshot eyes. *I didn't set you up. I never meant for this to happen!* If only she could say the words out loud. Tell him to his face. But would he believe her? Would any of them understand?

Chase laid out the mat. Aroha baulked—they hadn't cleaned off the bloodstains from yesterday. And Chase's karakia seemed even more dismal. From the corner of her eye, she glimpsed Tautaru grinning to himself. *You're not a father. You're a monster.*

First Jonno. Would he survive another chiselling? He looked sick. Aroha squirmed at each strike of the mallet. She lowered her head and watched the colour drain from her hands as fast as the ink blackened Jonno's skin. What was Chase chiselling on his chest? It wasn't the usual Gang insignia. More like an animal—possibly a bird.

Next Ollie. Then Mikie. Wally. And Dan. Tautaru's hands writhed with excitement as each boy had a chicken tattooed on their chest along with the freshly embellished tā moko on their faces.

'Ka pai, bro!' Tautaru slapped Chase on the back when he laid down the chisel. 'Great job!'

Aroha's legs shook. When she stood up, her toes dipped in puddles of blood flowing from the dais. Her eyes darted randomly and her head dropped.

'Are you okay, Aroha?' Her mother leapt up and caught her as she passed out.

The familiar sound of her father blazing brought Aroha back to life. *'Blood and ink! Blood and ink!'*

Everything was a blur at first. Aroha squinted at the boys as they stumbled off the dais. When she saw their faces, she wanted to collapse again. Blood ran into their eyes from the wounds on their foreheads, and they tripped on the

   David Whittet

wooden stairs. Perhaps they wouldn't see her with all that blood clouding their vision. She could tell they were too frightened to wipe it away. The slightest smudge would mean another round of chiselling.

Ngaio took Aroha home and laid her on her bed. 'Don't cry, my angel. You *tried* to do the right thing. I'm proud of you.'

The distinctive tapping noise of the chisel—the uhi—haunted Aroha throughout her childhood. It was there wherever she went and whatever she was doing. The endless echo of the mallet striking the albatross bone. Would it ever go away? Would she ever find peace? Or would it be there for the rest of her life?

❧ ❧ ❧

Rere Falls, East Cape, New Zealand, 1994.

Twenty years on and the thump of the mallet continued to ring in her ears, a rumbling tinnitus that refused to go away. Living rough, trudging aimlessly through dense bush for days on end, Aroha gravitated to the Rere Falls. The only place on earth where she could find peace, where the pounding of the waterfall drowned the incessant noise of the chisel.

Still she was tied to the Gang. The Gang that stole her childhood. Aroha had sworn they wouldn't claim the rest of her life. She'd come so close to freedom. Just a couple of years earlier, here at the Rere Falls, a chance meeting had promised her a new beginning. Then everything came crashing down around her. Her dreams shattered and escape further away than ever.

She felt the spray on her face. As a child, the endless deluge had brought her comfort, caressing her soul and tingling her skin with its pure, clean touch. Today, the ice-cold water only served to reflect the chill in her heart.

Wandering downstream, Aroha's life flashed before her. The familiar landscape transformed into a teeming montage of images. Love and hate. Hope and betrayal. Cascading as fast as the torrent of water hit the rocks. Visions so intense she almost lost her footing on the riverbank. She was back with her impish cousin, racing down the rockslide. How could that fun-loving rascal have turned into such a shameless playboy?

A glimpse of her first kiss with Amiri under the falls. She could still hear his voice. *Aroha. What a beautiful name.* Such a charmer. She sat down on the rock at the very spot where they'd met. *Amiri and Aroha. Love and the East Wind.* He was her soulmate. Or was he? Could she really have got everything so wrong?

Aroha threw a stone into the rapids. Why had she turned to her great aunt Kāterina for help in her hour of need? Kāterina had done nothing but blacken Amiri's name. What did that old witch know about anything? She may have been a revered Māori diviner, but her latest ramblings were a load of crap. Hunapo, a hero? And Amiri, a power-crazed businessman? What balls. Kāterina had even tried to shock her, claiming Amiri would turn her beloved waterfall into a water bottling plant. Aroha didn't believe a word of it. She couldn't believe it. *Wouldn't* believe it. Hunapo was a monster. Amiri was a man of vision.

Aroha turned her back to the falls and walked away. *This isn't my happy place any more. Amiri could have built his factory here for all I care. The Rere Falls have brought me nothing but bad luck.*

The arrival of a car with a young family temporarily distracted Aroha. Although it was fifty kilometres away from Gisborne, the nearest city, Rere had become a popular destination for weekend outings. Aroha watched the father park the car and take a hamper out of the boot. The mother laid a blanket on the grass in front of the waterfall. The two children tucked into the picnic, smearing their faces with Marmite from the sandwiches. After they'd finished eating, the kids splashed around in the water while the parents lay back on the rug, reading their books and basking in the sunshine.

More day trippers arrived. Aroha sighed as they climbed to the top of the falls and took photos. They all looked so happy. So *normal.* Lucky sods. Why couldn't she have been born into another time or another place? Anywhere but into the Gang.

          David Whittet

Chapter Two

Rere Township, East Cape, New Zealand, 1975.

'What's wrong with being a girl?' Aroha raised her eyes to her mother while they folded the laundry in the scullery.

'Nothing! Don't be silly!' Ngaio paused from reloading the washing machine and returned Aroha's gaze. 'What's got into you?'

Aroha rocked on her heels. 'I see the way Dad looks at me. I can see it in his eyes. He hates me. And all because I'm a girl.'

'Nonsense!' Ngaio put down the washing and flung her arms around Aroha. 'Your father loves you. You mustn't talk like this!'

'But it's true.' Aroha pulled back from Ngaio's embrace and frowned. 'And it's not just me. I've watched the way he looks at you. He's angry with you for not giving him a son. Why does he blame you? It's not your fault. It's so unfair!'

'He's a bloke. Men don't know how to show their feelings.' Ngaio shrugged, grabbing another pile of clothes. 'Come on, help me hang these on the washing line.'

Aroha eyed her dubiously as they moved outside. 'Why does he keep going on about needing a son?'

'He needs an heir—someone to take over from him when he's gone.'

'Dad's going away?'

'No, silly. When he … um … passes away … I mean … retires.' Ngaio dropped a shirt in the mud. 'Damn!' Her fingers trembled as she picked it up and brushed off the dirt. 'Don't be too hard on your dad. He's under a lot of pressure at the moment. That's what makes him so grumpy.'

Aroha shook her head as Ngaio fumbled with the pegs. She knew her mother didn't believe what she was saying. Covering for her dad always made Ngaio jittery.

'Take that basket back into the kitchen for me,' Ngaio continued, 'and fetch your exercise books. It's time for your lesson.'

Aroha went over the conversation in her head while she spread the books across the kitchen table. So her dad needed a boy to take his place. An *heir*, whatever that meant. A sudden thought brought a smile to her face. If her old man couldn't have a son—and Ngaio had said she was too old for another baby—then the Gang would come to an end.

Yay! Aroha got up and danced around the table. *I'm so glad I'm not a boy!*

A boy. The word triggered an echo in her head. Boys. Tattoos. The tap of the mallet on the chisel. She gasped with relief. At least she didn't have to go through all that. Yes. Thank God she was a girl.

Aroha doodled in her notebook. She often wondered what it would be like to have a brother or a sister. Would things have been different? Maybe. At least she would have had someone to talk to. Ever since trying to help the boys with the kawakawa paste, her father had scarcely allowed her out of the house.

'Why can't I go to school like the other kids?' Aroha grumbled as her mother hovered over her. 'It would be much more fun than this. I could have friends.'

'Ask your dad,' Ngaio said, eyeing Tautaru who had come in to grab a beer from the fridge. 'He's the one who insists you're homeschooled.'

Tautaru took a swig from his bottle and let out a loud belch.

Ngaio looked up at him as he put on his jacket. 'I can't do this. She needs a *proper* teacher.'

'She needs to learn her place in the Gang,' Tautaru said as he made for the door. 'Nothing more.'

'At least get her a tutor,' Ngaio shouted after him. 'I never learnt to read and write when I was a kid. How can I teach Aroha?'

Tautaru gave her the finger and left.

Ngaio groaned and fetched a Māori history book off the shelf. She sat down next to Aroha. 'Read this page to me.'

   David Whittet

'*The marae is the focal point of the Māori community, a meeting ground sacred to the iwi.*' Aroha read in a staccato, disjointed voice, running her finger along the line under the words. 'Mummy, what's an *iwi?*'

'It means the tribe. Try to keep going. You need to finish the page.'

Aroha stammered through the rest of the text. She wanted to impress her mother with her reading, but the words were all so long and difficult.

Ngaio frowned when Aroha finally reached the end. 'Your father just wants you to be a submissive wahine like me,' she muttered, clearing away the books and setting the table for dinner. 'Well, that's not going to happen. You're worth far more than that.'

Aroha could never understand why her mother maintained the kitchen was the heart of the gangland home. Her father's henchmen always overran their house. Mealtime was worst. Hiding behind the stove, Aroha watched her mother jostle for space with the gangsters. How did they expect Ngaio to cook when they kept pushing her out of the way?

With Ngaio's smock as cover, Aroha peeped at her father.

'I got one over on that bastard Maahanga,' Tautaru bragged to his lackeys. 'Had Bill tell him there's a price on Hunapo's head.'

'You mean you *haven't* hired a hitman yet?'

'Come on, Tautaru! You're slipping!'

The men raised their bottles, thumped the table and slapped Tautaru on the back. Aroha shuddered as the rabble collapsed into raucous laughter. They were on to their third crate of beer—and that was nearly empty. She covered her ears when the younger guys started singing. She didn't understand the words, and she didn't want to. They sounded nasty. Before long, the men were all flinging their arms around, beating time with the song. Aroha backed away. That was scary—what if they hit her?

The gangsters were a greedy bunch. Ngaio's fry-up smelt so good, but it was all gone before Aroha could get any.

'Never mind,' Ngaio comforted, heating a bowl of yesterday's stew.

Tautaru leant back in his chair and patted his fat belly. Ngaio cleared the dishes, beckoning Aroha to help.

'Ngaio! How many times have I told you?' Tautaru said. 'Leave the room when we are talking business. Gang affairs don't concern you!' His eyes shifted to Aroha. 'You too. Get out, both of you!'

Ngaio dumped the dirty plates in the sink and hustled Aroha away.

'Talking business! Yeah, right,' Ngaio mumbled as she closed the door behind them. 'All those bloodsuckers care about is the free booze and tucker!'

Aroha scratched her head as her mother took her to her room. *Why does she let Dad walk all over her? No way will a man boss me about like that when I grow up.* She took a deep breath and tugged on Ngaio's arm.

'Dad's friends freak me out,' Aroha said. 'I can tell they scare you too. Why don't you tell Dad they can't come to our house?'

'I have to choose my battles,' Ngaio said. 'And that's one I'd never win.'

'Choose your battles?' Aroha frowned at her mother. 'What does that mean?'

'Don't ask.' Ngaio tucked her into bed and pulled up the ragged bedclothes.

Aroha laid her head on the pillow. 'I wish they wouldn't get so drunk.'

'Me too.' Ngaio switched off the main light and turned on Aroha's night light. 'We're better off out of there when your father's doing business.'

Aroha rolled over in bed. 'Business? Is that what they're doing?' She bounced on the mattress. 'I thought they were just having a party.'

'That too.' Ngaio stroked Aroha's hair and kissed her goodnight. 'Now, off to sleep.'

Aroha could never sleep while the men were still in the house. She would get out of bed and gaze out of the window until the last of them had left. When she closed her eyes that night, though, something else kept her awake. It was her mother shouting in the hallway.

'Is leading the Gang really more important to you than your own daughter?'

Aroha crept to the door and listened through the crack.

'Leave it, Ngaio,' she heard her father say. 'Now will you get out of my way?'

     David Whittet

'She's growing up, hun,' Ngaio said. 'She sees the way you look at her. Tell her you love her. Talk to her. She's your only child, and you don't even know her.'

Aroha punched the air. *Good on you, Mum!* Ngaio always stuck up for her, nagging Tautaru to show her some affection. It never worked. Aroha heard the front door slam. That meant her father would be down at the tavern for the rest of the night.

A few minutes later, she heard Ngaio go to her room. Aroha snuck into her mother's bed. She'd have to go back to her bedroom before Tautaru arrived home, but for now, she felt safe snuggled in Ngaio's protective arms.

Aroha was drifting off to sleep when she heard her mother talking to herself.

'What's going to happen when she meets other kids?' Ngaio mumbled. 'They'll crucify her.'

Aroha raised her head. 'What do you mean?'

'Nothing, my angel.' Ngaio stroked her daughter's forehead. 'It's just—I worry about you. And that keeps me awake even more than your father's snoring.'

Aroha giggled. Tautaru's snoring. Her room was at the other end of the house and it kept her awake too!

But meeting other kids. That frightened her as well.

'Hey, Aroha! You're a smart-arse. Give us the low-down on Governor Hobson.'

'What?'

A crowd of schoolgirls accosted Aroha as she walked to the local store on an errand the following week. She gazed blankly when they bombarded her with questions.

'Hobson. The Treaty. Come on. Don't mess with us.'

'Stop kidding that you don't know.'

Sara, a bold eleven-year-old with dark-rimmed glasses, pulled Aroha aside. 'We've got an assignment for cultural studies. Quit pissing about and help us.'

'Yeah, spill!' Amy butted in. 'We have to hand it in on Monday. And I'm bloody well in detention already.'

'Hobson?' Aroha screwed up her face. 'Yes, I think I saw his picture in a book.'

'So you *can* help with our homework,' Sara said. 'Give us the juice on the signing with the Māori chiefs.'

Aroha began to sweat and tried to shuffle past the girls. 'I'd love to help you … if I could … but I really don't know much about it.'

Sara stamped her foot. 'Don't believe you. You just want to show us up.'

Amy stuck her tongue out. 'Miserable cow!'

'No, honestly.'

The girls jeered Aroha as she pushed past them and into the store to order the groceries.

Aroha overheard them talking when she scurried home, laden with shopping bags full of provisions.

'How come she hasn't heard of the Treaty of Waitangi?' Sara said. 'Her old man bangs on about Māori rights—she *has* to know about the Treaty.'

'She knew,' Amy scoffed. 'Selfish bitch! She can't bear us getting ahead.'

'No.' Lani, the oldest of the bunch at twelve, eyed Aroha lumbering down the street. 'Didn't you see her eyes? She hadn't a clue what we were talking about. What *is* her mother teaching her?'

Glimpsing back over her shoulders, Aroha caught Lani's gaze. She ran the rest of the way and held off her tears until she was inside the house.

        David Whittet

Chapter Three

He was back. That man. Loitering in the yard. Aroha looked away. Tried to avoid his eyes. She felt him watch her every move, his eyes as muddy as the puddles at his feet and his moustache as dirty. He slouched against the fence, cigarette hanging from his mouth. He was always dribbling, wiping the slobber on his sleeve. *Yuk*. And he stank. Aroha pinched her nose. A sweaty man-smell. All her father's men smelt bad, but Eru was by far the worst.

Her mother had slipped out to the store, and her father was supposed to be looking after her. That was a joke.

'I don't want you skiving off inside,' Tautaru had told her, locking the front door before taking off in his ute. 'You can clean the windows when you've finished sweeping the yard.'

Perhaps Eru would become bored and leave her alone if she just got on with her work. Turning her back on him, Aroha picked up her bucket and scrubbed the windows as fast as she could, praying he'd go away. But he didn't. He stubbed out his cigarette with his Doc Martens boot and lit another. She shivered as he came closer. What could she do? He had her cornered. Glancing down, she saw there was a ladder on the ground. Aroha grabbed it, leant it against the wall, and climbed to the top.

A horn blared. Aroha almost lost her footing. Her father's ute pulled up in the yard and he leapt out of the cab.

'Eru! What the hell are you doing here? Get out! There's no free beer today!'

Any other day and Aroha's heart would sink when her father came home. That afternoon she could have kissed him.

She emptied her bucket and rinsed the mop under the tap by the back door. The freezing cold water made her shiver. Growing up the only child of a notorious gang leader was hard enough without his men chasing her. There had to be more to life than this. And she was going to find it.

I am going to escape the Gang. Aroha wielded her mop, fighting an imaginary battle. *One day, I'll be free. Just wait and see! Nobody can stop me!* She stood tall for a moment before putting her cleaning stuff away in the scullery. *Even if it takes the rest of my life.*

More strife awaited when she reached the kitchen. Her mother was back and arguing with her father. Couldn't they go for more than a couple of hours without shouting at each other?

'For such a powerful man, you can be incredibly stupid,' Ngaio scoffed. 'I bet you drove halfway around the valley to dodge Maahanga.'

'What if I did?' Tautaru said.

'You live down the road from him,' Ngaio said. 'You're bound to keep bumping into each other!'

Aroha shook her head. Nobody had told her why her father hated his only brother. Uncle Maahanga was mighty scary, but that wouldn't bother her father. They were both bullies. With so much in common, they should have been buddies, not enemies. Besides, they were both in the Gang. And they didn't talk to each other. Shouldn't they be working together instead of fighting?

Ngaio shot Tautaru a wicked grin. 'Maahanga hasn't got the plague, you know. You won't catch some nasty disease from just setting eyes on him!'

Aroha stepped back. Her father was about to explode.

'Tūtakina ake!' Tautaru shoved Ngaio against the pantry wall.

'Don't tell me to shut up.'

Aroha squinted at Ngaio, amazed at the fresh determination in her mother's eyes. *That's right, Mum. You let him have it!*

'Scared of him, aren't you?' Ngaio added, ducking her head.

Tautaru pressed his enormous beer gut against her belly, intimidating her with his bulk.

'Maahanga doesn't frighten me. I could have the bastard shot.' Tautaru curled his lips with icy contempt. 'I should've given the order long ago.'

　　　　　David Whittet

Aroha flinched. *What? Dad wants to kill Uncle Maahanga?*

Ngaio pushed Tautaru back, goading him through clenched teeth. 'Shooting Maahanga won't get you a son.'

A son. Yes! Aroha remembered what her mother had told her: 'He needs an heir—someone to take over from him when he's gone.' *But what has that got to do with Uncle Maahanga?* She began to piece it together while her parents continued fighting. Of course. Maahanga had a son—her cousin, Hunapo. So her uncle had an *heir*, and her father didn't. *That's it! Dad's frightened Maahanga is going to use Hunapo to take over the Gang.*

'Kai hamuti!' Tautaru spat the expletive in Ngaio's face, showering her with saliva. 'Thanks to you, I've more important things on my mind than executing that low life. Besides, a bullet would be far too quick for Maahanga. The bastard needs to suffer.'

The quarrelling continued over the dinner table. Aroha looked down at the stingy scrap of meat and dollop of mashed potato on her plate. Chewing that scraggy leftover beef would be as painful as listening to her parents' bickering. She eyed her father's juicy steak. It was so unfair.

Tautaru pointed his fork at Ngaio. 'Bloody Rere! I hate this godforsaken backwater.'

Not that again. Aroha was sick of her father moaning about living in the small settlement. There were only a few houses in the township, plus a school and a shop. But that didn't matter. Just down the road were the Rere Falls.

'Don't blame me,' Ngaio hit back. 'It was your precious Gang that landed us here.'

'What choice did I have? With the fuzz on our tails,' he said. 'It's still a bloody dead end. And Rere's not big enough for both me and Maahanga.'

Ngaio raised an eyebrow. 'I'd like to bang your frigging heads together. Why can't you sort it out like grown men?'

Tautaru threw his knife and fork on the table and picked up the steak with his hands. Aroha covered her eyes as he regurgitated the gristle back onto his plate, then peeked through her fingers to see him use a dirty fingernail as a toothpick.

'Bloody women. This place is full of them.' Tautaru waved the bone at Ngaio. 'Busybodies. Gossips. Mouthing off to everyone who'll listen.'

Ngaio began clearing the table. 'You can swear about Rere all you like. But you're stuck here.' She turned to Aroha. 'Come on, help me with the dishes.'

Aroha followed her mother to the kitchen sink. 'I'm glad we came to Rere,' she said as they washed the pots. 'I love those waterfalls.'

Ngaio smiled. 'Your happy place.'

'Yes. I don't know what I'd do without the falls.' Aroha paused and gazed at her mother. 'But why does it make Dad so grumpy?'

'Your father hates living in a small community, where everyone knows everyone else's business. He thinks they're all plotting against him.'

Aroha screwed up her face. 'If Dad hates it that much, why *did* we move here?'

Ngaio explained how, a few years earlier, there'd been a police operation in Gisborne to shut down the Gang. They had a crack team—whatever that was, working on a sting— whatever that meant, all to catch her father. Why was her dad always in trouble? Protection rackets. What were they?

Aroha couldn't really follow Ngaio's story. It was all far too involved for her to understand. The upshot seemed to be that it forced Tautaru to move Gang headquarters from Gisborne to Rere to get away from the police.

More interesting was how her mother positively glowed when she mentioned Commander Rutherford, the police chief in charge of the raid.

'He was a good man,' Ngaio said. 'He spent his entire career trying to stop your dad being naughty.'

So, was Rutherford some kind of superhero? Aroha smiled to herself. If Commander Rutherford's raid was the reason they came to Rere, then he was her champion too.

Ngaio took off her rubber gloves when they finished the washing up. 'Now, you dry the dishes while I fetch some firewood.'

Ngaio bustled out of the kitchen. Aroha reached up to the rack for a tea towel. She broke out in a cold sweat when she glanced through the window and caught sight of Eru.

Aroha watched her father stride into the yard and confront him.

 David Whittet

'What are you doing here again?' she heard her father say. 'I've told you. There's no more free beer.'

'I brought you this,' Eru replied.

Aroha cringed when she saw Eru sidle up to her father and hand over a discreetly wrapped package.

'Good man!' Tautaru said. His scowl disappeared, replaced by a hearty belly laugh as he pocketed the plunder and thumped Eru on the back. 'Come in.'

Aroha ran to her mother.

'What's the matter with you, Aroha?' Ngaio said. 'Don't be so silly. It's just your father and one of his mates.'

Aroha caught Eru's smug grin when her father fetched him a beer from the fridge.

'Cheers, bro!' Eru and Tautaru raised their beer bottles.

Ngaio took Aroha's hand. 'You look like you've seen a ghost.'

Aroha wanted to answer, but her mouth dried up and her tongue stuck to the roof of her mouth. Couldn't her mother see what Eru was like?

Every day. *Every single day* Eru was there with his drooling mouth and stinking breath. Aroha couldn't stand the sight of his wriggling fingers. He was always edging closer, and the thought of him touching her made her feel sick.

Whenever she heard someone bang on the door, Aroha ran to the storeroom and bundled herself into a large trunk. She felt safe nestled amongst musty old clothes and moth-eaten sheets—until her mother's spring cleaning bust her cover.

'What are you doing in there?' Ngaio shouted. 'Come out. I haven't got time to play hide-and-seek. Can't you see I'm busy?'

Aroha found fresh places to hide, in cupboards and under tables, but none brought her the security of that mouldy old chest. She even resorted to locking herself in the toilet.

'Hurry up and get out of there,' Tautaru bawled. 'I need to take a dump.'

‘Listen, dear,’ Ngaio told Aroha as they cleared away the lunch dishes. ‘I’ll be out this afternoon.’

Aroha shook. ‘Can’t I come with you?’ She peered through the kitchen window and covered her mouth with her hands. Eru was there, hovering in the yard. ‘Please! I’ll be good.’

‘No. It’s grown-up stuff. Your father will look after you.’ Ngaio turned to Tautaru as he came inside, lugging a heavy crate of beer. ‘Take care of Aroha. I’m late for a meeting. I’ll only be away an hour or so.’

Tautaru grunted. ‘A meeting?’ He glared at her accusingly. ‘Where? And who with?’

‘Just women’s stuff.’ Ngaio snatched her bag. ‘A hui on the marae.’

Aroha clung to her arm. ‘Please, Mum. Don’t leave me.’

‘I *have* to go. For heaven’s sake, don’t make things more difficult.’

‘Enough, Aroha,’ Tautaru growled. ‘Find something to do.’

Aroha crouched in a corner when Ngaio left. She glanced up as her father marched back into the yard. Her chest tightened when she caught what he said to Eru.

‘Make yourself useful and keep an eye on Aroha. I need to follow Ngaio and see what she’s up to. I don’t trust her.’

Aroha curled up in a ball in the space under the kitchen sink. *Perhaps he won’t find me here.* She knew he would. This was the moment he’d been waiting for. Nothing would stop him now.

Footsteps approached. Growing louder. Aroha held herself, scared the sound of her pounding heart would give her away. The stench of stale sweat, beer and cigarette smoke became even more overpowering as he got closer. Aroha pinched her nose. Too late. She sneezed.

‘There you are!’ Eru grabbed her arms and dragged her from under the sink. ‘You tease.’

‘Get off me!’

    David Whittet

Aroha seized his legs. *Pull! Tug! Yank! Trip him up!* Eru lost his balance and slumped against the washing machine. *Run! Get out of here! While you've got the chance!*

Aroha flew out of the kitchen and into the backyard. She heard Eru wheezing behind her. He was getting closer. *Faster. Go faster!*

She felt his hands touch her chest. The dreaded moment. His grubby paws on her skin.

Eru spun her around. 'Come on, stop fighting.'

'Let go of me. My dad will be back soon.'

'I don't think so.'

Towering over her as he taunted, Eru slobbered on her hair. She wanted to wipe the spit off as it trickled down her forehead, but he grabbed her wrist.

'Help! Someone! Help me!' Aroha screamed.

Eru gagged her with his hand. He fondled her with his other hand, working down her body, tearing her clothes. What was he going to do to her? How far would he go? If he ripped off any more of her clothes, she'd be naked.

'Stop! Please!'

He tightened his grip on her mouth.

'Why are you doing this to me?'

Her cries didn't get past his fist. The caressing grew more intense. The stink even more sickening as he began to sweat. She felt his breathing quicken. He pressed against her. Her body convulsed when his hand reached her groin.

Aroha bit his hand, sinking her teeth into his leathery flesh with all the strength she could muster.

'Like it rough, do you, bitch?' Eru squealed. 'Well, so do I!' He licked the blood from the tooth marks and used his body weight to shove Aroha over an old wooden barrel.

Noise. A vehicle. A door slammed. Eru froze. Aroha's heart missed a beat.

Voices. Thank God. She turned her head and saw Kaine, one of her father's henchmen, jump over a fence and into the yard.

'Filthy bastard,' Kaine bellowed. 'Get off her, you scumbag!'

Lunging forward, Kaine tried to pull Aroha free.

Eru fought back, landing Kaine a kick in the balls. 'Get the hell out of here, Kaine. Or I'll tell the old man it was you.'

'Son of a bitch!' Kaine groaned, falling backwards and losing hold of Aroha.

Another kick from Eru sent Kaine to the ground.

More noise. Aroha glanced across the yard. More vehicles. More gangsters arriving. She could breathe again.

'You even fight like a girl!' Kaine was back on his feet when the other men arrived and aimed a hefty punch at Eru's gut. 'Take that, you perv!'

The gangsters joined in enthusiastically, chorusing insults and trampling him underfoot.

'Pig! Scum! Slimeball! Meamea! Pōkōtiwha!'

Kaine spat on Eru's bruised body. 'If I catch you anywhere near Aroha again, you're dead meat.' He put his arm around Aroha and led her away as the men continued to stomp on Eru with their boots. 'He won't bother you again. Now let's find your mother.'

Aroha was still shaking when Kaine took her inside the house.

'Looks like nobody's home,' Kaine said.

'Mum's gone to a meeting.' Aroha wiped her eyes on her torn sleeve. 'And Dad went after her. They left me with Eru.'

'Well, your father will be home soon,' Kaine said, his hand still on her shoulder. 'We've got a meeting. That's why we're all here.'

Her father. What would he say? Would he blame her for leading Eru on?

'What is it, Aroha?' Kaine asked.

'Please don't tell Dad,' she whispered.

Tautaru had punished her for *fraternising* with the boys at the tattooing ceremonies. Being half-naked with one of his men would be much worse than that. She'd get a thrashing for sure. He wouldn't understand that she wasn't to blame.

David Whittet

Unclean. Soiled. Violated. Aroha couldn't look in a mirror. Telling herself the attack wasn't her fault didn't help. Why did she feel so guilty?

Her mother nagged her for not brushing her hair.

'Here, let me do it,' Ngaio said, wielding the hairbrush over her head.

'No, Mum.'

Aroha backed away. How could she let anyone near her hair when Eru had slobbered all over it? She shuddered. That smell. The sticky trickle of saliva seeping through her scalp.

I have to get him out of my body. Wash him away. She found a bottle in the kitchen cupboard. Concentrated household bleach. That should work.

'What on earth are you doing?' Ngaio demanded when she discovered Aroha scrubbing herself aggressively in the bathtub. 'Stop that at once! You're going to hurt yourself! Give me that bottle!'

'I'm sorry, Mum,' Aroha mumbled, reluctantly handing over the bleach. 'It's just … I feel dirty … I have to wash it away.'

'Wash what away?' Ngaio interrupted. 'What's the matter with you, Aroha?'

'I want to be clean again.'

'What do you mean?' Ngaio continued to scold Aroha as she hauled her up and out of the bath. 'You have beautiful skin, Aroha.'

'No, it's not beautiful … my skin is bad … filthy … rotten!'

'Nonsense,' Ngaio snapped. 'Thank goodness you haven't harmed yourself. Bleach is dangerous stuff. I expected better from you!'

'Mum, there's something I need to tell you.'

Aroha opened her mouth to continue, but Ngaio sounded off again before she could find the words.

'What is it? I want no more excuses.'

'Don't be angry with me. Please. There's a reason I feel so dirty …' Aroha dribbled to a standstill. She caught her mother's disparaging frown. *Don't you want to know what's wrong? Why can't you listen?* If only she could say the words out loud. Instead, she said what she knew her mother wanted to hear. 'It's nothing, Mum. I won't do it again. I promise.'

Aroha saw the relief on Ngaio's face.

'All right,' Ngaio said. 'You've learnt your lesson.' She wrapped Aroha in a blanket and squeezed her. 'We won't say another word about it.'

❧ ❧ ❧

Rere Falls, East Cape, New Zealand, 1994.

The picnickers had all gone home, and Aroha was alone again with her memories. As an eleven-year-old, she'd struggled to understand her mother. It had hurt that she couldn't talk about Eru and explain the reason she was purging herself in the bath. Why wouldn't Ngaio listen?

At age twenty-nine, it made sense. Poor Ngaio. Tautaru blamed her for everything that went wrong in the house. Her mother couldn't handle the stress. Let alone take on more angst from her daughter. Ngaio just wanted it all to go away.

That didn't stop Aroha from wanting to shake her mother when things got out of hand. She still couldn't understand why Ngaio let Tautaru get away with such abuse.

Roles had reversed when Aroha reached her teens. Unrest made Ngaio clumsy. She kept dropping the pots and pans.

'Come on, let me help you,' Aroha had said when she found her mother crying in the corner. 'Cheer up, please. I'll make dinner. There'll be trouble if it's not on the table when Dad gets home.'

Growing up didn't make it any easier to understand her father. The burning resentment in his eyes had continued to mess with her head.

She'd overheard the women elders gossiping about Tautaru's childhood when Ngaio had taken her to a hui on the marae.

'Tautaru never got on with his father,' one woman said. 'Maahanga was the favourite. The old man was always praising Maahanga and putting Tautaru down.'

 David Whittet

When Tautaru was in his early teens, his parents had split up. Maahanga had gone to live with his father, but they left Tautaru with his mother.

'Maahanga was the red-blooded male who'd earned his place with his father,' the woman had continued. 'I heard the old man wouldn't have Tautaru in his house. Staying with his mother did Tautaru's head in. He was the older brother and couldn't understand why *he* wasn't the one with his father.'

Aroha had edged closer and cocked her ears when she heard the women laugh about Tautaru being bullied at school. The other kids had roughed him up because he was fat and a sissy—and his mother was always turning up at school and fussing over him. Worse still, Tautaru was crap at sport. Maahanga was in the premier rugby team.

No wonder he hated Uncle Maahanga!

Would her father have been different if he hadn't been bullied? If the women were telling the truth, those kids had done some mean things to him—forced him to wear a dunce's hat and made him the slave of an older boy.

'My uncle was caretaker at the school,' another woman had said. 'He helped Tautaru down when the kids tied him to the top of the flagpole. Not that he got any thanks from Tautaru. "Don't worry, son," Uncle Wiremu had said. "It's your turn today. But it'll be someone else's tomorrow. Then you can have a jolly good laugh." Tautaru spat in my uncle's face. "I'm not your son!" he had said,' the woman concluded.

For a moment, Aroha almost felt sorry for her father. From the women's gossiping, it was obviously Tautaru's *turn* for humiliation every day. Was that why he revelled in the boys' pain at the tattooing ceremonies? A kind of delayed payback for the torment his classmates had inflicted on him? Would he have been kinder to women if his mother hadn't mollycoddled him?

Aroha shrugged. Was revenge the only thing men thought about? It certainly felt that way. All the men in her life had let her down. Why couldn't her father have risen above the bullying and broken the vicious cycle of violence and intimidation? That would have shown true leadership and brought him mana. Then she and countless others would have been spared a lifetime of misery.

Aroha watched the sun disappear behind the falls. There had been happier times in her childhood. For as long as she could remember, she'd accompanied her mother on visits to a distant relative, a recluse who lived in the wilderness. Those wonderful expeditions into the forest! The only time she had her mother to herself. Quality time with a parent. Mother-daughter repartee. This had been an entirely new experience.

As a toddler, the visits were a welcome relief from the grim reality of life at home. Aroha never forgot the first time she stepped into her great aunt Kāterina's caravan. Ornate trinkets. Old books. Gems. Everywhere.

'Quite an Aladdin's cave, isn't it?' Kāterina had said, taking Aroha's hand and leading her inside the *Gypsy Rose*.

Aroha had gazed at the ornaments, her eyes darting from one curiosity to the next. 'Aladdin? Who's that?'

Kāterina had rolled her eyes and turned to Ngaio. 'Surely you've told her about Aladdin?'

Aroha remembered how her mother had looked down and shaken her head.

Kāterina had taken a dusty old picture book off her shelf. 'Well, we must fix that,' she'd said, blowing away the cobwebs. 'You'll love hearing about *Aladdin and the Magic Lamp*. And *The Arabian Nights*.'

When she was seven, Aroha started to ask questions about the mysterious relative and her crystal ball. She'd pestered her mother for answers. Could this old woman really see into the future? Or was it just another of those silly fairy tales grown-ups told children?

Dusk brought a chill to the falls. Aroha walked away. With hindsight, perhaps there was some truth in her great aunt's ramblings. Two of Kāterina's prophesies had already come true. Both had changed Aroha's life irrevocably.

As she climbed the path, Aroha cast her mind back to the first of Kāterina's predictions. The relationship with her cousin Hunapo. Aroha's only childhood companion. The boy who had promised her so much but caused her such unspeakable pain. Why had it all gone wrong? And could she ever forgive him?

     David Whittet

Chapter Four

Urewera Forest, East Cape, New Zealand, 1975.

'This is *fun*,' Aroha said, climbing into the cab next to her mother. 'Why can't we do this every day?'

Ngaio stalled the four-wheel-drive vehicle. 'Your dad wouldn't let me. He's scared I'll dent his precious ute. I'm pushing my luck to use it once a month.' With a rev of the engine, they were out of the yard and on their way. 'Your father thinks I'm a lousy driver.'

'That's not fair,' Aroha said. 'Daddy always picks on you. Why do you let him?'

Ngaio shrugged. 'It's easier that way.'

Perched high in the passenger seat, Aroha felt so grand as they drove down the bumpy road along the banks of the Wharekopae River.

'Hold on tight,' Ngaio said, swerving to miss a pothole. 'Goodness, that was a big one!'

'You see, you're not a bad driver,' Aroha said. 'Dad would have hit it for sure.'

'And got a puncture!' Ngaio said.

Aroha giggled. 'Then he'd start swearing. And blame you.'

With a wicked grin, Ngaio mimicked Tautaru's raging. *'This is all your fault, Ngaio! You made me do this! Wahine kore tuki!'*

Aroha watched her mother roar with laughter as the vehicle hurtled down the road into the forest. At home, Ngaio didn't even smile.

'Your father's a cheeky devil,' Ngaio said, 'calling me a stupid woman.'

Aroha clapped her hands in delight. Her mother was a different person when she got away from Tautaru.

Ngaio pulled up and parked the vehicle in a clearing. 'Out you jump. Remember, we have to walk the rest of the way.'

Aroha groaned. 'Can't you go a bit further? My feet hurt.'

'I daren't,' Ngaio said. 'You know the drill. There's just a dirt track from here on. Your dad really would go mad if I crashed his pride and joy.'

Aroha climbed out of the cab. She was about to complain again, but then decided time with her mother was too precious to spend moaning. Instead, she ran down the path into the forest, waving a branch she had picked up.

'Catch me if you can,' Aroha said. 'Come on! You can do it!'

'Wait!' Ngaio huffed and panted as she chased Aroha, her feet catching in the undergrowth. 'Mummy's not as young as she used to be!'

The long trek through the Urewera forest soon had Aroha out of breath too.

'Are we nearly there?' Aroha said. 'I'm starving!'

'We're not even halfway.' Ngaio mopped the sweat from her forehead with an old handkerchief. 'And you know your aunty Kōkā's a vegan. She's a health freak too. So there'll be no cookies. Or lollies.'

Aroha made a face. 'Why does she have such a funny name, anyway?'

'Kōkā is a nickname. Her proper name's Kāterina. Kāterina Kururangi.'

'Kāterina? That's such a pretty name.' Aroha shook her head as they continued walking. 'So why do you call her Kōkā? That's ugly.'

'She could never sleep when she was a little girl. She used to spend all night outside looking at the stars. So her father called her a tohunga kōkōrangi. That's Māori for an astronomer. It got shortened to Kōkā. And the name stuck.'

'Kāterina is much nicer.' Aroha put her hands on her hips. 'And that's what I'm going to call her from now on.'

'Suit yourself,' Ngaio said. 'We'd better get moving. It's another half hour's walk at least.'

  David Whittet

'Wow! I haven't seen those before!' Aroha's spotted some age-old binoculars the moment they entered the caravan. Every visit to the *Gypsy Rose*, Kāterina had something new and exciting to show her. 'Can I look through them?'

'Yes, but be very careful. They're precious.' Kāterina pointed to the scene engraved on the metal casing of the binoculars. 'See those brave warriors with their spears? They were your ancestors.'

'My what?' Aroha asked.

'Your forefathers.' Kāterina moved closer so Aroha could get a better look. 'And those are the waka they used to cross the mighty ocean.'

'Waka?' Aroha said. 'They look like tiny boats to me.'

Kāterina frowned. 'My goodness, Aroha. You need to learn your Māori history. Waka are canoes. Imagine being at sea for months on end in one of those.' She handed Aroha the binoculars. 'These glasses belonged to Kamaka. A fearless explorer and a founder of this beautiful land. I'll tell you his story. But first, your mother's gasping for a cup of tea.'

Using the binoculars, Aroha watched Kāterina boil the jug. Extraordinary— even the tiny stove looked gigantic. She zoomed in on Kāterina's face. Aroha always thought her great aunt looked very grand, with eyes shining as brightly as any of the trinkets in her travelling home. But through the binoculars, her lines and wrinkles looked like mountains and valleys. Gross!

'Be a good girl and fetch the teapot,' Kāterina said.

Aroha handed Kāterina the old brass pot and put the binoculars back to her eyes. Rays of sunlight caught Kāterina's outline, but her long flowing hair looked different through the glasses. Aroha hadn't noticed how white it was before. She knew Kāterina was older than her mother. The binoculars made her great aunt look positively ancient.

Why do old ladies have grey hair? Aroha turned the binoculars to her mother. Ngaio was going grey too. *I hope my hair doesn't go grey when I grow up!*

Kāterina took a picture book off the shelf and beckoned Aroha to sit beside her. As her great aunt recounted Kamaka's adventures, a model hand with writing all over it caught Aroha's eye.

'What's that?' Aroha asked.

Kāterina put down the book and picked up the curious object. 'It's a perfect replica of a human hand. I use it for my palmistry readings.'

A what? 'I'm sorry, Kāterina,' Aroha said, 'I don't understand.'

Kāterina showed Aroha the symbols on the cast. 'You see those little marks? They guide me when I examine a client. I can tell how long someone will live, just from looking at their hands.'

'You can?'

'Absolutely!'

Aroha jumped up and down. 'That's awesome!'

Kāterina beamed. 'Wait till you see my *precious!*'

Ngaio sighed. 'It's getting late, Kōkā, and we've things to discuss.'

'You haven't finished your tea. A good brew shouldn't be rushed. We'll talk in a minute.' Kāterina fetched her crystal ball from its fancy plinth. 'My precious is magic, Aroha. It can see into the future.'

Huddled together on a stool, Aroha shielded her eyes, momentarily dazzled by a mighty glow.

'*Whoah!* That's bright!' She peeked through her fingers. 'Can it tell my future?'

'Of course. My precious can tell everyone's future. But all in good time.' Kāterina got up and put the crystal ball back on its stand. 'First, you need to learn about Kamaka.'

Aroha rolled her eyes. 'I'd rather you told me about my future.'

'Patience, my child.' Kāterina pursed her lips. 'Before you can appreciate the future, you must understand your past. Maybe I'll let you look into the crystal ball later if your mother's not in too much of a hurry to get home.'

'I've finished my tea,' Ngaio interrupted, clicking her fingers. 'You need to play outside, Aroha. Kōkā and I have to talk. Grown-up stuff.'

'*Oh!*' Aroha pulled a face. 'We haven't finished the story.'

'Next time, Aroha. I promise.' Kāterina closed the book. 'Your mother's getting restless.'

       David Whittet

'Okay!' Aroha skipped down the steps out of the caravan. She didn't really mind. The forest was a fantastic playground. She climbed trees, paddled in streams, and picked forest flowers. She gazed up as a native bird warbled a melody. *It's singing just for me!* As the tūī flew away, Aroha waved her arms in the air. Deep in the forest, she was free too. Free to play, free to laugh, free from her father and the gangsters with those scary tattoos on their faces.

Before they left for home, Kāterina called Aroha back into the *Gypsy Rose*.

'Yay!' Aroha bounced on her stool when Kāterina sat her down in front of the crystal ball. 'Will I really see my future?'

'Yes—but careful.' Kāterina steadied the ball on its pedestal. 'Now concentrate and tell me what you see.'

Crouched over the ball, Aroha struggled to see anything other than her own reflection.

'I'm not sure.' She moved her head closer and strained her eyes. 'I can't see anything.'

'Look harder!' Kāterina ran her fingers over the ball and chanted a Māori blessing. 'Haere mai ki ā mātou, e ngā wairua atawhai! Kia pono ki o matapae!'

Although Aroha had no idea what the words meant, they sounded so lyrical tripping off Kāterina's tongue that she joined in, humming the melody.

'What does it mean?' Aroha asked.

'I'm inviting the spirits to join us,' Kāterina explained. She chanted the verse again in English. 'Come to us, merciful spirits! Be truthful with your predictions.'

Aroha couldn't keep still, overwhelmed by Kāterina's energy.

Kāterina slowly withdrew her fingers from the crystal ball. 'The spirits are with us now. Your future awaits.' Aroha saw a host of dazzling images emerge from the crystal ball. Mountains, castles, magnificent palaces. Vivid colours. So much brighter than anything she'd seen before.

'I see a prince!' Aroha jumped off her stool. 'My knight in shining armour!' She'd heard the women elders use the expression and always wanted to repeat it. 'He's coming to rescue me from the Gang!'

Ngaio threw her arms in the air. 'For heaven's sake, Kōkā, don't fill her head with such foolish nonsense!'

Aroha was far too excited to take any notice of her mother. She turned to Kāterina. 'Is this really going to happen? I can't wait!'

'Calm down, Aroha,' Kāterina said, caressing the crystal ball again and chanting another incantation. Her voice rose in such a crescendo that the trinkets on the shelf vibrated along with the tune.

Aroha gasped when Kāterina removed her hands again. The palace had disappeared, replaced by a tree. And it wasn't a prince she saw, but a boy not much older than she was, perched high amongst the branches.

'What's happened to my prince?' Aroha cried. 'Bring him back.'

'No, Aroha,' Kāterina said with a frown. 'What you see is the truth. Not a prince in a far-off land but a local boy … from your own whānau.'

'What?' Aroha scowled at Kāterina. 'I don't believe it!'

'I told you, it takes an open mind to confront your destiny.' Kāterina gave Aroha a dark look. 'Perhaps you're not ready to discover your future.'

'Damn right, Kōkā!' Ngaio sprang to her feet. 'Not another word. Aroha is far too young for these ridiculous ideas! She's just a baby!'

'A *baby*?' Aroha glared at her mother. 'I'm almost eleven! I'm not a baby any more!'

Ngaio pulled Aroha away from Kāterina and cuddled her protectively. 'You will always be *my* baby. And you're not old enough to be thinking about boys!'

'But she's not too young to dream,' Kāterina said, tapping the bench with her fingers.

'What do you know about bringing up children, Kōkā?' Ngaio flashed her eyes at Kāterina. '*Nothing!* I'm doing my best to teach Aroha about the real world, and you feed her mind with fantasy.'

'That's not fair!' Kāterina's voice cracked as she fought back. 'I've shown Aroha her roots. Told her about her tangata whenua.'

'But you couldn't stop at that, could you?' Ngaio retaliated, gritting her teeth. 'You had to pretend you could see into the future. You're a charlatan.'

          David Whittet

'I'm no fraud!'

Aroha didn't know where to look. The two women who meant most to her were fighting like kids. Her mother paced up and down the caravan, making the floorboards creak. It was almost a relief to leave.

'A local boy, indeed,' Ngaio muttered. 'None of those Gang boys are good enough for my angel.' She helped Aroha into her coat. 'Hurry up. Put your beanie on. We're going home.'

What was wrong with her mother? The silence was unbearable during the endless trudge back through the forest.

Aroha took a deep breath. 'What is it, Mummy? Didn't you like what we saw in Kāterina's ball?'

'You can't believe everything Kōkā tells you,' Ngaio said. 'She can't really see into the future.'

'You told me she could,' Aroha said. 'What was it you called her? A *mata-something*?'

'A matakite,' Ngaio said. 'Now hurry up. I want to be back at the ute before it gets dark.'

'What's a *matakite?*' Aroha asked.

Ngaio hesitated. 'A diviner … a clairvoyant … Anyway, it's all gibberish.'

Aroha scratched her head. 'I thought you said she advised some famous people.'

'She did.' Ngaio stopped to tie up a shoelace. 'Kōkā has the gift of the gab. She could talk anyone into anything. She used to have a string of Māori leaders hanging on her every word. Not any more.'

'So, what went wrong?'

Ngaio sighed. 'I guess they realised it was all bunkum. You can't fool people forever.'

Aroha's legs ached. The trek home seemed so much longer. Her jandals rubbed against her blistered feet. Would they ever reach the ute?

'Why does Kāterina live so far away?' Aroha sighed.

'Her caravan's been stuck in that ditch for years,' Ngaio said.

'So why doesn't she move it?'

'Maybe she likes living out in the back of beyond.' Ngaio took Aroha's hand as they neared the clearing. 'Mind you, she hasn't always been out in the sticks. Visiting her was much easier when she had her caravan in a paddock next to the waterfalls. She was there for ages. Never told me why she shifted.'

Aroha raised her eyebrows. 'I don't know why anyone would leave the Rere Falls.'

Ngaio unlocked the door when they reached the vehicle and lifted Aroha into the cab.

Aroha fastened her seatbelt and stared at her mother. 'I still don't know why you were so angry with Kāterina.'

❧ ❧ ❧

Looking back two decades later, Aroha understood why her mother had been so upset. Ngaio's attempts to teach Aroha about her Māori heritage were so dull. But with her gift for storytelling and dramatic imagery, Kāterina brought Māori culture alive in a way that Ngaio never could. That must have hurt. No wonder her mother was jealous.

Aroha had always looked forward to visiting the *Gypsy Rose*. Kāterina's crystal ball took her to distant lands and transported her into a world of magic. It showed her places far removed from gangland and brought colour to her otherwise drab everyday life.

Chapter Five

Rere Township, East Cape, New Zealand, 1976.

Aroha sat cross-legged on the floor, not knowing where to look. Insults flew backwards and forwards between her parents. They'd been at it all morning. Shouting. Blazing. Threats and curses. Aroha was sick of it.

Tautaru slammed a fist on the kitchen bench. 'A woman's place is in the home. You are not going to that hui.' He glared at Ngaio. 'Wahine kore tuki!'

Ngaio rolled her eyes. 'Not that again. I am *not* a stupid woman!'

Aroha could tell her father was about to explode. He'd gone that purple colour. His eyes looked so threatening. What was he going to do?

Tautaru slapped Ngaio's face and shoved her against the wall.

'Dad! Stop it! Please!' Aroha grabbed her mother's arm and pulled her away from him.

Tautaru shifted his glare—and his fists—towards his daughter. 'Get out, Aroha. Go on! This is grown-up stuff.'

Aroha had wanted to leave the house since she first got out of bed. But was her mother safe? Would he hit her again?

'Go,' Ngaio mouthed. 'I'll be okay.'

The dismal grey clouds reflected Aroha's mood as she ran down the familiar track to the Rere Falls. Each step of the brisk thirty-minute walk usually lifted her spirits. Today she fretted all the way. *Grown-ups!* Why shouldn't her mother go to the women's meeting if she wanted to? Why did her father have to control Ngaio's every move? And how dare he hit her? Pausing for breath, Aroha wondered why her mother let him trample all over her. After all, Ngaio was much smarter than her father.

Aroha gazed up at the vast arc of the waterfall spanning the mighty Wharekopae River. Hidden away in a remote corner of the Tairāwhiti region, they were hers and hers alone.

Thank God for the Rere Falls. Clean, rugged and dependable. They were everything her home was not. She watched the pounding water. The roar of the falls blotted out all the things that upset her so much. Her father blazing, her parents fighting, the hideous noise of the mallet hitting the albatross bone. They all disappeared, and her heart beat in sympathy with the endless flow.

Aroha skipped through the spray, dancing to the roar of the thrashing torrent. She felt so brave going behind the cascading water. Several days of heavy rain had swollen the falls, and their force took her by surprise. When a sudden deluge of water landed on her head, she lost her balance and fell onto the rocks.

Apart from a few scratches, she'd only hurt her pride. After nursing her bruises, Aroha scrambled over the slippery boulders and wandered aimlessly along the riverbank. And there, perched high in a tree, was her cousin Hunapo.

'Me Tarzan, you Jane,' Hunapo said, jumping down from the tree and landing in front of her.

Aroha stepped back. 'Don't be silly. I'm Aroha, and I know you're Hunapo.'

'It's from *Tarzan of the Apes*,' Hunapo grinned. 'Haven't you seen it? It was on the telly last week.'

'My dad hardly ever lets me watch TV,' Aroha sighed. 'Anyway, what are you doing here?'

Hunapo laughed. 'Same as you, probably. Getting away from my old man.'

Aroha stared at him, suddenly feeling small. With his impish smile and his fading T-shirt celebrating Te Hoetere, a Māori rock band, he looked much more grown-up than her.

David Whittet

Hunapo's grin broadened. 'There's a rockslide just up the river,' he said. 'I've wanted to have a go on it for ages, but it's no fun on your own. Come with me. It'll be the ride of your life!'

Aroha blushed. 'Come with *you?*'

Hunapo nodded. 'The rockslide's insane!' He pointed downstream. 'Have a go! You won't regret it!'

'I'm not sure,' Aroha mumbled, shuffling awkwardly. His high spirits were too much for her. He was addressing her like a long-lost friend, and they hardly knew each other. They'd met at Gang functions but had never been allowed to talk. She felt a tinge of resentment. He was invading her private space. Rere Falls were *her* escape. 'I can't, Hunapo. I have to go back home.'

'Come on, Aroha,' Hunapo persisted, his eyes twinkling. 'You know you want to.'

That face. The bewitching expression. How could she resist when he smiled at her like that?

'Don't, Hunapo … Stop, please!' Aroha covered her face with her hands. She couldn't let him see she was close to tears. 'I have to go back home.' She uncovered her face and met his gaze. His soulful eyes cut straight through her tears. 'But I don't want to go home. There's always trouble … fighting. My dad's always angry.'

Hunapo put his arm on her shoulder. 'So's mine. It's just the same at our place. Ranting, raving, arguing. It never stops!'

Aroha dried her face on her sleeve and tilted her head. 'It's like that for you too?'

'Our house is a war zone! Never a dull moment.' Hunapo's eyes rolled skyward. 'My father's always blazing about something. Actually, most of the time he's badmouthing your dad!'

Aroha giggled. 'You're so naughty, Hunapo.' She felt herself warming to her cousin. 'Do you know why our fathers hate each other so much?'

'Search me.' Hunapo shrugged. 'Maybe because they're such morons. To hell with the bastards! Mete pōkokohua! Kai a te ahi!'

'Hunapo!' Aroha took a step backwards and crossed her arms. She knew boys copied their fathers and swearing in Māori made them feel grown-up, but somehow it felt wrong coming from one as young as Hunapo.

'Well, they are arseholes! And full of crap!' Hunapo stood tall, clasping his hands together. 'Anyway, I thought you'd be used to that kind of language from your father.'

'I am.' Aroha's eyes welled up again. 'I just want to get away from it. For a little while at least. That's why I come here.'

'Sorry, Aroha.' Hunapo took her arm gently and led her down the riverbank.

Secretly, Aroha was delighted to have someone call their family squabbling for what it was. Her father would have gone mad. Following Hunapo down the path, Aroha wished Tautaru could have heard it. Because it was true.

'Don't look so worried.' Hunapo gave her hand a squeeze. 'We're going to have fun. I promise you!'

'I hope we won't get lost,' Aroha said. 'I've never been this far before.'

'Trust me.' Hunapo stopped when they reached a bend in the river. 'Close your eyes.' He guided her a few paces further. 'Now open them.'

'Wow!' Aroha gazed at the sixty-metre-long natural rockslide. Children coasted down the rocks on all sorts of home-made devices, boogie boards, inner tubes, mats, inflatable cushions. Families picnicked on the grass.

This must be what normal kids do. Play. Have fun with their friends and families.

Hunapo stood at the water's edge. 'Ready for a thrill?'

'I can't do that!' Aroha panicked as she watched some kids bouncing down the rocks on an old mattress and crashing on a boulder. 'It's *way* too scary!'

'Of course you can. Where's your sense of adventure?'

She watched Hunapo run off and chat with some mates. He came back dragging an old tyre.

'Your chariot awaits,' he announced proudly.

'We're going down the slide in that?' Aroha said. *'Seriously?'*

'Too right. In you get.'

Aroha's legs shook as she clambered into the tyre. Hunapo pushed it to the edge of the rockslide, then jumped in beside her. Aroha couldn't look ahead as they began to move. It wasn't too late to get out. But then Hunapo would think she was a sissy. She couldn't have that. *I have to see this through.*

To her amazement, Aroha felt an overwhelming sense of freedom as they jetted down the rockslide at high speed. Water sprayed into their faces, temporarily blinding them. She clung to Hunapo for dear life, screaming in both terror and exhilaration—and relief when they came to an abrupt halt at the bottom.

'That was wild!' Aroha exclaimed as Hunapo helped her out of the tyre. 'I wouldn't have missed it for the world.'

'Told you,' Hunapo grinned.

'I need to sit down,' Aroha said, holding her reeling head. Lying on the grass, they watched some more kids glide down the waterslide. 'It's getting late. I need to get home.'

The sun slipped behind the hills as they wandered back. Aroha grabbed Hunapo and hugged him when they parted.

'Thank you! That was *amazing,*' she said. 'In fact, it was the best day of my life!'

Aroha skipped her way home. *It is possible to escape from the Gang—at least for an afternoon!* She danced in the field before running the rest of the way home. *Someone else knows how it feels to belong to the Gang! Hunapo understands! We're so alike!*

A sudden thought stopped Aroha in her tracks. Her mind went back to the first day Kāterina had allowed her to gaze into the crystal ball. What was it her great aunt had said? *A local boy from your own whānau.* Aroha had been so disappointed at the time that she'd done her best to forget about it. Now it all fell into place. Kāterina was talking about her cousin and she was right. Hunapo was far more fun than some stuffy prince in an imaginary castle. He was real—and he wanted to get away from the Gang as much as she did.

At least her parents had stopped fighting when she got home. Her mother was cooking dinner.

Aroha took a deep breath. 'You'll never guess who I met at the falls.'

Ngaio looked up from the stove. 'Who?'

'Hunapo,' Aroha said. 'We had this crazy ride down the rockslide.'

Ngaio stopped stirring the pot. 'That boy will never make you happy.'

'He will,' Aroha said. 'Today was the best day ever.'

Ngaio waved the spoon at Aroha. 'He's a scoundrel. I don't want you seeing him.'

'Mum!' Aroha glared at her mother. 'You'd like him if you knew him. He's fun. Kāterina told me I'd meet someone from the family. And I have—just like she said.'

'I told you not to take any notice of Kōkā,' Ngaio said. 'I wouldn't be surprised if the old witch didn't set the whole thing up. She's devious enough. I bet she told Hunapo to follow you.'

Aroha rolled her eyes. Ngaio was always telling her off for being silly. Now her mother was being stupid. 'He didn't follow me. He was already there. Hiding in a tree—just like he was in the crystal ball.'

'Whatever.' Ngaio scowled and ladled the stew onto the plates. 'You'd best keep out of his way if you know what's good for you.'

Keep away from Hunapo? No way. Aroha had felt alive when she was with him this afternoon. Other kids had mates. Why couldn't she?

Aroha ate her dinner in silence. If only she had a close friend she could talk to. Boasting about her adventures with Hunapo would be wicked.

So what if Hunapo was a rascal? He brought a smile to her face. That was all Aroha cared about. Her father called him a rebel. She wasn't sure what that meant, but if it was someone who stood up to the Gang, then Hunapo *was* a kindred spirit.

     David Whittet

Rere Rockslide, East Cape, New Zealand, 1994.

Still looking for answers at age twenty-nine, Aroha stood at the top of the Rere Rockslide. It seemed a lifetime since Hunapo persuaded her to coast down the rapids in an old tyre. So much had changed since that reckless afternoon, and none of it made sense.

Kāterina's prophecy for a start. Was her great aunt really playing cupid as Ngaio had suggested? Aroha began to wonder. Had Kāterina told Hunapo to hide in a tree and wait to surprise her?

Aroha kicked a stone down the rockslide and told herself not to be so ridiculous. It was simply a coincidence that Hunapo had shown up the way he'd appeared in the crystal ball. Worse, if Kāterina really could see into the future, that would mean her latest revelations were right as well. What a bloody nightmare.

A bunch of kids turned up. Their makeshift surfboards were a little more elaborate than Hunapo's clapped-out tyre, but judging by the shrieks, the thrill of the ride was the same. When they reached the bottom of the slide, each claimed they'd been the most daring. That hadn't changed either.

Further downstream, some kids were skipping stones across the river. Aroha counted the bounces as they took turns. None were as good as she was. She used to play that game with Hunapo, and she always won.

'How old are you?' Aroha had asked Hunapo when his stone sank on the second bounce.

'Twelve,' Hunapo had replied. 'Nearly thirteen.'

'I'm eleven,' Aroha said. 'You're almost two years older than me. So why aren't you better at this?'

Hunapo had promptly picked up another stone and skimmed it across the water. *'Yes!'* he crowed as it bounced six times. 'Beat that if you can!'

'Watch me.' Aroha chose a flat stone, aimed carefully and threw it sidearm. She grinned as it glided effortlessly downriver and clapped her hands when it rebounded on the water for the twelfth time.

'I'm bored with this,' Hunapo had said. 'Let's do something else.'

Typical Hunapo. He always gave up when he was losing. But she'd put the cheeky monkey in his place for once. And that was cool.

What was decidedly uncool was how the women elders had made fun of the relationship. Aroha refused to believe it when she heard them joke that it was only a matter of time before Tautaru split them up. How could she have been so naïve? Her father would stop at nothing when it came to the Gang. Maahanga was just as ruthless. Neither of them cared how much damage they caused their children in their determination to get one over on the other.

She used to lay in bed wondering if Hunapo was still awake. Did he think about her as much as she thought about him? Was he making it up when he said his father wouldn't let him play with girls? Could his home life possibly be as bad as hers? Or was he pushing it to get her sympathy?

At age eleven, Aroha prayed her friendship with Hunapo would never end. Eighteen years later, she wished it had never begun. Did she really mean that? She'd always known the fun-loving rascal would grow into a gangster, but never imagined he'd hurt her so cruelly. Yet despite everything, deep down, she was desperate to believe Kāterina's plea that he was innocent. That was impossible— she'd seen the evidence.

Aroha took a last look at the now deserted rockslide. She was no nearer understanding Hunapo. Or finding the truth.

David Whittet

Chapter Six

Rere Township, East Cape, New Zealand, 1976.

'Where the bloody hell have you been?' Maahanga waived his fist as Hunapo rode into the yard on his bicycle.

'Just riding my bike. Down by the falls.' Hunapo's wide grin disappeared as he eyed his father. 'And I had a go on the rockslide. It was awesome.'

'The trouble with you, Hunapo, is that all you think of is pleasure,' Maahanga growled. 'Pleasure and squandering every opportunity I give you.'

'What if I don't want to lead the Gang?' Hunapo muttered under his breath, propping his bike against the fence.

'Well, don't just stand there,' Maahanga said. 'Help me! Do I have to run this place on my own?'

Hunapo pulled a face at his father. If only his impish smile worked on his old man.

Maahanga scowled back. 'You can start by loading the truck. Fetch those boxes from the shed. All of them.'

Hunapo stepped into the shed, rolling his eyes. *An unpaid hand. Is that all I'm good for?* He gazed at the stacks of packing cases. 'Bloody hell! There are masses of them! It'll take forever!'

'Then you'd better get your arse into gear,' Maahanga said. 'There's no dinner for you until the job's done.'

Hunapo glanced sideways at his father. 'So what are they? Drugs?'

Maahanga turned away and attached a trailer to the back of his truck. 'Never you mind.'

'I'll take that as a yes.'

'They ain't lollies. That's for sure.'

Hunapo lifted a box and promptly dropped it. 'It's bloody heavy!'

'Don't be such a wimp!'

'I'm not a bloody packhorse!' Hunapo panted as he struggled to move the packing cases. They were far too heavy for drugs. Weapons more like. 'Are they guns?'

Maahanga grunted. 'I told you. None of your business.'

'You're always banging on about me being the next Gang president. So I think it *is* my frigging business.'

'Just get on with the job.' Maahanga secured another packing case on the trailer with some rope, covering the load with a tarpaulin. 'It's getting late. I want it finished before dark.'

Hunapo paused for breath after humping half a dozen boxes. He scratched his head. 'Dad, are you sure you know what you're getting yourself into?' He stammered as his eyes met his father's, 'I mean … trading firearms … this could get us into a heap of trouble.'

Hunapo stepped back. He expected an explosive response, but it didn't come. Maahanga just sighed and shook his head.

'You're such a pussy, Hunapo. Will you ever be man enough to lead the Gang?'

Hunapo looked up at the stars as he helped his father fasten the last packing case. His muscles ached, his limbs drooped, and he gagged on the smell of his own sweat.

Maahanga thumped him on the back. 'You've earned your supper tonight, son. Come on, there's stew on the stove.'

Globules of fat floated on his plate as Maahanga ladled the stew from the pot. Hunapo didn't care. It was food and he was starving. He chewed on the beef. Tough and leathery. They ate in silence—apart from a few belches from his father.

Swallowing the last mouthful, Hunapo looked up from the table. Yesterday's soup spilt all over the stovetop. Last week's dishes piled up in the sink. Stains on

     David Whittet

the wall. Mud on the floor. How he missed his mother. She would never have allowed them to live in such a tip.

His eyes fixed on a fading black-and-white photograph stuck to the fridge with a magnet. His seventh birthday. How he remembered that day. His mother had given him a new bicycle. The pride in her eyes. She must have saved up for ages. It was the best birthday present he'd ever had. In fact, it was the *only* birthday present he'd ever received.

Hunapo shifted his gaze back to his father. Maahanga would never understand how much he loved that pushbike. It had taken him to the Rere Falls. And to Aroha.

Maahanga opened another beer bottle. Hunapo watched him swig it down. Was his father in a good mood? Booze sometimes made the old man happy, but more often it made him grumpy.

'Dad,' Hunapo began, watching his father's expression. 'When I was at the waterfall, I, um …'

Maahanga eyed him suspiciously. 'What? Spit it out.'

'I met my cousin. Aroha.' Hunapo bit his tongue the moment the words left his mouth. The twitching vein above his father's right eye told him he should have remained silent.

'No wonder you're turning into such a pussy,' Maahanga said. 'I don't want you having anything to do with her.'

Hunapo stared back at his father. 'She's my cousin!'

'How many times have I told you?' Maahanga said. 'We steer clear of Tautaru and his family.'

Hunapo scratched his head. 'Tautaru's your brother, and you're both in the Gang. Surely you have to get along.'

'Chance would be fine thing,' Maahanga said. 'The bastard's shut me out. He even tried to get me in the clink.'

'That's not Aroha's fault,' Hunapo said. 'She's different.'

Maahanga snorted. 'Balls! She's a wuss. Just like her father. He's all bluster and bullshit.'

Hunapo drew himself up and eyed his father. 'No, Dad. She's my friend.'

Maahanga slammed his fist on the table. 'I thought I laid that feminine crap to rest when I got rid of your mother. If I catch you anywhere near that sissy again, you *know* what will happen.'

Hunapo rubbed his back. He knew—the scars were still raw.

⁂

Hunapo remembered the arguments before his mother left. As he lay in bed, he used to bury his head under the pillow to dampen the noise of his parents fighting. There was one night he could never forget. It was just a week after the excitement of his seventh birthday.

'I'm warning you, Kiri,' he heard his father shout. 'You're not turning my son into a ponce—'

'Hunapo's no ponce,' Kiri hit back.

Bloody right I'm not, Hunapo seethed, sitting up in bed.

'Why can't you accept Hunapo for what he is?' Kiri continued. 'He's different. He's not just another gang kid. I wish you could see that.'

'Bullshit! It's you. Teaching him to think like a woman. Filling him with effeminate horseshit.'

As he listened, Hunapo visualised his father menacing Kiri. He wanted to go and help her, but it wouldn't do any good. Maahanga reminded him of the Incredible Hulk. Like the Hulk, his old man knew how to use his body to intimidate. Hunapo had learnt that to his cost. He curled up under the sheets as Maahanga's voice continued to reverberate through the house.

'From now on, you leave Hunapo to me. I'll beat that feminine crap out of his body if it's the last thing I do.'

Hunapo cringed. Not another hiding. He heard Kiri spring to his defence.

'Beating the poor kid won't change him.'

'Then maybe it's you who needs a thrashing. I'll take the strap to both of you.'

　　　　David Whittet

Surely Maahanga wouldn't use the belt on his mother?

Kiri's voice. 'You should be proud of your son, instead of trying to change him into something he's not. Hunapo's going to be a New Age boy. What do they call them? A *metrosexual.*'

A what? Hunapo hadn't heard the word before, but whatever it meant, he was quite sure he wasn't one. *Metrosexual indeed.* His mother had been reading too many women's magazines.

Maahanga was swearing at Kiri again. 'Kai hamuti! Go shit yourself!'

Hunapo's imagination ran riot as the fight continued. He could picture his father pinning her against the kitchen sink. Kiri's small plump stature was no match for Maahanga's Herculean physique.

'How dare you feed him with this crap? Metrosexual be damned! Now you listen to me, Kiri. Hunapo *will* be a warrior, and the more you fill him with this pansy shite, the harder I will have to beat him.'

'That's not fair! Hunapo's never going to be one of them. Face up to it.'

'Don't push me, Kiri!'

'Haven't you looked in his eyes recently? Hunapo has a kind heart and a generous spirit.'

'Tō teke! Bullshit! Just get your fat arse out of my sight.'

Quiet at last. But Hunapo couldn't sleep. Was he a New Age boy? No. He was as masculine as the next boy and no less of a pushover. He gave as good as he got in a fight and more. But that didn't mean he couldn't be sensitive too, and no way would he treat women the way his father did. If that was being a man, perhaps he had a feminine side like his mother said. It was all far too confusing. Hunapo jumped out of bed and paced around his bedroom until daybreak.

※

Hunapo studied his mother as she cooked breakfast the next morning. She looked tired. He guessed she'd been awake all night too. He looked for the telltale bruises. Her arms were purple. God knew what horrors she was hiding underneath her apron.

'Hunapo!' Maahanga thumped the table, his mouth full of black pudding. 'There are going to be some changes in this house. You're going to think like a man. Like a gangster. Like a true Gang president in the making.'

Hunapo almost choked. Egg yolk ran down his chin. *What if I don't want to be the Gang president?* If only he dared to say how he felt. But the old bugger would never understand.

'*I* will teach you everything you need to know,' Maahanga continued. 'You don't take any notice of your mother. There'll be no more of this namby-pamby nonsense. Fetch your jacket. Your training starts today. You're coming on a job.'

Hunapo looked at his mother. She closed her eyes and groaned.

Maahanga rose from the table and gave Hunapo a yank. 'Come on. What are you waiting for?'

Hunapo wiped the egg from his face with his shirt. 'All right. I'm coming.'

Gang training. Going on a job. Hunapo shook his head and grabbed his anorak. What did gangsters do all day? He'd seen gun-wielding gangsters on television, but none of them were remotely like his old man. They didn't spend their lives mouthing off and drinking beer.

So his father was to be his role model. All the miserable bastard had taught him so far was a load of Māori swear words. Every one of them nasty.

'Watch and learn,' Maahanga instructed, parking the truck on a run-down street of ageing state houses. 'Collecting Gang dues will be your job one day.'

Gang dues? What the hell were they?

His mother had told him about Jehovah's Witnesses going from house to house, hammering on the door and preaching the word. But did gangsters do that too?

          David Whittet

'Ignore them. Pretend we're out,' Kiri used to hiss whenever the Witnesses called on them. 'I'm sick of hearing about eternal damnation.'

Nobody ignored his father. Everyone they called on came to the door. Most looked nervous. To Hunapo's amazement, they took his old man's ranting seriously. *Incredibly* so. A few choice expletives from Maahanga and they all scuttled into a back room, returning moments later with an envelope. With a smirk, his father would stuff it in his pocket and leave without another word.

❧

'What on earth have you been doing? You're covered in mud!' Kiri exclaimed when father and son arrived home. 'And what's happened to your face?'

'He's learning to fight like a gangster!' Maahanga ruffled Hunapo's hair. 'Not chicken out like a little girl.'

'Come here, Hunapo. Let me wipe your face and get those dirty clothes off you.' She sniffed as she pulled off his T-shirt. 'You need a bath.'

Kiri shooed him into the bathroom, quizzing him about the day as she ran the water.

'Actually, it was quite fun,' Hunapo admitted as he hopped into the tub. 'We met loads of people up the coast.'

'And fleeced them, no doubt,' Kiri muttered. She stared at the scars on his back. 'You'll get more beatings if you follow in your father's footsteps. You're no gangster.' Her voice grew more urgent as she continued. 'You don't have to do what your father says. I know you're different. You're like me. We could run away together—'

A sudden thump on the bathroom door almost took it off its hinges. Maahanga barged in and screamed at Kiri.

'I heard that! Whakianga mai! Get out of my house!'

Hunapo froze as Maahanga slapped Kiri across the face.

'Go on! Get out!' Maahanga grabbed Kiri's arm and yanked her out of the bathroom.

Hunapo grabbed a towel, wrapped it around himself and followed them out. He clasped his hands over his head as he watched Maahanga drag his mother into the yard and throw her to the ground, spitting on her as she writhed in the dirt.

'E mero! You piece of shit!' Maahanga cursed, then marched back into the house and bolted the door. Hunapo stood shivering, his body still wet from the bath. 'Go to bed, Hunapo. This is your fault. I told you not to listen to your mother. She's full of shit.'

Hunapo's lips quivered. *My fault? What crap!* He opened his mouth to protest, but nothing came out. His heart thumped. He wanted to shout and scream. *How dare the bastard treat his mother like that?* But speaking up would only result in a beating. He rubbed his eyes on the towel and staggered to his bedroom in silence.

Hunapo held a vigil throughout the night. Where was his mother? How was she feeling? He gazed at the stars through his window. When would she come back?

Morning broke. Just as bleak. Silence at the breakfast table. Chores as usual. Gang training. How could they carry on as if nothing had happened?

Going on the job with his father wasn't fun any more.

'Did you have to be so rough with the old women?' Hunapo asked as they drove home. 'I thought Mrs Brown was going to have a heart attack.'

'She was just trying it on,' Maahanga said. 'Those women know when their protection money is due. You need to harden up, son.'

Hunapo shuddered. Mrs Brown wasn't trying it on—she was terrified. What would have happened if she'd died? Would they have arrested his father? Would he have been in trouble too?

So the old man wanted him to harden up. Hunapo knew he could never be that hard.

 David Whittet

'Dad …' Hunapo and Maahanga sat at opposite ends of the kitchen table. Dirty dinner dishes and the remains of burnt sausages between them. Maahanga reached for a can and rubbed his swollen belly. Hunapo took a deep breath. 'Where's Mum? When's she coming home?'

Maahanga swigged his beer. 'She's … er … She's gone to stay with a friend.'

'Who?'

'Her aunt, Isabella.'

'Will she be back soon? I miss her.'

Maahanga clenched his jaw. Hunapo knew the answer before his father spoke.

'No. It's just you and me for now. That's cool. We can do man stuff together.'

Man stuff. *Yeah, right.* Terrorising women. That's *not* cool.

Hunapo got up and took the dishes to the sink. He wanted to weep, but he was a boy. *Boys don't cry.* And he daren't show weakness in front of his father.

Weeks passed. Suspicion drove Hunapo crazy. *Where is she?* Was his father lying to him? Hunapo was sure that Kiri had told him Isabella was sick. Dying. Kiri had gone off to visit her, armed with flowers and grapes. That was last year. She had to be dead by now.

Maahanga's yelling interrupted his thinking.

'Get a move on, Hunapo. We're going up the coast today.'

Hunapo shrugged. That meant more bullying and misery for the locals. And grief for him, too. He thought about making a run for it. Too late. His father had him cornered.

'Get in,' Maahanga said. 'There's no time for daydreaming.'

Hunapo stumbled on the step as he climbed into the truck. He had to say something. He watched Maahanga slam the cab door shut and put the key in the ignition. Fidgeting with his seat belt, he swallowed hard. 'I want to see Mum.'

Mahanga grunted and revved the engine.

'Why hasn't she come home? I heard Isabella died ...' He broke off momentarily, catching his father's glare. He couldn't stop now. 'So where is she?'

Maahanga's knuckles tightened on the steering wheel. 'Don't know. Don't care.'

'Dad! She's my mother. Why can't I see her?'

Maahanga put his foot down on the accelerator. The vehicle veered out of the yard and through the township. 'I told you. I'm not having her mollycoddling you again. Filling your head with dreams. Kiri had her chance, and she blew it.'

Hunapo stared out of the window throughout the two-hour drive. He couldn't bear to look at his father. Houses flashed past, so run-down he half expected them to collapse. He pressed his head against the window, watching the women hang out their washing.

Hunapo's heart suddenly froze. Then it raced. He wound down the window and waved frantically. 'Mum! Mum!' He pulled on his father's arm. 'Dad! Stop! Please!'

The car swerved across the road.

'What the hell are you playing at?' Maahanga shouted. 'Are you trying to get us killed?'

'You've got to stop the car. It's Mum!'

'That's not your mother,' Maahanga snorted, hitting the accelerator even harder.

'It *is!*' Hunapo hung his head out of the window, trying to catch a last glimpse of the woman. Squinting, he saw something that made him pull his head back inside the cab. The woman had a baby in her arms. Perhaps it wasn't his mother after all. Or maybe it was someone else's baby she was holding.

Hunapo knew he was kidding himself. His mother had moved on. Found another man and had his child. Worst of all, Hunapo wondered if she had forgotten all about him.

He was still searching for answers when they pulled up at a fishing community outside Tolaga Bay. A group of bikers loitered outside the village store. He watched them ogle the storekeeper's daughter. They blew cigarette smoke in her face, and she blew them a kiss in return.

     David Whittet

Hunapo cringed. One of those goons could be his mother's new man. They looked just as mean as his father. Why did she always pick losers? If she found a good man, she could come and rescue him.

'Those bastards don't know what's coming to them,' Maahanga smirked, jumping out of the truck. He beckoned for Hunapo to follow. 'Come on, son. Buck up.'

Hunapo heard the men shouting as he clambered out of the cab.

'Bro! It's old man Maahanga!'

'The Crusher!'

'We're out of here!'

The roar of bike engines revving up was deafening, and Hunapo lost his footing. He scrambled to see the men disappear on their Harley Davidsons in a cloud of petrol fumes.

Maahanga waved his fists after them. 'The bastards think they can escape from me. No matter.' He turned to Hunapo with a broad grin. 'We'll just get the money from their wives.'

Hunapo dodged. So they were going to spend the day victimising women. Everything was wrong as he trudged behind his father. From the pitiful looks on the women's faces to the glint in his father's eyes when he took their money. Was this his life now?

It was dark when they drove home. The ride seemed endless. Hunapo stared into the darkness, praying for a glimpse of his mother in the shadows as they rattled through the coastal settlements.

Lying awake in bed that night, Hunapo wondered if Kiri had been wrong to go on about him being a sensitive boy. Was that why his father called him a wimp? Hunapo rolled over in bed. He didn't believe in bullying old ladies and stealing their savings, but that didn't make him a wuss.

If only Kiri had kept quiet. Then Maahanga wouldn't have been so angry all the time, and he might not have thrown her out.

I would still have a mother, and my life wouldn't be such hell.

Five years on and Hunapo was still doing his father's dirty work. Stacking boxes and delivering parcels. All of them undoubtedly full of plunder. Taking messages to people who didn't want to receive them. And now he was twelve, the dreaded Gang initiation was less than a year away. Hunapo shuddered at the thought. Maahanga promised him that his tā moko would be excruciating. Future presidents had to show their mettle.

At daybreak, Hunapo watched his father drive off in his truck. The trailer, loaded with contraband, rattled along behind. He sighed as they disappeared into the distance, then turned to get on with the tasks Maahanga had left him. There had to be more to life than this. There was: Aroha.

What was it about his cousin that had so captivated him? Was it merely that they were both miserable at home? They certainly enjoyed pulling their fathers to pieces whenever they were together. Aroha had even picked up a few of his swear words, which gave him a kick.

But the attraction was more than that. He'd never met anyone like her before. Aroha always seemed to know what was right. And unlike him, she did it. She reminded him of Kiri.

Keeping their friendship secret was impossible. The Gang had spies everywhere, and his father had eyes in the back of his head. *I can't see her again; I have to see her again.* The argument raged through Hunapo's head. *Damn their petty feud! We're going to hang out. Whatever the consequences.*

Their clandestine meetings had a chilling air of foreboding. For Hunapo, forever looking over his shoulder was inexplicably exciting and terrifying.

Nothing came close to the thrill of a bicycle ride with Aroha holding on to him for dear life.

'Wow … *slow down* … be careful!' Aroha had screamed as they tore down a hill.

 David Whittet

He'd laughed and peddled even faster. Turning a corner at high speed, they crash-landed on a bank.

Was she hurt? Was she mad at him? Hunapo turned his head to look at her. Thank goodness she was smiling.

'You are a clown,' she said. 'That was scary. And you've broken your bike.'

Hunapo got up to inspect his bike, the handlebars embedded in the riverbank and the back wheel still spinning.

'Is it going to be okay?' Aroha asked.

'Couple of twisted spokes. Nothing I can't fix.'

'Good.' Aroha lazed back on the riverbank. 'Because that was kind of … fun.'

'My mother gave me this bike,' Hunapo said, pulling it out of the mud. 'The only birthday present I've ever had.'

Aroha sat up. 'Tell me about your mother. Where is she? I don't think I've ever seen her.'

'My father threw her out. I was only seven.' He broke off. Blinked back a tear. 'I can still remember that day. I waited and waited for her to come back. But she never did.'

Aroha put an arm on his shoulder. 'Oh, Hunapo. I'm so sorry.'

Hunapo could tell that she *was* sorry. The gentle touch of her hand told him she cared.

'I heard later that she'd tried to come home and see me,' he said. 'My aunt said she'd tried to get me back. Looked for a lawyer but couldn't find anyone willing to pick a fight with the Gang.'

'So you haven't had a mother all these years?'

Hunapo shook his head. 'And now I think she's forgotten about me.'

Aroha patted his back. 'You've got *me* now. Nobody's going to scare me off. We're friends.'

Hunapo smiled. 'Yes. Best friends forever.'

Chapter Seven

Aroha never forgot that bike ride. The wind rushing through her hair as she clung to Hunapo. Her heart raced as fast as the bike tearing along the riverside track at full speed. The thrill was almost as wild as jetting down the rockslide.

What a crazy afternoon, Aroha had scribbled in her diary when she got home. *Hunapo's such an idiot!*

She'd seen the crash coming. Why didn't he take any notice when she told him to slow down? They could both have been seriously hurt. She should have given him a good telling off for being so irresponsible. Instead, they'd talked about his mother and she'd been so touched by his story.

Aroha drew a picture in her diary. The two of them riding on Hunapo's bicycle. Underneath she wrote: *Best friends forever.*

❧

Three months later, Aroha wanted to tear the page out of her diary. She lay on her bed, chewing her pencil. She wiped a tear from her eye and began a new page.

Dear Diary, what's the matter with Hunapo? Why doesn't he want to play with me any more? Have I upset him?

These days, Hunapo just sat on the riverbank for hours on end, watching the water flow past. She'd lost her fun-loving rascal.

'Come on, let's bounce some stones down the river,' she'd said one afternoon, pulling on his arm.

Hunapo shook his head.

She gave him a cheeky grin. 'Why not? Because I always win?'

 David Whittet

Hunapo had snorted and walked away.

Aroha leafed back a couple of pages in her diary. Just a few weeks ago, they'd invented their own make-believe gang.

'Doesn't sound much fun to me,' Hunapo had said when Aroha suggested the idea. 'I thought you wanted to escape from the Gang. Not invent a pretend one.'

'Our gang will be different,' Aroha had said.

'We can't play at gangs with just the two of us.'

'You've got mates,' Aroha said. 'Get them to join in.'

Hunapo shuffled his feet. 'S'pose.'

Aroha scratched her head. 'We need a name for our gang.'

Hunapo smiled. 'How about Hunapo's Heroes?'

'Be serious,' Aroha said. 'I know. The Rere Rescuers.'

Reliving the adventure through her diary was painful.

'This is more fun than I thought,' Hunapo had said when they staged a mock raid in an old barn. He stood guard over two local kids who'd volunteered to act as hostages, using a dusty power drill he found on a shelf as a fake gun. 'Move and you're dead!'

'All right, Hunapo.' Aroha noticed the worried look on the boys' faces. 'That's enough. Time to let them go.'

Hunapo grunted. 'Do I have to? I'm enjoying this.'

'Of course you do,' Aroha said. 'I told you, our gang will be fair. We're The Rere Rescuers. We have to do the right thing.'

'Spoilsport!' Hunapo pointed the power drill at her before putting it down. 'Still, it was fun while it lasted.'

Aroha stuffed her diary away in a drawer. Ngaio told her she had to practise writing every night. How could she bother with homework at such a time? All she could think about was Hunapo and how to get him back.

I have to talk to him. Getting up off her bed, Aroha pressed her hands against her forehead. *But what can I say?*

The next morning, Aroha grabbed the mop and raced through her chores. *I'll make him talk to me.*

She found him in his usual position by the river. She crouched down beside him and put a hand on his shoulder.

'What is it, Hunapo? Why so serious?'

She watched his gaze follow the river. Why wouldn't he look at her?

At last, he glanced back at her. 'Nothing.'

'I've missed you,' Aroha said. 'I bet your mates miss you too. We had fun, pretending we were a good gang. Why won't you play with us any more?'

'I've grown up,' Hunapo said. 'You should too.'

'This isn't you. What's up?'

Hunapo shrugged. 'You don't want to know.'

'I *do*. Tell me. I know something's wrong.'

Hunapo threw a stick into the water and watched it float away.

Aroha looked down. 'I thought we were friends.'

Hunapo continued to gaze downstream. 'We can't be friends. Not any more. I have to be a leader. That means I can't go on seeing you.'

Aroha felt her eyes well up. It took her a moment to catch her breath. 'But we're friends for life! For *life*, we agreed!'

Hunapo turned towards her. 'The last few months—they've been great. We've had fun. Pārekareka.' His eyes darted from Aroha back to the river. 'But we know it can't last forever.'

'It *can* last! We can make it last! Please, Hunapo!'

'We pretend it can, but we know it can't.' Hunapo turned to face her again. 'Surely you can see that.'

'No!' Aroha rubbed her swollen eyes, rummaging in her pocket for a handkerchief. 'You don't know what you're saying.'

'My father's told me not to see you again.' Hunapo took a deep breath and

                David Whittet

gritted his teeth. 'He thinks you're turning me into a wuss. *Feminine side my arse,* he keeps growling at me, *you won't learn to be a gangster playing sissy games with girls … I'll beat that weak-kneed crap out of you!*'

Aroha couldn't stop herself giggling at Hunapo's imitation of his father, but immediately regretted it.

Hunapo frowned at her. 'This is no joke. He'll beat me till I change—until I'm a real man. I have to be a leader. It sucks, but there's nothing I can do about it.' His bottom lip jutted out, and he stammered, 'if my father knew I was here with you, we'd both be dead.'

'Bull! You're his son. He'd *never* kill you!'

Hunapo shook his head. 'You don't know my father.'

Aroha reached out and grabbed his arm. 'I know what it's like. My father hits me too. Look.' She rolled up a sleeve to show Hunapo her bruises. 'My dad's as mean as they come, but he wouldn't kill me.'

'So what?' Hunapo said. 'My old man wouldn't think twice about doing me in.'

'Don't be silly,' Aroha replied. 'Like you just said, he wants you to lead the Gang. You can't do that if you're dead.'

Hunapo pushed her away. 'The old bugger's damn near killed me already. And if he caught us together, he'd crucify both of us. *Our families.* They're poison for each other.'

Aroha's throat tightened. Her breathing quickened. 'What was it you told me?' she said. '"Our families are a bunch of idiots! Morons the lot of them." Yes, that's what you said. "To hell with the bastards!"' She watched Hunapo blush and hang his head. 'I can't believe you're chickening out. You *are* a wuss!'

Hunapo looked up. 'Oh, Aroha,' he groaned. 'You've got an answer for everything!'

An answer for everything. If only she had. Back then, Aroha was so caught up in their friendship that she couldn't see the danger. She should have done. Her father had often threatened to have Hunapo killed, and the hatred in his eyes told her he meant it.

Looking back, Aroha realised Hunapo must have known what was coming. Why hadn't he run away while he still had the chance? Instead, the very next day after that fraught meeting on the riverbank, he was around at her house at five in the morning, knocking on her bedroom window.

Rubbing the sleep from her eyes, Aroha could tell at once that he was changed. Broken. There was blood on his shirt and judging by his bloodshot eyes, he'd been crying. So he wasn't making it up about his father beating him. Why hadn't she believed him?

Aroha glimpsed the scars through his torn clothing and immediately covered her face. What had Maahanga done to him?

Chapter Eight

Hunapo thought his head would burst as he rode home on his bicycle. How could he persuade Aroha that their friendship had to end? *I don't want to hurt her, but I have to.*

He'd thought about showing her the wounds from his latest beatings. They were still raw and weeping pus. Surely that would convince her there was no future for them. He'd been about to lift his shirt and let her see for herself what happened to him when he disobeyed his father. One look in Aroha's eyes and he knew he couldn't do it. It was too cruel. He'd tucked his top firmly back in his shorts.

Aroha had taught him so much, opened his eyes, shown him things he had never noticed before. Gripping the handlebars as he got closer to home, Hunapo told himself she was worth the pain and the indignity of his father's thrashings. She'd looked so sad when he'd left her on the riverbank. Even with her swollen eyes and matted hair, he thought she looked beautiful. Hunapo couldn't conceive of a life without her.

※

The belt. That familiar thick leather belt. The reflection of the sun's rays in the buckle almost blinded Hunapo as he swung into the yard. Before he could dismount from the bike, Maahanga was on top of him. Lashing him again and again. The force sent him crashing to the ground, landing on top of his bicycle.

'You've been with *her*, haven't you?' Maahanga demanded, grabbing Hunapo by the scruff of the neck and dragging him up from the mud. 'Kai a te ahi! Answer me, you little turd!'

'No. I was just out riding my bike …' Hunapo stuttered, dodging the belt.

'Don't lie to me!' Maahanga shot back, continuing to flog Hunapo.

'It's the truth.'

'Do you think I'm stupid?'

'No. I can explain.' Hunapo put up his hands to fend off his father. 'I was just sitting by the river. Aroha came up and started talking to me.'

'I warned you, Hunapo.' Maahanga tore off Hunapo's shirt and struck him soundly on his back.

'It wasn't my fault … I didn't ask her to come … and I couldn't get her to go away.'

'Just tell her to bugger off. She'll go running back to her mother.' Maahanga stepped back and put the belt down. 'Fetch that broom and help me clear the shed.'

The old shack was a tip. Hunapo began sweeping, avoiding his father's probing eyes throughout the afternoon.

After a couple of hours, they sat down on a crate for a rest. Maahanga shuffled on the box, edging closer to Hunapo.

'Listen, son. One day you'll thank me. Let this be a lesson to you.'

Hunapo didn't answer. He sat in silence, nursing his wounds.

'Once you're Gang president, you can have as many girls as you like,' Maahanga continued. 'You'll get the pick of the bunch. They'll be all over you.'

After an uncomfortable pause, Hunapo got up and went back to work.

'We've earned ourselves a brew.' Maahanga put his hand on Hunapo's shoulder when they finished. 'Off you go inside and put the kettle on. I'll finish up out here.'

One moment he's lashing out, the next he treats me like his mate. Hunapo filled the jug and put it on the stove. While waiting for the water to boil, he wiped the blood off his back with his torn shirt and put on a new one. *I have to say something.*

'Dad …' Hunapo chose his moment. He handed his father a mug of tea.

'Cheers, son.'

They sat down at the kitchen table. Maahanga picked up a newspaper and slurped his tea. Eyeing his father, Hunapo took a sip then put his mug down. The old man looked calm enough as he scanned through the paper.

 David Whittet

'I know there's shit between you and Tautaru,' Hunapo began, his eyes fixed on his father. 'But I don't see what—'

'Damn right there's shit,' Maahanga interrupted. 'If you knew what the bastard had done to me, you'd understand. Tautaru's resented me since we were kids. Stolen everything that's mine. Destroyed my business. Threatened to have me shot.'

'I understand, Dad. But—'

'Now he wants to rob you of your birthright,' Maahanga continued. 'He'd do anything to stop you being the next president.' He put the newspaper down and leant towards Hunapo. 'We have to stand up to the bastard. For your sake.'

Hunapo hesitated. 'What I was trying to say is … I don't see what this has got to do with Aroha. Why won't you let me see her?'

Maahanga slammed his fist on the table. 'Because I've had enough of women turning you into a pansy—'

Hunapo flinched. 'Dad! Nobody's going to turn me into a pansy.'

Maahanga picked up the newspaper and waved it at Hunapo. 'First, your mother. Teaching you to think like a woman. Now that bloody cousin.'

'That's bullshit. Aroha's got more balls than most boys. She even beat me at arm wrestling.'

'Defeated by a woman?' Maahanga screwed up the newspaper and brandished his fist. 'That proves my point. You *are* a pussy, Hunapo!'

Hunapo raised his palms in defiance. 'Back off. She's my friend. And I've never had a friend before.'

'She's your enemy.'

'No. You don't understand. She's fun to be around. And I need some fun. Like other kids—'

'Fun?' Maahanga interrupted. 'Gangsters don't have *fun*. You're not here for a good time!'

'Why do I have to be different?'

Maahanga's eyes burnt. 'Because *you* have to be a leader. Gang presidents don't have friends. They have henchmen.'

Hunapo slumped his shoulders. 'That's not me, Dad.'

Maahanga stood up and slapped Hunapo across his face. 'Go to your room. Tomorrow you're going to be a real man. This crap stops now.'

Hunapo slammed his bedroom door and rubbed his stinging cheek. He aimed an imaginary punch at his father. *Up yours, you old bastard! I'm not giving up on her, whatever you do to me.*

Aroha was worth far more than another beating. Besides, his father would find an excuse to thrash him whatever he did. Actually, he'd got off lightly today. A few lashes with the belt when he'd got home and a slap on the face when he'd talked about Aroha. He'd expected worse. Perhaps his old man was running out of steam.

'Shit!' Hunapo caught his toe on a nail protruding from the bare floorboards. He sat on his bed and wrapped his bleeding foot in a sheet.

He had to think fast. There had to be a way for him to go on seeing Aroha. But how? *Maahanga's got eyes in the back of his head. The bugger won't let me near her again. What am I going to do?*

Hunapo rolled over, the rusty springs on his mattress squeaking. His face suddenly lit up. *We'll be blood cousins! That way, the miserable sod can never separate us.*

Five in the morning. His father's snoring reverberated throughout the house. Thank God. That meant the coast was clear. Hunapo snuck out, cursing the creak when he shut the front door. He sprinted across a paddock to Aroha's house, praying Tautaru and Ngaio were asleep too.

Hunapo crept around the house, looking for Aroha's bedroom. The room with the night light. That had to be hers. He gently tapped on the window. No

    David Whittet

response. He peered inside. Aroha was sound asleep. He knocked again, louder this time. At last her head stirred, and she rubbed the sleep from her eyes.

He beckoned her to come over. She dragged herself out of bed and peered through the window.

'Hunapo! What are you doing here? It's the middle of the night.'

'Open the window. I've something to tell you!'

'I must be dreaming,' Aroha mumbled.

He saw her fumble with the window latch and cringed at the scraping noise when she opened it.

'Careful! Don't let anyone hear you!' Hunapo glanced over his shoulder nervously. 'Come outside. We need to talk.'

'Okay.'

Hunapo watched Aroha disappear through her bedroom door. His heart stood still as he waited for her. Was she coming? Had she copped out? Had Tautaru woken up and stopped her?

Hunapo breathed again when she emerged from the back door, clutching a jacket over her nightdress.

'You came, Aroha! You're such a trooper!' Hunapo beamed at her in the moonlight and put his arm on her shoulder. His father was wrong. Aroha had guts.

Chapter Nine

'Blood cousins?' Aroha gazed at Hunapo in amazement. 'What do you mean?'

They'd snuck into Tautaru's shed. It was bitterly cold, and she huddled up close to him on a wooden box.

'We'll bond together. Share blood.' Hunapo squeezed her hand. 'Once we're blood cousins, no one can tear us apart. Our souls will be together for eternity!'

'Eternity?' Aroha couldn't believe her ears. She jumped in the air and clapped her hands, dancing amongst the crates and motorbike parts. 'That's beautiful, Hunapo!'

'Shush, you'll wake your old man,' Hunapo whispered. 'Come back and sit down.'

Aroha knocked over a toolbox in her excitement. 'I can't help it. It's wonderful. Together forever!'

'Yes, well,' Hunapo said, 'our souls will be together forever, but our bodies may have to follow different paths.'

Aroha sank back on the box beside him. 'Different paths? What does that mean?'

Hunapo took her arm. 'It's just, we have to prepare … for when we have to part.'

'No! Never!' Aroha glared at him. 'I want you here with me forever.'

'I'm sorry. I'm not explaining this very well.' Hunapo bit his lip. 'Listen, you've been the best friend I've ever had, and we'll always be friends.' He pressed his hand against hers. 'But we haven't got long. We'll have to be friends apart. Soon.'

'Don't say that!' Aroha covered her ears. 'You're breaking my heart.'

'This is hard for me, too. My old man won't let me see you again. That's why I've had to come out in the middle of the night.'

Back on her feet, Aroha shook. 'Stop it! You can get around your father. Don't give up on me.'

 David Whittet

'I'm not.' He buried his hands in his hair, stumbling on his words. 'But the old bastard's going to split us up, and there's nothing we can do about it. He'll make me a prisoner rather than let me go on seeing you. That's why we must bond. Before it's too late. That way, however far apart we are, we'll always be there for each other.'

Aroha suddenly froze. 'What's that?' She pointed to a red stain seeping through his shirt. She'd seen it through her bedroom window, but it had grown much bigger. 'You're bleeding!'

Hunapo shrank back. 'It's nothing.'

'I want to see,' she said.

'Leave it. Please.'

'I need to look.' Aroha stepped forward. Fighting him off, she lifted his shirt and gasped. Gashes, sores and bruises covered his body. The more recent wounds were bleeding, the older ones oozing foul yellow gunk that stank. 'Hunapo!' She drew back so fast that she almost fell over. 'Your father did this to you? Because of me?'

Hunapo hung his head, trying to hide the wounds with his hands. 'I didn't want you to see.'

'I feel sick!' Aroha held her breath, trying not to inhale the vile smell.

Her mind drifted back to the tattooing ceremonies. Hunapo's injuries looked even more brutal than the ones the boys suffered when they got their tā moko. She could still see their faces and hear the thump of the mallet.

'It's all right, Aroha.' Hunapo put his arm around her shoulder. 'I don't mind the beatings. I can take them for you.'

Aroha stared into his eyes. Those sad, soulful eyes. 'I can't let you go through another beating. Not for me.' She pulled away from him and got up to leave the shed. 'You were right. We can't go on seeing each other.'

Hunapo caught her arm and pulled her back. 'Don't go. We can't part like this.'

'We have to …'

'A sudden break would be far too cruel,' Hunapo insisted, still tugging on her arm. 'Don't worry. I've got a plan.'

Aroha felt her body go limp, and she slumped down beside him. 'Are you sure?'

'Yes. But we have to act fast.' Hunapo rubbed her hand. 'We *will* be blood cousins. And our souls *will* be together for eternity.'

Aroha dabbed her eyes and looked up at him. 'Oh, Hunapo …'

'What?'

Aroha rested a hand on his knee. 'Nothing.'

Hunapo lowered his brooding eyes. He was hurting too but was thinking more about her than himself. Aroha knew then that with a maturity beyond his years, he would make an outstanding leader. Hunapo could change the Gang for the better—if only he could escape from Maahanga.

Aroha almost fell off the box when Hunapo described his bold plot for a secret ceremony at the Rere Falls. It could never work. They'd be caught and punished. Or would they? A delightful tingle ran down her spine. Hunapo had thought of everything.

'We have to meet before it gets light,' Hunapo said. 'You need to leave about five. Don't let the old folks see you. Have you got a watch?'

Aroha shook her head.

'Here. Take mine. Don't lose it. It belonged to my uncle. Just make sure nobody sees you.'

Dawn was breaking when they crept out of the shed.

Aroha threw her arms around Hunapo as they parted, tears in her eyes. 'Promise me you'll take care of yourself,' she said. 'Don't let your old man catch you and beat you again.'

'I can look after myself.' Hunapo nudged her towards the back door. 'Now hurry. Back to your bedroom before anyone wakes up.'

Aroha shivered. 'I don't want you to leave me.'

'You must. Until tomorrow. At Rere.'

'I'll be there.'

❧

　　　　　David Whittet

Aroha hurried back to her bedroom, her heart racing. *Blood cousins.* She'd heard about *blood brothers.* Gang boys often shared blood. More for a dare than anything else. But *blood cousins?* A secret ceremony at her beloved waterfall. That was so special.

'You look tired, Aroha,' Ngaio said at the breakfast table. 'Didn't you sleep very well?'

Aroha shook her head and hid her face behind a cereal packet.

The day dragged. Why had Ngaio given her so much work? Today, of all days. While scrubbing the kitchen floor, she fretted about Hunapo's wounds. With the thrill of the plot, she'd put the horror to the back of her mind. The ceremony would put Hunapo at risk of an even worse beating. She couldn't let that happen to him. Perhaps she shouldn't go to the falls in the morning. No. She'd promised Hunapo, and she couldn't let him down.

All remaining doubts disappeared when Tautaru and his minions took over the house that afternoon. They were drunk and, as usual, Tautaru threw Aroha and Ngaio out while they discussed 'Gang business'.

Aroha grinned to herself. In just a few hours, thanks to Hunapo, she would thumb her nose at her father and his men. That felt wicked. Deliciously wicked.

The familiar path felt different in the dark. Aroha stumbled over stones and overgrowth as she ran, her heart thumping against her chest. She prayed it wouldn't explode or her legs give out before she got there.

She'd never seen the falls at first light before. Amber rays of the early morning sun emerged from behind the hills and highlighted the endless flow. The stillness and calm amplified the sound of the cascading water.

The shrill ring of Hunapo's bicycle bell made her jump. Looking over her shoulder, Aroha watched him get off his bike and prop it up against a tree. He looked different. Proud. Dignified, even. And what on earth did he have tied to his belt? Aroha took a step back. Could it be? Surely not—it looked like one of the ceremonial swords she'd seen in Kāterina's historical picture books.

'What's that?' she asked as he walked towards her.

Hunapo drew the mighty sword from its sheath. 'My great-grandfather rode into battle with this sword.'

Aroha shielded her eyes, dazzled by the sparkle of the ornamental diamonds and the sun's reflection on the golden blade.

'Maahanga let you take it?' she said, peaking through her fingers.

Hunapo grinned. 'He doesn't know.'

He took a pace towards her. They stood facing each other for a few moments in front of the falls.

Aroha's eyes remained fixed on the sharp blade. *What's he going to do with it?* She sighed with relief when he laid the sword on the ground.

Hunapo took her hands in his and put them together in prayer. He gazed into Aroha's eyes.

'We have been drawn to each other for a purpose,' he said, his voice trembling. 'Our souls belong together. I will always look out for you, Aroha. I will be there for you whenever you need me. If you are ever in trouble, I will rescue you.'

Aroha felt her eyes filling with tears. She shouldn't cry on such a solemn occasion, though. She wanted to tell Hunapo that she'd be there for him too, but she couldn't get the words out.

She shuddered when he picked up the sword and pointed the blade up to the heavens. Another shiver. Not fear this time, but the thrill of expectation.

Hunapo grasped her right hand and held it high in the air. Slowly, he drew the blade closer. Aroha felt a bead of sweat on her forehead. How would it feel? Would it hurt? Would it change her forever?

'Ow!' A sharp jab. A moment of pain. A drop of blood oozed from her thumb. And yes, she felt different.

Hunapo passed the sword to Aroha. 'You must do the same to me.'

What? Me? Cut you? Aroha stepped back. 'No. I couldn't.'

		David Whittet

'I'll help you.'

Hunapo positioned the sword in Aroha's hand. It was so heavy she thought she would topple over into the water. How could anyone use such a monstrous weapon in battle?

She felt a strange sense of power as Hunapo guided the blade toward his right thumb. For the first time in her life, she was totally in command. Blood spurted from the incision. Deep, pure red. So different from the horrible sticky blood on his scars.

Hunapo rinsed the blade in the waterfall and placed it on the rocks. He pressed their bleeding thumbs together and held them skyward.

'This morning, we have shared blood,' he said. 'Our bond that will last forever.'

Aroha watched the blood trickle down their wrists. 'Forever and ever.'

⁂

Rere Falls, East Cape, New Zealand, 1994.

Aroha retraced her steps down the path and over the rocks. She felt as dizzy as she had the morning they'd shared blood. She kicked off her shoes and walked barefoot in the mud. She half expected to see the skid marks from Hunapo's bicycle. Or a drop of blood immortalised on the ground. All trace of their secret ritual had disappeared, but she could still hear Hunapo's voice.

⁂

'We did it! *Yay!* No one can separate us now!' Hunapo had flung his arms in the air and danced on the water's edge. 'Come on, we're going for a ride under the waterfall.'

At first, she'd been reluctant to join Hunapo on the victory lap after the ceremony. But as usual, Hunapo had talked her into it.

'I can't,' Aroha had said, sitting on the bank nursing her thumb. 'I'm still bleeding.'

Hunapo had hastily bandaged her hand with an old handkerchief from his pocket. 'That should do the trick.' He fetched his bicycle. 'Now jump on and hold tight! Prepare for the ride of your life!'

Aroha had clung to Hunapo as they rode across the rocks directly beneath the pounding water. She'd soon forgotten her throbbing finger. She felt free and liberated as the cascading torrent doused them.

'This is *fun,*' she had screamed. 'Faster! *Faster!*'

She'd let go of Hunapo for a moment to splash her hands in the plunging deluge, balancing precariously behind him. Branches of the overhanging trees swept past, brushing against her face. By now, the sun was high in the sky and beat down on their drenched bodies.

'Oh, Hunapo! If only we could do this all day!'

'If only,' Hunapo had sighed. 'But I have to get you home. Before anyone misses you.'

One last circuit through the falls. A final moment of reckless abandon. Then Hunapo had peddled towards Tautaru's place and the real world. Still soaking wet, they sang a blessing as they sped along the winding path.

Aroha had blinked a tear when Hunapo dropped her off a safe distance from the house.

'I'll never forget today, Hunapo. Never. It was beautiful. Paradise. I wish it could last forever.'

Hunapo had opened his mouth, but nothing came out. He gave Aroha a hug and cycled away.

How empty she'd felt when he left.

     David Whittet

Aroha could forgive Hunapo a lot for the joy they had experienced that day. And over the following years, she had enough to forgive him for.

Looking back, the ceremony had marked the end of their childhood. Whatever Maahanga did to punish Hunapo for performing the rite, her only friend was never the same again. That mischievous rascal was gone forever.

Chapter Ten

Maahanga's Place, 1976.

How do I get the old man off my case? Stealing the sword and getting out of the house unnoticed had tested Hunapo's ingenuity to the limit.

Hunapo usually gobbled a rasher of bacon in a single mouthful. The morning before the ceremony, though, he could barely hold the knife and fork. He eyed his father across the breakfast table and took a deep breath.

'Dad, the yard's a mess. I got my foot stuck in a possum trap the other day. Would you like me to tidy it up?'

'What?' The sausage fell from Maahanga's mouth onto his plate. 'What are you after, Hunapo?'

'Nothing. I just want to help.'

Was that too obvious? Have I blown it? Hunapo scratched the back of his neck. Maahanga followed him around all day. *I have to get that sword. The ceremony's meaningless without it. Why can't the bastard leave me alone?*

Hunapo tiptoed into the living room at four in the morning. Every creak of the floorboards was like a landmine about to explode. He pulled open the cupboard. There it was. The golden blade gleaming in the moonlight. Hunapo claimed his prize. He was out of the door and madly peddling his bike to the Rere Falls.

Hours later, the ceremony was over and Hunapo had to get the sword back before his father noticed it was missing.

Please, God. Let the old man be still sleeping.

 David Whittet

Hunapo slowed down as he neared home. Beads of sweat broke on his forehead. He got off his bike behind the house and laid it on the ground. The slightest noise and he was dog tucker. With a last admiring gaze at the sword, he ran his fingers across the blade. *Damn.* His thumb was still bleeding. He stuck it in his mouth and sucked hard until it stopped.

The house was dark. Hunapo slid the sword back into its sheath and stuffed it down his pants. He took off his shoes at the back door. Still no sign of Maahanga. Thank God the bastard was a heavy sleeper. Hunapo took a deep breath and stepped inside.

The scullery was empty. A tap dripped. Hunapo crept into the kitchen. Last night's dishes remained piled up in the sink, just as he'd left them.

Hunapo snuck into the living room. His legs wobbled as he edged toward the cabinet. The latch clicked when he fumbled to open it in the dark. What had happened to that shaft of moonlight?

Hunapo was about to return the sword to its spot on the shelf when he sensed a dark shadow draw over him. He glanced up and froze. Before he could take another breath, Maahanga was on top of him, like a monster emerging from the abyss.

The belt. The dreaded leather belt.

'How many times do I have to beat the crap out of you before you listen to me?' Maahanga yelled, thrashing Hunapo mercilessly. 'Haven't you understood a word I've told you? Didn't I beat you hard enough? Because this won't stop until you learn!'

'Dad, please! You're going to kill me!'

'You might as well be dead if you carry on like this! You're a disgrace. You've turned me into a laughing stock—'

'Bullshit! People laugh because you and Tautaru squabble like spoilt kids …'

'How dare you answer me back, you little shit!' Maahanga swung the belt so violently Hunapo could no longer dodge the strokes. 'Bloody women and their big mouths. I can't even go for a pint without some son of a bitch bullshitting me. *Sensitive soul,* my arse! I thought I'd laid that crap to rest when I threw Kiri out.'

Hunapo wrapped his arms around his body to protect himself.

Maahanga grabbed Hunapo's hand. 'What's this?'

Hunapo clenched his fist. 'It's just a cut. I must've scratched it on a tree.'

'Don't lie to me!' Maahanga said. 'Kai hamuti! Do you take me for a fool?' He forced Hunapo's fingers apart. 'It's a clean cut.'

Hunapo swallowed. 'Let go! All right—yes. I cut it. On purpose.'

Maahanga's face turned puce. 'You've shared blood, haven't you? With that bitch Aroha?'

Hunapo freed his hand and eyeballed his father. 'You can beat me all you like, but you'll never get Aroha out of my body now!'

'I'll skin you alive!' Maahanga thrashed Hunapo with the belt. 'I'll bleed you to death if that's what it takes to get the bad blood out.'

'You can't!' Hunapo gritted his teeth as the leather bit into his skin. 'She is part of me now. Forever. And there's nothing you can do about it.'

'We'll see about that!' Maahanga threw the belt on the floor. He walked over to a chest, unlocked a drawer, and pulled out a gun. 'You leave me no choice. You're unclean. Contaminated with the blood of our enemy!'

Hunapo's eyes bulged. He backed away. Trembling. Quick, jerky steps. Surely his father wouldn't kill him in cold blood. Maahanga leant forward and aimed the gun at Hunapo.

The bastard's going to shoot me! He is! He's going to do it!

'Kill me, and you'll have nobody to lead your precious Gang,' Hunapo spluttered, retreating into a corner. As he collapsed against the wall, something dug into his thigh. He slid his hand inside his pants and drew out the sword.

Maahanga shrank back. His face twitched as Hunapo aimed the sword at him.

Maahanga's eyes bulged. 'Put that down, Hunapo!'

'I thought you were a warrior. Man enough to face anything.' Hunapo stepped forward, brandishing the sword in front of him. 'Not such a superhero now, are you?'

'Just give it to me,' Maahanga said.

Hunapo pointed the sword at Maahanga's hand. 'Drop the gun.'

Maahanga let go. The gun fell to the ground.

 David Whittet

Hunapo felt his heart pounding. *It's him or me.* He pressed the blade against his father's neck. 'What? Scared *I'll* skin *you* alive?'

A drop of blood appeared on Maahanga's throat. Hunapo held his breath. What had he done?

Maahanga grabbed Hunapo's wrist and prised the sword away from his throat.

Hunapo yanked the blade back towards his father. *You've got to do it now. Before the old bugger gets the upper hand.* He watched the colour drain from Maahanga's face as he made another strike. More blood trickled down his father's chest.

Go on! An inner voice rang through Hunapo's head, goading him. *It's self-defence. One more thrust and there'll be no more beatings. Ever.*

Hunapo closed his eyes for a second. *I can't do it. He's my father.*

He inched the blade away from his father's neck. His arms went limp and Hunapo dropped the sword to the ground.

Maahanga wiped the blood off his neck with his sleeve and booted Hunapo onto the floor.

'You've tarnished our heritage!' Maahanga picked up his prized sabre and examined the blade. 'I can't believe you'd use our sacred weapon for some childish sham. And with *her*. Our enemy.' He kicked Hunapo again. 'Our ancestors won this sabre in battle. Men with balls. Not little boys who play with girls.'

Maahanga took a cloth and cleaned the blood from the blade, still cursing as he polished the decorative jewels on the hilt with his spit. 'Kai hamuti! I'll never forgive you for this.'

Hunapo curled into a ball, his head buried in his arms. *Why didn't I finish him off while I had the chance? I've blown it.*

Glancing through his fingers, Hunapo watched Maahanga admire the shining armament.

'Stained by a tyrant's blood!' Maahanga grunted, returning the sword to the cabinet.

Hunapo sat up and glared at his father. 'Yes! Your blood!'

'You miserable pōkokohua!'

Maahanga lunged at Hunapo, grabbing the back of his son's neck and dragging him outside into the yard.

'Let go! I can't breathe!' Hunapo pleaded.

Maahanga threw him to the ground. He landed in a puddle, almost choking as the muddy water went up his nose and into his mouth.

What's happening to me? The pool of blood by his head told Hunapo that his father was still chastising him. So why didn't he feel the pain? The belt had lost its sting. Hunapo could hardly feel it lashing his back. He scarcely flinched when Maahanga trampled on him. Had his body finally given up? Was he dying?

Even the verbal abuse faded into the distance. 'This bullshit ends tonight. When my father gave me a thrashing, I took it like a man. I've been too soft on you. How can I turn a snivelling crybaby into a warrior? Whakianga mai!'

Expletives flowed from Maahanga's mouth like bad poetry. After a last kick, Hunapo heard his father stomp back into the house. It was over. For now, at least.

Hunapo closed his eyes. The back door slammed. Then nothing.

Too sore to move and too confused to think, Hunapo looked up at the sky. How long had he been lying in the mud? Was it only this morning that he'd been heading to the Rere Falls to meet Aroha? The stars had looked so bright then. Now the clouds were gathering. Grey and murky.

It was getting dark. He must have been out cold all day. Cramp in his legs finally forced him to shift. Stumbling to his feet, Hunapo hobbled towards the house. He peered in the kitchen window. Through the ragged curtain, he saw his father warming some stew on the stove.

Hunapo had seen a rat scurry across the bench the previous day. It had freaked him out. Now it made him grin. *I hope the rat drowned in the stew and gives the bastard the plague.*

     David Whittet

He watched his father sit alone at the table and pick at his dinner. The old man obviously wasn't enjoying it. Good. If he hadn't thrown Kiri out, he wouldn't have to eat rat-infested leftovers.

Maahanga suddenly stood and stared at a fading picture of Hunapo's seventh birthday, stuck to the refrigerator with a magnet. Hunapo knew precisely what was going through his father's mind. The bastard always had a guilt trip after a beating. But it never lasted. His old man didn't really have a conscience.

Hunapo watched his father tear up the photograph and throw it in the trash along with the rest of his dinner.

Damn you! That was the last picture of my mother! And Kiri looked so happy in that photo. There'd been precious little happiness after she left.

Cold and hungry, Hunapo wanted to go inside. But he wasn't ready to face his old man again. Still staring through the window, he saw Maahanga light the fire and rub his hands in front of it. Outside, Hunapo shivered. *I hope the bastard burns his fingers!*

Hunapo sat on the doorstep. Was Maahanga really going to shoot him earlier that morning? Would he be dead if he hadn't had the sword? Hunapo shuddered. Should he have killed his father? He hated the old man enough. But even with a gun pointed at him, he couldn't do it.

Hunapo was still trying to make sense of it when he heard his father unbolt the door. He looked up as Maahanga beckoned him inside.

'Hunapo, son. Come in. There's some stew left on the stove.'

'I'm not hungry,' Hunapo said.

'Don't be like that,' Maahanga said. 'I had to do it. For your own good.'

'Bullshit!' Hunapo pushed past his father and slammed his bedroom door behind him.

Hunapo took off his cold and damp clothes. His mother would have put him in a hot bath and rubbed liniment into his wounds. She always did that after his father beat him.

Why did you leave me, Mum? I need you now more than ever before.

Chapter Eleven

WE SHARED BLOOD! Aroha wrote in her diary in large letters. *Does that mean nothing?* She scribbled underneath: *Why won't he see me again?*

She knew the answer already. *His father's given him another beating. Poor Hunapo. I could kill Maahanga.*

Writing about it didn't help. She threw the diary on the floor.

Aroha dreaded going to sleep. Ngaio made her cocoa at bedtime and told her to think about nice things. It didn't work. Besides, there was nothing *nice* about her life.

Every night she had the same horrific nightmare. Maahanga's belt digging into Hunapo's flesh. The foul yellow gunk oozing from the wounds. She woke up shouting. 'Stop it! Get off him! You bully!'

Too frightened to go back to sleep and bored with staring at the cobwebs and peeling wallpaper, Aroha climbed out of bed and gazed at the stars through her window. Kāterina had told her how the Southern Cross guarded against evil. 'Help Hunapo, please—and me,' Aroha whispered, her eyes fixed on the constellation.

She'd prayed her cousin would rescue her and fulfil her lifelong dream of escape from the Gang. Now it seemed *she* would have to save *him*. To do that, she'd have to find him first.

Weeks dragged into months. Chores. Lessons. Homework. Bed. And still not a glimpse of Hunapo. Instead of chewing her pencil when she wrote in her diary, she began biting her nails.

'You need to stop that, Aroha,' her mother growled when she tucked her into bed.

'Yes, Mum.'

'I don't know what's got into you. You're not concentrating on your lessons or your homework. And you're out of the door as soon as my back's turned.'

Aroha tossed around in her bed. Should she confide in her mother? She had to talk to someone.

'Mum …' Aroha took a deep breath. 'I'm looking for Hunapo. He's been avoiding me.'

Ngaio jumped upright. 'You stay away from that boy. Hunapo's no good for you.'

'But Mum! He's my friend.'

'He's bad news.'

'Mum!'

'He'll break your heart.' Ngaio raised her hand and waved a finger at Aroha. 'I don't want you seeing him again. Promise me.'

'No!' Aroha covered her head with her pillow.

'What about Jonno?' Ngaio pulled the bedclothes off Aroha's face. 'You liked him, didn't you? Remember how upset you were when he got his tā moko?'

Aroha looked at her mother suspiciously.

'He's a nice boy,' Ngaio continued. 'Why don't you go and see him?'

Aroha shook her head.

Ngaio got up abruptly and marched towards the bedroom door. 'In that case, you're grounded.'

Aroha cursed herself for trusting her mother. She thought Ngaio would never let her out of her sight. When the women elders came around for afternoon tea, Aroha's eyes lit up.

'I'll just play outside.' Aroha ran out of the house before Ngaio could answer. *And I'm not coming back until I've found him.*

She looked everywhere. All his usual haunts. The barn, the shed, the riverbank, the swing, the treehouse. She was about to give up when she thought of one last place. The old outhouse at the back of Maahanga's land. She raced across the paddock and there, on the doorstep, sat Hunapo. His eyes were cold and distant. His forehead furrowed and his fingers steepled. Was he sulking? Or just thinking?

After looking around to make sure they were alone, she ran up and flung her arms around him.

'Hunapo! I've missed you so much!'

'Shove off!' His voice was cold, and Aroha noticed his hand was shaking as he pushed her away. 'You're not welcome here.'

'You don't mean that, Hunapo!' Aroha sat down on the step beside him. 'That's your father speaking, not *you!*'

'Maybe it is. And he'll give me another hiding if he catches you here! Now piss off!'

'I'm not leaving.' Aroha shuffled closer. 'I'm going to help you fight back …'

Hunapo rolled his eyes. 'Can't you understand? This isn't some childish game.'

'I'm not stupid.'

'But you haven't a clue how much shit we're in.'

'I *do*. That's why we have to be strong.'

'Get real. We're screwed.'

'Don't say that.'

'What do you want me to do? Lie to you? Pretend everything's okay?'

'Of course not. But you have to stand up to your father.'

'You've got to be bloody kidding! My old man's damn near killed me already.' Hunapo raised his head towards her, sighed and looked away. 'You don't know the Gang like I do.'

'Bullshit!' Aroha jumped up from the step, flailing her arms in the air. 'Have you forgotten I'm the Gang president's daughter? I've had to sit there. Forced to watch boys getting tattooed. Not even allowed to close my eyes.'

'All right. Calm down. I'm sorry.' Hunapo turned his back on her, clenching his fists. 'But believe me, those ceremonies are small fry.'

'That shows how much you know.' Aroha stepped away, shifting from one foot to the other. 'I've seen parents carrying those kids off bleeding to death.'

 David Whittet

'That's nothing.' Hunapo bit his fingernails and cast her a black look. 'You've no idea what goes on out of sight. You'd shit your pants.'

'No idea?' A tear trickled down Aroha's cheek. 'No kid should have to watch their father beating up his mates just because they upset him …' She glared at Hunapo. There was so much more she wanted to tell him. How she'd laid awake in bed crying because there was nothing she could do to stop her father's cruelty. How she'd punished herself for her father's crimes, cutting her skin with a knife. She wiped the tears from her face. 'I thought we were kindred spirits.'

Their eyes finally met.

'We are … *were* …' Hunapo stood up. He took a pace towards her, stopped and swallowed hard. 'You've seen it all before, have you? Well, look at this.' Hunapo pulled off his shirt. 'This is what happens to you when you defy the Gang.'

Aroha felt her heart thumping. She shrank back. Covered her eyes. 'I can't look.'

'You must.' Hunapo grabbed hold of her and pulled her towards him.

Why was she so frightened? She'd seen the result of Maahanga's floggings before. The foul smell told her this would be much, much worse. She pinched her nose, but the stench wouldn't go away.

Hunapo clasped her head between his hands, forcing her face into his festering wounds.

'Stop it, Hunapo!' she cried. His grip was so strong that she struggled to breathe. 'You're hurting me!'

Her cheeks rubbed against his rotting flesh. She thought she was going to choke. No. Throw up.

Hunapo pulled her head back and glared into her eyes. 'Now can you see why we can't be together?' He let go of her and she swung away. 'Maahanga went ape when he found out we'd shared blood. The bastard thought he could purge your blood from my body if he beat me hard enough.'

Aroha hung her head over the edge of the step, covering her mouth to stop herself retching.

Hunapo rubbed her back. 'I didn't mean to frighten you. But you have to see things how they are.'

Aroha wiped her face. She scrambled to her feet and walked away. Damn. Her feet caught in the long grass. She didn't want him to see her stumble. She just wanted to get away. Yet she couldn't stop herself from looking back over her shoulder. What was he thinking? Was this the end of everything? Was he sad? Or was he glad to see the back of her?

Hunapo got up and took a couple of paces towards her.

'It's for the best,' he said. 'Go while you've still got the chance. I'd only bring you a lifetime of misery and unhappiness.'

She watched him kick a clod of mud. She thought she saw tears in his eyes, but perhaps she was mistaken. Boys don't cry. At least, that's what Hunapo always said.

He buttoned up his shirt and began to trudge home.

Those scars. Those *horrible* scars. Aroha couldn't bear it a moment longer and bolted off in the opposite direction.

Minutes later, Aroha was back with a fistful of kawakawa leaves.

'This will ease the pain,' she said, dragging him back to the doorstep.

'Bloody hell!' Hunapo exclaimed, his mouth wide open.

Aroha sat him down and rolled the leaves between her fingers, making them into a paste.

'Here, rub this into the wounds. You'll soon feel better.'

'Aroha … I don't know what to say …'

'Don't say anything. Come on. Let me do it for you.' Aroha took a dollop of the balm and began gently massaging it into his back. 'Let the kawakawa work its magic.'

'Why are you so good to me, Aroha?' Hunapo sighed. 'I don't deserve you.'

'Maybe not. But you *need* me. Who else is going to look after you like I do?'

     David Whittet

Hunapo shrugged. 'Nobody.'

Aroha took another dollop of the poultice and daubed it onto his broken skin. She dabbed her eyes, afraid her tears might spill into the wounds.

She handed him his shirt when she finished up. 'You can put this back on. But you can't go back to your father.' She wiped the paste from her hands and raised her eyes to his. 'Let's run away together. Today!'

Hunapo took a deep breath. 'I wish things could be different. My old man—' He looked at the blisters on his hand while doing up his shirt. 'As long as we go on seeing each other, it'll just get worse.' He picked at a scab before tucking his top into his pants. 'Thirteen years old. Scarred for life and scared shitless.'

Aroha wanted to hug him. Make everything better. But he backed away from her.

'It's over.' Hunapo almost choked on his words. 'We're history. We can't be seen together again. Never.'

The words she had dreaded. Aroha rocked her head.

Hunapo slapped his hands over his eyes. 'I have to be a leader. I have to do the right thing. Learn to lead the Gang to a better place. You've taught me that. Help me make the right choice. Please.'

'Going back to Maahanga is *not* the right choice,' Aroha replied. 'Not after what he's done to you!'

She saw his body tense. Heard him mutter something under his breath about the sacrifices he would have to make for the Gang.

'I have to go back,' he said eventually. 'My old man says he'll kill you if he catches us together again. And he means it. I can't let him do that to you.'

Before Aroha could take in what he'd just said, Hunapo had staggered to his feet and was running away across the paddock.

⚘

Uncle Maahanga wouldn't dare kill me. He's far too afraid of my father. Aroha tried to make sense of what Hunapo had said as she raced home. *It's all bullshit.*

Hunapo's just making excuses. Besides, she'd rather be dead than face the miserable life that waited for her back home.

I have to do the right thing, Hunapo had said. *Learn to lead the Gang to a better place. You've taught me that.* Did he really mean it? Or was that just more of his crap?

I thought you were different, Hunapo. Seems you're just like the rest. No, that wasn't fair. It was just … she'd prayed Hunapo would stand up to his father. *Do the right thing.* That would never happen with his father goading him. *She would have inspired Hunapo to be a just president.* Together they would have led the Gang to a better place, away from the bullying and corruption. Now, she was out of his life.

Aroha didn't even notice her mother berating her for breaking the curfew when she slunk back into the house. She went straight to her room and shut the door. After picking up her diary from the floor and grabbing a pencil from her bedside table, Aroha crashed onto her bed. Starting a new page in her diary, she wrote the heading in capitals: *SCARRED FOR LIFE.* She paused and bit the end of her pencil.

Scarred for life and scared shitless. Hunapo's words felt as appropriate to her as they were to him.

ઝ ઝ ઝ

Rere Falls, 1994.

Something was different. Aroha had seen it the moment she returned to the Rere Falls. An arborist had cut down their tree. The native rimu where Hunapo had first appeared, climbing down from the branches like a scene from a B-movie. Using his penknife, he'd carved their names in the wood with a love heart. That's where it all began. And now it had gone.

Was this a sign? Perhaps it wasn't only the Gang and their parents who had torn them apart. The tree surgeon had it in for them too. She'd always found peace at the Rere Falls. Now they looked bare and ugly without the weeping branches of the rimu and their red seed cones. Nothing was the same any more. Had the landscapers felled their love as well as their precious tree?

Aroha feared they had. The next time she'd come face to face with Hunapo after that disastrous day, the circumstances had been very different, and she'd had even more to forgive him for.

Were their fates destined to remain intertwined? Aroha shrugged. Yes, their paths would continue to cross, but in her heart she knew they would never again enjoy the unbridled freedom they had shared as blood cousins.

Part Two

Blood and Ink

Chapter Twelve

Urewera Forest, 1976.

'Hurry up and get ready,' Ngaio urged. 'We're going to see Kōkā.'

Aroha pulled a face. 'Do we have to?'

Aroha had always looked forward to visiting Kāterina with her mother. Not now. And definitely not today. Judging by Ngaio's expression, her mother wasn't too happy about it either.

Ngaio hit more potholes than ever. That always happened when her mother was in a mood. They didn't speak during the ride to the clearing or on the trek through the forest. Aroha had nothing to say. Her feet ached. And when they arrived, she would have to sit through another of Kāterina's stories. They weren't fun any more. Tales of courage and adventure were the last thing she wanted to hear. And after that, they'd have to walk back to the ute. More blisters.

As always, Kāterina was standing at the door of the *Gypsy Rose* waiting for them. Aroha took off her shoes without a word and climbed the steps into the caravan.

'What? No hugs for your Aunt Kōkā?' Kāterina's face dropped. 'Whatever's the matter?'

'Don't ask.' Ngaio took off her coat and slumped on a stool. 'Just don't ask!'

Kāterina put her arms around Aroha and gave her a squeeze. 'Tāku tamaiti! My precious child! Tell your aunty what's wrong.'

'I can't.' Aroha peered up at her mother. 'Not with …'

'I understand.' Kāterina followed Aroha's eyes towards Ngaio. 'Be an angel, Ngaio. Pop outside and boil the kettle on the barbie. The stove in here's out of gas and I'm dying for a cuppa.'

Ngaio grunted. Aroha ignored the scowl as her mother left the caravan.

Kāterina pulled Aroha closer. 'You can talk now. We're on our own.'

Aroha pushed back. 'What's the use?'

'Perhaps I can help you,' she answered, stroking Aroha's tangled hair. 'Try me.'

'Promise you won't say anything to Mum? Or Dad?'

'Of course I won't,' Kāterina said. 'You can trust me.'

'It's Hunapo,' Aroha blurted out. 'I've been seeing Hunapo …'

'I was right!' Kāterina jumped off her stool, almost dropping Aroha onto the floor. 'Did he climb down a tree, just like I told you?'

Aroha nodded, hooking her feet around the stool to steady herself.

'This is nothing to be sad about!' Kāterina exclaimed, using a musty old handkerchief to dry the tears on Aroha's face. 'I know your parents won't approve, but they'll come round. Hunapo's a good boy. He'll make you happy!'

'You don't understand.' Aroha dabbed her eyes with her hands. 'It's over between Hunapo and me. He's dumped me!'

'Dumped you?' Kāterina shook her head. 'Why?'

'He says I'm turning him into a wuss. Holding him back from being a leader.'

'That's Maahanga speaking—not Hunapo!'

'His father's going to kill him.'

Kāterina rubbed her chin. 'I've heard Hunapo's father mistreats him.'

'Mistreats him?' Aroha almost choked on her words. 'You should see his back—it's all bent out of shape.'

'He showed you?'

Aroha nodded.

'Murua ahau. My poor child.' Kāterina held Aroha tight against her bosom. 'He shouldn't have subjected you to that.'

'He didn't mean to—at least, not at first.' Aroha rubbed her face against Kāterina's chest. 'His body's covered in scars. I almost threw up!'

'Whakarihariha tēnā! Disgraceful!' Kāterina patted Aroha's back. 'I'm so sorry.'

Aroha flinched when she heard her mother step back into the caravan.

'Tea's made,' Ngaio said.

　　　　David Whittet

Aroha slid to the floor as her mother handed Kāterina a mug of tea. Listening to the two women's conversation while they slurped their tea, she wanted to scream.

Ngaio eyed Kāterina. 'I hope you've been talking some sense into Aroha. She won't listen to me.'

Aroha glared at her mother. *What does Mum know? She hasn't a clue what I'm going through.*

Kāterina put her mug down on the bench. 'We need more time on our own,' she told Ngaio. 'Could you pick some vegetables from the patch? I was going to make us some minestrone soup for supper.'

Ngaio sighed. 'Just remember Aroha's vulnerable right now. I don't want you filling her with nonsense. She needs a firm hand.'

Aroha turned her head to see Kāterina nodding. *She doesn't get it either. I need someone to understand how I feel.*

She watched her mother leave the caravan again. Ngaio's face looked even more miserable this time.

Kāterina beckoned Aroha back to her lap.

'I *want* Hunapo to be a leader.' Aroha got up off the mat and moved to Kāterina. 'I *want* him to take the Gang to a better place. But that will *never* happen with Maahanga goading him!'

'Then you must work on him,' Kāterina said.

'No.' Aroha buried her head in Kāterina's breast. 'He's shut me out of his life. Forever.'

Kāterina hummed a tune and rocked Aroha in her arms. 'How can we bring a smile back to your lovely face?'

Aroha wiped her nose on Kāterina's dress. 'You can't.'

'We'll see. Just a moment, Aroha.' Kāterina stood up and fetched her crystal ball from its plinth.

Aroha settled back on Kāterina's lap and watched her stroke the ball like a beloved pet.

'Awhinatia ahau ki te whakamarie i a Aroha!' Kāterina crooned. 'Help me to comfort Aroha!'

Aroha had always enjoyed listening to Kāterina singing. It was usually so lyrical. Today it sounded just plain raucous.

'Mum'll go mad if she sees you messing around with the crystal ball,' Aroha said. 'You know what she's like.'

'Yes, I do.' Kāterina ran her hands across the shining sphere. 'But today's...different.'

'Mum won't think so.' Aroha shrugged her shoulders. 'Anyway, it doesn't matter. I don't care any more.'

'Don't give up, Aroha. I see hope in the crystal ball …'

Aroha lowered her head. 'I don't want *hope*. I want *Hunapo!*'

'Perhaps Hunapo is not the boy for you after all. Maybe we can find someone better.'

Aroha rubbed her bloodshot eyes and watched Kāterina's gnarled fingers follow the curves of the ball.

'Come on, old girl,' Kāterina muttered, her hands moving faster and faster. 'You're not past it yet.'

Aroha wished she'd just stop. 'Kāterina, please—'

'Wait!' Kāterina pointed at a blurred reflection in the ball. 'I see something here … a tall, dark stranger …'

Aroha covered her eyes. 'If it's not Hunapo, I don't want to know.'

'Look.' Kāterina gently pulled Aroha's hands away from her face. 'He's *very* handsome, and he's come all the way from the east, just to meet you.'

Aroha threw her arms in the air. 'I don't care if he's come from the North Pole.'

Kāterina frowned. 'Don't be like that.' She tilted her head and put her ear to the crystal ball. 'Can't you hear the East Wind? Blowing him to Rere.'

'It's no use, Kāterina,' Aroha sighed. 'I know you're just trying to cheer me up and it's not working. I'm not a baby any more.'

'Of course you're not. But this is real, Aroha. The wind is blustering the *Gypsy Rose*. Can't you feel the caravan shaking?'

     David Whittet

Aroha watched Kāterina banging the floor with her foot.

'You're doing that on purpose!' Aroha snorted.

'No, I'm not,' Kāterina shot back indignantly. 'Something magical is happening.' She rubbed her hands together dramatically, a wicked glint in her eyes. 'A force beyond our reckoning is at work. A power we cannot resist. Stop fighting it.'

Aroha stopped listening. Normally, she would have lapped up Kāterina's antics. Today she just wanted the old woman to shut up.

Then suddenly the caravan swayed. Violently. What was going on? This time it wasn't Kāterina doing it. Was the mysterious stranger really coming for her?

Aroha jumped off the bench. 'I don't like it,' she shrieked. 'Make it go away! I want Hunapo back! No one else. I want Hunapo!'

Ngaio burst into the caravan. She took Aroha in her arms and glared at Kāterina. 'What the hell is going on?' she demanded. 'What have you done to her, Kōkā?'

Kāterina lowered her head. 'I was just trying to cheer her up.'

'Cheer her up? Just look at her!' Ngaio shook her head. 'Why did I trust you?'

'I would never do anything to harm her,' Kāterina hit back defiantly. 'You know that. She's hurting and she's got things she's afraid to tell you. She needs you to understand.'

'I don't need a parenting lesson from you, Kōkā,' Ngaio snapped.

Aroha listened to Kāterina and her mother arguing over what was best for her. What did either of them know about what she needed?

'Get your coat, Aroha,' Ngaio said. 'Hurry up! We're leaving. We'll be late home as it is. I want to get back before dark. There'll be all hell to pay from your father if his dinner's not on the table when he gets home!'

Aroha tripped on the rucked mat as she fetched her coat from a peg by the caravan door.

'Quickly! Here—let me help you.' Ngaio grabbed Aroha and buttoned up her coat.

As she left the caravan with her mother, Aroha felt Kāterina tug on her arm.

'Be strong, Aroha,' Kāterina urged. 'Tōku taonga! My treasure! Farewell! E noho rā!'

What a ghastly afternoon. With so many thoughts racing through her head, Aroha thought her brain would explode. As if getting over Hunapo wasn't enough, Kāterina had to torment her with stuff and nonsense about some dark, handsome man.

Only her sore feet and frozen ears took Aroha's mind off things during what felt like an endless trek back through the forest. Ngaio scarcely breathed a word to her the whole way.

At last, the clearing where Ngaio had parked the vehicle was in sight. For once, it would be a relief to get home. The distant rumble of a horse galloping broke the forest's eerie silence. Aroha glance back over her shoulder. The horse neighed. She'd know that sound anywhere.

'It's Cleo,' Aroha exclaimed, nudging her mother. 'Look!'

Ngaio didn't look. 'Just keep walking.'

Amidst a cloud of dust, Kāterina appeared riding her horse, Cleopatra, one hand on the reins, the other clasping her crystal ball. Aroha shielded her eyes, dazzled by the glow of the ball in the twilight.

'Stop! Ngaio! Come back!' Kāterina's cry rang out, echoing through the trees. 'I need to warn Aroha …'

When she finally caught up with them, Kāterina looked so excited that Aroha thought she was going to fall off the horse.

'What now?' Ngaio groaned.

Kāterina held the crystal ball high in the air. 'My precious has shown me things—'

'No more,' Ngaio interrupted. 'Just go home, Kōkā.'

'This is important!' Kāterina caught her breath. 'I told Aroha she would meet someone new. A stranger from the east. Turns out he might not be good for her. I've just seen it in my crystal ball.'

David Whittet

Aroha raised her eyes to the heavens. Had Kāterina really ridden all this way just to spout more rubbish?

'Go home, Kōkā,' Ngaio repeated. 'I'm not listening to another word.'

'Why won't you hear me out?' Kāterina pleaded. 'You used to call me your rock. Have you forgotten?'

'That was then.' Ngaio grasped Aroha's hand and strode down the path toward the vehicle.

Aroha felt more confused than ever as her mother bundled her into the ute. Did Kāterina really believe what she was saying? Was she going to meet some dark stranger and was he going to bring her trouble?

'That wretched woman,' Ngaio fumed, starting the vehicle. 'Don't take any notice of Kōkā and her ridiculous stories.'

Aroha scowled. 'I *didn't* take any notice. Kāterina still thinks I'm a little girl and believe in her fairy tales.'

'Good for you, Aroha. Kōkā is just a foolish old woman.'

'I told Kāterina, I don't care about some prince from a far-off land. It's Hunapo I want. *Hunapo!*'

'Hunapo is *not* the boy for you,' Ngaio growled. She revved the engine, struggling to get the ute out of the mud. 'Believe me! He will *never* make you happy!'

'He *would*—if you gave him a chance.'

Aroha turned away and gazed out of the window for the entire journey home. She couldn't bring herself to look at her mother again, let alone speak to her. Ngaio continually jammed the gearbox in frustration, the graunching noise punctuating the mood within the cab as the ute bounced over the rough terrain.

The experience unsettled Aroha. She did her best to forget about Kāterina's prediction. It was just an old woman's fantasy. But what if it wasn't? After all, Kāterina had been right about Hunapo scaling down a tree in front of the falls.

Whenever the East Wind blew over her face, Aroha wondered about the dark, handsome man whom Kāterina had described to her so vividly. Would she ever meet him? And what was the dire warning Kāterina had seen in her crystal ball?

❧ ❧ ❧

Rere Falls, 1994.

Returning to the falls hadn't provided any answers. Fifteen years on and Aroha was still no closer to understanding the madness of the months following that fateful visit to the *Gypsy Rose*.

Why had she come back to Rere? What had she expected? Maybe she'd hoped the spray from the waterfall would anoint her with knowledge and wisdom. Only then could she make sense of the dark chain of events that turned her life upside down.

Dipping her toes in the water, Aroha remembered the emptiness she'd felt when Hunapo disappeared from her life. How she'd grieved for their friendship. Then, when she'd finally come to terms with the loss, they were suddenly thrown back together. An arranged marriage with Hunapo—it should have been a dream come true. So why had it ended in disaster?

At the time, it was all a gigantic muddle. Why did Tautaru and Maahanga hate each other so much? And why were the women so keen to see her marry Hunapo?

It wasn't until her early twenties that Aroha pieced together the snippets of gossip and conversation she'd overheard. Her mother had always maintained the kitchen was the heart of the gangland home. Aroha quickly realised, though, that the real powerhouse was the verandah, where the women gathered when

David Whittet

the men kicked them out during Gang meetings. The women missed nothing. They dissected and digested everything over afternoon tea.

The more she discovered, the more convinced Aroha became it was Moana Kingi, the women's leader, who was responsible for her appalling predicament.

Aroha had never liked Moana. She was stuck-up and self-centred and delighted in putting everyone else down. Moana was especially mean to Ngaio. Aroha could see how much the constant barbs hurt her mother.

Moana was so scary that Aroha had avoided her whenever she could. The old dragon thought she owned the marae. When Moana had caught Aroha skipping with her rope in the courtyard, the tongue lashing was so severe that she wet herself.

If she'd known the whole story back then, Aroha would have hated Moana even more.

It was Lilly who eventually told Aroha about the ill-conceived meeting on the marae where the women's conspiracy was hatched. Dear Lilly. The one member of the women's circle with the courage to speak out.

'How could Moana be that evil?' Aroha exclaimed, clinging to Lilly when she learnt the truth.

'Moana's a callous bitch,' Lilly said. 'She could turn any situation to her advantage. She had no qualms whatever about manipulating your relationship with Hunapo for her own ends.'

Chapter Thirteen

Moana's Place, Rere Township, 1978.

Lilly squatted uncomfortably on the deck. She was equally ill at ease with the tone of the meeting and didn't join in the women's gossip as they drank their tea.

'What's the latest on Aroha and Hunapo?'

'It's like *Romeo and Juliet's* come to Rere!'

'Maybe it'll end in a duel to the death between old man Tautaru and Maahanga!'

'Who'd win? My money's on Maahanga. Tautaru's all mouth.'

'I'd laugh if the dickheads killed each other!'

'Yay! No more protection money!'

'Shut it all of you.' Moana glared at the women, her eyes as black as the storm clouds overhead and as threatening as the tā moko on her chin. 'This is no joke.'

'Don't be such a spoilsport, Mo!' Rona protested, biting into a savoury muffin. 'We haven't had this much fun in ages.'

'Yeah, lighten up, Mo.' Erina put down her teacup with a sigh. 'Sometimes you just have to laugh …'

Lilly shook her head. Didn't the women realise they were talking about living, breathing people? She glanced up at Moana. Dressed in a dark, rusty-gold jersey coat over a black dress embellished with an ornate Māori pattern representing fire, Moana stood apart from the rest of the women. Lilly understood why she was so cold and aloof. The feud between the two brothers had ruined her and her husband, Hori. Before the fall out, Hori had invested substantial funds in Maahanga's businesses. Financial disaster struck when hostilities escalated and Tautaru demanded his men divest their interests in anything belonging to Maahanga.

Lilly shrugged. Perhaps if something like that had happened to her, she'd have been equally hard-nosed.

'Does anyone know how the feud started?' Erina asked.

Rona shook her head. The others joined in.

'Haven't a clue.'

'Me neither.'

'Lost in urban legend, I'd say.'

'No.' Moana silenced the women with a stroke of her hand. 'It was greed. Pure greed.'

'No surprises there,' Rona muttered, pulling a face.

'Come on then, Mo. Spill!'

Moana sighed. 'It all began with a heist,' she said, settling into her chair and leaning against the verandah railing. 'Hori told me about the night the Gang nicked a whole truckload of priceless Māori artworks from a visiting exhibition.'

Lilly closed her eyes as Moana described the robbery. She didn't want to know how the vendetta had started. She'd seen how it ended.

'Tautaru bribed the security company's guards,' Moana explained. 'Promised them a share of the takings if they disabled the alarm. The entire operation was Tautaru's baby. He'd done his homework—Māori art was in high demand. And Tautaru had the underground network to flog the pieces.

'Hori smelt trouble the moment he went to help Tautaru load the canvases onto a truck. He couldn't believe his eyes when he caught Tautaru kissing the paintings. That's right. The bastard had the canvases in his hands, and there he was slobbering all over them. "You *beauty!*" Tautaru had drooled. "You're going to make me rich—*very rich!*"'

Moana tapped her fingers on the railing. 'That's when it all went wrong. Tautaru wanted it all for himself. He refused to give the security guards their cut.'

'Bloody hell!' Erina raised her eyebrows. 'Typical Tautaru. Selfish bastard. How come the guards didn't kill him?'

'Tautaru made himself scarce,' Moana continued. 'Too busy counting the spoils. As usual, it was Maahanga who copped it. The boys were out celebrating the haul at Smash Palace. They all took a dreadful bashing. My Hori too.'

Lilly took a deep breath and held it in. Her partner, Matt, had been at Smash Palace that night. He'd come home with a black eye and a broken nose. His nose was still crooked.

Moana went on to recount what she'd heard from Hori about the riotous party at the tavern. Maahanga had torn off his shirt and danced on the top of a table, singing a bawdy song at the top of his voice. Some women joined him on the tabletop, flashing their cleavage in his face. The men had raised their bottles in the air, showering one another in beer. Maahanga toppled off the table, smashing a chair with his fall.

'I knew something was up when Hori wasn't home by daybreak,' Moana said. 'So I went looking for him. They were all still at Smash Palace. And it wasn't a pretty sight. Our boys comatose on the ground. Broken beer bottles everywhere. And that was before they got busted. Poor devils didn't know what hit them.'

Lilly felt even more distant from the rest of the women. They were all lapping up Moana's story as if it was just an entertaining diversion. Hadn't their partners suffered injury on that night too?

'I was just in time to see the security men ransack the place,' Moana said. *"Screw you,"* they screamed, kicking our lads with their hobnail boots. "Where are the goods, you double-crossing bastards?"

'Maahanga held his head and groaned. "What's the hell's going on?"

'"Check the cellars," the men said, pulling panels off the walls and tearing the seating apart. "I bet the bastards have hidden the gear down there …"

'I remember this giant roughneck picking Maahanga up and pinning him against the bar. "They're not here—believe me," Maahanga kept repeating. "Bugger off! You'll get your money …"

'The goon spat in Maahanga's face. "We're doing a job up in Whakatane tomorrow night. If we don't have the brass before we leave … Well, nobody bullshits us and gets away with it."'

        David Whittet

Lilly's legs had gone to sleep. She always ended up crouching on the deck. The other women invariably pushed her out of the way in the scramble to get a chair. Today's session had gone on longer than ever. She rubbed her calves and tried to shuffle into a more comfortable position.

Pania, the rubberneck amongst the women, took up the story. 'My Bill was there when Maahanga had it out with Tautaru. I'd have given anything to have been there too.'

Lilly groaned as Pania told the women how Maahanga had charged round to Tautaru's place to confront his brother. Pania was an even better storyteller than Moana, and the women were enjoying every minute of her recount.

'Tautaru was in the backyard, loading the spoils onto a trailer,' Pania said. 'Bill said he scarcely acknowledged their presence.

'Maahanga let rip. "What the bloody hell are you playing at, Tautaru? Are you *trying* to get us all killed? Pōkokohua!"

'"Bugger off!" Tautaru shook his fist. "Everything's under control."

'Bill thought Maahanga was going to explode. "Under control? Kai hamuti! You should have been at Smash Palace. We all got the bash. We're in the shit if those bastards stitch us up!"

'"My brother! Fancies himself a warrior and he's shitting himself over a bunch of mercenaries!" Tautaru snorted. "You'll get your cut if that's what you're worried about."

'"You don't bloody get it, do you?" Maahanga retaliated. "What good's the money if we're all in the clink?"

'Bill watched them continue to fight while Tautaru secured the last of the paintings on his trailer.

'"I might have known you'd bottle it," Tautaru said.

'"You're a dickhead, Tautaru!" Maahanga replied. "Those punks won't take it lying down. They'll grass! They're turning the screws already!"

'"Our men can look after themselves. Just butt out, Maahanga. Leave this to me."

'"Damn you! You're not bulletproof. These men are bruisers. You can't order them around as if they were your minions."

'"Bruisers, are they?" Tautaru gave Maahanga the finger as he drove off. "I didn't realise you were such a chicken."

'"Give the bastards their share, you son of a bitch," Maahanga shouted after him. "We've only got a few hours! Whakianga mai!"'

Pania dissolved into a fit of giggles as she wound up her story. 'And the best bit—when the men grassed, I heard Tautaru and Maahanga spent the night next door to each other in the cells.'

The women clapped and joined in the laughter.

Lilly covered her face. It wasn't the least bit funny. The feud had destroyed the lives of those closest to her—especially her dear friend Ngaio. And Ngaio's beautiful daughter, Aroha.

'So how come they're not still in prison?' Erina asked.

'A bent lawyer. How else?' Moana said. She wasn't laughing either. 'And the pricks have been fighting ever since.'

'Actually, it started long before that,' Neina said, leaning forward. In her late eighties, Neina was the oldest member of the group. With her steel-grey hair and high cheekbones, she had mana. 'They've hated each other since they were kids.'

'Perhaps Maahanga had a bigger dick,' Rona hooted.

'Rona!' Moana reprimanded as the women collapsed with laughter.

'Maahanga was an attractive man in his youth,' Neina said in her rasping voice. 'He was lean, slender, athletic and virile. Everything that Tautaru was not …'

'I heard Ngaio had an affair with Maahanga,' Erina chipped in. 'No wonder they hate each other.'

Lilly felt her muscles tense. How could they mock her friend this way?

Pania laughed. 'Aye, Ngaio has a past all right. I heard there was a love child.'

'You made that up,' Moana scolded. 'You need to watch your mouth. It's going to get you into a heap of trouble.'

'Yeah, Pania.' Erina toyed with a lock of hair. 'You're dead meat if Tautaru hears you talking like that.'

Lilly leapt to her feet, glaring at the women. 'Stop it!' She grasped the table

 David Whittet

to steady herself, almost falling over with cramp in her legs. 'How dare you? Ngaio is my friend. And she's a respected member of our circle.'

'Lilly's right.' Neina raised her hand. 'This is no joke—'

'It certainly isn't,' Moana interrupted. 'But it could be just the opportunity we've been waiting for.' She paused for a moment. Her features suddenly lit up, and she banged the table to get everyone's attention. 'I want you all at the marae tomorrow afternoon for a hui. Two o'clock on the dot. And not a word to anyone. Especially not your men.'

Lilly slumped to the floor again. She'd seen that look on Moana's face before. What was the conniving battleaxe up to now?

❧ ❧ ❧

Matara Marae.

Lilly had a bad feeling as the elders arrived in huddles at the marae the next day. She'd been awake all night, second-guessing Moana's plans. The women gossiped with one another as they removed their shoes before entering the ornately carved meeting house. Had any of them given a thought to why Moana had summoned them to the meeting? Did any of them care?

Moana was there at the entrance, insisting they all swear an oath of secrecy.

Lilly sighed. 'Is this really necessary?'

Moana held up a piece of paper. 'Just read it out and swear it.'

'Bloody hell, Mo.' Pania pushed her way to the front. 'What's going on? Don't you trust us?'

'You, too, Pania,' Moana said. 'Swear it on your life. Not a word to anyone. Especially not Tautaru or Maahanga.'

Lilly tucked herself away at the back as the thirty-odd women sat cross-legged on the floor in the cramped meeting room. Moana stood tall, towering above the elders as she addressed the hui.

'We have all suffered because of the bad blood between Tautaru and Maahanga,' Moana began. 'Like many of you, Hori and I lost our life savings and our home.' She drummed her fingers on the wooden lectern. 'Remember the good times before those two dickheads started their vendetta? When profit drove the Gang, not infantile squabbling? Now we struggle to put food on the table for our mokopuna.'

Lilly had to admit Moana was a charismatic speaker. The elders applauded enthusiastically. Lilly glanced up at the rafters. If Moana's voice got any louder, it would blow the cobwebs off the sculptured panels of the ceiling.

'The men are frigging useless,' Moana continued. 'None of them have the balls to stand up to Tautaru. *We* have to fix this.' She paused and took a deep breath. 'And the solution is staring us in the face. Aroha and Hunapo …'

Lilly buried her head in her hands. *I thought as much.* It was the thought of Moana dragging Aroha into her half-baked scheme that had kept Lilly awake the previous night. Thank God the other women seemed equally shocked. Lilly watched them shake their heads and look at each other in disbelief.

'Aroha and Hunapo?' Pania jumped to her feet. 'Are you out of your mind, Mo?'

'No, strangely enough, I'm not.' Moana raised her palms to the women. 'Aroha and Hunapo are our one chance to end this fiasco once and for all. We've all watched and laughed. Maybe it's just a childhood crush, but we can use it to bring the family—and the Gang—back together.'

'No!' Lilly wiped a bead of perspiration from her forehead and stumbled to her feet. She'd never spoken out at a meeting before. 'You can't do that to Aroha. She's just a child.'

'Yeah, Mo. Get real,' Pania said. 'It's not going to happen. Tautaru would go raving mad. And we all know what happens then. We get the bash from his heavies.'

Lilly watched Pania walk up to the rostrum and push Moana aside. She'd never had much time for Pania before, but she had to admit, standing up to Moana took guts.

'Whatever were you thinking?' Pania continued, eyeballing Moana. 'Have you got a death wish or something?'

Moana climbed back onto the rostrum and tapped on the lectern. 'Actually, I'm thinking about an arranged marriage.' She stared straight ahead at the women. 'Come on, my friends, we're the women of the Gang! We can outsmart those stupid arseholes! We're the ones with the brains!'

Lilly was speechless. She wanted to jump up and down, but her legs wouldn't move. Or scream, but her mouth wouldn't open either. Why didn't she have Pania's nerve?

'Tell me you're not serious, please,' Lilly spluttered.

Her friend Evie, a small woman with a large heart, came to her rescue, putting her arm on Lilly's shoulder.

'This is madness, Mo,' Evie said. 'It couldn't possibly work. Tautaru wouldn't stand for it. We'd have an all-out war …'

Erina was next on her feet. 'Evie's right. I'm not one for rocking the boat.'

'Bloody right,' Anika said. 'I haven't got over the last beating yet.'

'And it's not just Tautaru,' Pania said. 'What about Maahanga? He'd go crazy too. And if he gets wind of this, he'll never let Hunapo near Aroha again.'

'We all know how Maahanga treats Hunapo,' Evie sighed. 'He's already beaten any romantic feelings out of Hunapo.'

'I thought my women had more balls than their men,' Moana said. 'Seems not.' Her dark eyes radiated a mesmeric gleam as she focused on each of the women in turn. 'My plan *will* work! I am going to *make* it work!'

'Don't look at me like that!' Pania screwed her eyes shut. 'You don't fool me with your mind tricks.'

Lilly shielded her eyes from Moana's stare. But she sensed the mood of the meeting was changing. One by one, Moana was sucking the women in.

'We have to do something,' Erina said.

'Damn right, we do,' Rona added. 'Tautaru's bleeding us dry.'

Evie flung her arms in the air. 'Yes, but a *marriage!*'

'Why not?' Rona said. 'It's a Gang tradition.' Her eyes suddenly lit up. 'Perhaps that's why Hunapo and Aroha met. I've always believed everything happens for a reason.'

'Don't give me that bull!' Pania growled.

Rona pulled a face. 'So what would you have us do? Sit back and do nothing while our children go hungry?'

Erina glared at Pania. 'Have you got a better idea?'

'Of course she hasn't!' Moana clasped her hands on the lectern, her eyes still locked on the women. 'So I suggest we start making plans.'

Lilly had a sinking feeling in her stomach. *Do something. Don't let Moana win.* But what could she say that would make any difference?

Before Lilly could find the words, Hana, a newcomer to the women's circle, was on her feet and challenging Moana. That girl had bottle.

'Is this legal?' Hana asked. 'How old are they? I thought Aroha was only fourteen...'

Pania snorted. 'Since when was anything the Gang does legal? Gang rule is all that counts around here. You'll soon learn that, Hana.'

Hana shook her head. 'It still doesn't make it right.'

'Don't talk to me about what's right!' Moana pounced on Hana, jumping off the rostrum and pointing a finger at her. 'Who the hell do you think you are? Coming here with your posh accent and your fancy outfits. You're not in Auckland now. You haven't lost everything like us. Our kids are starving—that's not *right*.' Moana moved back to the rostrum and leant forward over the lectern. 'Well, now we have the means to put things right. Aroha and Hunapo. Who cares if it's legal or not? Arranged marriages are happening in gangs throughout the country, often with kids a lot younger than Aroha!'

'What about Ngaio?' Evie said. 'You can't do this to her.'

'Evie's got a point,' Anika jumped in. 'Ngaio will never allow it.'

'She'll have no choice.' Moana dismissed Anika with a wave of the hand. 'Where is Ngaio anyway? Absent as usual. She never comes to our meetings.'

You bitch! This time, Lilly didn't hesitate. Grabbing Evie's arm for support, she was back on her feet in an instant, her voice trembling. 'How can you say that? You know why she's not here. Tautaru won't let her attend!'

 David Whittet

'Exactly!' Moana gritted her teeth. 'Tautaru has Ngaio under his thumb. And for that reason, there is no way she can usefully contribute to our affairs. I propose we expel Ngaio from the group.'

Lilly's jaw dropped. *You are a bitch!* 'Take that back, Mo. If Ngaio goes, I'm leaving too.'

'Me too,' Evie added, standing beside Lilly. 'None of us will agree to that.'

All the women joined in, jeering and shaking their heads at Moana.

Anika raised a fist. 'That's harsh, even for you, Mo.'

Moana took a step back. 'Okay. Calm down. I didn't mean that.' She took a deep breath. 'But whatever we feel about Ngaio *personally*, she's still Tautaru's stooge. We cannot let her dictate our policy or interfere with our plans. Remember, this is for us. For our whānau! For our children! Our tamariki! Our mokopuna! They're all *still* hungry!'

Moana's powerful voice resounded through the marae. Lilly watched the women's heads beginning to nod in agreement. Damn Moana—yet again she had the elders exactly where she wanted them. Lilly sank back to the floor in despair.

'Our children are our future,' Moana declared. 'Let's do this for them!' She raised her hands in the air. 'There's no time to lose. I move we take a vote on it!'

Lilly didn't need to look at the show of hands. She already knew in her heart that Moana had won.

The women joined hands as they left the marae and gathered in a huddle outside.

'Have we just made the biggest mistake of our lives?' Anika asked. 'What have we just agreed to?'

'God help us,' Lilly said.

Pania swung around, breaking away from the group. 'Bloody fools! Why the hell did you let Moana fool you? It'll take more than God to get us out of this mess!'

Would God help them? Lilly repeated her prayer in Māori as she wandered home alone. 'Ka awhina te Atua i a matou.'

Chapter Fourteen

Lilly's Place, Rere Township, 1993.

Aroha pressed her hands to her cheeks. She couldn't take it all in at first. Lilly's recollections cast new light on muddles and worries that had haunted Aroha for so many years. Half-heard conversations suddenly made sense. Contradictions fell into place. Why hadn't she pieced it together before?

Lilly leant forward. 'If only I'd been stronger,' she said. 'I should have stood up to Moana. Stirred the other women into action.' She put her arm on Aroha's shoulder. 'I'm so sorry. I could have saved you all this misery.'

'Don't blame yourself,' Aroha said. She noticed a tear in the corner of Lilly's eye. 'None of this is your fault.' She paused for a moment, remembering the incident with the skipping rope on the marae. 'Moana's the scariest woman I know.'

Lilly shook her head. 'Pania saw what was coming. I think the rest of the women did too. They were just too afraid to admit it.'

'So how did Moana pull it off?' Aroha asked. 'How did she dupe Tautaru into accepting the marriage?'

'She got Hori to do her dirty work,' Lilly said. 'As usual. I'd give anything to have been a fly on the wall when the poor guy got home from work that night.'

Aroha frowned. 'I still don't see how she did it. Tautaru hated Hunapo. He was always mouthing off about Hunapo being a threat to his leadership. Said he was going to get rid of Hunapo once and for all.'

'Moana was clever,' Lilly said, settling herself in the chair. 'Hori told my Matt how she shamed him into going along with her plan. She sent him on a guilt trip. Said they lived in a pit because Hori didn't have the guts to stand up to Tautaru. Everything was Hori's fault. According to her, he should never have bailed out on Maahanga

David Whittet

when Tautaru gave the order. Now he had the chance to make good—by convincing Tautaru that the ultimate revenge on Maahanga was to take Hunapo away from him.'

'And Hori really believed he could hoodwink Tautaru?' Aroha said. 'He didn't know my old man.'

'According to Matt, she even convinced Hori that her plan would bring down both Tautaru and Maahanga. Everyone would hail Hori as a hero. The one who brought prosperity back to the Gang. And he'd be the next president.'

Aroha raised her eyebrows. 'As if Tautaru would fall for that. Hori *really* didn't know my father.'

Lilly giggled. 'Hori told Matt he was convinced Moana had found a new lover, and it was all a ploy to get him bumped off.'

'I'm amazed Tautaru didn't kill him,' Aroha said.

'I was there when Hori confronted Tautaru,' Lilly continued. 'Matt and I were having a drink at Smash Palace. I remember Hori poking his head through the door. Tautaru was propping up the bar, surrounded by his cronies and full of his usual hot air. I watched Hori stand there, waiting for the right moment. His face said it all. Then I saw the moneybag, tucked under his arm.'

'He wanted to put Tautaru in a good mood?' Aroha asked. She'd noticed how her father's minions always had the telltale satchels in their hands when they needed a favour.

'Exactly,' Lilly said. 'No better way to suck up to Tautaru than giving him the spoils of a drug run. Hori sidled up to the bar and asked Tautaru for a word in private. You should have seen old man Tautaru's eyes light up when he saw the bag. The pair of them disappeared into an alcove. I could hardly see them through the layers of smoke, but I caught a few snippets of what they were saying.'

Aroha held up a hand. 'Wait. I'm not sure I'm ready for this.'

'You are.' Lilly gave Aroha's shoulder another stroke. 'Knowing what happened will help you understand. I promise.'

Aroha looked down at the floor. That didn't make listening to the story any more comfortable.

'Perhaps Tautaru was too busy counting the money to take in what Hori was saying,' Lilly continued. 'But I tell you, he exploded when Hori convinced him Maahanga was plotting a coup.'

Lilly mimicked Tautaru sounding off. *'Maahanga and Hunapo leading the Gang as father and son? Never! I'll tear the bastard limb from limb!'*

Lilly paused for a moment, then added, 'Everyone in the bar looked up. But they soon lost interest. Tautaru berating one of his men was nothing unusual. But I kept listening.

'"There's another way to get back at him, Tautaru," I heard Hori say. "Take Hunapo away from him. Bring Hunapo into your whānau! Watch Maahanga grow old as a broken man. A tired and lonely loser! Watch him sink into despair. He's always had a weakness for the bottle. How long till he's a drunken old sozzle?"

'I watched Tautaru down the last of his beer and wipe his mouth on his sleeve. "You could be right," he muttered, or something like that. "This might be the answer."

'Moana must have told Hori exactly what to say. He was word perfect. "You always said putting a bullet in Maahanga's head would be too quick for the bastard. Now's your chance to make him really suffer. Thrashing Hunapo is the only pleasure the old bugger has left in life. Take it away from him."'

Lilly's story triggered a memory. Back when she was fourteen, Aroha had been trying to fall asleep when she heard her father burst in through the back door and berate her mother. That was nothing unusual, but it stuck in her mind because they were arguing about her and Hunapo.

Now it fell into place. Tautaru must have just come home from the tavern after that meeting with Hori. Tautaru could never resist an opportunity to rub Ngaio's nose in it. And that night he had a bombshell.

Aroha had crept out of bed and pressed her ear against the door.

     David Whittet

'That pig Maahanga thinks my daughter isn't good enough for his precious Hunapo,' she'd heard her father shout. 'Well, I'm going to teach that pōkokohua a lesson!'

'Of course Hunapo's not good enough for Aroha,' Ngaio had replied.

'Making him a wuss, is she?' Tautaru hit back. 'I'm going to get my own back on the bugger once and for all! There's going to be an arranged marriage between Aroha and Hunapo.'

An arranged marriage? To Hunapo? No way. It couldn't possibly be true. Had she misheard it? Was she dreaming?

Aroha pictured Tautaru pinning Ngaio against the wall, the way he always did when he was mad. But her mother had sounded unusually calm.

'Just let it go,' Ngaio said.

'Did you not hear me, woman? An arranged marriage! Aroha and Hunapo!'

Aroha hadn't imagined it. This was for real. And for the first time, her mother had the last word.

'Been talking to Hori, have you?' Ngaio said. 'They're taking you for a fool. I've heard the women talking. "Trick the old bugger into arranging a marriage between Aroha and Hunapo." Everyone's laughing at you behind your back.'

Aroha had covered her ears, waiting for the inevitable expletive from her father. But it didn't come. Instead, she heard the back door slam. She looked out of her bedroom window to see him pace around the backyard like a caged chicken, kicking the burnt-out tyres that littered the ground.

She heard him raging. 'Hori! The bastard! Why did I listen to the pōkokohua? I bet he's in cahoots with Maahanga again. Bloody traitors!' Tautaru mimicked a strangling action with his hands. 'Watch your backs, you bloody backstabbers!'

Aroha couldn't help laughing when her father headbutted the shed door, almost knocking himself unconscious.

Now that she thought about it, Aroha remembered going grocery shopping with her mother the next day.

'You should have seen the bastard's face,' Ngaio crowed when they met up with a few of the other women outside the village store. 'I thought the old bugger was going to burst an aneurysm when I told him we were all laughing at him.'

The women broke out in spontaneous applause.

'Bravo, Ngaio!' Evie exclaimed, giving her a hearty handshake. 'About time someone took Tautaru down!'

'Good on you, girl!' Ruby said. 'I'd give anything to have seen the bastard's ugly nose put out of joint!'

'Don't get too cocky,' Pania interrupted. 'Tautaru won't give up that easily. No doubt he's plotting his revenge as we speak.'

'Yeah, watch out, Ngaio,' Rona said. 'There'll be payback.'

Ngaio flinched and dropped her shopping bags. 'Damn,' she cursed as a milk carton leaked over her dress.

Aroha helped her mother pick up her groceries and wipe the milk off her clothes.

'And Mo won't give in without a fight,' Pania added.

The women nodded in agreement. 'It's not over yet.'

Aroha remembered thinking at the time that the women were right. Her father would never admit defeat. And nor would Moana.

She recalled how Neina had put her arm on Ngaio's shoulder. 'What have you got against Hunapo? He's not a bad boy. In fact, he's the pick of the bunch.'

Aroha had immediately warmed to Neina. She'd wanted to put her arms around the old lady and kiss her wrinkled face. But before she could, her mother pulled her away.

'Best of this lousy lot, maybe,' Ngaio said. 'Come on, Aroha. You deserve better.'

Aroha mouthed a 'thank you' to Neina as her mother led her down the street.

'Neina's a wise soul,' Pania called after them. 'You should listen to her.'

Ngaio had grumbled all the way home. 'Damn Pania. Neina too.'

Don't listen, Aroha told herself. Neina could see the good in Hunapo. Why couldn't her mother?

David Whittet

Back home, Aroha had sat at the kitchen table and watched her mother rummage through a cupboard and pull out some flour and yeast.

'Mummy,' Aroha asked, surprised by the force with which Ngaio was kneading the dough. 'Why do you always make bread when you're angry?'

'It helps me cope with your father,' Ngaio said. 'Now fetch me the rolling pin from the drawer.'

'It looks fun,' Aroha said. 'Can I have a go?'

'Maybe next time,' Ngaio said. 'Come over here and watch how I do it.'

Aroha studied her mother. Was her mood getting better? The smell of baking usually calmed her down.

'I want to ask you something,' Aroha said. 'And please don't shout at me.' She paused and took a deep breath. 'Why do you hate Hunapo so much?'

Ngaio thumped the table with the rolling pin. 'That boy is trouble …'

'He's not!'

'Enough, Aroha. Get ready for bed.'

Ngaio flung the bread into the oven and slammed the stove door.

❃

'Goodness, is it supper time already?' Aroha asked when Lilly emerged from the kitchen carrying a tray. 'I was miles away.'

'Help yourself to the cookies,' Lilly said, handing Aroha a mug of cocoa.

'Thanks.' Aroha took a sip of her drink. 'You know, back then I couldn't understand why Ngaio had such a downer on Hunapo. Mother's instinct, I guess. Now I can see she was right.'

Lilly sighed. 'Yes. She knew Hunapo would bring you nothing but grief, and I should have stood by her.'

Aroha noticed the mug shaking in Lilly's hand.

'I'm sure you did your best,' Aroha said.

Lilly's lips quivered. 'I should have done more. I would have done. If only

'I'd known then what Hunapo would do to you.'

Aroha put her mug on the table, leant forward and put her hand on Lilly's knee. Lilly's eyes darted around and wouldn't meet hers.

'I'm surprised you can be so calm about it after everything that's happened,' Lilly said. 'Poor Ngaio. She didn't want you forced into a terrible marriage the way she'd been.'

Aroha flinched. She hadn't heard this before. 'The Gang made Ngaio marry Tautaru? How?'

Lilly lowered her head. 'You don't want to know.'

'I do.'

'Well …' Lilly hesitated. She looked up and their eyes met. 'You know Ngaio was once in love with Maahanga? Long before she married your father.'

'I thought that was just vicious gossip,' Aroha said. 'I never believed a word of it.'

'Maahanga swept Ngaio off her feet when she was a young girl. He was so handsome in his youth.'

'So how did she end up with my father?' Aroha asked.

'It was a drunken party. A one-night stand with Tautaru.' Lilly paused again. 'I've said too much. Are you sure you want me to go on?'

Aroha nodded. 'I have to know.'

'Ngaio found herself pregnant,' Lilly said.

'With me?'

'Yes.' Lilly rubbed her forehead. 'The Gang's rife with double standards. You know that. It was even worse back then. The men could have as many conquests as they liked, but the women—we were expected to save ourselves for them. Before Ngaio could think for herself, the elders branded her a slut and bullied her into a marriage she knew could never work. Saddest part is, Ngaio was such a carefree girl before Tautaru.'

'I've often wondered what Mum would have been like if she hadn't married my father,' Aroha said.

　　　　　David Whittet

Lilly smiled. 'Ngaio once told me she'd have killed Tautaru if he wasn't your father.'

I wish she had. Tautaru was a rotten bloody father.

Aroha scratched her head. 'I never figured out why Ngaio always gave in to him.' She picked up her mug and took another slurp of cocoa. 'Anyway, if Moana's scheme turned my old man into such a laughing stock, how come I still had to go through with that wretched ceremony?'

'Kaine talked him into it,' Lilly replied. 'Or at least, that's what Matt told me.'

'I wonder how Kaine did it?' Aroha said. 'Tautaru was mighty angry the night my mother got the better of him. I watched him storming around the yard.'

'Kaine was—is—Tautaru's most loyal ally,' Lilly said. 'I guess he knew your old man well enough to push the right buttons. They met in private, so I can't tell you for certain. But I can tell you this—' she giggled '—Kaine started by getting the old bugger on the back foot.'

Aroha raised her eyebrows. 'How?'

'Matt was down at Smash Palace with his mates. Their usual Friday night drinks. Tautaru was waving his fists at Kaine. That was quite normal too.'

Lilly paused for a bite of her biscuit.

'Go on,' Aroha said. 'Did Matt hear what they said?'

'Tautaru was going on about the farmers up the coast growing cannabis and keeping the profits for themselves.' Lilly pulled a face and once again imitated Tautaru's bellowing voice. *'Now listen to me, Kaine, I want these farmers punished. It's our land, and that money belongs to the Gang. Make an example of the bastards. Show everyone what happens when they cheat the Gang!'*

'Kaine told him there'd always be a few that tried it on. Everyone in the bar heard Tautaru's reply. "Then sort the buggers out! And damn quickly if you know what's good for you."

'This is where the story gets really entertaining,' Lilly continued. 'Matt said Tautaru went all twitchy.

'"By the way, Kaine," Tautaru began. "I was talking with Hori last night."
Matt had to pinch himself to stop laughing. "Now let's be absolutely clear about
this," Tautaru went on. "What I'm about to say stays in this room. You don't
breathe a word to anyone …"

'Kaine couldn't contain himself. "Stays in this room? Everyone's talking
about it! Oh, Tautaru. I can't believe you fell it. I thought you'd have known
Hori's missus had him right under her thumb."

'Matt saw Tautaru's jaw drop and struggled to keep a straight face. That was
even harder when Tautaru came out with his lame attempt to save face. "Under
her thumb? Moana has him by the short and curlies!"

'The entire crowd joined in the fun. The jeered even louder when Tautaru
pretended he hadn't believed a word Hori had said.'

'God, I wish I'd been there!' Aroha said. She couldn't remember when she'd
laughed so much. She could just picture her father, his face crimson with fury
at such a public humiliation. And all because a group of women had outwitted
him. 'I bet he wanted to kill someone.' Aroha burst into another fit of giggles.
'Thank you, Lilly. That's made my day.'

'That's where the fun ended, I'm afraid,' Lilly said. 'Tautaru and Kaine
disappeared into a private room at the back of the tavern. When they came out
an hour later, the arranged marriage was back on. And—well, you know the rest.'

'Yes.' Aroha looked down at her feet. Nobody knew revenge like her father.
Why did he always have the last word? She looked at her watch. 'It's getting
late. I'd better make a move.'

Trudging home, Aroha kicked a stone down the street. Why was her life
such a bloody awful mess? If only Ngaio had stood up to her father when it
really mattered. Everything could have been different.

Aroha lay awake that night thinking about what Lilly had said. And about
Hunapo. *Especially* about Hunapo. Could she ever forgive him after everything
that had happened? A sham marriage, an assassination attempt, an arson attack.
Could he change? Would he ever be a better man?

 David Whittet

When she was twelve, just after he dumped her, every night Aroha would drift off to sleep wondering what was going through Hunapo's mind. She hadn't seen him since that dreadful day when she'd tended his wounds with the kawakawa leaves, and he'd told her it was over. Did he miss her as much as she missed him? Did he ever think about her?

Chapter Fifteen

Mangatu Forest, 1978.

Hunapo took aim; his eyes squinting at the deer. He'd been waiting for the stag to emerge from its hiding place behind the giant tōtara tree. At last. Hunapo raised his arm, his father's gun in his hand. He squeezed the trigger, grinning as the buck winced and fell to the ground.

'Yes! I got it, Dad!' Hunapo said, jumping up and down.

'Nice one!' Maahanga replied, thumping him on the back. 'It's venison for tea tonight!'

They ran through the clearing to claim the trophy.

Dad was right, Hunapo thought to himself. *Aroha was turning me into a wuss. Well, not any more.*

Hunapo looked forward to the hunting and shooting expeditions with his father. Everyday cares disappeared deep in the forest. He'd even grown closer to his father since finishing with Aroha. His father's praise meant everything. Aroha wouldn't have approved of him bagging a red stag. He could hear her chiding him. *How could you, Hunapo? Killing innocent animals.*

It hadn't been easy. The first few weeks of separation were the worst. Aroha was his first—his *only*—true friend, and they'd shared blood.

Hunapo frowned. Perhaps the split had been for the best. She wouldn't like the other things he was doing for his father these days either. He could picture her nagging him.

You can't do that, Hunapo …

No, Hunapo. I won't let you …

Hunapo, I'm disappointed in you …

     David Whittet

Hunapo, you have to do the right thing …

There were distinct advantages to obeying his father: the beatings were less frequent and not nearly so harsh.

'You've got a hunter's eye, son,' Maahanga said when they carried the carcass home. 'In for the kill. We'll make a gangster out of you yet!'

Hunapo smirked. Maahanga had said the same thing to him yesterday when they were out collecting protection money from some elderly women. His old man hadn't seen him secretly handing the money back to the ladies. He felt warm and fuzzy inside. Aroha would have been proud of him.

Maahanga put his rifle down on the kitchen bench and hung the dead animal upside down on a makeshift meat hook. Hunapo watched him rummage in the drawer and pull out a butcher's knife.

'Here.' Maahanga made the first incision. 'Let me show you how to skin a deer.'

Hunapo held his nose when his father pulled out the animal's innards. *Gross!* Perhaps he wasn't cut out to be a hunter after all. Hunapo sighed with relief when a loud hammering on the door interrupted further gutting of the beast.

Maahanga twitched. Looked around him. 'You go, Hunapo. And if it's—'

Hunapo had seen the look on his father's face before, and Maahanga was clenching the knife so hard his knuckles were white. He wasn't worried about debt collectors this time. Or even the cops. What was his old man so scared about?

'Yes, Dad,' Hunapo said. 'I know the drill. You're not home.'

Hunapo went to the door, whistling a tune. That would make him seem relaxed and grown-up. 'All right! I'm coming,' he shouted as the banging got louder. 'Keep your hair on!'

Hunapo recognised the men the instant he opened the door. They were half a dozen of Tautaru's most vicious men. Tonight, with the dark grooves of their facial tā moko heightened by the twilight, they looked meaner than ever.

'What do you want?' Hunapo stammered.

'Not you!' The ringleader, a giant bruiser, shoved Hunapo out of the way.

'Stop! You can't go in …' Hunapo held his arms against the walls, trying to stop them from getting any further. 'My father's not here!'

The men laughed. 'Like hell he's not!'

Hunapo backed down the hallway. The sadistic grins on the gangsters' faces were even scarier than the scars that covered their bodies.

One of the men threw Hunapo to the floor. 'Stay out of this, kid, if you know what's good for you.'

Another henchman kicked Hunapo in the groin. 'I'll show the little shit what's good for him.'

Rolling over on the floor and holding his throbbing balls, Hunapo watched the men trash the place, smashing the furniture with a baton and throwing crockery on the floor.

Not that mug, please. That was my mother's.

Hunapo looked up when he heard his father's voice.

'Get out!' Maahanga yelled, still clutching the butcher's knife. 'You heard me!'

Go for it, Dad! Hunapo saw his father step forward, brandishing the blade at the men's faces. *You can do it!*

'You miserable pōkokohua!' The ringleader gave Maahanga the finger. He turned to his men. 'Get the son of a bitch!'

The gangsters pounced on Maahanga. Hunapo could scarcely bear to look. In a flash, they had his father restrained on the floor. And they were pointing the knife at Maahanga's neck.

The gun! Hunapo suddenly remembered the rifle. His father had left it on the bench. If only he could get his hands on it. The gangsters were so busy bashing Maahanga, maybe they wouldn't notice.

Hunapo crawled across the floor. The sound of his father's groaning grew louder. That told Hunapo he had to succeed. Just a bit further. The weapon was almost within reach. He glanced back at his father.

'Kai hamuti! Kai kurakura!' the men shouted and spat on Maahanga's face.

'Don't you call my father a shit!' Hunapo had the rifle in his hands and aimed it at the men. 'Get off him!'

 David Whittet

'Put that down, kid.' The ringleader edged towards Hunapo. The rest of the men raised their hands.

'Stop!' Hunapo pointed the barrel at the leader's head, his finger twitching on the trigger. 'Another step and I'll shoot!'

The ringleader continued to push forward. 'No, you won't.'

Hunapo felt the sweat roll off his forehead. *Pull the trigger! Kill the bastard! Now! Before he gets any closer.*

Hunapo's heart pounded so loud it almost deafened him. His finger tightened on the trigger. Then a sudden excruciating pain. What the hell was happening? It was a moment before Hunapo realised that the bastard had landed him another exquisite kick in the balls. The gun swung upwards and fired into the ceiling, shattering the electric light bulb and showering them in plaster.

Writhing in agony on the floor, Hunapo made a last vain attempt to hold on to the rifle as one of the minions yanked it out of his hands.

'Get out of here, Hunapo!' Maahanga yelled, wiping a mixture of blood and masonry from his eyes. 'Go to your room!'

'You heard your old man. This is no place for a kid.'

Hunapo hobbled to his bedroom. The pain in his bollocks was as bad as one of his father's thrashings. Gangsters certainly knew how to incapacitate a guy. Instantly.

What the hell did the bastards want, anyway? Why were they abusing his father? Amidst the screams and threats, Hunapo overheard something that made his blood boil.

'We'll take the stag for our supper,' one of the men said. 'Cheers for bagging it for us!'

The bastards were stealing the deer! His trophy! How dare they?

No matter how long Hunapo lay in bed that night, sleep would not come. Fragments of what he'd picked up during the fight preyed on his mind. What the hell was Tautaru planning? What did his despised uncle want with him? And even more baffling, what did it have to do with Aroha?

Chapter Sixteen

Tautaru's Place, 1978.

'Help me clear the table, Aroha,' Ngaio said when they finished dinner. 'Your father will have to make do with that cold ham when he gets home.'

Aroha shot up from the table and got to work washing the dishes.

Be quick, she told herself. *Get to bed before the old man's back.*

Tautaru was in an even worse mood than ever these days. He was always shouting and throwing empty beer bottles at Ngaio. Thank God he was so drunk that he usually missed. Ngaio had taken to flinging pans back at him.

Aroha was sick of it. A couple more pots to dry and she'd be in her room.

Too late. She heard his voice booming in the yard.

'Whakianga mai! The women will laugh on the other side of their faces when they see what we've got in store!' Tautaru burst through the door. 'Thought you could get the better of me, did you?' He shoved her against the kitchen stove. 'Nobody makes a fool of me and gets away with it. Wahine kore tuki!'

'Don't call me a stupid woman!' Ngaio held up her palms to protect her eyes from Tautaru's spit. 'It wasn't *me* making a fool of you. It was the women.'

'Whatever! It makes no difference.' Tautaru stepped back and grabbed a beer out of the fridge. 'I'm going to teach you a lesson you won't forget.'

Ngaio grabbed Tautaru's arm and pulled him towards her. 'Not Aroha. I'm begging you.' She attempted to embrace him. 'Do what you want with the Gang, but don't do this to my Aroha!'

What was her mother on about? What was her father going to do to her? Was she in for another thrashing? Her wrists were still sore from the last time her father hit her. She slid her hands into her pockets before he could strike and hid behind the washing machine.

'Don't kid yourself, Ngaio,' Tautaru said. 'This marriage will happen! Get that into your thick skull.'

Marriage. Aroha took a deep breath. So she hadn't got it wrong when she overheard them arguing a few nights back.

'You've done some mean things in your life,' Ngaio said. 'But committing your own daughter to a lifetime of misery just to—'

'It's your own bloody fault,' Tautaru hit back. 'You and those damn women. Meddling in affairs that are none of your business. Undermining my leadership. Goading my enemies. This is about uniting the Gang behind *me.*'

'You don't need Aroha for that,' Ngaio said. 'You've had no difficulty getting rid of your rivals in the past.'

Aroha slid further into the corner as her parents continued to hurl insults at each other. *They're talking about me as if I wasn't here.*

'Aroha is part of this whānau,' Tautaru said. 'She can't escape her responsibilities.'

'She's just a child,' Ngaio said.

'She has a duty to the Gang like everyone else.'

'*Duty!*' Ngaio's voice trembled as she repeated the word.

Was her mother going to cry? Aroha peered from behind the washing machine. She flinched when Tautaru threw Ngaio across the kitchen. Watching her mother collapse against the bench, Aroha wanted to hug her. A glare from her father told that wasn't safe.

'Go to bed, Aroha.' Ngaio lifted her head. 'I'll come and see you later.'

Even with her head under the pillow, Aroha could still hear her father's voice thundering through the house.

'This isn't just about bringing Maahanga down. This union will send a message to those bloody traitors …'

Was Tautaru still talking about the arranged marriage? What did he mean about Maahanga? It suddenly occurred to Aroha that he hadn't mentioned Hunapo all night. Her heart missed a beat. Surely they weren't going to marry her to someone else? She took her head out from under the pillow. Her mother was still pleading with him.

'Stop this,' Ngaio said. 'I'm begging you.'

'Too late now,' Tautaru said. 'The men have already paid Maahanga a visit.'

'No!' Ngaio groaned.

'And they've taken care of Hunapo,' Tautaru added.

What had they done to Hunapo? Aroha clutched her chest. Had they—? No, they couldn't have—

Before she could think it through, Tautaru sounded off again.

'I'm going to tell Aroha in the morning …'

Tell her what? That he'd killed Hunapo?

Too upset to listen, Aroha retreated under the covers. The arguing raged on in the distance. How could she get through the night not knowing what had happened to Hunapo? Tautaru was always going on about getting rid of Hunapo once and for all, but she never thought he'd do it. Could her father really be that evil?

Aroha punched the air under the bedclothes. She wanted to march back into the kitchen and demand the truth.

The sound of Tautaru cursing at her mother brought Aroha back to the present.

'Kai hamuti!' Tautaru said. 'Now get up off the floor and cook my dinner. If you think I'm having cold ham, you can think again. Come on. Get your finger out.'

'Get your own dinner, you bastard,' Ngaio shot back. 'You're sick!'

Aroha heard a slap. Had her mother just hit her father? Ngaio must have been desperate. About time someone stood up to the brute. *Give him another one from me.*

Aroha pretended she was asleep when she heard her mother's footsteps approaching her bedroom. Squinting through the sheets, she watched Ngaio

David Whittet

grab anything she could find. Chairs, books, even the bedside table—Ngaio used them all to barricade the bedroom door.

'My angel,' Ngaio whispered, snuggling under the blanket beside Aroha. 'I won't let anyone harm you.'

Ngaio held her so tight that Aroha could feel her mother's snivelling throughout the night. Aroha felt like crying too. She didn't want to sleep. She'd only have nightmares of her father's hitman assassinating Hunapo.

Tautaru barged into the bedroom the next morning, smashing Ngaio's makeshift blockade and demanding she cook his breakfast.

'Take that, you fat slob!' She grabbed one of Aroha's shoes from the floor and threw it at Tautaru.

Tautaru ducked and raised a fist to Ngaio.

'Don't you come near me!' Ngaio made a strangling motion with her hands. 'I won't be responsible for my actions.'

Aroha had never seen her mother as angry before. Why couldn't she have put up a fight like this sooner? She could have saved everyone so much misery.

Tautaru's hands dropped to his sides, and he left the bedroom without another word.

'Are you okay, Mum?' Aroha asked as she got dressed. 'I've never heard you talk to Dad like that before.'

'I want better for you, my darling.' Ngaio wrapped her arms around Aroha. 'I've failed miserably. Never had the guts to break away. I can't let that happen to you.'

Ngaio combed Aroha's long black hair and tied it back. Aroha stared at her mother's red eyes.

'You've been crying all night,' Aroha said. 'What has Dad done?'

Ngaio wiped her face. 'Nothing, sweetheart. Off and do your chores. Mummy needs to think.'

The kitchen floor looked even worse after Aroha had mopped it than it did before she started. How could she carry on as usual with so much on her mind? What was her father going to tell her? And how much longer did she have to wait in agony?

She heard vehicles arriving and glanced out of the window. It was her father's minions. Doubtless here for a meeting. That meant they'd all get drunk and it would be even longer before Tautaru spoke to her.

Aroha went into the scullery to empty her bucket. The kitchen would be out of bounds with the men there. She threw her mop on the floor in frustration. Then she felt a hand on her shoulder. If it was her mother telling her off for doing a lousy job cleaning the floor, she didn't care. She turned to see her father.

'Come with me,' Tautaru said. 'I have an important announcement to make.'

The men all looked so serious as they sat around the table when Tautaru paraded her into the kitchen. What had they done to Hunapo? Was she next?

Tautaru seated himself at the head of the table. Aroha shifted from one foot to the other as she stood on ceremony beside him. She could feel the gangsters staring at her.

Kaine, who sat on Tautaru's other side, got up and fetched a stool. 'Here, Aroha. Have a seat.'

Surely Kaine—the man who'd rescued her from Eru—wouldn't be involved in anything as dreadful as killing Hunapo?

Aroha's eyes darted around the table. The men each helped themselves to a bottle of beer from the crate on the otherwise empty table. Hori looked especially pleased with himself. What was he laughing about? She glanced down at her mother who sat huddled on the floor in a corner. Her face was puffy from crying and her eyes were blank.

'Listen to me carefully, Aroha,' Tautaru said in that voice he always used when he wanted to sound big. 'I have chosen you for an essential role in the Gang's unification. We need to provide a united front to our enemies and show our strength to those who would deny the power of the Māhiti Gang. As part of a strategic alliance within the Gang, you will marry Hunapo in the spring.'

Aroha almost fell off her stool. So they hadn't hurt Hunapo. And she wasn't mistaken when she heard her parents arguing about an arranged marriage. She steadied herself when she heard her mother's voice.

 David Whittet

'It's not right.' Ngaio pulled herself up from her squatting position on the ground. 'And it's not legal. You know that, Tautaru …'

'Shut it, Ngaio!' Tautaru glared at her as he rose to his feet and rallied his men. 'Raise your bottles, my friends, to Aroha and Hunapo. And to the supremacy of the Māhiti Gang!'

'To Aroha and Hunapo! And the Māhiti Gang!' the men cheered, their raucous celebrations drowning Ngaio's objections.

Hunapo's alive! And I'm going to marry him! Aroha felt so ecstatic that she thought she might dance on the kitchen table if all the men weren't there. Instead, she gave her father a kiss on the cheek. She couldn't remember the last time she'd done that.

Why did her mother look so miserable? Aroha tried to ignore the moaning when she helped her to clear up the empty beer bottles after the men had left. Why couldn't Ngaio share her joy?

Aroha wrote in her diary that night. The first entry in months. *I'm going to marry Hunapo!* She scrawled the words across the page, then paused and sucked the tip of her pencil. How would Hunapo react to the news? Would he be as excited as she was? What if he wasn't? Aroha dismissed the thought with a stroke of the pencil. Hunapo had only dumped her because he thought it was the right thing to do for the Gang. Now everything was different. They could start again. Carry on from where they left off.

Aroha closed her diary. She couldn't wait to see Hunapo again.

Chapter Seventeen

The moment Hunapo dreaded had arrived. He'd been on edge since the night Tautaru's henchmen invaded their home. They were coming back for him. He'd overheard that much. Whenever he heard footsteps approaching the house, Hunapo had taken to climbing through a hole in the kitchen wall and hiding in the cavity. Usually, it was just the postman with a bunch of bills. But today felt different.

'You can come out, son,' Maahanga said. 'It's just some women.'

Hunapo poked his head through the gap in the plaster. Maahanga had open the door to Moana and a group of the elders.

'I think you know why we're here.' Moana barged into the kitchen, her entourage following behind. 'We'll be looking after Hunapo until the wedding.'

The wedding? Hunapo's jaw dropped. So that's what those thugs were talking about.

'Go to hell!' Maahanga said. 'Hunapo is not marrying Aroha.'

Moana grabbed Hunapo's arm, pulling him through the crack. 'You're coming with us. Hurry up and fetch your things.'

'Get off me!' Hunapo pushed her away and collapsed onto a chair, his head reeling so violently he thought it would explode.

Marry Aroha? How could this be? He'd mourned the loss of her friendship, and at last the grief had passed. He'd moved on. Dedicating himself to becoming a Gang leader gave him purpose. And doing what Maahanga told him simplified his life; there were fewer beatings and recriminations.

Hunapo was fond of Aroha. *I care about her … of course I do … but she does my head in! Why does she have to be so intense?* He shuddered at the thought of more profound and meaningful conversations with Aroha. Yet she could be

  David Whittet

such fun when she wasn't on a crusade. If only they could simply be mates, like ordinary cousins.

Hunapo glanced up. His father was still shouting at the women.

'I might have known Tautaru would send a bunch of women to do his dirty work. Pōkokohua! The bastard hasn't the balls to come here himself.' Maahanga spat in Moana's face. 'Haere atu! Get out.'

Moana didn't budge. 'We can do this the easy way, or do you want me to call Tautaru's men again?'

'Whakianga mai!' Maahanga swore. 'You're not taking Hunapo anywhere!'

Moana turned to Hunapo. 'I told you to get ready. We're leaving.'

Hunapo's breathing quickened as the women surround him.

'Like hell you are!' Maahanga pushed the women aside and snatched Hunapo, crossing his arms over his son's chest.

Moana put her hands on her hips. 'I should have thought one visit from the men was enough, but if you want another pasting, that's up to you.' Moana turned to the women. 'Come on, my friends. Maahanga's going to regret choosing the hard way.'

Hunapo breathed a sigh of relief as the women left. Moana was scary. He'd never seen a woman that intimidating before.

When she reached the door, Moana turned back. Hunapo felt her piercing eyes target his deepest fears.

'You know, Hunapo,' she said. 'You could save your father a lot of pain. You saw what happened last time. They won't go so easy on your dad next time. Save him the heartache. Come with us now!'

'No way!' Hunapo said.

'You think about it.' Moana walked up to Maahanga and ran her fingers over his bruises. 'I'm not sure how much more your father can take.'

She'd won. Hunapo knew another thrashing would kill his father.

'All right, I'll come with you,' Hunapo said, his voice trembling. 'But you won't stop me seeing my father.'

'Hang in there, son!' Maahanga gave Hunapo a last hug. 'I'll rescue you. Somehow.'

'I don't think so,' Moana said. 'Come on, Hunapo.'

Hunapo raised a fist high in the air as Moana frogmarched him out of the house.

'I'll find a way, Hunapo!' Maahanga called after them, staggering to the door. 'Believe me! We'll lead the Gang together! You and me, father and son! Believe me!'

Hunapo looked back and nodded. He knew his father's promises were empty. Tautaru had won. He wanted to cry, but Gang boys don't cry. That would disrespect his father even more.

'Where are you taking me?' Hunapo demanded as the women huddled him into the back of a ute.

'You'll be staying with Olivia Winiata,' Moana said. 'She'll be looking after you till the wedding.'

'But she's an old woman,' Hunapo groaned.

'Don't be so rude,' Moana said. 'She's not old, and you'll do as she tells you.'

Hunapo took a lighter from his pocket and began singeing the blisters on his arms. He smiled to himself when the women held their noses at the smell of scorched flesh.

⚘

Could he make it? Hunapo looked around him when the ute drew up at Olivia's place. Moana jumped out and laid into Olivia, who was waiting at the front door.

'I hope you're up to this,' he heard Moana say to Olivia.

It's now or never. Hunapo pushed past Pania and legged it down the street. He turned the corner and ran straight into Kaine.

'Where the hell do think you're going?' Kaine grabbed his ear and twisted it. 'Try that trick again and you'll regret it.'

                    David Whittet

'Let go!' Hunapo protested as Kaine marched him back to Olivia's house. 'I'm not afraid of you.' His pounding heart and throbbing ear, though, told him he was.

'You should be scared,' Kaine said. 'I've got my eyes on you.'

Moana gave Hunapo a slap when Kaine handed him over. 'Take that, you little shit.' She turned to Olivia. 'Don't take any nonsense from the miserable brat.'

'Don't call him that.' Olivia ruffled Hunapo's hair and greeted him in Māori. 'Nau mai! Nau mai!'

Hunapo pushed her hand away from his head. He didn't want those gnarled fingers anywhere near his hair. 'Don't do that!'

'I'm sorry,' Olivia said. 'Come in and make yourself at home.'

Hunapo stepped back, not wanting to go inside. Pania gave him a push.

'Time for us to go,' Pania said. 'Let them get to know each other.'

Hunapo watched the other women nod in agreement. They were obviously all in this together.

'Remember what I said,' Moana reminded Olivia. 'You call me at once if there's any trouble.'

'Yes, Moana.'

Hunapo saw the way Moana eyeballed Olivia. What a mean bitch! She was treating Olivia with the same scorn she'd shown his father earlier that afternoon. He noticed how Moana repeatedly looked back over her shoulder as she walked down the garden path with Pania and the rest of the women.

Looking down at his feet, Hunapo followed Olivia inside. She shut the door and extended an arm towards Hunapo.

'It's so good to have you here,' she said.

That's a lie. It was obvious from what he'd seen that the women had press-ganged her into it. 'You don't need to pretend.' Hunapo dumped his rucksack on the floor. 'This must be as difficult for you as it is for me.'

'No!' Olivia said.

'Well, it's true, isn't it? You don't want me here any more than I want to be here.'

'Not at all!' Olivia beckoned him to follow her. 'You're very welcome here. I want you to call me Aunty.'

Hunapo shaded his eyes as they walked through the living room. 'Blimey! You need your sunnies in this house. Everything sparkles.'

Olivia smiled. 'Not like that at your home?'

'Hell no. My old man's place is a train wreck.' Hunapo ran his fingers over the polished furniture. 'I don't believe it. Not a broken chair. Jeez, there's even ornaments on the mantlepiece.'

'I like to keep my home looking nice.' Olivia opened the door to Hunapo's bedroom. 'I hope you'll be comfortable in here.'

Hunapo gasped. There were sheets on his bed. 'Holy shit! I've never seen anything like this before!'

Dinner that evening was a novel experience too. Knives and forks. What did you do with them?

'You can use your fingers if you like,' Olivia said. 'I don't mind.'

'Thanks, Aunty.' Hunapo picked up the steak and bit into it.

Olivia heaped a second helping of mashed potato onto his plate. 'You're a very special boy, Hunapo,' she said. 'Did you know that?'

Hunapo spat a mouthful of meat back on the plate and flung the words back at her. 'I am *not* special! I don't want to be special!'

'But you are the chosen one,' Olivia said.

The chosen one! Hunapo despised those words. His father had called him that too, and he hated it as much then as he did now.

'No! *No!* I'm not!' Hunapo protested, slamming his fist on the table. 'Don't ever say that again!'

'I just meant …' Olivia stammered. 'You're our one hope—'

Hunapo felt a surge of rage flood through his body. He seized an ornate china salt cellar from the table and threw it to the floor.

Without a word, Olivia bent down and picked up the shattered pieces.

Hunapo noticed a tear in the corner of her eye. It must have been precious. 'I'm sorry, Olivia … I mean, Aunty,' he mumbled, lowering his head. 'I didn't mean to do that. I hope it wasn't valuable.'

'It all right, Hunapo,' Olivia reassured. 'No harm done.'

'It just makes me so angry,' Hunapo said. 'Other kids hang out with their mates. Lucky sods. Why do I have to be different? The *chosen one*—don't make me laugh! I'm no bloody messiah. They say it's my destiny. Well, I don't want it.'

'I understand.' Olivia beamed at Hunapo and squeezed his hand. 'I wish I could do something to help.'

'You can't,' Hunapo replied, slamming his hand on the table. 'Nobody can help me.'

'They could,' Olivia said. 'If you'd let them.'

Hunapo stared at Olivia. She was still fondling the brown fragments of china. The look on her face was too much. He got up from the table and tore off to his room.

Chapter Eighteen

Lilly's Place, 1993.

'Poor Olivia,' Aroha said, blinking back a tear. 'It was a gift from her late husband?'

'Yes,' Lilly replied. 'Olivia treasured that salt and pepper set. Her Jack gave it to her on their silver wedding anniversary. And Hunapo broke it the first night he was in her house.'

Typical Hunapo. Aroha took a deep breath and held it in. 'She didn't deserve that.'

'No,' Lilly said. 'What we did to Olivia was unforgivable. Like I said, Moana would use anyone to get what she wanted.'

Aroha felt heavy in her chest. It was all so unfair. Olivia had been so kind to her as a child. Treated her like a daughter and Hunapo like a son. It was too painful to think about.

'Time for a cup of tea,' Lilly said, getting up and walking to the kitchen.

Aroha had been so upset by her last visit that she swore she wouldn't go back to see Lilly. All that talk about Moana and the arranged marriage left Aroha feeling sick to her stomach for days. Less than a week later, and she was back for more. Moana's treatment of Olivia was even more shameful. Should she just get up and go home? No. Aroha needed the truth. It was the only way she'd ever get peace of mind. And Lilly was the only person she could trust.

'So why did Moana choose Olivia to look after Hunapo?' Aroha asked when Lilly brought the tea in on a tray. 'I'd have thought Olivia would have been her last choice.'

     David Whittet

'She was,' Lilly said, pouring the tea. 'Everyone else refused. None of them wanted Hunapo messing up their children. You should have heard their excuses.'

'I can imagine,' Aroha said with a sigh.

'Pania was quick off the mark,' Lilly said. She imitated Pania's voice. *'He can't stay with us. My Nikora is in enough trouble as it is, without Hunapo egging him on.'*

'That's Pania to a tee,' Aroha said.

'The rest of them were just as bad,' Lilly said with a smile. '"I can't take him either," Sylvia said. "The doctor has just put my Ihaka on Ritalin. I won't have Hunapo stealing his pills!" Then Marie went on about her kid being on pills too.'

'Moana must have been furious,' Aroha said.

'She was,' Lilly said. 'We were all sitting on the floor in the marae. Moana prowled around like a vulture, sniffing out weakness. I covered my eyes when she eyeballed me. "So not one of you is prepared to take him on?" she said. Nobody answered. "If you're all so worried about your kids, remember we're doing this to feed our families. Put food on the table." Did she seriously think any of us believed that crap?'

'So how come Olivia got roped in?' Aroha asked. 'Pity she didn't have an excuse.'

'She wasn't there. Olivia never came to our meetings.' Lilly paused, hiding her face behind her greying hair.

'What is it?' Aroha said.

'It was me.' Lilly dropped her chin to her chest. 'I suggested Olivia. I thought she would be good for Hunapo.'

Aroha rested a hand on Lilly's arm. 'And she was.'

'Yes, but at what cost?' Lilly looked up at Aroha. 'Of course, all the other women jumped at the idea. Moana wasn't so happy. She dismissed the idea with a wave of her hand. "Olivia Winiata? Surely not! She has no experience with kids. Let alone one like Hunapo."

'"That's why she's perfect," Pania chipped in. "No children of her own. Nobody for Hunapo to screw up."

'That didn't convince Moana. "I'm not so sure," she said. "Olivia lacks the strength of character to stand up to Hunapo. He'd walk right over her. The boy needs discipline."

'I wasn't going to let her get away with that. "He needs nurturing," I told her.

'Evie backed me up. Urged them to give Olivia a chance. "She's a kind soul. She'll take good care of Hunapo."'

'She tried,' Aroha said, slumping her shoulders. 'God knows, she tried.'

Nobody knew that better than Aroha. Olivia was there for her when Tautaru did his level best to turn Hunapo into a monster. It was Olivia who begged Hunapo to show Aroha some respect.

Lilly wiped away a tear. 'I should never have done that to Olivia. I wish I'd taken Hunapo in myself. I would have done if I'd known what was going to happen to Olivia. I was just frightened of getting the blame when it all went wrong. And I knew it would end in disaster.'

Aroha helped Lilly clear away the tea things. She thought Lilly was going to cry when they began washing the teacups.

'I had to break the news to Olivia,' Lilly said. 'I'll never forget the panic in her face. "Why me?" she protested. "You've all got children of your own. I haven't a clue how to look after a teenager!"'

'You were close to my mother,' Aroha said. 'She wouldn't talk to me. Have you any idea what was up with her?'

Lilly sighed. 'The women always made me do their dirty work. They sent me to talk Ngaio into accepting your marriage.'

'But she never did,' Aroha said.

'No.' Lilly pulled the plug out of the sink. 'And I wish I'd never tried. Pania went on about how they were all relying on me. "Don't let your feelings get in the way," she kept saying. "Ngaio has to face up to her responsibilities like the rest of us."'

'So you went to see Ngaio?' Aroha dried the last of the dishes and folded the tea towel. 'I bet that didn't go well.'

     David Whittet

Lilly sighed. 'It was horrible.' She put the cups and saucers on the shelf and led Aroha back into the living room. They sat down on the settee and Lilly began the story. 'When I got to the house, I thought Ngaio was dead. She just sat there. Slumped over the kitchen table. The place was a tip. And Ngaio was usually so house-proud. I'd never seen it look so awful.

'I gave Ngaio a pat on the back. Thank God she was still breathing. I'd brought her some fruit and put it on the table. I don't think Ngaio even noticed I was there.

'"What's up?" I said, trying to sound chatty. "We haven't seen you around in ages."

'I sat down beside her. It seemed like forever before she spoke, and when she did, she hardly lifted her head.

'"You know what it is," she said. "Don't pretend. Mo sent you, didn't she? I might have known you'd all gang up on me."

'I didn't know what to say. I moved my chair closer and tried again. "Don't be like that. We need a good catch up, you and me."

'"It's my Aroha, as if you didn't know," Ngaio said. "Forcing her to marry Hunapo isn't right. They're first cousins and they're both still children."

'I tried to explain to her how it was all about healing the wounds, bringing the whānau together, but she wouldn't listen.

'"Tautaru and Maahanga will never stop fighting," she said, pointing a finger at me. "I know that even if the rest of you don't."

'In my heart, I knew she was right, but I had to keep trying. "Don't you want to see the whānau back together?" I knew straight away I'd said the wrong thing.

'"That was a kick in the guts," Ngaio said. "Nobody has put more into this whānau than me. I expected better from you."

'I'd have given anything to have disappeared into a hole in the ground. How could I have made such a mess of it? I wanted to tell Ngaio that arranged marriages were a Gang tradition, and that if Aroha didn't marry Hunapo, she'd be hitched to another much less desirable gangster down the track.

'"Hunapo's a good boy," I said eventually. "And Aroha likes him. She's the envy of all the other girls."

'"Hunapo will break her heart," Ngaio said, "and it's totally illegal."

'I couldn't argue with that. But I saw a way of turning it to my advantage. "Well, perhaps that's a good thing," I said. "If they're not *legally* married, it'll be easier for Aroha to get away if it does all go wrong."

'"What planet are you on?" Ngaio growled at me. "Get away from the Gang? If this goes ahead, Aroha will be bound to Hunapo forever—far more than she would in any civil marriage. You can't divorce the Gang!"

'I knew I was beaten. I was just about to leave when she grabbed hold of me.

'"Please help me, Lilly," she said. "You're my oldest friend. The women will listen to you. You can make them change their minds."

'I thought she would never let go. "I'm sorry," I said. "You know I can't. Mo's determined. We're all struggling to put food on the table for our kids, just because Tautaru and Maahanga can't settle their differences. The women won't stand for it any longer."

'"That's it then, is it?" Ngaio cut me down with her eyes. "You and the rest of the women have condemned Aroha."

'I wanted to hug her, make everything go away, but I couldn't. "We can't part like this," I said, wracking my brains for something positive. "At least Tautaru will be kinder to you when he doesn't have to stress about not having a male heir—"

'Ngaio pushed me away. "I think you should go now," she said "I mean it. Get out!"'

Lilly buried her head in her hands when she finished the story. Aroha could hear her sniffling and put an arm around her shoulder.

'I'm sorry, Aroha,' Lilly said. 'I let you down. I should have understood how your mother was feeling and helped her. And I should never have listened to Moana.' Lilly lifted her head and their eyes met. 'I suppose … I just thought … kidded myself … that you and Hunapo really were made for each other.'

     David Whittet

'Hunapo could have been good for me,' Aroha said. 'If Tautaru hadn't got to him.' She leant back on the settee, still trying to piece everything together. 'What happened next? I mean, to my mother. Before she … you know—'

'She turned to Maahanga,' Lilly said. 'He was her last hope. She seduced him. At least, that's what I heard. Next thing we all knew, the two of them were down in Hawke's Bay canvassing. Maahanga still had loyal supporters down there. Men with grievances against Tautaru. She got the numbers. Enough to topple Tautaru. But who could have imagined things would turn out the way they did?'

Aroha rubbed the tā moko on her chin. Who indeed?

Chapter Nineteen

Tautaru's Place, 1978.

Aroha was desperate to see Hunapo again and share the glad tidings. Two weeks had passed since Tautaru broke the news of the marriage and still no sign of Hunapo. Why hadn't he been to see her? Perhaps he wasn't as excited about the wedding as she was. Or maybe he simply didn't know what to say after they'd been apart for so long.

The house seemed to be filled with more gangsters than ever. Meeting after meeting. Aroha took to pressing her ear against the kitchen door. Above the raucous laughter and the clinking of beer bottles, she could hear her father going on about arranging an event on the marae to announce the wedding.

'It's time to make a statement,' Tautaru said. 'This union will show the succession of the Māhiti Gang is secure. A declaration of strength with the Gang united behind *me!*'

How did he manage to make everything about him?

She didn't need her ear up against the door when Tautaru sounded off again. 'I seem to remember, Kaine, you told me that bastard Ngatoro and his sidekick were biding their time to kick me out. Waiting in the wings, are they?'

Aroha rolled her eyes. Tautaru was always frightened that Henare Ngatoro or Pita Rutene would take his place. From what she'd heard, either of them would make a far more just leader than her old man.

Her father again. 'Those bastards won't know what's hit them if they challenge me! I rule this Gang!'

All this talk, but still nothing about Hunapo.

'Dad,' Aroha asked when Tautaru came out for a fresh crate of beer, 'I want to see Hunapo.'

'All in good time,' Tautaru said. 'You and Hunapo will be guests of honour at the announcement of your engagement. All eyes will be on you. I don't want you letting me down. Understand?'

Aroha nodded.

Tautaru took her into the kitchen where the gangsters still sat around the table. 'You must greet the visitors with a hongi. Then there's the mihi. You'll need to practise.' He gestured to Chase. 'Take her back with you and make her practise the mihi. And don't let her go until she can say it backwards.'

What? Go with Chase? The monster that delighted in torturing the boys with his chisel? Do I have to? The look in her father's eyes told her she did.

Aroha flinched when Chase grabbed her arm and led her away. The touch of his hand made her skin crawl. She recited the mihi to herself. She'd have it word perfect super quick if it meant getting away from Chase faster.

She could still hear her father boasting to his men when they were halfway down the street.

'Make no mistake, my friends,' Tautaru said. 'This will be *big.*'

Announcing their engagement should be a joyful affair, Aroha thought, *not a show of the Gang's strength.*

When the day arrived, Aroha realised just how enormous the ceremony would be. She curtsied politely and gave all the Māori elders from the neighbouring tribes a hongi until her nose was raw. Was there no end to the line of visitors?

Her father always got himself into a flap at formal Gang events. He wore his māhiti, an almost threadbare cape, over his ceremonial cloak. Ngaio had told Aroha the māhiti, made from the long white hair of dogs' tails, was created especially for the Gang's founder. Did the old cape have some mystical power? Otherwise, how could such a scruffy outfit have given the Gang its name? And dogs' tails! Aroha held her nose. *No wonder it stinks!*

'Where the hell is your mother?' Tautaru demanded. 'She's meant to be here with you, greeting our guests.'

Aroha shrugged. 'I haven't seen her all morning.'

Tautaru turned to Kaine. 'Find Ngaio. And for Christ's sake, no more cock-ups.'

Aroha bowed her head. Even on such a special day, her parents were fighting.

'Smile, damn you,' Tautaru hissed in Ngaio's ear when she eventually took her place at Aroha's side.

Aroha sighed. She guessed Ngaio would rather scream than smile.

Why couldn't they get on for just one day? Although cross with her father for bullying her mother yet again, Aroha still couldn't understand why Ngaio refused to share her happiness.

A sudden roar of motorbike engines drew Aroha's attention away from her parents and the guests. Petrol fumes clouded the horizon. Bandanas flapped and brakes screeched.

'It's the Wairoa Warriors,' Tautaru said. 'What the hell are they doing here? We didn't invite the bastards.'

The bikers parked their Harley Davidsons in the paddock adjoining the marae. Aroha shuddered as her father approached their leader, and the two of them wrestled their fists in a gang salute. Did that mean there was going to be trouble?

Aroha heard Tautaru whispering to Kaine. 'The bastards owe me money. Hit them up. Make them pay. Or we take their bikes.'

Trust her father. Aroha shook her head. *No Dad. Not today. Please. Not on my special day.*

Deliberately turning her head away from her father, Aroha watched the guests gasp with delight as they filed into their pews. The women elders had decked the marae with flowers, and the afternoon sun highlighted the ornamental carvings. She'd never seen it look so beautiful, yet it felt strangely empty. There was still no sign of Hunapo. Where was he? The ceremony was due to start in a few minutes. Her heart suddenly stood still. What if the entire event was just another of her father's sick jokes and his men really had bumped Hunapo off?

 David Whittet

She told herself not to be so silly. Even her old man wasn't that twisted, and he definitely wouldn't have invited all these people if he'd done something that nasty.

Then she caught sight of Olivia. That meant Hunapo couldn't be far away. Yes! There he was. Olivia held his arm and escorted him to the stage. Aroha had waited so long for this moment. She felt like jumping in the air. But why did Hunapo look so pained? Was it just the seriousness of the occasion? Or was it something else?

Moana appeared and beckoned Aroha to join Hunapo on the stage. Aroha noticed Hunapo looked skinnier than ever. Hadn't he been eating?

'What's the matter?' Aroha said, sitting down next to him.

Hunapo stared into the distance. 'I'm sick of being pushed around by the Gang.'

'Pushed around? What do you mean?'

Moana scowled at them. 'Quiet, you two. The ceremony's about to start.'

The women elders joined them on the stage. Why couldn't everyone just go away and give her a few minutes alone with Hunapo?

Tautaru stood up and made a long introductory speech. Aroha watched Hunapo flinch when her father went on about the prosperity and stability the marriage would bring to the Gang.

She wanted to hug Hunapo. That would make him feel better. She gave him a gentle nudge.

'Don't look so sad,' she whispered in his ear. 'We're going to be happy together.'

He didn't answer. She felt him push her away. She knew he was hurting, but did he have to shut her out? She'd gone to the marae so full of hope. Now she could weep.

At last, Tautaru finished his speech. The crowd applauded and stamped their feet in appreciation.

'Your turn, Aroha,' Tautaru said. 'Time for your mihi.'

Aroha clutched her arms to her chest. How could she recite the mihi when she was so distraught about Hunapo? She stood up and glanced around at the elders. All so elegant, dressed in their traditional costumes, and all waiting for her. Her eyes returned to Hunapo. He was staring at the floor.

Aroha cleared her throat and stammered through the words. She'd practised for so long, but it all came out wrong. Hunapo didn't so much as look at her during the performance. He would think it was all false and made up. But it wasn't. She meant every word of it.

Aroha covered her face when she sank back into her chair. How was she going to survive the rest of the proceedings? Speeches, singing, dancing. How much longer? What was the point anyway if Hunapo didn't want to marry her?

I have to talk to Hunapo after the ceremony. That thought was all that kept her going. She was on her feet the minute the closing prayers finished.

'Hunapo! We need to—'

He was gone. She watched him disappear through a side door, with Olivia in hot pursuit. Aroha went after him too. She'd just got down from the stage when she felt her father's hand on her shoulder.

'Not so fast, Aroha,' Tautaru said. 'You need to come and farewell our guests.'

I need to be alone. Aroha couldn't bear to look at the visitors, let alone say goodbye to them. Why couldn't her father hurry up?

'I'm sorry, Dad,' she said. 'I'm feeling a bit funny. I need to get a drink of water.'

Before he could reply, Aroha was off to the kitchen at the back of the marae. She glanced out of the window. Moana and the women elders were squatting on the deck outside. They were talking about the ceremony. She caught enough of their conversation to get the gist of what they were saying. They sounded just as upset about Hunapo as she was.

'I'm not surprised Hunapo wants to run away,' she heard Evie say. 'Parading him around like a trophy. It's enough to make anyone bolt.'

'Then what do you suggest we do about it?' Moana snapped.

'Give the poor boy some space,' Lilly said. 'If we want Hunapo and Aroha to rekindle their friendship, they need time to get to know each other again—and not with all of us watching them!'

Aroha could have burst into their meeting and kissed Lilly. She would have done so if she hadn't overheard Moana sounding off.

'More space? Bloody nonsense. The little devil needs pulling into line!'

     David Whittet

Lilly must have won the argument. She was on their doorstep first thing the next morning.

Tautaru grunted and went to open the door. 'What the hell do you want?' he said. 'Ngaio's still in bed.'

'It's not Ngaio I've come to see,' Lilly said.

Aroha listened to their conversation. What? Lilly was going to take her to meet Hunapo at the Rere Falls? They'd have time alone together? Aroha wanted to jump for joy. Her mind brought her down to earth. She couldn't bear a repeat of yesterday, and if Hunapo was still in a mood, it would be.

She lagged behind Lilly as they walked to the falls.

'Cheer up,' Lilly said. 'I thought this was what you wanted.'

'It was—is,' Aroha said. 'I'm sorry. I just don't think Hunapo will be very pleased to see me.'

'Of course he will,' Lilly reached for Aroha's hand. 'Now come on, or we'll be late. Olivia said she'd be there with him at half past ten.'

Despite everything, Aroha's heart still missed a beat when she caught sight of him. Silhouetted against the falls, Hunapo looked every bit the hero she wanted him to be. She had to stop herself from running and flinging her arms around him. That would be a mistake.

'Come on,' Lilly said to Olivia. 'Time for us to take a walk.'

Aroha took a deep breath once they were alone. 'Oh, Hunapo!' The words came out in a gush. Why was it so hard to talk to him? 'Remember how we played here? You were such a monkey! We had our own gang. What did we call it? The Rere Rescuers, wasn't it?'

Hunapo looked away. 'I've got the real Gang to deal with now,' he muttered, stuffing his hands in his pockets.

'I know you have.' Aroha ran her fingers through her hair. 'Why is everything so horrid? Your father. My father. The Gang.'

Hunapo didn't answer. He continued to stare down the river.

Aroha drew another long breath. 'We used to talk about how different the Gang would be if we were in charge … Well, now we *are* in charge—or at least, we *will* be. You are going to be the new leader! We can change things, make everything better …'

'No, we can't,' Hunapo snapped. 'Don't be so stupid. We're just puppets. I know that even if you don't.' Hunapo signalled to Olivia and Lilly, who were watching in the distance. 'I'm sorry, but I want to go home now. I can't talk about any of this.'

Aroha watched him walk away. Did he know how much he was hurting her? Was being Tautaru's right-hand man more important than his feelings for her? One thing she knew for sure: the mischievous rascal she had loved so much was gone forever.

'What is it?' Lilly wrapped her arms around Aroha. 'Didn't it go well?'

Aroha rubbed her eyes. 'He won't talk to me.'

'Just give him time,' Lilly said. 'Hunapo has a lot to think about, but he'll come round, you'll see!'

Aroha shook her head. 'I don't think he will. Not now. He thinks I'm stupid.'

'Of course he doesn't.'

Aroha glanced downstream. 'Look.' She pointed at Olivia, who was struggling to keep up with Hunapo. 'He couldn't get away fast enough.'

Lilly shrugged. 'Let's get you home. I wonder what your Mum's got for your dinner?'

Aroha didn't care if she never ate again.

'Try not to worry,' Lilly said as she walked Aroha home. 'Olivia's been talking to Hunapo. He cares about you. He just doesn't know how to show it.'

Aroha sighed. 'Really?'

'Yes, he does,' Lilly repeated. 'Boys aren't like us. They bottle everything up. They don't know how to talk about their feelings.'

'Are you sure?' Aroha scratched her head. 'Hunapo used to talk to me a lot.'

Lilly raised her eyebrows. 'Boys can talk all right, but not about anything *important!*'

 David Whittet

Aroha hunched her shoulders. 'We used to talk about important things. How we'd take on the Gang and make it better.' Aroha paused, her lips quivering. 'You know, Hunapo and I could have been perfect for each other. We'd have changed things, made the Gang fair.'

'You still will, I'm sure of it,' Lilly squeezed Aroha's hand. 'Don't give up. Just be patient until everything settles down. You'll see Hunapo again next week. He'll have cooled down by then. Now off you go and run inside.'

❈

How do I get through to him? Aroha spent the following week rehearsing what she was going to say to Hunapo. She had to get it right for their next meeting. *'Be strong. Fight the Gang.' No, I can't say that. He'll just laugh at me.*

When the day came, Aroha put her shoulders back, her chest out and raised her chin. That's what her father did when he was talking to his men.

'I'm not stupid, Hunapo,' she began as they walked along the riverbank. 'I know how much you're hurting. But I can help you—if you'll let me in.'

'Let you in?' Hunapo replied, rolling his eyes.

'Yes, let me in,' she repeated. 'I know you boys find it difficult to talk, but I can support you …'

'Where did you get this bullshit?' Hunapo sneered. 'What do you know about boys, anyway?'

'More than you think, and it's not bull!' Aroha answered, her face hot. 'Boys find it hard to express feelings close to their heart. It's true. We were best friends, remember? We used to talk for hours, but I never really knew what was going on inside your head.'

'Of course I remember!' Hunapo threw his head back. 'You were always on my case.' Aroha thought she could see a faint smile on his face. 'But things are different now. You need to understand that. I have to be a leader. Everyone is looking to me to save the Gang. We can never go back to where we were.'

'I don't want to go *back*,' Aroha said, her hands on her hips. 'I want to go *forward*. With you!'

'You won't want to be with me when I fail … and I'm going to fail!'

'You won't fail, Hunapo!' Aroha tried to put her arm around him, but he pulled away.

'They're setting me up to fail,' he said. 'How do they expect *me* to patch up a family dispute that has been going on all these years? I can't. It's going to end in disaster.'

'No! Don't say that. We can do this together, you and me. You'll be a hero! I know you will!'

Hunapo snorted. 'I'm no hero. You can't help me. Back off. I have to do this myself.'

'But I want to be there for you. *Please*, Hunapo, let me help you.'

'You're doing my head in!' Hunapo held his hands to his ears and gave a loud grunt. 'You think you have all the answers, but you don't. I'm never going to be a leader—just a fall guy. A pathetic whipping boy for the Gang.'

'No, that's not you … *never*.' Aroha almost choked on her words. 'You'll make a great leader!'

'No, I won't,' Hunapo replied, digging his foot in the ground.

'Why won't you let me help you?' Aroha shook her head and crossed her arms. 'I don't understand you. I'm going to be your *wife*.'

'You were a good mate, but a wife? Face it, that's never going to work.' Hunapo walked away from her. 'This is all too heavy. You need to give me some space.' He turned back and glared at her. 'I'm *not* a hero, and I don't want to hear you saying that again.'

Aroha felt naked, exposed, her deepest fears laid bare. She couldn't face home when Lilly and Olivia arrived to take them back.

'I'd like to stay for a while,' she told Lilly. 'I like to look at the falls. They clear my head. I'll make my own way home.'

The Rere Falls had no magic answer for Aroha. As a child, watching the pounding waters had brought her peace. Today they felt cold, uninviting and empty.

Chapter Twenty

Olivia's House, 1978.

Soaking in the bathtub, Hunapo ran his fingers over the scars on his body. The grooves in his skin still smarted. He looked down at his chest, his nipples disfigured by all the wound contractions. A couple of years back, he'd told Aroha he was thirteen and scarred for life. Nothing had changed.

Everything his old man had taught him was bullshit. His father flogged him, then the gangsters thrashed his father. Bloody crazy. And now he had to live with an old woman because Maahanga hadn't the guts to fight off his uncle Tautaru. His father was a coward and a hypocrite.

Everything Olivia said or did irritated him. He didn't want to hurt her, but he was so wound up that when she asked him to do something, however undemanding, he flew into a rage.

'Blame it on my father—it's all his bloody fault,' Hunapo yelled as they argued about cleaning the kitchen floor. He knew how much she hated his coarse language, but he couldn't stop himself. 'I'm only here because the pōkokohua couldn't stand up to a pack of women!'

'That's not fair and you know it,' Olivia retaliated. 'Your dad had no choice.' She thrust a mop in his hand. 'There's a bucket in the yard and detergent in the cupboard. Now get on with the job.'

Hunapo glared at Olivia. No woman had ever spoken to him like this before. Maahanga had not cleaned their house since his mother left. So what if Olivia wanted to keep her home spotless? Why did he have to help? Sloshing the water on the linoleum floor, Hunapo pretended the mop was a spear and Maahanga the target.

Gangsters don't do chores. Another of his father's lies.

Olivia put her hand on his shoulder when he wrung the mop in the sink. 'You need to talk to your father, Hunapo. All this bitterness is eating you up.'

'I know, Aunty.' Hunapo lowered his head. 'You're right. I should go and see him.'

When he wasn't cursing the bastard, Hunapo worried about his old man. How would the bugger cope on his own?

He felt Olivia's hand stiffen on his back.

She hesitated. 'Of course, we'll need to clear it with Moana first.'

Hunapo flung the mop to the ground. 'What?'

'Moana made me promise ... You need supervision with your father ...'

'Stuff Moana. She can't stop me seeing my father ...'

'I can't go behind her back.' Olivia bent down to pick up the mop. She shook as she got up and met Hunapo's glare. 'Don't worry. The women won't interfere. They'll just chaperone you ... They won't come between you and your father.'

Hunapo exploded. 'Bloody women!' He tore the mop from her hand and threw it to the floor. With a kick, he overturned the bucket, flooding the floor with soapy water. 'Nobody chaperones me! Whakianga mai! I'm going to see my father.'

'Come back ... Please ... You're going to get me in so much trouble ...'

Hunapo stopped for a moment. Perhaps he should go back. Olivia didn't deserve the grief. But he didn't trust Moana. She'd do anything to stop him from seeing his father. He slammed the door and raced down the garden path.

There was no sign of his father when Hunapo arrived at Maahanga's place. Where the hell was he? Fumbling in his pocket for the key, Hunapo let himself in. The kitchen and the living room were both empty. With a knowing sigh, he wandered through the deserted house. *I bet the bastard's down at the tavern.*

     David Whittet

Hunapo yawned. He was in for a long wait and settled himself down in a chair. He'd almost dropped off to sleep when he heard creaking floorboards. What the hell was that? Hunapo got up. He held his breath. What if it was the thugs back for his father? He crept into the kitchen and armed himself with a club—a weapon Maahanga had frequently used on him.

The noise seemed to come from his father's bedroom. Hunapo put his ear to the door. It didn't sound like the thugs. More like a squeaky mattress. But his father never went to bed this early. And instead of his father's habitual snoring, there was a weird moaning. Sounded more like a woman.

'*Yes. Yes. Yes. Don't stop … I'm coming …*'

Then a high-pitched cry.

Hunapo flung back the door and immediately covered his eyes. *Yuk!* Everyone knew Maahanga was a regular at the local brothel, but he hadn't brought a bimbo home before. Or had he? Hunapo peaked through his fingers. Maahanga was on top of the woman. They were both stark naked and his father's buttocks clenched as he thrust into her. *Gross.* The way their bodies bounced across the bed, it amazed him they didn't land on the floor. The woman continued to shriek, more and more furiously. Hadn't she seen him? Then suddenly her entire body convulsed. Hunapo was about to leave when he saw her face. It was Aroha's mother, Ngaio.

Hunapo struck the bedpost with his club. 'Bloody bugger! Pūrari paka!'

Maahanga froze. 'Son! It's not how it looks …'

Ngaio hung her head and grabbed a sheet to cover herself.

Hunapo shook his head. 'You're one sick bastard.'

Maahanga jumped off the bed. He grabbed his pants and used them to wipe his groin. 'I can explain …'

Hunapo brandished the club at his father. 'Don't come near me.'

Maahanga pulled on his shirt. 'We need to talk. Please, Hunapo! Come back!'

Hunapo was already out of the door. He couldn't bear to look at his father a moment longer. In the distance, he heard Maahanga shouting at Ngaio.

'Sprung by my own son! This is your fault, Ngaio! Just go home!'

Hunapo stumbled through the township, still swearing to himself. *Kai a te ahi! Filthy pervert!*

Where could he go? He couldn't face Olivia any more than he could his father. He needed to be alone.

❧

Hunapo walked for days on end, his shoes disintegrating until he threw them away. He thought about his mother. What would Kiri have said about Maahanga sleeping with his sister-in-law? Hunapo stopped in his tracks. Perhaps his father had been sleeping with Ngaio before Kiri left. Hunapo had heard the rumours, and Ngaio had sometimes stayed overnight when he was little. That was unforgivable.

What had happened to Kiri? Had she really started a new life with someone else? Right now, he'd give anything to see her again. She'd hold him in her arms and make everything right.

His feet blistered as he carried on barefoot, the pain temporarily numbing his senses. But as he scrambled over hills and waded through streams, nothing could remove the image of his father screwing Ngaio. Aroha's mother! Remembering how Aroha had used kawakawa on his wounds, he picked some leaves and sat on the long grass to rub it into his aching feet. Was his future mother-in-law going to be his stepmother too? Or was Maahanga simply trying to get his own back on Tautaru? Both thoughts were equally disturbing, and he wanted to get as far away from it all as he could.

After another day tramping through dense bush, Hunapo reached the township of Patutahi. As a child, he'd come here with his mother for picnics. He could still taste her Marmite sandwiches. Which reminded him it was a couple of days since he'd eaten. He pinched a bread roll from the village store and ran down the street.

 David Whittet

'Stop, you little bugger,' the shopkeeper shouted after him.

Hunapo gave him the finger and took a bite from the roll. Couldn't the man see he was starving? Besides, nicking bread when you were dying of hunger was nothing compared to what his father had just done.

The next morning, he arrived in Gisborne and collapsed exhausted at the harbour. He must have been walking for three days. Or was it more? He'd lost track. It was forty-seven kilometres from Rere to Gisborne. It felt twice as far.

He dossed down on the quay amongst the other vagrants. They all had blankets. Hunapo shivered with only the shirt on his back to protect him from the icy wind that blew in from the docks. A noisy party at a fishermen's tavern kept him awake. Not that he wanted to sleep. That would only bring back the nightmare.

A passing youth offered him his coat. 'Here. Take this. Looks like you need it more than me.'

Hunapo's jaw dropped when he looked up. It was his old mate, Jake Rata.

'Jake! What are you doing here?'

'I'm here with the band,' Jake said. 'Playing the drums at the gig. What about you? Don't say you've finally got away from your old man!'

❧ ❧ ❧

Lilly's Place, 1993.

'Have you any idea why Hunapo ran away?' Aroha asked.

'Not really,' Lilly said after a moment's hesitation. 'Of course, Olivia was blamed. She was in a dreadful state. She got me out of bed in the middle of the night when he didn't come home.'

Aroha rubbed her chin. She knew Lilly was hiding something.

'Olivia must have known what was going on,' Aroha said. 'Didn't she tell you?'

'No.' Lilly paused again. 'She was too upset. What with both Maahanga and Moana hounding her.'

Lilly's keen brown eyes conveyed a silent message. There was clearly more to this story. Aroha didn't want to push Lilly, but she needed answers.

'Tautaru went mad too when Moana came and told him Hunapo was missing,' Aroha said. 'But it was all hush-hush.' She leant forward; her eyes fixed on Lilly. 'I have to know what happened that night.'

Lilly scratched her head. 'I can only tell you what I heard. Olivia said Maahanga pushed his way into her house as soon as Hunapo disappeared. He broke the chain on her door and ransacked the house. Pania told me Maahanga was out all night, waking up all Hunapo's mates.'

'But none of them knew where he was?' Aroha asked.

'Not according to Pania,' Lilly said. 'And Pania always had her ear to the ground for gossip.'

'Go on,' Aroha prompted.

'Next thing I knew,' Lilly continued, 'Olivia was hammering on my front door. It was one o'clock in the morning. She'd just had a rollicking from Moana. I told her there was nothing more we could do until morning. I stayed up all night, making her cups of tea.

'Moana summoned all the women to her place the next morning. Everyone else avoided Olivia, but I sat next to her on the verandah.

'"Hunapo is missing," Moana sounded off, pointing at poor Olivia. "And we all know who's to blame."'

'What a bitch,' Aroha said. 'So, what happened next?'

'Moana divided the women up into search parties. She reckoned he couldn't have got far with no money. Told us not to leave a stone unturned until we found him. Evie and I took Olivia home. Tried to persuade her it wasn't her fault.'

Aroha sighed. 'It wouldn't have been Olivia's fault. Nobody can stop Hunapo when he's in a mood.'

'I remember telling Olivia that Hunapo would come back when he was ready,' Lilly said.

'Did he come back of his own accord?' Aroha asked.

          David Whittet

'More or less,' Lilly said. 'A few days later, we were all down at the marae weaving flax when Hana burst in, waving her hands in the air. She'd seen Hunapo sleeping rough in the old railway yard. She took great delight in telling us how he'd been dossing with a bunch of hobos.

'"You could smell him a mile off," Hana's daughter added.

'Everyone rushed to find Moana. There was pandemonium. We'd all had enough.

'"I could wring Hunapo's neck for putting us through this," Erina said.

'Moana arrived and took charge. Told us to concentrate on getting Hunapo home.

'"Just drag the bastard back and lock him up," Pania said. "And throw away the key until after the wedding."'

'Typical Pania,' Aroha said. 'So they did force him to come home?'

'Not exactly,' Lilly said. 'Actually, it was all down to Evie. Moana swore she wouldn't let Hunapo stay with Olivia again. Evie's son Jake had been at a gig in Gisborne over the weekend. He'd found Hunapo with a bunch of vagrants at the docks. Hunapo told Jake he'd only come back for Olivia. He wouldn't stay with anyone else.'

'I'd love to have seen Moana's face,' Aroha said.

'It was a picture,' Lilly said with a smile. 'I can promise you that.'

Walking home from Lilly's that night, Aroha still didn't understand what had made Hunapo run away. She was sure it had something to do with her mother. But for the life of her, she couldn't think what.

Chapter Twenty-One

Olivia's House, 1978.

Hunapo flung his arms around Olivia. 'Thank you for taking me back, Aunty. You're one in a million.'

'It's good to have you back, Hunapo.' Olivia gently brushed the unkempt hair off his face. 'I was worried about you. Out there in the cold, all on your own.'

'It's not much fun living on the streets,' Hunapo agreed, glancing down at his feet. 'It's opened my eyes to a lot of things.' His bloodshot eyes caught hers. 'I'm sorry I ran away, and I'm sorry I got you into trouble. It's just all been too much for me. I had to get away. I didn't mean to worry you.'

'I know that, Hunapo,' Olivia said. 'Everyone has been putting far too much onto you. Now, why don't you take a bath and wash off all that grime? I've ironed you some clean clothes.'

Hunapo picked the calluses off his feet in the bathtub. How far had he walked over the past couple of weeks? Wandering the streets had done his head in. Too much time to think and his mind was still in a mess. Damn his father. Why couldn't the scumbag control his cock?

He had to get away from his old man. Living rough had taught him that much. Life with Maahanga would just be more of the same. Beatings. Until they killed him. Hunapo ran a flannel over his torso, his skin wrinkled in the soapy water. Perhaps the wedding might not be such a bad thing. At least it gave him a chance of a new life. Tautaru was a bastard too, but he couldn't possibly be more of a bully than his father. But what if he failed to meet Tautaru's—and everyone else's—expectations?

Hunapo lifted his weary body out of the bath and reached for a towel. The sores on his feet bled as he rubbed them dry. What about Aroha? Could he cope

     David Whittet

with her, full-on, twenty-four seven? He thought back to the day they'd met. How he'd pretended to be Tarzan, and she'd no idea what he was talking about. He could still see her expression—half thrill, half horror—when they raced down the rockslide. They'd had such fun. Until Maahanga ruined everything.

Hunapo pulled on his T-shirt. Yes. The marriage had to be a better option than the train wreck his life had become.

Olivia smiled when he came back into the kitchen. 'That's more like it. You look much better.'

'I feel … almost human again.' Hunapo shuffled from one foot to the other. 'Aunty, I've decided. I've accepted the arranged marriage. And I'm going to do my best for the Gang.'

Two weeks on and no second thoughts. Hunapo wanted nothing more to do with his father.

Someone was approaching the house. Hunapo froze. He'd know those footsteps anywhere. Many a time he'd taken cover when he'd heard them coming. Hunapo looked out of his bedroom window. Yes, that was his old man hammering on the door.

He heard Olivia telling Maahanga he couldn't come in.

'Bugger off!' Maahanga's voice echoed through the hallway. 'Bloody woman! Nobody stops me from seeing my son.'

Olivia was clearly doing her best to stop him. 'Please go,' she said. 'I'm in enough trouble as it is.'

Maahanga's voice got closer. 'Get out of my way. Which is Hunapo's room?'

Hunapo didn't move when his father burst into his bedroom. He sat on his bed and continued to pick the school sores on his legs.

'Hallelujah, son,' Maahanga gave him a hearty thump on the back. 'We've done it! We've got the numbers to smash Tautaru's little pantomime!'

'It's no good, Dad,' Hunapo drew blood from one of his scabs. 'I've decided that marrying Aroha is the right thing to do. For the Gang and the whānau.'

'Did you not hear me?' Maahanga waved his arms. 'We can destroy Tautaru and the marriage. You're free!'

Hunapo licked the pus off one of his sores. 'I'll never be free.'

Maahanga growled and stomped his foot on the floor.

Hunapo shrugged. *Make as much noise as you like. But don't expect me to take any notice.*

'Are you all right, Hunapo?' Olivia called from outside the door. 'Do you need help?'

'No, Aunty, it's all right!' Hunapo shouted back. 'Don't you worry. I can look after myself. My father doesn't frighten me any more!'

Maahanga paced up and down the bedroom. 'What's the matter with you, Hunapo? I've been out there, breaking my back to get support for your future, while you sit on your backside picking your filthy scabs!'

'Breaking your back? Yeah, right!' Hunapo rolled his eyes. 'Breaking your back screwing your sister-in-law!'

Maahanga raised a fist. 'You little shit!'

'I caught you in the act,' Hunapo snorted. 'How could you? With Aroha's *mother?*'

Hunapo watched his father's face turn scarlet and his neck veins bulge. One day his old man was going to overdo it and burst something.

'You don't understand,' Maahanga said. 'Ngaio's been helping me round up the troops to crush Tautaru. She hates the bastard as much as we do.'

Hunapo smirked. 'It's a pity that's not all she was helping you with.'

'What about you?' Maahanga hit back. 'Aroha is *not* the right girl for you.'

'Why not?' Hunapo said. 'Because she's the daughter of our enemy? Well, you picked the wife of your enemy!'

'Pōkokohua!' Maahanga slapped Hunapo across the face.

'Anyway, I'm glad I chose Aroha,' Hunapo rubbed his cheek. 'She's shown me stuff. Opened my eyes.'

'Don't start,' Maahanga said. 'You're surrounded by bloody women, that's your trouble. I have to get you out of here.'

'The womenfolk have been great,' Hunapo said. 'Olivia, Lilly and Evie. They've taught me so much.'

'Bloody nonsense! I've had a gutful of your feminine crap. You're a disgrace to the whānau!'

'A *disgrace*? Bollocks!' Hunapo rolled his eyes. 'You're the one sleeping around! What if I tell Tautaru that you're shagging his wife?'

'Tō teke!' Maahanga spat the expletive in Hunapo's face. 'Once Tautaru's out of the way, you can say goodbye to Aroha.'

'Bullshit. You'll never beat Tautaru. However many men you've got, Tautaru will always have more.'

'Damn you!' Maahanga stepped back and tripped over the pile of Hunapo's dirty clothes on the floor. 'I told you, we've got the numbers.'

'Listen, Dad.' Hunapo helped his father back onto his feet. 'You could stop this. It's not too late. Make your peace with Tautaru. Put an end to all the fighting. Then you'd be a *real* man!'

'Make peace with Tautaru?' Maahanga snorted. 'Are you out of your mind? The power-crazed bastard's had it in for me since we were kids. Get rid of me, and the Gang's his!'

Hunapo threw his arms in the air. 'None of this would have happened if you and Tautaru weren't so bloody pig-headed!' Why couldn't his father understand? 'Frigging spoilt kids, both of you.'

Maahanga grabbed Hunapo by the scruff of the neck and shook him. 'Do you really think Tautaru is going to stand aside and let you take over the Gang? Once you've outlived your usefulness, the bastard will have you shot.' Maahanga let go and Hunapo fell to the floor. 'He hired an assassin to have you killed when you were a baby!'

Hunapo covered his ears. His father was just trying to frighten him. It was all bullshit. It had to be. If Tautaru had really wanted him dead, he wouldn't have given up. Would he? What if Maahanga was right and Tautaru was just biding his time before getting another hitman to bump him off?

'Not so cocky now, are you?' Maahanga pulled Hunapo's hands away from his head. 'See what happens when you disobey me! You played into Tautaru's hands!'

'Please, Dad!' Hunapo said. 'No more!'

Hunapo just wanted his father to leave. Should he call Olivia and get help? No. He had to fight his own battles.

Maahanga bent down and picked Hunapo up off the floor. 'Damn Tautaru. And damn those women, too. You're coming home with me.'

'Get off me!' Hunapo broke out in a sweat. He fought with his hands and kicked with his feet, but his father's arms were like clamps. 'I'm not going back with you.'

'Kai hamuti! You'll do as you're told!' Maahanga slung Hunapo over his shoulder and charged out of the bedroom.

'Aunty! Olivia! Help!' Hunapo shouted. Why hadn't he called her before?

The front door swung open.

'Stop right there!' Moana stood at the foot of the corridor, flanked by Olivia and the women elders. 'Put Hunapo down. And get out!'

'And don't come back,' the rest of the women chorused, jostling Maahanga and pulling Hunapo away from him.

Moana snapped her fingers. 'Come on, move it!'

'You can't stop me from seeing my son.' Maahanga fended off the women with one hand and kept hold of Hunapo with the other.

Moana stepped forward and eyeballed Maahanga. 'I can, and I will stop you bullying Hunapo.'

'If I had my way,' Lilly said, 'you'd be facing the courts for child abuse.'

Hunapo freed an arm and pushed his father away. 'It's no use, Dad. Just go. Before you get yourself into more trouble.'

'No way,' Maahanga said. 'You're coming home with me.'

　　　　　　　　David Whittet

Olivia clutched Hunapo's arm. 'Don't worry, Hunapo. Your father's going to leave without making a fuss.' She turned to Maahanga. 'Aren't you?'

Maahanga shoved Olivia aside. 'Like hell!'

'Enough!' Moana stamped her foot. 'Cut the crap. Just put Hunapo down and go.'

Maahanga glared back. 'Never! I'm not giving up on you, Hunapo. I have to get you away from these bloody women. They're ruining you.'

Hunapo screwed his eyes shut. Why couldn't his father see the women had won?

The old man was still ranting. 'It's time to be a man, Hunapo … show them some balls …'

Opening his eyes, Hunapo saw the women closing in. He wriggled free and fell into Olivia's arms.

Maahanga tried to snatch Hunapo back, but Olivia had her arms wrapped tightly around him.

'Hunapo … listen to me …' Maahanga stammered.

'I'm staying here,' Hunapo said. 'With Olivia.'

Moana gave Maahanga the finger. 'You heard him. Go!'

Maahanga's face turned a bright purple. The way it always did before he lashed out. Hunapo shuddered. Surely his father wouldn't try it on in front of all the women?

'Don't do it,' Hunapo mumbled.

'Kai a te kurī!' Maahanga spat in his face. 'You are no longer my son! I'm done with you.' With a finger to the women, he barged past them and slammed the back door in their faces.

'Kai hamuti! Kai kurakura!' Hunapo could still hear his father swearing outside in the street.

Alone in his bedroom, Hunapo punched the wall with his fists. *You are no longer my son!* The words cut to the core. His father had beaten him repeatedly but had never disowned him before.

So I'm no longer your son! Hunapo tore the greenstone pendant from his neck. *Then you're no longer my father.* The pendant was the one gift he'd received since the bicycle and the only thing his father had ever given him. Maahanga had said it was a symbol of their bloodline. Hunapo threw it to the floor and trampled it with his boot. *Damn you to hell, Maahanga! You've never been a father to me. Mete pōkokohua!*

'Dinner time,' Olivia called from the kitchen.

Hunapo didn't take any notice. He wasn't hungry. Eventually, she came to his room.

'Hunapo!' she gasped. 'What have you done to that beautiful pounamu?'

'It was my father's.' Hunapo looked down at the shattered fragments on the floor.

'I know how much he's hurt you,' Olivia said.

Hunapo pushed her away. 'You know nothing.'

'Come and have something to eat,' Olivia said. 'That'll cheer you up. I've got you a nice steak.'

Dinner *did* make him feel better.

'How was it?' Olivia asked.

Hunapo picked the last morsel of meat off the bone with his teeth. 'Great. Thanks, Aunty.'

Screw this. The next couple of weeks drove Hunapo crazy. Olivia taught him one thing, Tautaru the opposite. Were they trying to turn him into a schizo?

'Don't let anyone see your weaknesses,' Tautaru told him with a thump on the back. 'That's the most important lesson a gangster can learn. Particularly when it comes to women. Especially Aroha.'

David Whittet

Did that apply to Olivia too? She might be just a woman, but like Aroha, Olivia had changed him. Made him a better person. And she cared about him. One night, when he got up to go to the toilet, Olivia's bedroom door was ajar. She was kneeling at her bedside, praying. What was it she said? 'Dear God, help me to do my best for him.' Or something like that.

As if being the prized son that Tautaru never had wasn't enough, the other kids mocked him.

'Nobody's telling me who I can marry.'

'Especially not to that goody-goody.'

Hunapo came home in a foul mood after a fight with one of the boys and kicked the washing machine until it spun across the floor.

'Whakianga mai!' he swore. 'Dickhead! Just wait till I'm Gang leader. I'll rub that motherfucker's nose in the shit.'

Olivia drew a long breath and drummed her fingers on the kitchen table. 'I don't know what they're teaching you in the Gang, but you are a guest in this house, and you will treat me and my property with respect.'

Hunapo froze. Ducked his head. He'd never been told off like that by a woman before. He looked up at her red-rimmed eyes.

'I'm sorry, Aunty,' he said. 'I hope the washing machine's not broken.'

'Come on,' Olivia said. 'You can help me put it back. And I will not have that kind of language in my home.'

'Do I have to spend the day with Aroha?' Hunapo asked when Tautaru picked him up the next morning. 'Can't I come on the job with you?'

Tautaru shook his head. 'Not today. I want you to take Aroha in hand. Wāhine need to be taught their place in the whānau. Remember. Aroha is just a little girl. A kōhine. You will be a warrior.'

Hunapo sighed. He'd been looking forward to going into town with the gangsters.

Ngaio arrived with Aroha. Hunapo felt Ngaio take him apart with her eyes. 'You take care of her, Hunapo,' Ngaio said.

Hunapo shifted his gaze to Aroha. What did she have around her neck?

'Look, Hunapo,' Aroha began, catching hold of his arm. 'I've got these fantastic binoculars. My great aunt Kāterina lent them to me. They belonged to Kamaka. See that dent on the barrel? My aunty told me that came from a spear aimed at Kamaka's head in the great Māori Land Wars.'

Give me strength. Aroha was so gullible. Did they even have binoculars during the Land Wars?

'We can be great adventurers like Kamaka,' Aroha continued. 'We're so lucky to have his binoculars.'

Hunapo rolled his eyes. 'Get real, Aroha. You'd believe anything.'

He watched her face fall. She was trying hard not to cry. He took her arm, and they left for the riverbank, carrying a chilly bin.

Tautaru beckoned Hunapo back. 'Don't give her any special treatment because she's my daughter.'

Hunapo scratched his head. Aroha could be bloody irritating. But it wasn't so very long ago he'd promised to look after her. Now her father was telling him to boss her around. How weird was that?

   David Whittet

Chapter Twenty-Two

Aroha gazed at Hunapo as they finished their picnic overlooking the Rere Falls. Was this the same boy who pledged he'd always be there for her?

'Don't let my dad turn you into something you're not,' she said, edging closer to him. 'You're not one of them.'

Hunapo pulled away. 'I am what I am.'

'No,' she said. 'You've got a kind heart. You'll *never* be one of them.'

'Leave it.'

She watched Hunapo kick a stone down the riverbank.

'I heard what my father told you,' Aroha said. 'He told you not to give me any special treatment because I'm his daughter. You're better than that, Hunapo.'

'What would you know?' Hunapo said.

'Olivia told me you were okay about the marriage,' Aroha said. She wished he'd look at her when she was talking to him. 'I thought you were going to give it a go.'

'I was … I am …' Hunapo leapt to his feet, waving his arms. 'For fuck's sake, I don't know what I'm doing. Olivia says one thing, Tautaru tells me another—to harden up. How the hell am I supposed to know what to do?'

'Hunapo!' Aroha's jaw dropped. *He must be hurting to talk like that. He knows how much I hate it.* Not knowing where to look or what to say, she got up and put a hand on his shoulder.

'Piss off.' Hunapo walked away. 'I knew today was a mistake.'

That was Tautaru speaking. Not Hunapo. Aroha knew that. Perhaps she'd pushed him too far. Best give him a minute to cool down. She wandered to the water's edge and looked at the waterfall through the binoculars.

'Come and have a look,' she shouted, waving the binoculars in the air. 'They make everything look so beautiful.'

Hunapo walked towards her, and she handed him the binoculars. He held them up to his eyes. That had to cheer him up. Surely. But he didn't appear to be looking through the glasses. Hunapo suddenly swung his arm and threw the binoculars into the river.

Aroha's heart stood still as the ripples spread and the binoculars disappeared.

Still shaking, she looked at Hunapo. Her father really had got to him. *Don't give her any special treatment because she's my daughter.* He'd taken that to heart.

'My mother will kill me for this,' Aroha wailed. 'Kāterina too. She told me to guard them with my life.'

For a moment, Hunapo lowered his head. Was he feeling guilty? Ashamed? Was he going to do the right thing and dive into the river and find the binoculars?

'Precious, were they?' Hunapo grabbed Aroha with both arms. 'Then you'd better get in there and find them!'

She fought back, desperately trying to free her hands, but Hunapo was strong. He picked her up and threw her into the river.

The ice-cold water took her breath away. She'd never learnt to swim. Gagging, choking, gasping for air, she fought to keep her head above water. 'Help me! Hunapo! I'm going to drown!'

I will always look out for you, Aroha. I will be there for you whenever you need me. That's what Hunapo had said when they shared blood. Did that mean nothing now? Was he going to leave her to die?

'Stand up, Aroha!' Hunapo said. 'It's not that deep in there! You're such a little girl!'

Embarrassed beyond belief, Aroha felt like a drenched rat when Hunapo paddled into the water and helped her back onto her feet.

'I'm sorry,' Hunapo lowered his head. 'I shouldn't have done that.'

'No, you shouldn't.' Aroha gave him a hard stare and bolted.

　　　　　　　David Whittet

Panting and shivering, Aroha collapsed on the kitchen floor. She'd made it home. Just.

'Aroha, my darling!' Ngaio leapt to her feet. 'What's happened to you? Where's Hunapo? Why hasn't he brought you home?'

Aroha opened her mouth to reply, but the words wouldn't come out. Just water. Lungfuls of water.

'You're soaked.' Ngaio rested her hand on Aroha's forehead. 'And frozen.'

Ngaio wrapped her arms around Aroha. Her mother was warm and cuddly, and it felt good. But Aroha couldn't rest until she'd owned up.

'Don't be angry with me,' Aroha said, her teeth still chattering. 'Please, Mum … but I've lost Kāterina's binoculars.'

'What?' Ngaio raised her eyebrows. 'Kōkā will go mental …'

'Will she hate me?'

'Of course not,' Ngaio said. 'She'll be upset at first, but she'll get over it. But how did you lose them?'

Aroha felt her throat closing in. 'They fell in the river.'

Ngaio shook her head. 'So why didn't Hunapo go in and find them?'

'Hunapo threw the binoculars in the river,' Aroha said. 'And then he threw me in.'

Ngaio clenched a fist. 'Dirty rat! Wait till I get my hands on him.'

Tautaru wandered into the kitchen, swigging his beer. 'Sounds like Hunapo's been teaching you a lesson in survival,' he said. 'Good on him.'

'You bastard!' Ngaio glared at Tautaru. 'You absolute bastard! And don't just stand there, get a towel. And a blanket! Can't you see the state she's in?'

Aroha coughed up some more watery spit. She was just as angry with the old man as her mother was. Tautaru was turning Hunapo into a monster.

'Aroha needs to toughen up.' Tautaru flung a towel and some bedcovers at Ngaio. 'I told Hunapo to play rough with her.'

Ngaio picked up the towel and dried Aroha. 'I knew this would happen,' she said. 'I told you Hunapo would be no good for my baby!'

But he could have been, Aroha thought, if her father hadn't led him astray.

Tautaru fetched another beer from the fridge and seated himself at the kitchen table. He took a slurp and glanced down at Aroha. 'Don't look so miserable. Hunapo's showing you the way of the world. You should thank him!'

Ngaio threw the towel at him, catching him on the cheek. 'What kind of man are you? She's your daughter. Your flesh and blood! How can you let him treat her like that?'

Tautaru stood up and pointed a finger at Aroha's face. 'You must be tough when you're the Gang president's wife. Not weak like your mother. And the sooner you learn, the better.'

Ngaio spat in his face. 'Kai angaanga! Kai upoko!'

Aroha had never heard her mother curse like that before. She watched Tautaru wipe the spit off his face. Then he grinned at them. What ghastly punishment was he dreaming up?

'Come on, Aroha,' Ngaio said wearily. 'You're still shivering. Let's take those wet clothes off and get you into a hot bath.'

'This time I'm leaving him,' Ngaio muttered as she scrubbed Aroha's back in the tub.

'Are we going to run away, Mummy?' Aroha asked.

'I wish we could,' Ngaio said, gently combing Aroha's hair. 'Just you and me. We'd be so happy. Away from all of this.'

'So why can't we?' With her father turning Hunapo into such a brute, Aroha would have given anything to get away.

'Your father wouldn't let us,' Ngaio gave a half-hearted shrug. 'He'd find us wherever we went. He's got spies everywhere.'

Aroha put on her pyjamas. At last, she felt warm. Her mother tucked her into bed. Ngaio looked every bit as miserable as Aroha felt.

'Mum,' Aroha said. 'Can we go and see Kāterina? I want to explain about the binoculars.'

'I don't think so,' Ngaio said. 'Let me find the right moment to tell Kōkā.'

Lying awake that night, Aroha thought it would be much better if she told Kāterina. And the sooner, the better. Why couldn't her mother see that?

　　David Whittet

'Wake up, Aroha!' Ngaio burst into her bedroom the next morning. 'We're going to see Kōkā.'

Aroha rubbed the sleep from her eyes. 'Are we really? I thought you said—'

'But mind, you'll have to play outside,' Ngaio interrupted. 'There's something I need to discuss with Kōkā.'

❧

What's the matter with Mum? Aroha watched Ngaio grind the gears and curse under her breath as they drove into the forest. *Perhaps she'll lighten up when we get there.*

Ngaio continued to ignore Aroha on the long trek through the undergrowth. *Why is she shutting me out?* Aroha wracked her brains for an explanation as they trudged down the path in silence. Gone was the mother-daughter repartee that she had enjoyed so much on their previous trips to the *Gypsy Rose*.

Aroha was desperate to talk to Kāterina and come clean about the binoculars. And if anyone could tell what was wrong with her mother, it was Kāterina.

'You're not coming in,' Ngaio said when they finally reached the caravan. 'I told you you'd have to play outside.'

'Oh!' Aroha's face fell. 'I must talk to Kāterina. Just a few minutes. Please.'

'No. Kōkā and I have important business to discuss.'

Tears brimmed in Aroha's eyes. 'But—'

'But nothing.' Ngaio climbed the rickety steps into the *Gypsy Rose* and closed the door behind her.

Seated on the bottom step, Aroha passed the time pulling grass out of the ground. A forest bird chirped in the distance. She watched the kōkako flex its wings, perched on a treetop. When she was a little girl, Aroha used to think the birds were singing only for her. Now, her mother's shouting drowned the birdsong. Why was Ngaio so mad at everyone these days? The kōkako flew away. How Aroha wished she could do the same.

Aroha could *feel* the tension spilling out from the caravan. Still cross with her mother for not letting her have a good heart-to-heart with Kāterina, Aroha

Gang Girl

was beyond caring what they were fighting about. She covered her ears to blot out their voices. But the arguing grew louder, and Aroha got sucked in when she picked up fragments of their conversation.

Kāterina's voice rose in a crescendo. 'Human life is sacred!' That was nothing new. She'd heard Kāterina say it many times before.

But what was her mother saying? 'Incest. That's what it is.'

Incest. What was that? Had she misheard it? Maybe it was *unrest* her mother had said. No, there it was again.

'This isn't *incest*,' Kāterina said, 'it's an extended whānau ...'

What on earth were they talking about?

Then another word she hadn't heard before. 'Stop calling it a venereal disease,' Kāterina said. 'It's a child.'

Venereal. What an ugly word. And Ngaio and Kāterina were batting it backwards and forwards like it was one of her father's swear words. Except Kāterina *never* used naughty words.

'Get me an abortion,' her mother said, 'I'm begging you.'

Abortion. Aroha had heard of that. She was just beginning to piece things together when her mother burst out of the caravan. Ngaio looked dreadful. Her dress was torn. And why was her face so white? What had they been doing in there? Aroha had only seen one person so pale before, and that was her great-grandmother on her deathbed.

'Come on, Aroha,' Ngaio said. 'We're going straight home!'

'What?' Aroha replied. 'Can't I say goodbye to Kāterina?'

'No! Kōkā's not herself. She's ... out of sorts. Leave her be.'

Ngaio may have looked as though she was on her last legs, but Aroha couldn't believe the force with which her mother moved her down the path.

'Come back!' Kāterina called after them. 'You'll haemorrhage!'

'*Haemorr*— what?' Aroha looked up at her mother, her mouth wide open. 'What's Kāterina on about?'

'Nothing you need worry about,' Ngaio said. 'Try to keep up.'

　　　　　David Whittet

'You're hurting my arm!'

Aroha glanced back. Kāterina stood in front of the caravan, her voice echoing through the forest.

'Murua ahau! Murua ahau!'

Kāterina always repeated those words when she was upset.

Ngaio kept stumbling on the undergrowth, and Aroha wondered if they'd make it back to the clearing where they'd parked the vehicle. Unable to bear the silence between them any longer, Aroha took a deep breath and asked the question that was driving her crazy.

'Mummy, why were you talking about an abortion?'

'What?' Ngaio stopped dead in her tracks and glared at Aroha. 'I taught you not to listen to other people's conversations.'

Aroha backed away. 'I wasn't. I didn't *want* to hear. You were shouting so loud I couldn't help it.'

'How dare you talk to me like that?' Ngaio waved a finger in Aroha's face. 'I expected better from you. It was grown-up talk. Nothing to do with you!'

'You're just like Dad,' Aroha said. 'He's always telling me off for listening to him and his mates. As if I cared what they were talking about.' She paused and bit her lip. 'But I would like to know why you were talking about an abortion. Is Kāterina having a baby? Or is it you?'

'None of your business.' Ngaio clenched her teeth. 'Don't you breathe a word of this to anyone. Especially not your father. If you do … I swear I'll …'

Ngaio broke off without finishing her sentence and strode ahead.

Aroha could sense her mother's rage. Stuff that. Aroha was angry too. She was fourteen, and Ngaio still treated her like a child.

'Mum!' Aroha said. 'If only you'd talk to me, perhaps I could help you.'

'If only you could.' Ngaio stopped and turned to face her daughter. 'I'm sorry, Aroha. You're a good girl. It's just … I've just got so much on my mind at the moment.'

Aroha looked up at her mother's face. 'Tell me. I understand more than you think.'

'I know you do.' Ngaio hugged Aroha tight against her body. 'Don't worry about me. I'll be okay. But you *must* promise not to say anything to your father. Especially not about abortions.'

'I promise.'

Aroha nestled her head on her mother's tummy. She hadn't done that in ages, and she began to relax. Had today simply been a ghastly nightmare? Of course it had. Kāterina was far too old to have a baby, and when Tautaru had gone on about wanting a son, Aroha had heard her mother say she couldn't have more children. Yes, it was all a bad dream, and she hoped she'd wake up soon.

As she tried to work it all out, Aroha felt something sticky on her face. 'Mummy, what have you spilt on your dress?'

Ngaio didn't answer. More oily liquid oozed onto Aroha's cheeks. She moved her head and looked up at her mother. Ngaio's face was grey and lifeless, her eyes as dead as tombstones.

'What is it, Mum?' Aroha put her hand on Ngaio's stomach. 'You're bleeding!'

Keep calm. Mummy must have her monthly. Aroha had just started having them herself. Why did they always come at the worst possible moment?

When Ngaio collapsed, and the blood continued to flood through her dress, Aroha realised it was much more than a bad monthly.

'Mummy! You're dying! Don't leave me!' Aroha grabbed hold of her mother, her fingers slipping on the blood. 'Try to get up.'

Ngaio gasped for breath. 'It's no use, Aroha. Cuddle me one last time …'

'Please don't die!' Aroha pressed her hands against Ngaio's belly. Perhaps if she pushed hard enough, she could stop the bleeding. She glanced around. Kāterina might have followed them. No sign of anybody. Just eerie shafts of moonlight breaking through the trees, the cold rays highlighting Ngaio's deathly appearance. And the blood flowed even faster. Aroha heaved Ngaio up from the ground, her arms struggling with the dead weight. 'What am I going to do?'

'We'll die together,' Ngaio whispered. 'It's best this way.' Her head dropped and her body slid back. 'No more hurt. No more pain …'

     David Whittet

'You can't give up!' Aroha could hardly bring herself to look at her mother's face. Just a couple of hours back, those eyes had been full of fire. 'I won't let you!'

Ngaio beckoned Aroha to lie beside her, her arm shaking. 'Don't fight. We'll be together for eternity. Nobody can harm us any more …'

'No!' Tears streamed down Aroha's cheeks. She made a last desperate attempt to pull her mother to her feet. When that failed, she closed her eyes.

Alone in the middle of the forest, Aroha couldn't bear to watch her mother take her last breath.

❧ ❧ ❧

Lilly's Place, 1993.

Aroha paced up and down the living room. 'My aunt Kuini died after a botched abortion. Do you think that's what happened to my mother?'

Lilly shook her head.

'I do,' Aroha said. 'But it still doesn't make sense. Ngaio was fine when she went into the caravan. When she came out, she was bleeding to death.'

'It could have been a miscarriage,' Lilly said. 'Brought on by all the stress.'

'No.' Aroha took a sharp breath. 'Someone gave her an abortion in the caravan that afternoon while I sat outside on the step.'

'That's impossible,' Lilly said. 'Kāterina wouldn't have anything to do with an abortion. And she wouldn't let anyone else touch Ngaio. Especially not in her beloved *Gypsy Rose*. Besides, you said yourself there was nobody else in the caravan.'

'I know.' Aroha scratched the back of her neck. 'I don't suppose I'll ever get my head around it.' She sighed and sat down next to Lilly. 'I thought Ngaio was going to die in my arms. She went mad, telling me we'd die together.'

'But she didn't, did she?' Lilly said. 'Tell me what happened. How did you get home?'

Aroha stared down at her hands. Talking to Lilly had reopened the wounds.

'I went back down the path to fetch Kāterina. It was all I could do. I only got a little way when Kāterina arrived on her horse. She'd been worried Ngaio wouldn't make it home and came looking for us. We managed to get Mum onto the horse and rode back to the vehicle. Then Kāterina drove us home.'

'What did Tautaru say when you got back?' Lilly asked.

'All I remember was him going on about all the blood on the upholstery of his new ute. He made Kāterina clean it up. But he must have known.' Aroha felt a lump in her throat. 'It was just a couple of days later that Ngaio disappeared. My father killed her. I'm sure he did.'

'You really believe that?' Lilly said.

'Yes.' Aroha turned her head and gazed into Lilly's eyes. 'You're not hiding anything from me, are you? You'd tell me if you knew what happened to her?'

'Of course I would,' Lilly said.

Aroha wiped her eyes. 'I'll never forget the morning I walked into Ngaio's bedroom and found she'd gone. I wanted to die. She was right. We should have both died together in the forest.'

Lilly put her hand on Aroha's wrist. 'Don't say that.'

'My father said she'd gone to hell. The place bad girls go when they disobey the Gang. Callous bastard. Even at that age, I knew he was lying. Ngaio would be in heaven. But I couldn't bring myself to believe she was dead. I kept looking for her. Emptied cupboards thinking she might be hiding. Searched my father's sheds in case he'd locked her up. I know it sounds ridiculous, but sometimes I still look for her, even now.'

'That's not so crazy,' Lilly said. 'She was my friend and I miss her too. We both need some closure.'

'As if we'll get that after all these years,' Aroha said with a wave of her hand.

'Someone must know what became of her,' Lilly said. 'I'm going to grill Pania. If anyone knows, it's her.'

Aroha rolled her eyes. 'Pania? You can't trust a word she says.'

'I know she's an awful busybody, but you have to hand it to her, she has a

　　　　　　David Whittet

knack for digging up the truth.' Lilly leant forward. 'Hunapo lost his mother too. He never knew what happened to her, either. And he was even younger than you were.'

'I know.' Aroha paused for a moment. 'And Tautaru ruined his life as well. It was just after Ngaio disappeared that he gave Hunapo his sixteenth birthday present. And we all know what that was: a couple of hookers. Sometimes, I think my father didn't have even the tiniest shred of human decency.'

Aroha stood up to leave. Was Hunapo born bad or was he corrupted by her father? He seemed to have chosen the gangster's life.

Another thought crossed her mind as she put on her coat. She turned to Lilly. 'When Ngaio was dying that night, she told me how we'd be together for eternity. Hunapo had promised me that too. He said we were bonded for eternity. And look how that turned out.'

Chapter Twenty-Three

Olivia's House, 1979.

'Sixteen today!' Olivia burst into Hunapo's room with a tray of bacon, eggs and black pudding. 'Breakfast in bed!'

Hunapo wiped the sleep from his eyes. 'Thank you, Aunty. That looks yummy.'

And it was. Hunapo lay back on the bed and patted his stomach when he'd finished. He was about to get up when someone hammered on the front door. He heard Olivia protesting.

'You're not bringing them into my house.'

'Out of my way. Wahine kore tuki!' It was Tautaru's voice and there was giggling in the background.

Hunapo jumped out of bed and flung on some clothes. Too late. Tautaru burst into his bedroom with two gorgeous girls in the skimpiest outfits Hunapo had ever seen.

'Welcome to the perks of being a Gang leader.' Tautaru gave him a hearty thump on the back. 'Happy birthday!'

The girls had his shirt off before he could button it up. 'You won't be needing that.'

'I give you a *boy*,' Tautaru instructed the girls as he left. 'Make him a *man*.'

Hunapo thought his eyes would burst when they stripped off. Those fishnet stockings … They went all the way up to their suspender belts! And those G-strings! Hunapo gasped. Did all women wear them? The knickers came off. *Holy crap!* Those pussies. He couldn't stop himself gawping at them.

The girls grinned as they climbed on top of him.

'First time with two girls?'

'First time ever.'

David Whittet

His raging adolescent hormones went into overdrive and in minutes his body exploded.

Bloody hell! That was frigging unbelievable!

❧

Hunapo lay on his bed after the girls had gone, his entire body still tingling and glistening with an ungodly mixture of sweat and sticky secretions. A wicked thought entered his head. He would *never* have had that much fun with Aroha. She would be far too pure for anything like that. He rolled over and buried his head in the pillow. Aroha was the only girl he'd spent any time with up till then. Maahanga had taught him pain was a substitute for sex. *Gangsters don't have fun. You're not here for a good time!* Not that it seemed to apply to his father. He looked like he was having fun with Aroha's mother.

Things were different now. Those two girls had shown him the joys of the flesh, and Hunapo wanted more. Much more. But he was going to *marry* Aroha. How would that work? Would he be allowed a bit on the side *after* they married?

A knock on the door.

'Hunapo!'

It was Olivia and she didn't sound happy. Hunapo covered himself with a sheet.

'Okay, Aunty. Come in.'

Olivia's face blazed. Her voice trembled as she spoke.

'It may be your birthday, but I will not have my house turned into a bordello.'

'It wasn't my fault … it was Tautaru … I didn't ask him to bring the girls … He said it was my birthday present.'

'Then you can tell him from me that if he's intent on turning you into a shameless playboy, he can do it somewhere else. I will *not* have those tarts in my home again.'

Hunapo couldn't stop himself smiling. Olivia was magnificent when she was all fired up.

'All right, Aunty. I understand.'

He was already thinking about a certain deserted barn. It would make the *perfect* love nest.

❄

'You're the hottest girl I've been with.' Hunapo stroked Cindy's face as they lay naked on the floor, all passion spent.

'Bullshit.' She got up and retrieved her discarded clothes. 'I bet you say that to every girl you've laid.'

'No, Cindy. You were special.' He rolled over on the straw and reached for a pack of smokes from his shirt pocket.

Cindy sniggered. 'At least you remembered my name.'

Hunapo lit his roll-up and watched her get dressed. 'Don't go.'

'Might as well.' Cindy looked down at him and snorted, pointing her foot at his wilting groin. 'You've shot your load.'

Hunapo blushed. 'I can come again. Give me a minute.'

Cindy pulled up her knickers. 'Much as I'd love another shag, I've got to go.' She thrust a leg into her jeans. 'I have to collect firewood for Aunt Lydia.' She heaved her top over her head. 'And I hate the bloody hag.'

'Don't be mean!' Hunapo sat up and stared at her. 'I know Lydia. She's a lovely old lady.'

'She's a freaking witch.' Cindy ran a hand through her hair. 'She scared the shit out of me when I was a kid. Still does.'

Hunapo smirked. 'You must have been as wicked back then as you are now. She used to give me lollies when I was little.'

'Lucky you!' Cindy threw a bale of hay at him. 'Well, if you think she's so bloody wonderful, you can go and get the bitch's firewood yourself!'

                    David Whittet

Hunapo stubbed out his cigarette and put on his pants. 'All right, I will.'

He was about to suggest they fetch the wood together when she unbolted the barn door, blew him a fake kiss and left. *Damn*. He shook his head and buttoned up his shirt. Aroha would never have been so disrespectful towards one of her elders. She would have done *anything* to help an old lady.

Hunapo grabbed his jacket and took in a sharp breath. What was he doing sleeping around with these bimbos? It was Maya last week. With a miniskirt that covered less than a belt would and legs to die for, Maya was shit-hot. Everything had been so exciting at first. The girls made him feel alive. But once they'd had sex, it left him empty and alone.

He felt worthless when he wandered out of the barn after Cindy left. None of those girls could hold a candle to Aroha. Today he had the chance to do the right thing, and he hurried to Lydia's house.

'How nice to see you again, Hunapo.' Lydia's eyes sparkled when he loaded the kindling into her hearth. 'Thank you so much. I was feeling the cold.' She rubbed her hands together as Hunapo lit the fire. 'I thought my niece was bringing me some firewood days ago. But Cindy's a law unto herself. Now tell me, Hunapo, will you stay for a cup of tea?'

'No, Lydia. I'd best get home.' He gave her a kiss on the cheek and handed her an envelope. 'Here, this is for you.'

She opened it and cried. 'Bless you, Hunapo.'

He smiled all the way home. Aroha would be so proud of him.

Hunapo picked at his dinner that evening.

'Not hungry?' Olivia asked.

'I want to tell Aroha I'm sorry. I just don't know how.' Hunapo's soulful eyes met Olivia's. 'What can I say to her?'

Olivia finished clearing the supper dishes and sat down beside him. 'Why do you find it so difficult to talk to her?'

Hunapo tensed his shoulders. 'Sometimes she's just … too much. Keeps on and on about cleaning up the Gang and I can't hack it.'

Olivia put her hands on his. 'That's just who she is.'

'I know. It's what makes her such a good person.'

'Why don't you tell her that?'

'I wish I could show her how I feel. But whenever we're together … I just seem to make everything worse. Sometimes I think it's better if I don't see her.' Hunapo covered his face with his hands. 'I've been so mean to her. Will she ever forgive me?'

Olivia frowned and rubbed her chin. Her face suddenly lit up. 'Why don't you ask her to come over for dinner? I'll cook something special.' She patted him on the back. 'I bet she could do with some company now her mother's gone.'

Hunapo gulped. He'd heard about Ngaio's disappearance. Why hadn't he gone to comfort Aroha? He felt sick in his stomach. He had promised he would always be there for her, but once more he had let her down when she most needed him.

'Aroha adored her mother.' Hunapo blinked back a tear as he stumbled over the words. 'She'll be a wreck.' He remembered how he'd waited and waited for Kiri to return. 'God, I felt like shit when my mother never came back.'

Olivia took his hand. 'Invite her for tea on Thursday. She needs you. Now more than ever.'

Hunapo frowned. 'How do I ask her? I'll only mess things up if I go and see her.'

Olivia got up from the table and opened a drawer in her sideboard. 'Write to her.' She handed him a pad of her best stationery. 'All girls like getting elegant letters. Especially when there's an invitation to dinner included.'

     David Whittet

Chapter Twenty-Four

Aroha held the letter to her face and sniffed its delicate perfume. Such beautiful notepaper. Olivia had brought it around that morning. It must have taken Hunapo ages to do, his writing was so neat and tidy. If only Ngaio could have seen it. Would it have changed her mind about Hunapo?

Not that Hunapo had been making things easy for her over the past few weeks. She'd seen him snogging Maya outside the local store. Cocky Maya. How could he?

And the embarrassment when the shopkeeper glanced at her over his bifocals. 'Was that Hunapo I saw out there? I thought he was marrying *you* … not Maya … or one of his other girls …'

She'd flung the groceries in her shopping basket and fled from the shop.

The next day she picked some flowers to give to Angie, an elder recently home from hospital. There were some lovely snowdrops and pansies down by Ben Brown's farm. She dropped all the flowers she'd collected when she saw Hunapo disappear into the barn with Cindy.

Perhaps she should decline the invitation to Olivia's if that was how Hunapo was carrying on. But Aroha hoped with all her heart the letter was a sign that he was turning over a new leaf. She had to give it a go.

Tea was at six o'clock on Thursday, and Aroha spent all day in preparation. She put her hair into a bun. She'd seen it in a women's magazine and thought it looked so grown-up. And it did. Aroha gazed into the mirror with pride. She put down the hairbrush and rummaged through an old makeup bag she'd found on Ngaio's bedside table. Ngaio had hardly ever worn makeup, but today Aroha would put the kit to good use. She even attracted a few whistles from the boys when she walked down the street to Olivia's place.

Hunapo opened the door when she arrived. 'Aroha! You look … amazing! I … er … Come in!'

When she saw his eyes almost pop out of his head, Aroha felt taller than she ever had before.

Olivia gave Aroha a hearty bearhug. 'Haere mai! I'm so glad you could come. And you do look stunning.'

Aroha wrapped her arms around Olivia. 'Thank you for inviting me, Mrs Winiata.'

'Call me Aunty. That's what Hunapo does.'

Olivia led her into the dining room. 'That smells wonderful,' Aroha exclaimed as the aroma wafted through from the kitchen. 'I'm starving!'

'It's roast lamb with all the trimmings. Hunapo told me it was your favourite.'

Aroha stifled a tear as she sat down at the table and Olivia served up. The spread was just like her mother used to make it.

'I'm full to bursting,' Hunapo said when they finished eating. 'That was terrific. Thank you, Aunty.'

'You're very welcome.' Olivia began taking the dishes through to the kitchen.

Aroha offered to help with the washing up, but Olivia insisted she stay and talk with Hunapo.

Alone together on the settee, Aroha watched Hunapo bite his thumb. She used to do that too when she was nervous. His eyes darted around the room. At last, he turned and looked at her.

'I was so sorry to hear about your mother …' He broke off, still fidgeting with his hands. He lifted his head and started again. 'I was a wreck when my mother left.' He shuffled towards her and put a hand on her shoulder. 'Life will never be the same, but it will get easier.'

'Will it?' Aroha dabbed her eyes. 'Are you sure?'

'It will. I promise.'

Aroha's voice croaked. 'Some days I don't think I can bear it any more.' She paused and took a deep breath. 'I think my father killed her.'

      David Whittet

'What?' Hunapo said. 'I know he's a bastard, but—'

'He was always threatening to do it, and she was so frightened of him. I knew something was going on, but Mum wouldn't talk about it. She said I was too young to understand.'

Hunapo took her hand and gave it a squeeze. 'I kept praying Kiri would come back after my father threw her out. You need to do the same. Don't lose hope.'

'But your mother didn't come back, did she?' Aroha said. 'And mine won't either. Not if she's dead. Maybe it wasn't my father. It could have been the abortion.'

'Abortion?' Hunapo's jaw dropped. 'What the—'

'She almost bled to death in the forest.' Aroha exhaled, trying to blow away the memory. 'I thought she was going to die in my arms.'

Hunapo stared at her. 'Are you sure it was an abortion?'

Aroha began to cry. 'Of course I'm sure.'

Olivia rushed back in from the kitchen.

'What is it, sweetheart?' Olivia sat down beside Aroha and gave her a hug.

'It's just ...' Aroha looked up at her warm brown eyes. 'I didn't even get to say goodbye to my mum. No note. No words of comfort. Nothing.'

Olivia rubbed Aroha's back. 'My poor darling! I know how you feel. My husband died suddenly, and I never got the chance to say goodbye either. But I know my Jack is up there somewhere, looking down on me. And I bet your mum is thinking of you wherever she is.'

Aroha nodded, smiling through her tears. 'I hope so.'

'My mother didn't leave a note either,' Hunapo said. 'But then, I pretty much knew why she left.' He rolled his eyes. 'She couldn't stand living with my father a day longer, and I can't say I blame her!'

'Hunapo! You're such a monkey!' Aroha dried her eyes. She had glimpsed that impish rascal of old.

When it was time for Aroha to go home, Olivia kissed her on both cheeks. 'I'm always here if you want to talk. Remember—I'm your *aunt*.'

There was a bite in the air as Hunapo walked Aroha home along the moonlit streets.

She squeezed his hand. 'Olivia's lovely. You're so lucky to have her looking after you.'

'Tonight was her idea,' Hunapo admitted. 'She's been more like a mother to me than an aunt.' He stopped and grinned. 'But don't you dare tell her I said that!'

'Oh, Hunapo! I've missed you so much.' She gave him a high-five. 'Even your cheek.'

'I've missed you too.'

'Honestly?'

'Yes.' Hunapo skidded to a halt as they reached her place. 'You know, we've got so much in common, you and me. We've both lost our mothers and our fathers are mean bastards.'

Aroha undid her bun and shook out her hair. 'It's worse for you, Hunapo.' She walked through the yard and looked into the kitchen. Tautaru was there, boozing with his mates. 'I only have one father. That's bad enough. You've got two.'

Hunapo followed her to the back door. 'Yeah. Maahanga first and now your old man. I don't know which is worse.'

'Thank God for Olivia. She'll help us through this.' Aroha gave him a kiss on the cheek before opening the door. 'Thank you for tonight. It was awesome.'

Snuggling up in bed, Aroha wanted nothing more than to drift into a blissful sleep, but her father and his cronies were so rowdy she couldn't settle. She went over the evening in her head. Why was Hunapo so shocked when she'd mentioned the abortion? Did he know something he wasn't telling her?

Aroha buried her head in the pillow. Another niggling worry refused to let go. Would Hunapo ever give up his girlfriends? Or would he always juggle a double life? She tossed and turned on the mattress. Why couldn't she get rid of the feeling that everything was going to blow up again sometime soon?

David Whittet

Chapter Twenty-Five

Aroha was sick of hearing about Hunapo's sixteenth birthday party. He'd already had his present. Those awful girls had done enough damage without another of her father's overblown celebrations. Hadn't that ghastly event on the marae to announce their engagement been enough? It was the most unnatural thing Aroha had ever experienced. Now she had to go through it all again with a bridal waltz at Hunapo's birthday party.

Her father's men took over the kitchen every day to plan the grand celebration. That was a joke. They left all the preparation to the women. The men just sat around the kitchen table drinking beer and listening to her old man boasting.

'This party will show everyone that the Māhiti Gang reigns supreme,' Tautaru said. 'I'd like to see that bastard Ngatoro put on a show like this. Or old man Rutene, for that matter.'

The men cheered and raised their bottles.

Aroha raised her eyebrows. Not that again. Why did her father still have it in for nice Mr Ngatoro? Or kind Mr Rutene? She folded her arms. How much longer would this go on? She just wanted them to leave so she could get on with cooking dinner.

For Aroha, the only decent thing about the party was the beautiful frock the women made her for the occasion.

'She has to look like a princess for the bridal waltz,' Tautaru had said to the women's sewing group. 'Are you sure you're up to the job?'

The silky white material felt so soft in Aroha's hand. She gasped when she tried it on and looked in the mirror. Embroidered with a twirly Māori motif and embellished with glass beads and sequins, the women had done a brilliant job.

'Are you okay?' Evie asked as she made some adjustments to the dress. 'Don't you like it?'

'I'm sorry. It's beautiful.' Aroha blinked back a tear. 'I just wish my mother could have seen me wearing it.'

Aroha sat in front of Ngaio's old dressing table on the day of the party.

Tautaru put his head into the room. 'Don't forget you're meeting Hunapo at five to rehearse your dance.'

'No, Dad.'

'I'm off to the hall now to run through the programme with Hunapo.'

She knew that meant an afternoon of heavy drinking for the pair of them. Aroha sighed. *Please God, don't let Hunapo get smashed and make a fool of himself.*

Aroha shed another tear for her mother when she put on the dress. She pressed her head against the tarnished mirror on the dresser. The black spots that blurred her image matched her mood.

Olivia arrived at half past four to escort her to the community hall.

'Doesn't it look beautiful?' Aroha gazed at all the flowers and festive lights. 'You women have done us proud.'

Olivia smiled. 'It had to be *perfect* for you and Hunapo.'

Five o'clock passed with no sign of Hunapo.

'You go home,' Aroha said. 'You need to get changed for tonight.'

'Are you sure?' Olivia replied. 'Will you be all right?'

'Of course I will,' Aroha grinned. 'I've got my fiancé to look after me.'

Olivia blew out her cheeks. 'If the wretch ever turns up. He left home hours ago.'

'He was supposed to meet my dad for a rehearsal.'

'A likely story.' Olivia shook her head and looked at her watch. 'I'd better go and get ready. I won't be long.' She hugged Aroha. 'And by the way—you look gorgeous.'

'Don't be late for the bridal waltz,' Aroha called after her.

Olivia looked back over her shoulder. 'Just try to keep me away!'

Aroha smoothed down her dress as she waited alone. Five thirty. Where on earth was the rascal? The guests would soon be arriving. She wandered through the empty hall. Six o'clock. She heard laughter in the distance. Giggling girls. And a male voice that sounded all too familiar. *That had better not be Hunapo.*

She followed the noise to a grubby anteroom at the back of the hall. She flung back the door and gasped.

'Hunapo! How could you?'

He was drunk. Smashed. And surrounded by a mob of adoring girls. Even worse, they were taking their clothes off.

'Aroha—I'm sorry!'

She watched him attempt to sober up and fend off the girls. They were all over him, and with so many piercings and facial studs, they tore his skin when they kissed him.

'Enough, Maddie,' Hunapo said. 'Get off me! You too, Kara! And you, Tia!'

Aroha stepped back, holding her head in her hands. This was the boy who had comforted her so tenderly just a couple of weeks ago.

Her cheeks flushed. She glared at Hunapo, pain, hurt and anger burning in her eyes. 'I thought you were better than this.'

More mindless cackling from the girls.

'It wasn't my fault … It was your old man … He got me plastered.'

'That's right, Hunapo. It's always someone else's fault.' Aroha maintained her gaze, refusing to break eye contact. 'When will you take some responsibility for yourself?'

She watched him squirm and search his brain for an excuse.

'I'm sorry … I, er … I …' His eyes shifted from Aroha to the girls and back to her. 'I didn't want this to happen.'

Tia started licking his neck. 'Of course you did! You're not the least bit sorry, are you Hunapo?'

'I *am!*' Hunapo put his hands up to shield himself from her. 'Shove off. All of you. I mean it. The party's over.'

'Oh no, it's not!' Maddie, a busty girl wearing a revealing lace and mesh bodysuit, pushed forward. 'It's only just begun.' She turned to Aroha and smirked. 'Don't be such a spoilsport. We're just warming him up for your wedding night!'

'Yeah, Aroha!' Sadie joined in. 'Want to see me kiss your *fiancé?*'

'Na.' Lola pushed Sadie aside and pulled off her baby-doll lingerie. 'She wants to see *me* make love to her betrothed.'

Aroha felt her body closing in on itself. Her eyes fixed on the raunchy tattoos that seemed to cover every inch of their bodies. Her mouth went dry. Her chest felt tight.

Maddie stripped off her bodice. 'Maybe she wants to see all of us screw him together.'

Aroha's hand tightened into a fist. She lunged forward. 'Get off him!'

Maddie grabbed her arm. 'Why don't you join in? You know you want to.'

'We can share him with you,' Sadie sniggered.

'Don't be shy.' Lola had Aroha's other arm. 'Here, let us help get your kit off.'

Aroha's eyes darted around. They surrounded her. There was no way she could get to the door. Maddie and Lola began pulling off her dress. She wrestled with them, but they were strong, and they all joined in the scuffle. She heard Hunapo's muffled voice in the background.

'Girls! That's enough! Leave her alone!'

None of them were listening. With a last tug, the dress ripped apart.

'My new frock!' Aroha broke out in a sweat. She bared her teeth at the girls and shoved them away. 'The women spent ages making it … specially for tonight. My father will kill me!'

'Don't cry!' Maddie yanked the dress off Aroha's shoulders. 'That's better. Now you can get in on the action!'

Aroha refused to let the girls see her cry. Pulling the torn gown back on, she charged forward towards Hunapo.

'I'm leaving, Hunapo. *You* can tell Tautaru how your girlfriends destroyed my ballgown and explain why I won't be dancing with you tonight.'

'Don't worry, babe.' Maddie pushed Aroha aside and flung herself on Hunapo. 'I'll dance the tango with you instead.'

'We could all do the Dance of the Seven Veils.'

    David Whittet

'With Hunapo's balls as the prize!'

'Served up on a plate!'

'Piss off, all of you.' Hunapo staggered to his feet, throwing the girls off him. 'Get out!'

Aroha shook her head as he crashed back onto the floor. 'You want everyone to think of you as a man, Hunapo! You're not a man. You're a loser. A miserable, drunken low life.'

She bolted out of the hall and into the street, clutching the remnants of the dress to her chest.

'Come back,' he called after her. 'Forgive me. I'm sorry.'

Like hell you are. The tears she had fought off so bravely now flooded down her cheeks.

Aroha walked through the township for what seemed like hours but was probably only a few minutes. What was she going to do? Tautaru really would kill her if she didn't go back to the community hall for the ball. But how could she with her dress torn to shreds?

She sat on a park bench, her head buried in her hands. She needed her mother. Someone to take her into their arms and make it all better. But if Ngaio were here, she'd only go on about Hunapo. *I told you all along, Hunapo is no good for you.* Right now, that was the last thing Aroha needed.

She stared at the ground. *I have to talk to someone.* What about Olivia? She'd have to be quick to catch her before she got back to the hall. Aroha got up, took a few steps towards Olivia's house, then stopped. Talking to Olivia would be awkward with her being Hunapo's foster mum. And although she was angry, she didn't want to snitch on Hunapo.

Who else? Lilly would understand. So would Evie. But they were both in the hall, and Aroha couldn't go back in looking like this. She slumped down on the bench.

Someone sat down beside her. Her eyes were closed, but she knew it was him. The telltale smell of sweat and stale alcohol. Hunapo's smell.

'Go away,' she said without moving.

Hunapo edged closer and attempted to put his arm around her. 'I never meant to hurt you, Aroha.'

Aroha pulled away to the opposite end of the bench. 'So you keep saying.'

'I didn't.' Hunapo clasped his hands together in his lap. 'Those girls mean nothing to me.'

'Don't they?'

'They're just after some fun.'

'Yes.' Aroha snorted so loudly she made him jump. 'Making fun of me gave them a terrific kick.'

'Oh, Aroha!'

'Maddie has *Hunapo* and a love heart tattooed on her back.'

'Mads is a law unto herself. I went ape when I saw her tattoo.'

'Your name, permanently engraved on her back.' Aroha gave him an icy stare. 'She won't give you up without a fight!' Talk of tattoos took her mind back to those ceremonies on the marae. 'I don't understand why anyone would *choose* to get a tattoo.'

Hunapo ducked his head. 'I tell you—Maddie, Tia, Sadie, Lola—none of them mean anything to me. You're everything.'

Aroha folded her arms and shuddered. 'It didn't look like that.'

'Honestly. It's true!'

Aroha stood up and confronted him head-on. 'Then promise me you will never see them again.'

Hunapo's chin dropped to his chest. 'I promise.'

'Look me in the eye and say it.' She watched him play with his hands. 'You can't do it, can you?' He didn't answer. 'I want you to go back into that hall and tell all of them it's over.' Still not a word. Aroha shrugged and took a few paces away. 'I'm not sharing you with them.'

Hunapo followed her down the street. 'Don't go. Please, Aroha. You come first.'

She turned back. 'Then promise.'

'I do.'

                    David Whittet

'Look at me.'

Hunapo slumped back onto the park bench and stared down at his feet. 'I can't. I'm sorry.'

Aroha stared at him, shook her head slowly, then looked away. 'I guess I don't mean that much to you, after all.'

'You do, Aroha! You do!' He took a deep breath and closed his eyes. 'But sometimes … you don't make it easy for me.'

'Hunapo! You're much better than this!' She stepped back and sat down next to him. 'Those girls—they'll never make you happy. They're just out for a good time. You're destined for so much more.'

Hunapo lowered his gaze. 'I can never be the man you want me to be.'

'Of course you can.' Aroha placed her hand on his. 'You're the one to unite the Gang, build a better future for all of us. Remember how we used to talk.'

'Why does everyone expect so much from me? Why can't they accept me for what I am? I'm just an ordinary boy.'

'No, you're not. You're the most extraordinary person I have ever met!'

Hunapo pulled back, his voice cracking. 'You've *never* understood me, Aroha! You're just like everyone else! You want to turn me into something that I'm not! Well, you can't. I'm no saviour. Why do *I* have to be the one to change the world? Why can't I just be myself?'

Aroha sighed. She glanced up at the stars, then down again. She was sitting right next to the boy who had given her so much grief and heartache. She still believed in him, but as she turned her head towards him, she could almost touch the giant gulf between them.

'Come on, Hunapo.' She got up from the bench and took his hand. 'I need to change. I've got an old party-dress at home. That'll have to do for tonight. If we're not back at the hall soon, we'll both get a hiding from Tautaru.'

Aroha did her best to hold back the tears as she danced the bridal waltz with Hunapo that night. The song that blared out over the loudspeakers was all about dancing cheek to cheek. She should have been in heaven, but she wasn't. Even as they twirled around the dance floor, she could see Sadie and Maddie winking at Hunapo. Had he noticed? She wasn't sure. But every time he smiled, she was convinced he was grinning at them and not her.

'What's up?' he asked as he whisked her up on her tiptoes. 'Why are you crying?'

'I'm not.' Aroha forced a smile. 'I didn't know you could dance, Hunapo.'

The waltz concluded, and the crowd broke out in applause. This time she was certain Hunapo and Maddie made eye contact. She couldn't bear to look at him any more. *He's a playboy. He's weak, and he's never going to change.*

She glanced around the hall. Her father was dressed up in that old ceremonial cape. As far as Aroha was concerned, that grotty māhiti stank as much as the gang named after it. There were people everywhere and most of them pretty drunk. Nobody would notice if she ran away. At least, not until she'd got a head start. She'd disappear, just like her mother had done.

Aroha grabbed some food from the buffet and stuffed it under her dress. She'd need it once she was on the road. She edged towards the door, making sure she mingled with the crowd. The music started up again. *Now or never.* She clutched her chest in apprehension and made a run for the door.

She could already smell freedom when she felt a firm hand on her shoulder. She let out a long, low-pitched cry as she turned around to confront her father.

'Not leaving, are you, Aroha? We can't have you sneaking away from the party early. You're the guest of honour!'

For the rest of the evening, she endured Tautaru parading her in front of a multitude of visiting gang dignitaries. She went through the motions—smiles, handshakes, the customary hongi—but inside she felt like her heart had stopped. She wished it had. Worst of all were the excruciating photographs with Hunapo. She was positive Maddie was smirking in the background.

Aroha wasn't listening to her father bragging when they trudged home that night.

'We socked it to the bastards! When did the Wairoa Warriors ever put on a show like that?' *Blah, blah, blah.* She wanted to cover her ears, but he was holding her hand. More and more of the same old rubbish. 'The Māhiti Gang reigns supreme …' *Blah, blah, blah* … 'We're invincible …' *Blah, blah, blah.*

Could she possibly feel any more pain? Would she ever be happy again? Aroha just wanted her mind to leave her in peace. But it wouldn't, forcing her to go through the day's events time after time. She would never stop caring about Hunapo, but how could she spend the rest of her life with someone with such ambivalent feelings towards her? And share him with those hateful girls?

Chapter Twenty-Six

Aroha watched a spider attack its prey. Staring at the barren walls of her bedroom, with torn posters and rotting wallpaper peeling away from the plasterboard, she felt as trapped as the fly in the web.

Will I ever be free? Under house arrest following her thwarted attempt to escape after the bridal waltz, Tautaru told her she'd stay there until the wedding. Alone and frightened, she spent the endless days gazing at the flaking paint and mould on the ceiling and tormenting herself about the ceremony. At the party, everyone was talking about a tattoo and giving her knowing looks. *What will they do to me? I have to know.*

She crept into the kitchen. Her father was there, fetching another beer from the fridge.

'Dad, I heard I'll get a tattoo on my face when I marry Hunapo.'

Tautaru turned to face her. 'You'll have a tā moko like all the gangsters' wives.'

Aroha's lip quivered. 'No, Dad, please. You know I hate tattoos. Especially on the face.'

'Women receive a tattoo on their chins. Hunapo will have the full facial tā moko.'

'Dad, I'm begging you. Anything but that.'

Tautaru waved his hand at her. 'How many times do I have to tell you? Blood and ink are sacred to the Gang.'

Aroha wished she hadn't asked. *Blood and ink.* The mere sound of those words drove her wild.

Lying on her bed, Aroha looked through some books Kāterina had given her. Maybe she could escape in her imagination. The first volume she opened was all about zoos. Aroha felt as caged as the tigers in the pictures. She tossed

David Whittet

it aside. The next was about a beautiful princess. She was in no mood for a happy ending, and that book ended up on the floor too. All of them were tales of courage and adventure. Make-believe. Only one of Kāterina's stories struck a chord. The wedding ceremony loomed over Aroha's head like the sword of Damocles.

Five days and she could take no more. She leapt off her bed when she heard Olivia at the door. Brilliant! Someone she could talk to. She raced down the corridor in time to see Tautaru slam the door in Olivia's face.

'Dad!' Aroha glared at her father. 'Olivia came to see me! Why didn't you let her in?'

'No distractions,' Tautaru said. 'You need to spend your time contemplating your future as the Gang president's wife.'

'I've tried, Dad—honestly. But I can't think of anything stuck in my bedroom. At least let me go for a walk. I need to get some air. I can't breathe in the house.'

Tautaru frowned and shook his head. 'Do as I tell you and go back to your room!'

Aroha could have hit his smug face. Arguing was useless—there had to be another way. *If I don't get out of here, I'll go mad.*

Kai. Food. Aroha gave her bedroom wall a high-five. *That's the way to get around the old man.* She endured another two days of imprisonment before the larder was bare.

'Dad, there's no food in the house. Let me go to the shop. I'll buy some stuff and cook us dinner. Like Mum used to do.'

Tautaru grunted.

Aroha opened the pantry door. 'See?' She drew closer to her father with a hesitant hug. 'I always *used* to go on errands, and it's just down the road to the store.'

Another grunt. He glanced across at the empty shelves. 'All right. Just make sure you come straight back.'

'Don't worry. I won't run away.'

Aroha scuttled out of the door before he could change his mind.

'You'd better not,' Tautaru called after her. 'I'll be watching you!'

❈

I'm free! Aroha skipped down the street. The sun was shining and the air smelt fresh. She was out of the house—for half an hour at least. She heard some girls giggling. That didn't dampen her spirits. At least, not at first. Surely Maddie and her friends weren't still after her blood. Or were they?

Aroha glanced around.

'It's her!' Maddie shouted.

'About bloody time,' Sadie added. 'I'm sick of being stuck in that shed.'

Aroha shuddered. Had they been spying on her all that time? And what did Maddie have in her hand?

Keep walking, Aroha told herself. *They can't do anything. Dad's watching.*

She caught snippets of their conversation.

'I know Aroha's a goddamn prude,' Sadie said, 'but why do you hate her so much?'

'Because Hunapo dumped me for her,' Maddie replied.

'He didn't exactly dump you.' That was Lola's voice.

'He's marrying the bitch, isn't he?' Maddie said.

Aroha ran the rest of the way and darted into the shop.

'You're as white as a sheet.' Mr Guthrie, the elderly storekeeper, took off his spectacles and stared at her. 'Is something wrong?'

Apart from being scared to death? 'No. I'm fine. I'm just here to pick up some supplies for Tautaru.' She gave him her shopping list and glanced back at the window. Maddie's face was pressed against the glass. Their eyes met.

Aroha rapidly turned her back to the window and loaded the groceries into the basket.

　　　　David Whittet

Mr Guthrie opened the cash register. 'Will that be everything?'

'Yes. Thank you. Just put it on my father's account.' Aroha shuffled from one foot to the other. *What am I going to do? I can't go back out there ... they'll kill me!* She lifted the basket and put it back on the counter. 'Actually, it's a bit heavy. Could you call my dad and ask him to come and help me?'

'No need to bother your father. I'll give you a hand.'

Why didn't Mr Guthrie want to call her father? He must owe him money— *everyone* owed Tautaru money. Aroha glanced back to the window. Maddie was still there. And looking meaner than ever.

'I'll just lock up the shop for a minute.' Mr Guthrie fumbled in his pocket for a key. He smiled and picked up her shopping basket. 'Let's get you home.'

Aroha wiped a bead of sweat off her forehead. She liked Mr Guthrie and didn't want to see him get hurt. 'Are you sure? My dad wouldn't mind coming to fetch me.'

'It's no trouble.'

He's a frail old man. He'll never scare off those girls.

The scene in front of her seemed to play out in slow motion when Mr Guthrie locked the shop door behind them. The girls surrounded her in a circle.

Aroha pulled on Mr Guthrie's arm as they got closer. 'Quick, Mr Guthrie. I want to go back inside.'

'Don't be silly, Aroha. You'll be home in a minute.'

The girls were on top of them in a flash.

'Get out of my way, old man!' Maddie shoved Mr Guthrie aside and slapped Aroha. 'Take that, bitch! Nobody shafts me and gets away with it.'

Groceries flew in all directions. Eggs smashed on the ground, milk flowed down the pavement, and lettuce leaves scattered across the street. Aroha screamed as Maddie and Lola pinned her to the ground. Then she saw something that made everything else fade into insignificance. She hardly noticed her father arriving with his minions, hurling abuse at the girls.

'Whaki/anga mai! Get your filthy mitts off my daughter!'

She was vaguely aware of the gangsters forcing the girls to pick the shopping up off the ground. What Aroha had seen was far more important. Maddie had dropped a pair of binoculars.

She picked them up and ran her fingers over the engravings on the casing. They'd got another dent, but they were *the* binoculars. She'd recognise them anywhere. Maddie must have found them washed up on the riverbank. And to think the wretch had been using those precious binoculars to spy on her. How dare she? As if leading Hunapo astray wasn't enough.

'You'd better watch your bloody back!' Maddie spat at Aroha before fleeing with the rest of the girls. 'I'll get you for this! Just you wait!'

Perhaps Maddie would get even one day. But right now, Aroha didn't care. She had found Kamaka's binoculars. She held them against her chest. *I have to get them back to Kāterina.*

❦

Tautaru put his arm around Aroha and took her home. She couldn't remember the last time he'd done that.

'Don't worry, Aroha,' he said. 'They wouldn't dare come near you again. They'll be dead meat if they try.'

He hugged her when they got back to the house. She didn't think he'd *ever* done that before. That was promising. She needed him in a good mood.

Aroha showed him the binoculars and took a deep breath. 'Can we take them back to Kāterina?' She felt his hand tense on her shoulder. 'Please, Dad. It would mean so much to her.'

Tautaru snorted. 'I don't want you seeing that stupid witch again.'

'You could come with me,' Aroha said. 'That way, you wouldn't have to worry about me running away.'

Tautaru took his hand from her shoulder and gripped her arm. 'I'm not having any more bullshit before the wedding.'

'But Dad! These binoculars are valuable. They belonged to Kamaka, a great warrior. He was Kāterina's great-great-grandfather, I think.'

She saw Tautaru's eyes light up.

'Valuable, are they?' he said.

'Yes, and Kāterina will be so happy to have them back.'

Tautaru grabbed the binoculars. 'Well, if they're a family heirloom, I'd better have them for safekeeping.'

'No!' Aroha tried to wrestle them back from his hands. She'd seen that greedy look in her father's eyes before. Once he got hold of the binoculars, she'd never see them again. 'I'm taking them back to Kāterina.'

Tautaru held them up out of her reach. 'I don't think so.'

Aroha jumped in the air, desperate to get hold of them. 'Give then to me! Dad!'

Everything returned to slow motion. Except this time it was blurred. Had she just hit her father? Or was it the binoculars that had struck his lip in the struggle? Whatever—his mouth was bleeding, and he was mighty angry. What was he going to do?

'Bitch!' Tautaru picked her up, threw her into her room and locked the door.

How long was she in there on her own? Aroha had no idea, but it felt like forever.

Even more cobwebs than before covered the ceiling. The giant spider, mercilessly devouring its victims, reminded Aroha of her father.

Curled up on her bed, she clutched her knotted stomach with one hand and held her aching head with the other. When she eventually drifted into a deep sleep, she didn't want to wake up. Because when she did, she knew Tautaru would have sold the binoculars.

Aroha stirred when she heard voices coming from the kitchen. Moana was shouting her head off. That ghastly woman's voice was almost as loud as her father's.

'What the hell were you thinking?' she heard Moana shout. 'Letting those girls loose on Aroha. No wonder she's gone crazy.'

'*You* are kaumātua for the women of this Gang,' Tautaru hit back. 'You need to get a grip on yourself. Those girls are *your* responsibility.'

Moana again. 'It's your fault, Tautaru. You sent those tarts to entertain Hunapo, and you encouraged them.'

Aroha tried not to listen. Tautaru, Moana, Hunapo. They were all the same. Blaming someone else for their own mistakes.

She heard the key turn in the lock on her bedroom door. Aroha rubbed her eyes and lifted her head to see Lilly walk in. *Thank God for Lilly.*

'They're arguing about me, aren't they?' Aroha said.

Lilly sat down on the bed beside her and held her hand. 'Don't take any notice of them.'

'They think I'm upset about those girls,' Aroha said. 'But it's not that.'

'What is it then?' Lilly ran her fingers through Aroha's tangled hair, knotted from several days' crying. 'I thought you were scared of them.'

'I am.' Aroha sat up. 'Or at least I'm frightened they won't leave Hunapo alone after our marriage.' She met Lilly's eyes. 'But it's the binoculars that are really worrying me.'

'The *what?*'

'I lost these precious binoculars and I only just got them back, and now my father's taken them. I'm sure he'll have sold them, and I so wanted to return them to Kāterina.'

'Leave it to me,' Lilly said. 'When did you last have anything to eat? I'm going to get you some lunch.'

Lilly left the bedroom door open, and now Aroha could hear everything that was going on in the kitchen.

'She says she wants to go and see her aunt Kāterina,' Lilly said. 'Something about returning some binoculars. Says her father won't let her.'

'Damn those bloody binoculars,' Tautaru said. 'I thought she'd forgotten about them.'

'She says you've taken them off her,' Lilly said. 'Is that true?'

'Yes,' Tautaru said. 'They were valuable.'

'Pawned them, have you?' Moana said.

 David Whittet

'Of course I haven't.'

'You *have,*' Moana said. 'Sprung!'

Pawned? What did that mean? Aroha blew out her cheeks. Had he sold them?

'This isn't a joke,' Tautaru said.

'Indeed it isn't,' Moana answered.

Lilly popped her head around the bedroom door. 'I've made you a Marmite sandwich and a nice hot cup of Milo.'

Aroha followed Lilly into the kitchen. Tautaru and Moana were seated at the table. A group of women elders squatted on the floor. They were all looking at her. Aroha kept her head down and sat at the other end of the table from her father. Lilly stood behind her, with her arm on Aroha's shoulder.

'She's starving.' Lilly glared at Tautaru. 'When did you last feed her? Go on like this and Aroha won't be at the wedding, she'll be in hospital.'

'She'll be at the wedding,' Tautaru said. 'Even if I have to drag her there with my own hands!'

'Not the way she's going,' Lilly said. 'You can't lock her up and then expect her to act normally at the wedding.' Lilly took off her jacket and wrapped it around Aroha. 'I'm taking her to Olivia's place. Olivia says she'll look after both Hunapo and Aroha until the wedding.'

Aroha gave a nervous smile. She knew what was coming from her father.

'No way,' Tautaru said. 'That miserable wahine has undermined everything I've taught Hunapo. She's ruined him.'

'She's been like a second mother to both Aroha and Hunapo,' Lilly said.

Tautaru thumped the table. 'She's not getting her hands on Aroha.'

'She might be your only chance,' Lilly said. 'Believe me, Olivia is the only one who can get Aroha to the wedding.'

Evie got up and knelt beside Aroha.

'You trust Olivia, don't you?' Evie said.

Aroha nodded. She felt a tinge of excitement, but that disappeared when her father opened his mouth.

'Well, I don't,' Tautaru said.

'Nor do I,' Moana added.

'So, do you have a better idea?' Evie said.

Tautaru wrung his hands together and glared at Aroha. 'Just leave her to me.'

'No, Tautaru,' Lilly said. 'We've tried your way and it doesn't work. Give Olivia a chance.'

Moana jumped up from the table. 'I need a word in private, Tautaru.'

I know what that means, Aroha thought as Moana and Tautaru stepped out into the yard. She strained her ears. What were they scheming? She could see her father flailing his arms in the air. But Moana seemed to be winning.

A couple of minutes later, they were back in the kitchen.

'We're not happy about this,' Moana said. 'Not by a long stretch. But we've decided Aroha will stay with Olivia until the wedding.'

Something in Moana's eye told Aroha this was too good to be true.

The women got up and stretched their legs.

'It's bad luck if you ask me,' Pania said. 'Aroha and Hunapo shouldn't be in the same house before the big day.'

Evie beckoned Lilly, and they each took one of Aroha's arms.

'Not so fast.' Moana reached for her jacket. 'I'm coming with you.'

'Are you really taking me to Olivia's?' Aroha asked. 'I hope she'll take me to Kāterina so I can explain about the binoculars.'

❧

Aroha couldn't rest until Kāterina knew the truth about her precious binoculars.

'Please, Olivia,' Aroha begged. *'Please, please, please.'*

Olivia glanced up from loading the washing machine. 'I can't. It's more than my life's worth. Moana's got eyes in the back of her head. Your dad too.'

'Oh!' Aroha scratched her head. *Think. How can I persuade her?*

'Please don't ask me again,' Olivia said.

     David Whittet

Hunapo wandered into the washing room. 'You could go tomorrow. Tautaru and Moana are going to a hui up the coast. Most of the gangsters, too.'

Olivia closed the washing machine door and added the detergent. 'Are you sure?'

'Positive,' Hunapo said. 'Tautaru thinks the coasties are stealing his money.' He put his arm around Olivia. 'Go on. Take her. I'll cover for you if anyone gets suspicious.'

'So can we?' Aroha asked. *Can we? Can we?*

Olivia started the washing machine without a word.

Hunapo rummaged in his pockets and handed Aroha a crumpled piece of paper. 'Give this to Kāterina.'

'What is it?' Aroha asked.

'It's a pawnbroker's ticket,' Hunapo said. 'I found it with Tautaru's things.'

Aroha screwed up her face. 'A pawnbroker? What's that?'

'Just give it to Kāterina, and she'll get her binoculars back.' Hunapo hung his head. 'And I'm sorry I threw them in the river.'

Olivia sighed. 'I just hope my old banger will get us there. Mind you, she's never let me down yet.'

'So we're going?' Aroha flung her arms around Olivia. 'You're an angel.'

❧

Aroha wondered whether Olivia's old Holden Belmont would conk out before they reached the forest. She held on to the grab handle as the vehicle chugged and spluttered its way down the bumpy track. Olivia parked in the same place her mother had used, and they trudged along the same path.

Aroha gripped Olivia's arm.

'You're thinking about your mother, aren't you?' Olivia said.

Aroha nodded. Why had she been so keen to come back?

They stopped to catch their breath, and Olivia took a flask from her backpack.

'Once all the fuss has died down,' Olivia said, 'I hope you and Hunapo find happiness. Maybe you could get away from this mess and start a new life somewhere else.'

Aroha lowered her head. 'I stopped thinking about all that a long time ago. Hunapo will never leave the Gang. It's in his blood. Those wretched girls are in his blood, too. He'll never change.'

'Don't give up on your dreams.' Olivia handed her a cookie and a mug of cocoa. 'It may seem a long way away at the moment, but one day you will escape from the Gang. I promise you.'

Aroha put her mug down on the ground and hugged Olivia. They stood there in each other's arms for several minutes. A gentle breeze rustled through the trees and blew through their hair.

'We'd better get moving,' Olivia said.

Aroha glanced over her shoulder. 'What was that?'

'I didn't hear anything.' Olivia looked around. 'I expect it was just the wind.'

'It was footsteps.' Aroha grabbed Olivia's hand. 'I'm scared!'

'Don't be silly,' Olivia said. 'There's nobody there. Come on, or we'll never get to the caravan.' She gave Aroha a gentle tug along the path.

'Someone's following us,' Aroha said. 'I know they are.'

They'd only taken a few steps when a booming voice echoed through the forest. *A better life somewhere else? Escape from the Gang?*

Aroha's heart stood still. 'It's my father. Run, Olivia!'

'No, Aroha,' Olivia said. 'He's got a gun.'

Aroha spun around. Everywhere she looked, there were gangsters.

Tautaru pounced on Olivia and spat in her face. 'Whakianga mai!' He pointed his gun at her head. 'Thought you'd run away with Aroha while my back was turned, you double-crossing she-devil! Pōkokohua!'

'Don't shoot her, Dad,' Aroha cried. 'Please.'

'No. A bullet would be too quick.' He beckoned to Kaine. 'Take her away.'

Kaine and another of Tautaru's men grabbed hold of Olivia.

                      David Whittet

'Stop!' Aroha tugged on Kaine's arm. 'You're hurting her!'

'Remember what I said, Aroha,' Olivia said as the men forced her hands behind her back. 'Don't give up on your dreams … stay strong …'

Tautaru stepped forward and hit Olivia on the head with the barrel of his gun. 'Shut up! Wahine kore tuki!'

Aroha punched her father. 'I hate you! I *hate* you! We weren't even trying to escape. We were just going to see Kāterina.'

'Bullshit!' Tautaru turned to Kaine. 'What are you waiting for? I told you to take her away.'

Aroha watched the men drag Olivia away down the track. 'Wherever you're taking her, I'm going too!'

Tautaru pulled Aroha back. '*You* will do as you're told.'

'Get off me!' Aroha lashed out and bit her father's wrist in a desperate attempt to get away. 'I'm going with Olivia!'

Tautaru slapped her face. 'I'll deal with you later.' He signalled to his minions. 'Take her back to Moana's place.'

Moana's place? No way! Aroha fought, but Kaine's iron grip gouged her arms. The birds in the trees crowed and took flight as the men escorted her back through the forest.

How had her father found out? She'd led Olivia straight into a trap. The men bundled Aroha into the back of a ute. Had Hunapo set them up? It was Hunapo who had said Tautaru would be up the coast that day. The question haunted Aroha as the vehicle lurched around corners and over potholes. No. It couldn't be Hunapo. He'd never do that to Olivia. He liked her. And although he'd done some pretty mean things recently, Hunapo wasn't entirely evil like her father. At least not yet.

The ute stopped with a jolt. Aroha looked up. Moana stood on the driveway, rubbing her hands together with that mean look in her eyes. Quick. Aroha scanned the street. She had to make a run for it.

She felt the men's grip on her shoulder. They lifted her out of the ute and put her down in front of Moana.

'She's all yours,' Kaine said. 'Don't let her out of your sight.'

'Don't worry. I won't.' Moana twisted Aroha's arm. 'You'll be staying with me from now on, and I don't tolerate any nonsense.'

Aroha pulled away from Moana. She'd almost freed her arm when a van suddenly swerved past, the tyres screeching as it careered down the street.

'It's Olivia!' Aroha said. 'I can hear her crying. What are they doing to her?'

'Never you mind.' Moana frogmarched Aroha into the house and dragged her up a staircase. 'Olivia will get what's coming to her.'

Locked in the attic, Aroha peered thought the shutters. Where were they taking Olivia? What would they do to her? Anyone who upset her father disappeared, and they never came back. *I may never see her again.* Aroha collapsed on the floor and wept. *This is all my fault. I'm sorry, Olivia.*

Stuck in that tiny room, every day seemed like a lifetime. Olivia had told her not to give up on her dreams. Aroha had never *wanted* to let them go, but what choice did she have?

More alone than ever on the eve of her wedding ceremony, Aroha lay plucking the mattress until her fingers ached. First Ngaio and then Olivia. The two women who meant most to her in the world, both gone within a couple of months. Neither would be there to comfort her in the morning. Just a brutal ritual that would bind her to the Gang for the rest of her life.

David Whittet

Chapter Twenty-Seven

Matara Marae, 1980.

Dawn broke, and a haunting song rang through the valley.

'Ka hari tenei ata! He ra o te tumanako me te koa! He huinga o nga wairua!'

Aroha felt the hairs on the back of her neck stand up as she translated the words: *Blessed is this morning! A day of hope and joy! A union of souls!*

For a merciful moment, Aroha forgot it was her wedding day and she was about to endure the savage chiselling. She stood in front of the marae, entranced by Marika's beautiful waiata.

Aroha had always looked up to Marika. At seventeen, she was just a couple of years older than Aroha, and already in demand as a musician. Marika had such a beautiful voice, and today, dressed in an exquisite korowai, a finely woven Māori cloak decorated with feathers and tassels, Marika's appearance was as stunning as her voice.

A day of hope and joy. A union of souls. The words brought tears to Aroha's eyes. Marika's music always reflected Aroha's mood. There was a sadness in Marika's voice whenever she performed at the tattooing ceremonies, and she'd promised Aroha something especially fitting for the wedding.

How Aroha wished the marriage *were* a true joining of their souls. It should have been. She was marrying her childhood sweetheart. Her blood cousin. But the Gang had destroyed all that.

Aroha trembled as the last strains of Marika's waiata faded away. Her father looked so pleased with himself welcoming the guests onto the marae, dressed in his black suit and patched leather vest. Crowds of gangsters had camped out on the lawn overnight, their Harley Davidsons gleaming in the early morning sun. They didn't want to be here. She could see that in their eyes when Tautaru gave them the Gang salute. The men downed the beer. The women drank the wine. None of them cared about the wedding—or about her. Perhaps if she hid behind the flagpole, it would all go away.

'Come here, Aroha.' Moana grasped her arm. 'The pōwhiri is about to start.'

Aroha stood with her hands clasped behind her back as the visitors assembled in the courtyard for the welcoming ceremony. The local iwi performed a haka, the traditional challenge to the guests.

When the crowd moved through to the meeting house, Marika chanted another stirring ballad. That brought fresh tears to Aroha's eyes, her heart beating to the rhythm.

Moana poked her in the ribs. 'Buck up, Aroha. This is no time for dreaming.'

Aroha scowled and followed her up the steps to the platform. Moana was the last person she wanted as a chaperone.

Tautaru and his special guests sat on a wooden bench, the paepae. Aroha turned her head away. She couldn't bear to look at them, all lined up in their finest Gang regalia. Across the platform, Chase squatted on the ground. Aroha came out in a cold sweat. Beside him, on a ceremonial cushion, lay the sharpened blade of the chisel, glistening in the shafts of sunlight that poured through the windows. And next to the chisel, the mallet. Just like the rituals throughout her childhood. Her body shook as much as the boys had when they faced their ordeal.

'Keep still,' Moana hissed. 'Everyone's watching.'

Pania escorted Hunapo onto the platform. He was trembling too. Was he feeling as scared as she was? She couldn't tell. He wouldn't look at her while Moana and Pania positioned the two of them at the centre of the platform. Hunapo was all dressed up for the occasion. Aroha had never seen him look so smart. He wore a clean, freshly ironed white shirt and smart navy pants. Most surprising of all, his unruly mop of hair was neatly combed and groomed. Why couldn't he be a *true* knight in shining armour and whisk her away from this hideous charade?

                          David Whittet

'Stand to attention, both of you.' Moana's gruff command dispelled any last thought of escape.

Tautaru signalled to Chase, who chanted a dignified karakia. Aroha felt her chest tighten as the guests joined in the incantation. Chase picked up the chisel. Its reflection almost blinding her.

The Gang bandmaster made a ceremonial drumroll. Aroha felt the drumsticks hammering against her skull, amplified a thousand times. She fell back onto her chair when the elders stripped off Hunapo's shirt and lay him on the customary handwoven mat, adorned with traditional Māori rafter patterns and stained with the blood of generations of boys.

She held her breath as Chase positioned the chisel over Hunapo's head. The crowd hushed. Aroha tensed. Everyone gasped the moment the albatross bone struck Hunapo's forehead. Blood streamed over his face. Aroha wanted to scream. Wave her hands in the air. Snatch the uhi from Chase's hand. Anything to make it stop.

Hunapo was used to pain. Aroha knew that. But the look in his eyes as the chisel dug deeper into his flesh told her it terrified him. The pained stare. The clenched fists. The curled toes. Aroha turned away towards the crowd. Even the toughest gangsters squirmed each time the hammer struck.

Aroha buried her face in her arms. She could still hear the relentless beat of the mallet. That awful pounding noise in her head. The rumbling tinnitus that had possessed her since she was a tiny girl. She clasped her hands over her ears, but it wouldn't go away.

Tears trickled down Aroha's cheeks when she, at last, looked up and gazed at the almost complete tā moko. She had lost her only childhood friend. The boy who used to make her laugh. Now they'd branded him for life. Just like all those other boys she'd watched being mutilated into a life of submission. She'd lost Hunapo the moment Tautaru got his grubby hands on him. But somehow the full facial tattoo made it final. 'Māhiti Gang' stamped across his forehead in black ink and deep grooves. And those curved lines over his cheeks and his chin. She still didn't know what they meant, but they scared her as much as they'd done as a young child.

Tautaru thumped Chase on the back when he laid down the chisel. 'Ka pai, bro. Ka pai te mahi!'

Hunapo lay on the mat, his face still bleeding. His body was so limp that for an awful moment Aroha thought he might be dead. She watched Tautaru beckon Pania to help lift Hunapo up and sit him on an ornately carved wooden chair at the front of the platform.

'I give you Hunapo, vice president of the Māhiti Gang!' Tautaru raised his arm in a Gang salute. The gangsters responded, holding their fists high in the air. The crowd rose to their feet, gawping at Hunapo as they broke out in applause.

Aroha leant forward and held out her arms towards Hunapo. Couldn't any of them see? He was still bleeding. He looked like he was about to pass out. Who was going to catch him when he fell off the platform?

A hand grasped her left arm. Her entire body shook as Tautaru towered over her. She tried to pull away. Moana grabbed her right arm.

'Today,' Tautaru said, 'we celebrate in blood and ink the marriage of my daughter to Hunapo. Aroha will now receive the Gang's tā moko on her chin to symbolise their union.'

Tautaru and Moana laid Aroha down on the mat, Hunapo's blood staining her white wedding dress.

'Fetch a towel,' Tautaru growled to Moana.

Aroha felt Moana let go of her arm. Tautaru's grip loosened too. This was her chance. Her *only* chance.

'Damn you!' Tautaru caught her in a rugby tackle as she fled from the platform. He pulled her head back by her hair. 'How dare you show me up in front of all our guests!' He spun around to Chase. 'Give her hell!'

'No, Dad! Please!'

Tautaru let go of her hair. 'You have defiled our ceremony. What have I told you about the sanctity of blood and ink?'

     David Whittet

Those wretched words again. Damn the blood! Curse the ink! Aroha jerked her head away. 'I don't care about your—'

Tautaru put his hand over her mouth to silence her. Aroha bit his wrist, drawing blood with her teeth. She heard him curse as she bolted from the platform.

'Whakianga mai!' Tautaru turned to his men. 'Don't just stand there! Bloody morons! Get her back!'

Aroha glanced back. They were gaining ground. She kicked off the fancy shoes she wore for the ceremony. *Run. Run for your life!* The muddy grass made it difficult. Her feet were slipping. *Keep going! Don't give up!*

Before she reached the end of the paddock, Kaine was on top of her. And moments later, she was back on the platform.

'Apologise to your father!' Kaine pointed a finger at Aroha. 'I know you're frightened but show him some respect. Moana, too. She's your kaiāwhina. She's here to look after you.'

I don't like Moana and I don't trust her. I didn't ask to have her watching over me. Aroha hung her head. 'Sorry, Dad. Sorry, Moana.' Her voice croaked as she forced the words off her tongue.

Why couldn't she have Lilly or Evie looking after her? Why had they taken Olivia away from her? But more than anything, Aroha wanted her mother. *Olivia had told her that Ngaio would be thinking about her wherever she was. Where are you, Mum? I need you! Now!*

Pinned to the ceremonial mat by three of her father's men, Aroha couldn't breathe when the chisel approached her face. She had a cute little dimple on her chin which she often admired in the mirror. In seconds it would be history. She screamed as the blade tore into her flesh. The pain was bad enough, but worse, each deposit of ink told everyone she belonged to the Gang. They'd tarnished her. Defiled her. No decent person would come near her. Never.

Every swing of the hammer brought a fresh wave of nausea. More blood spilt onto her dress. Her eyes grew heavier. Her head swooned. Everything seemed blurred and distant—and she couldn't feel the pain any more. Was she still alive? She hoped not. Perhaps she was bleeding to death. Her dress was absolutely sodden. She couldn't possibly have any blood left. Was this the eternal sleep she had prayed for? Had she finally broken free of the Gang?

A thundering voice called her back to life. And it wasn't her father. She raised her head to see what was going on.

'Kai a te kuri! You bastard!' Maahanga burst through the crowd and onto the platform where Tautaru was showing off Hunapo's tā moko to the visiting gang leaders. 'He's not your son—he's mine. My flesh and blood! Damn you to hell, Tautaru!'

Maahanga jumped on Tautaru. Before anyone could restrain him, he had his hands around his brother's neck.

'Get off me!' Tautaru's face turned purple as Maahanga continued to throttle him. He freed a hand and waved it at his minions. 'Tō teke! Get rid of him!'

Maahanga took a swipe at Hunapo as Tautaru's men dragged him off the platform. 'You're mine, Hunapo! You've disgraced the whānau!'

Still dazed, Aroha watched Maahanga retreat into the distance, punching the air with his fists.

'A plague on both whānau! Do you hear me? *A plague on both whānau!*'

Maahanga's curse rang through her head as loudly at it echoed through the valley. She sank back onto the mat. Why couldn't she just go back into that beautiful sleep?

'Get up, Aroha.' Moana handed her a cloth. 'Clean yourself up. You must look presentable for the hāngī.'

Aroha wiped the congealed blood from her eyes. The scene came back into sharp focus. She watched the elders lift the traditional hāngī out of the ground and felt sick. She was still very much alive, and her dream of escape once again shattered.

   David Whittet

Part Three

Love and the East Wind

Chapter Twenty-Eight

Urewera Forest, 1988.

Aroha kicked away the dense thicket and paused for breath. *What am I doing? Why am I here?* She gazed at the long winding track ahead. *I have to talk to someone.* She blew out her cheeks and exhaled slowly into the crisp forest air. *No, I don't. I'm just returning a family heirloom to its rightful owner.*

The path looked horribly overgrown. Much more so than she remembered from her childhood. Eight years on from the arranged marriage and now aged twenty-four, she'd parked her vehicle in the same clearing her mother had used when Aroha was a little girl. Her last trip to the Urewera forest had ended tragically with Olivia's kidnapping. As had the time before that when she overheard her mother arguing with Kāterina. Their angry voices still seemed to whistle through the trees.

A forest flower caught her eye. She knelt down and held the plant in her hand. The crimson petal of the *Clianthus* was the colour of her mother's blood, and the dew on the leaf had the same sticky texture. She vividly recalled how she'd felt it flow from Ngaio's tummy when they stumbled back through the forest.

Oh, Mum. What happened to you? Why did you abandon me?

So many terrible memories. Aroha let go of the plant and shook the dew off her skirt. She took her rucksack from her back and pulled out an old thermos flask. *Why am I putting myself through this? I could just turn back.* She had considered talking to Lilly but going back to the Gang's patch would be too dangerous. Setting foot in the Urewera forest was enough of a risk. She sat on a log and slurped the coffee. What was it Olivia had told her? *Don't give up on your dreams. One day you will escape from the Gang.*

That's right. Now's not the time to quit. Aroha slung the backpack over her shoulder and resumed the trudge through the undergrowth, her heart beating faster with each successive footstep. She looked down at her aching feet. When she made the trek in her childhood, they used to be covered in blisters from worn-out jandals. Now she wore brand-new, expensive trainers. But for all the recent changes to her life, was she any happier?

Pull yourself together, Aroha. You're just here to do a good turn for a lonely old hermit. And from the look of the track, nobody else had been to see Kāterina in a long time.

❧

'Tēnā koe kōtiro, nau mai!' Kāterina beamed at Aroha, kissed her on both cheeks and hugged her. 'Come in, come in. Haere mai! Welcome! It's so good to see you again. E noho. E noho.'

At first sight, Kāterina hadn't changed much. The same old time-worn face. A few more wrinkles, perhaps. But when Aroha got closer, there was a sadness in Kāterina's tired, watery eyes. Gone was the sparkle. As a child, Aroha thought they shone like diamonds. Not now. But her smile was just as warm. The trinkets still glistened in the sunlight. In fact, the *Gypsy Rose* was just as Aroha remembered it, decorated with ornate Māori carvings and full of memorabilia and curiosities. Her eyes scanned the feast of treasures. She caught sight of the palmist's model hand. She'd loved that when she visited with her mother.

'I've got something for you,' Aroha said. She rummaged in her bag and pulled out the old binoculars. 'I'm sorry they've got another dent. I wish I could say it happened in battle. You told me how they got damaged in the Land Wars—'

'You remember that story?' Kāterina said. 'I'm impressed.'

'Of course I do.' Aroha handed the binoculars to Kāterina. 'And I'm sorry it's taken so long. My father pawned them. I kept the ticket safe, but I've only just saved up enough money to redeem them.'

Kāterina gave her another cuddle. 'You shouldn't have worried. But thank you. You're an angel.'

Aroha shuffled. 'It was the least I could do.'

     David Whittet

Aroha felt Kāterina's eyes lock onto hers like magnets.

'Now tell me why you're really here,' Kāterina said.

Aroha gulped. The old woman had seen straight through her. She opened her mouth to reply, but nothing came out.

'Much as I'm delighted to have them back,' Kāterina continued, 'I'm sure you didn't come all this way just to bring me a pair of old binoculars.'

Aroha fell back onto a stool. 'I thought they were special … belonged to a great warrior.'

'They are. They did. But—' Kāterina shuffled backwards '—I'm not sure they even had binoculars back in those days.' She sat down on her bench with a thump. 'Well, they would have had a spyglass, but nothing flash like this.'

'So they didn't really belong to one of my ancestors?'

'Probably not.' Kāterina squirmed. 'Actually, that story about Kamaka—'

'You made that up too?'

Aroha gazed at the crystal ball sitting on its plinth. Was *everything* she'd seen in that mystic sphere false? Was *anything* Kāterina had told her true? But she'd been right about Hunapo. How he'd appear out of a tree. And now—what about the mysterious stranger from the east?

'Anyway, it doesn't matter,' Kāterina said with a shrug. She put the binoculars on a shelf, then leant forward and took Aroha's hands in hers. 'They've brought you back to me. That's what's important.'

Doesn't matter? So I've guarded that pawnbroker's docket with my life all these years for nothing?

'Tāku tamaiti,' Kāterina soothed. 'My child! I can see you're hurting, and you need to talk.'

'I don't.'

'Come on. You can tell me. We're old friends.'

Aroha stared blankly into the void in front of her. 'I shouldn't have come.'

'I'm glad you did.' Kāterina continued to massage Aroha's hand. 'Talk to me. You'll feel better for it. I promise.'

'I'm scared.' Aroha's voice cracked. She looked down at the floor. 'I've been frightened all my life and I'm sick of it.'

'E mōhio ana au, ki taku mōhio,' Kāterina said. 'I know. I understand.'

Aroha glanced up and met Kāterina's eyes. She'd almost forgotten how easily the old woman slipped between English and Māori.

'It's all so unfair,' Aroha said. 'I've tried so hard to turn my life around and break away from everything.' She dabbed her eyes with a handkerchief. 'Just when I dared to hope … pray … that I'd found a chance of happiness … it's all taken away. And all because they forced me into marriage before I knew what it meant. My father. Those wretched women. They say I broke a promise, but I was just a child.'

Kāterina screwed up her face. 'Slow down. I need to get my head around this. That was all such a long time ago. I heard you'd left Hunapo way back.'

Aroha snorted. 'You don't leave Hunapo or the Gang.' She rubbed the tā moko on her chin. 'I swear that ceremony will haunt me until the day I die. That's what gets me. I was *this* close to starting a new life … a new beginning … and it's being swept away from under my feet.'

Kāterina squeezed Aroha's hand and gave it a kiss. 'Start at the beginning. Kia kaha. Be strong. Tell me everything.'

Aroha pulled away. 'You can't imagine what it was like, being married to the playboy of the Gang. It wasn't a marriage. It was a sham. Hunapo and his bimbos. I kept asking my father for a divorce.'

'And he wouldn't help?' Kāterina asked.

'Of course he wouldn't,' Aroha said. 'He just went on about the marriage being vital to the Gang. That's all my old man cares about.'

'So what did you do?'

Aroha tensed her shoulders. 'I told Hunapo to grow up, or I'd run away. I don't think he cared if I went, but he knew he'd get if from Tautaru if I did. For a while, he pulled his head in. I even thought I could make things work.'

'But you couldn't?' Kāterina said.

 David Whittet

'I tried.' Aroha felt herself choking up. 'Lilly and Evie got me involved in the women's group. Those two women saved my life. I went to the embroidery class. I even joined the kapa haka group and learnt poi dancing. Our dance coach said I was a natural when we performed at the regional championships.'

'I was a poi dancer when I was young,' Kāterina said. 'Who'd have thought swinging tethered weights around could be so much fun.' She frowned at Aroha. 'So, if Hunapo was behaving himself, and you were getting on with the women, what went wrong?'

'I suppose I knew it was just a matter of time before Hunapo went back to his old ways.' Aroha hung her head. 'We were coming back from a day running errands in Gisborne. Lilly, Evie and I. It had been such a good day. I knew something was up as soon as I got home. Cheap perfume. I could smell it the moment I opened the door. Hunapo was making love to Maddie on our bed! *Our bed!*'

Kāterina reached out with her hands. 'Oh, Aroha! I'm sorry. You shouldn't have seen that.'

'And that's not the half of it.' Aroha blinked back a tear. 'Maddie has this grotesque tattoo on her back: *Hunapo* and a love heart. I'd seen it before at that awful engagement party. Well, now she's got another one. A sketch of her and Hunapo having it off, tattooed on her bum. And as if that wasn't enough, the bitch had a go at me.

'"Don't act so bloody surprised," she said. "If you weren't such a goddamn prude and gave him what he wanted, he wouldn't have to look elsewhere."

'I couldn't believe it. I must have stood there with my mouth wide open while she put her clothes on. And she didn't stop there.

'"You're the same stuck-up prig you always were," she said, with her nose in the air. "You're welcome to her, Hunapo. Come back to me when you get bored with the bitch."'

Kāterina shook her head. 'What did Hunapo say?'

'I didn't wait to hear,' Aroha said. 'I went straight to my father's place and told him I wasn't spending another night with Hunapo.'

'Surely even Tautaru had to do something after that,' Kāterina said.

'The bastard went on about young men needing to spread their seed.' Aroha almost fell off her stool at the memory. 'He told me it was my duty to stand by Hunapo for the sake of the Gang. The same old bullshit. And sure enough, a minute later Hunapo was there, saying it was all a stupid mistake and begging me to come back.'

'So what happened?' Kāterina asked.

'To cut a long story short, when I refused to go back with Hunapo, Tautaru insisted I moved back in with him.

'"You don't leave the house without my permission," he said. "And you don't tell anyone about this arrangement. You've done enough damage already."

'To make matters worse, Tautaru had brought in Rewa, one of his old flames, as a housekeeper. Live-in lover, more like. The cheek of the woman. She kept pretending to give me motherly advice. As if she could ever replace Ngaio.'

'I know Rewa,' Kāterina said. 'She's not all bad.'

'Maybe not,' Aroha said. 'But she knew how to wind me up.

'"Hunapo's telling everyone he threw you out," she said one night when we were washing the dishes. "Says you're frigid. Cheeky bugger. Look, I know your pride's taken a fall, but I know how you can get your own back." I could have throttled her.'

Kāterina looked edgy. 'But you didn't?'

'I came close to it,' Aroha replied. 'Who the hell did she think she was?

'"Hunapo's been blabbing," she said. "He's a loose cannon when he's drunk. Spilling secrets. We could get the bastard into a heap of trouble if we tell your old man what he's been saying."

'I flung the tea towel in her face and told her I'd had it with her stirring.'

Kāterina leant back against the bench. 'You said you were close to a new beginning. So something good must have happened.'

'It did.' For the first time since she arrived at the caravan, Aroha felt a smile creep across her face. 'I met Amiri. At the Rere Falls.'

　　　　David Whittet

Chapter Twenty-Nine

Rere Falls, 1987.

Six months after moving back to her father's house, Aroha stood on the riverbank gazing at the Rere Falls. Whenever the old man was out and Rewa wasn't looking, Aroha would escape to the falls, just as she'd done as a child. With their magical combination of tranquillity and unlimited energy, they were still the only place where she could escape from Hunapo, Tautaru and the rest of the Gang. She felt more alone than ever. As a kid, she'd thought Hunapo was a kindred spirit. She'd prayed he'd be the one to fulfil her dream of a life away from the Gang. How naïve was that? But he could have been—if Tautaru hadn't got in the way.

Aroha took a deep breath and soaked up the atmosphere. Why waste such a beautiful spring morning thinking about Hunapo?

As she sat on the grass munching an apple, Aroha was surprised to see a few people, dressed in yellow high-visibility jackets and protective headwear, examining the rocks at the top of the falls. Who were they? Outside visitors were a rarity at Rere. What was going on?

She continued to watch them over the following week. They returned every day and the equipment they brought with them looked more sophisticated each time they arrived at the site. Getting as close as she dared while remaining hidden from view, she studied their every move but still couldn't figure out what they were doing. She'd never seen such elaborate machines before. With the roar of the waterfall, there was no way she could hear what the men were saying. Then, as quickly as they'd arrived, one day they disappeared. Aroha shrugged and began wandering home. Now she'd never know what they were up to.

She took a last look over her shoulder. The amber rays of the setting sun looked more spectacular than usual as they struck the cascading water. She had to stay awhile and admire nature's golden light show. Mesmerised by their splendour, she stood transfixed for a full five minutes and was about to leave when she heard a voice behind her.

'Beautiful …' Startled, she spun around, and there stood a Māori man in his early thirties, his striking features silhouetted by the evening sun. 'The falls. Aren't they exquisite?'

'Yes, beautiful,' Aroha mumbled, trying to get a good look at him without appearing too obvious. 'I've loved these falls since I was a little girl. They're enchanting.'

He smiled. 'They *are* entrancing, aren't they? I've only been here for a few days, and I'm in love with them already!'

They stood motionless for a few minutes, admiring the cascading water. Aroha felt her heart racing. Tall and statuesque with dark wavy hair, she thought he embodied an almost Byronic charm. She caught his deep, alluring brown eyes. Large and expressive. Eyes that stared into the soul.

Get a grip, girl. What are you thinking? Aroha tried to pull herself together and walk away, but she couldn't. She shuffled, trying to think of something to say.

'What brings you to Rere?' she asked, her lip trembling. 'I've seen some men around in yellow vests. Are you with them?'

'Yes, they're all my men. I'm a business consultant, and we're surveying the land for commercial development.'

Aroha stepped back. Did her father know about it? There'd be trouble if he didn't. She forced a smile to conceal her surprise. 'What? Out here at Rere?'

'Yes.' He pressed his fingers to his lips. 'But it's classified information at the moment.'

Aroha sighed. Business consultants with private agendas would be out of her league.

'My time at Rere is almost over,' he said with a frown. 'I'll be going back to Auckland in the next couple of days.'

'Oh.' Aroha looked down at her feet. 'That's a pity.'

     David Whittet

'But I'll be back. This is just a preliminary inspection; it's going be a long-term project …'

'Good … yes … I mean …' Aroha dribbled to a standstill. A glance at her watch and reality hit her. 'I better get going. My old man will be waiting. Can you believe it? I'm twenty-two and still under curfew!' She gave him a wave and turned away to the path home. 'It's been wonderful meeting you. I'm sorry I disturbed your time here.'

He took a step forward. 'Stay. Please.'

Aroha stopped, uncertain of what to do. She wasn't ready to turn round and face him again.

He caught her arm. 'Why don't we sit and talk? We could watch the falls together.'

Aroha blushed and hid her face. She secretly pinched her arm while he took off his coat and laid it on the ground over the rocks.

'Come and sit down,' he said.

His thoughtfulness overwhelmed her. It was the first time a man had put something down for her to sit on. Hunapo would never do that in a million years. She pinched herself even harder. *You're dreaming, woman. Fantasies like this don't happen to people like me.* In romantic novels maybe, but not to a gangster's daughter. She looked away, expecting the fairy-tale scene to disappear. She turned back and Amiri was still there. Looking just as kind-hearted as before.

'I don't know what to say,' she mumbled.

'Why not start by telling me about yourself?' he said. 'Here we are, in front of these beautiful waterfalls, and I don't even know your name.'

'I'm Aroha,' she gulped. 'It means *love*.'

'Aroha. What a beautiful name! I'm Amiri. That means *the East Wind*. You said you've got to get back to your father. Do you live around here?'

'Yes, just down the road. I live—um …' Aroha broke off. She didn't want to frighten him away by mentioning her ties to the Gang. How could she explain about Hunapo? And Tautaru? How could she look him in the eye and talk about her family? She felt him studying her, waiting for a reply. He would find out soon enough anyway, and it was better he heard it from her. 'And yes, I live with my dad. He's … um … Well, he's kind of a well-known person in the area.'

Amiri looked impressed. 'A celebrity?'

Aroha edged away. 'If he found me talking to you, he'd go insane.'

'*Insane?* Why?'

Aroha turned to leave, but then twisted around again and blurted out: 'I'm the daughter of the Gang leader, Tautaru.' She almost tripped on the grass in her haste.

Amiri called after her. 'Don't go. What is it?'

Surprised, she turned to face him. It dawned on her that he was new to the area and perhaps had never heard of Tautaru. 'You don't know who my father is, do you?'

'No, sorry. I don't. Why are you so afraid of him?'

Once again, she hung her head low and answered in fragments. 'He's mean, and *very* scary. Everyone's scared of him, even his mates. No, actually … my father doesn't have friends, just minions. He's a violent man. An ogre.'

'He's not mean to you, surely?' Amiri said.

Aroha rolled up her sleeve to reveal multiple scars on her arm from past beatings.

Amiri gasped and covered his mouth. She saw the shock in his eyes. Why did she feel so embarrassed? Should she run? No. This stranger made her feel safe.

'What kind of man does that to his daughter?' Amiri said after an uncomfortable silence.

Aroha sighed. 'A Gang leader. I was born into the Gang.'

She paused. He was waiting for her to go on. Tentatively at first, she told him about her childhood. She watched him clench his fists when she told him how she'd cried at the tattooing ceremonies.

'That's sick!' he said. 'How could anyone treat young boys like that? And your father punished you for helping them? Bastard!'

Amiri put his arm around her when she told him about her forced marriage to Hunapo. How she'd tried to flee from the platform before they brandished her with the tā moko.

　　　　David Whittet

'What they did to those boys was bad enough!' he said. 'But to a girl on her wedding day!'

'And left me scarred for life!' Aroha rubbed her chin. 'With this hideous tattoo.'

'Actually …' Amiri hesitated. 'I think it rather suits you.'

'What?' Aroha almost fell off the rock.

'I mean, it's elegant. Complements your lovely black hair and highlights those beautiful dark eyes.'

Aroha stiffened. A Gang insignia elegant? Was he for real? 'Seriously?' she said. 'Do you know what it signifies?'

Amiri leant forward and traced the lines of her tā moko. 'That's a koru. New beginnings. A pikorua. Life's path. And a toki, for strength.' He took his hand away. 'It's a traditional Māori design. Nothing to be ashamed of.'

'No,' Aroha insisted. 'It's a Gang patch.'

'I can see it upsets you. So why don't you get it removed with laser treatment?'

Aroha snorted. 'And where would I find the money for that?'

'I'd pay.'

Aroha stared at him. 'You don't mean that …'

'I'd do anything to make you happy …'

'I wish I could get rid of it,' Aroha said. 'But my old man would kill me if I did. It would be … suicide.' Aroha relaxed and snuggled her head on his shoulder. 'But thank you!'

They sat there for at least another hour. The time went by so fast. She felt happy and safe, watching the falls with Amiri. He opened up about himself. How he grew up on the wrong side of the tracks. How his parents had struggled to feed him and his sisters. His determination to make something of his life and winning a scholarship to business school. And how the venture at Rere would make or break his career.

Aroha had never felt this secure before. *Am I still daydreaming?* She nearly said the words out loud. *He's suffered too. His childhood was just about as bad as mine. He knows how I feel—he's a kindred spirit.* She pinched herself a third time. So hard she almost drew blood. It was shaping up like one of the Mills &

Boon paperbacks she'd discovered stashed away in her mother's dresser. *Ngaio must have been dreaming about love too.*

Amiri ran his hand through her hair. 'Amiri and Aroha. Love and the East Wind.' He gazed into her eyes and repeated the words. 'Amiri and Aroha. Love and the East Wind. It fits us perfectly, don't you think?'

Aroha smiled nervously and blushed. 'What a lovely thought!'

'That's you and me, Aroha. A unique bond.'

Utterly speechless and tingling all over, Aroha glanced up. The sun had almost disappeared. Tautaru would be suspicious. 'I have to go back. My life won't be worth living if I stay any longer!' She didn't want to move. In truth, she never wanted to leave his side again, but the darkness brought her back to the real world. 'You said you're going back to Auckland. Will I ever see you again?'

'Of course you will,' Amiri said. 'I'll be coming back every couple of weeks to work on the project. And even if I wasn't, now I've met you, I have a reason to return.' He helped her up, and they stood facing each other. 'You're an extraordinary girl, Aroha.'

He must be kidding—he said I was extraordinary! Real-life is so much better than Mum's trashy novels! Aroha blinked back a tear. *Oh, Ngaio! If only you were still here! I could tell you about Amiri. Share this magic moment with you!*

They stared into each other's eyes. Amiri held her face tenderly in his hands and gently touched her lips—a moment she wanted to last forever.

'The East Wind will always find you,' Amiri said. 'It will rustle the leaves on its way to you, so you will know it is coming. It will blow through your long dark hair and rest on your lips, and you will know I am near.'

When he lowered his mouth to hers, it felt to Aroha as though a spark of lighting coursed through their bodies. She sensed something else too. An invigorating burst of wind. She could feel it blowing in from the east and surrounding them, swirling up from their feet to their heads as they kissed. She had never felt so alive or so happy.

'This is only the beginning of Love and the East Wind,' he said.

Aroha could still feel the ethereal wind on her cheeks. Nature itself had endorsed their love.

 David Whittet

Chapter Thirty

The Gypsy Rose Caravan, 1988.

Kāterina raised her arms in triumph, a broad, self-indulgent smile smoothing the wrinkles on her face. 'Didn't I tell you about the East Wind?' she exclaimed. 'And the tall, dark stranger you would meet at the Rere Falls?'

'You did.' Perched on the edge of her stool in the *Gypsy Rose,* Aroha crossed and uncrossed her legs. Perhaps not all Kāterina's prophecies were fake after all.

'Still, I bet Tautaru wasn't happy when he found out,' Kāterina said. 'To him—and to Hunapo—it would be like a red rag to a bull!'

'I couldn't tell him. At least, not straight away. He was waiting to pounce the moment I got home that night. I was still over the moon from meeting Amiri. I'd hoped to creep in unnoticed, but no, Tautaru was there, lurching against the back door like an oversized toad, ready to strike.'

'A toad? More like a bird of prey, I'd say.' Kāterina held her sides, laughing. 'Tautaru's a vulture when he's swooping on his victim!'

'He's a bloodsucker all right.' Aroha almost lost her balance on the stool. 'Normally I'd have been a quivering heap, but Amiri made me strong. Gave me the courage to stand up to the old bugger.'

'So, what happened?' Kāterina asked.

'He sounded off as usual,' Aroha said. She mimicked her father's tirade. *'Wahine waikorohuhu! Wretched woman! What time do you call this? I told you to be in before seven every night.*

'Rewa sat at the kitchen table, sorting the laundry. "Cool it, man," she said. "Your blood pressure will be through the roof if you carry on like this."

'"Shut it, Rewa," he said. "My daughter, a young married woman, out on the streets at all hours. She's a disgrace to the whānau."

'I wasn't letting him get away with that. *It's Hunapo who's shamed the family,* I told him straight. *He's the one sleeping around.*'

'I bet that went down well,' Kāterina said with a grin.

Aroha sighed. 'Imagine what the old man would have done if he knew I'd been hanging out with a man.'

'All hell would have broken loose,' Kāterina said.

'It did anyway,' Aroha said. 'He went on about the embarrassment I was causing him by not living with Hunapo.

'"I have to lie," he said. "Pretend you and Hunapo are still together."

'"So what's new?" I said. "You lie all the time."'

Kāterina raised her eyebrows. 'That was brave.'

'I'd never stood up to him like that before,' Aroha said. 'I guess meeting Amiri gave me strength. I didn't even care when he started swearing at me. And when he aimed a punch at my face, the bastard missed!'

'I told you the East Wind would protect you,' Kāterina said.

Aroha giggled. 'You should have seen the look on the old man's face when he slammed his fist into the wall. Rewa told him he'd have a stroke if he didn't calm down.'

'Sounds like Rewa had the measure of him,' Kāterina said.

'He treated her like shit,' Aroha said. 'Just the way he did my mother. He was always telling Rewa to get off her backside. But she had the last word. "Get off my backside indeed," she would say. "What the hell do you think I do all day while you perch your arse on a barstool?"'

'Good on Rewa,' Kāterina said.

'I was wrong about her,' Aroha said. 'After Tautaru stormed off to the tavern, I thanked Rewa for getting him off my case. I could see her staring at me. *What is it?* I asked her.

'"You've met a bloke," she said, "haven't you?"'

     David Whittet

'I must have jumped off my chair. *How do you know?* I asked.

'Rewa gave me a knowing smile. "Your eyes. I can see the sparkle in your eyes."

'I sighed. *Is it that obvious? Do you think my father noticed?*

'"Of course not!" Rewa said. "Tautaru's as thick as two short planks when it comes to matters of the heart. Your secret's safe with me!"

'I gave Rewa a high-five. She was a mate.'

'It's good you had someone to confide in,' Kāterina said.

'There's one thing I never understood,' Aroha said. 'I asked Rewa why she stayed with Tautaru when he was so crass.

'Rewa paused before she replied. "Power," she said. "Tautaru has power. And power is *very* sexy."'

Aroha continued her story while Kāterina heated some lentil stew on the stove for their supper.

'So I assume you didn't take a blind bit of notice of Tautaru's curfew,' Kāterina said. 'You went on seeing Amiri?'

'Too bloody right!' Aroha said. 'Whenever Amiri was back at Rere, we'd go for a picnic beside the waterfall.'

'And Tautaru didn't find out?' Kāterina asked.

'Not straight away.' Aroha grinned at Kāterina. 'Like you said, I had the East Wind to protect me. And it did. At first. We were so happy while it lasted. He never wanted to go back to Auckland. I remember teasing him about it ...'

'You're a naughty boy!' Aroha poked Amiri in the ribs while she cleared up the remains of the picnic. 'A couple of days ago, you told me you *had* to get back to Auckland. Won't you be in trouble?'

Amiri laid back on the rug and chuckled. 'No. I'm the boss.'

'Lucky sod.' Aroha sat down beside him. 'Tell me about this commercial development. You're not going to spoil our beautiful waterfalls, are you?'

'No, I would never do that,' Amiri said. 'These falls are where we met. They'll always be sacred to me.'

'That's a relief.' Aroha plucked a blade of grass from the ground. 'So what *are* you doing here?'

'It's all to do with the water and a rare mineral,' Amiri said. 'A super vitamin with phenomenal properties.'

She watched his face light up. He put his arm around her and pulled her close.

'And it's unique to the rocks at Rere,' he continued. 'It doesn't exist anywhere else in the world! Didn't I tell you our meeting place was one of a kind?'

Aroha raised her head and gazed at her beloved falls. 'I always knew they were *magical*. I just didn't realise how *miraculous*.'

'The possibilities are enormous,' Amiri said. 'We're working on a product that will bring health to some of the most disadvantaged people in the land.'

'Oh, Amiri, that's beautiful.'

They kissed. She felt a spark. Just as she had when they first met, and that same rush of wind.

The mystic breeze followed them as they walked home.

'Thank you for today,' Aroha sighed when they reached the township. 'I wish I didn't have to go home.'

'You don't have to,' Amiri said. 'You could come back to Auckland with me.'

⚘

        David Whittet

'I wish I had gone with him there and then,' Aroha said, picking at her lentil stew and looking up at Kāterina. 'I would have done if I'd known what was coming.'

'But you'd only just met him,' Kāterina said.

Aroha frowned. 'That's what Rewa said. Sometimes you have to seize the moment. Life doesn't always give you second chances. And I'd waited all my life for someone to take me away from the Gang.'

'But could you trust him?' Kāterina asked.

'Of course.' Aroha put her plate down on the bench and gazed at Kāterina 'Amiri is a man of vision. So different from a loser like Hunapo.'

Kāterina raised an eyebrow. 'You said you didn't go straight back to Auckland with him—'

Aroha pursed her lips. 'Not because I didn't trust him. I was scared of what Tautaru and Hunapo would do to him. Of course, Amiri wouldn't hear of it. He was furious when I said I was staying behind.' Aroha paused and looked down. 'In fact, that's the only time I've ever seen Amiri lose his cool.'

Kāterina shrugged. 'Why? What did he say?'

✤

'There's a whole new life waiting for you in Auckland,' Amiri said. 'Hunapo. Tautaru. The Gang. They're all rubbish. Leave them behind.'

Why was she hesitating? Aroha had dreamt of escape her entire life, and Amiri was the dashing hero who was about to make it happen.

She took a sharp breath. 'I want to. God knows how much I want to! But you don't know my father. He'd hunt me down. Drag me back and shoot me.' She stared into his eyes. 'Then he'd come after you. He'd kill you too.'

Amiri's hands clenched. 'I'd like to see him try!'

Aroha watched his eyes bulge. They'd had a fantastic day out together. Why did he have to spoil it? She'd taken him to the rockslide. Even persuaded him to slide down with her on an old tyre. She'd laughed when he went on about ruining his posh pants and how the whole thing was an insurer's nightmare. Now it was time to go home. Amiri must have known how much she dreaded their parting and picked his moment.

'I'll soon sort that mob out,' he continued. 'They won't know what's hit them when my lawyer gets on to them.'

Aroha sighed. 'It'll take more than a clever lawyer to bring down my father.'

'I'll make them pay for what they've done to you. Hunapo. Tautaru. All of them.'

She watched his muscles tense. 'All right, Amiri. No need to shout.'

'I'll see them crushed!' Amiri jabbed a finger at her. 'I'll destroy the bastards! Tautaru's not the only one with heavies!'

Aroha stepped back. 'You're frightening me! What's got into you?'

'Sorry.' Amiri put his hand to his mouth. 'I didn't mean to scare you. It just makes me mad the way they treat you.' He held her tight in his arms and kissed her on the lips. 'I will keep you safe, Aroha. Stay with me and nobody will ever hurt you again!'

Kāterina took Aroha's hand. 'But they did hurt you, didn't they?'

'Yes, they did,' Aroha said. 'But only because I didn't stay with him. Rewa had warned me to watch my back. Told me I'd been taking too many risks. That Tautaru had spies everywhere, and he was on the warpath.'

'I bet Tautaru went crazy when he heard about Amiri,' Kāterina said.

'He did.' Aroha shivered at the memory. 'I was a fool not to take any notice of Rewa's warnings. She told me I was getting too cocky for my own good and she was right. I guess I was still too starry-eyed. I just tried to laugh it off.'

     David Whittet

Aroha strode into the kitchen and grabbed a spoon to taste the soup Rewa was cooking for dinner. 'Mmm. That's delicious!' She watched Rewa turn up the heat on the stove. 'Don't worry. I can look after myself. Besides, I've got Amiri to look after me.'

Rewa glanced through the window. 'You'll need more than a guardian angel now. Tautaru's back.'

'Pōkokohua!' Tautaru, armed with a thick leather belt, burst into the kitchen and pounced on Aroha. 'You were seen this afternoon. Traitor!'

Rewa tried to hold him back. 'Leave her alone!'

'You stay out of this!' Tautaru threw Rewa out of his way and spun back on Aroha. 'Pūrari paka! Bloody bitch! You are bound to Hunapo for life! Bonded by ink! Tā moko is sacred to this Gang!' He thrashed Aroha with the belt. 'Bad enough you've deserted Hunapo. But hooking up with another man! Does the honour of the Gang mean nothing to you?'

'Honour?' Aroha dodged the belt. 'Amiri has more *honour* than anyone in the Gang.'

'Pōkōtiwha!' Tautaru towered over her, using his body mass to pin her against the wall. 'That son of a bitch is an enemy of the Gang—'

'Amiri is no enemy!' Trapped under his weight, Aroha could hardly get the words out. 'He's a lovely man. He's my soulmate. My kindred spirit. Nothing you say can change that.'

Tautaru slapped her cheek. 'You will not see the bastard again.'

Rewa pulled on his arm. 'Stop. Before you do something you'll regret. You're going to suffocate her.' Tautaru stepped back and Rewa steered him towards the kitchen table. 'I've made us some nice soup for dinner. Why don't you sit down and relax? You must be hungry.'

'Soup?' Tautaru grunted. 'No steak?'

Aroha sniffled and wiped her nose as she continued her story. 'Rewa tried to protect me, but it was no use. Tautaru banged on about how he'd given me too much freedom. That I didn't respect Gang traditions. He made me go back to Hunapo.'

'And you did?' Kāterina said. 'That can't have been easy.'

Aroha curled her fingers. 'I put up a fight, I can tell you. But I had no choice. I was under house arrest at Hunapo's place.'

'So was that the end of you and Amiri?' Kāterina asked.

'Hell no!' Aroha said. 'You don't know Amiri! He doesn't give in that easily! He came after me when I didn't show up for a date.'

Kāterina rubbed the back of her neck. 'How did he find you? How did you get away from Hunapo and Tautaru?'

'I'd almost given up hope,' Aroha said. 'Hunapo locked me away in a room when I refused to sleep with him. I would lay awake all night and listen to Hunapo's snoring coming through the wall. I didn't think much of it when I heard footsteps around the back and the crash of broken glass. It was probably one of the gangsters mad with Hunapo for stealing his girlfriend, I thought. That happened all the time. But when the key turned in the lock on my bedroom door, I panicked. Was it Hunapo or one of the other gangsters determined to force himself on me?'

The door burst open. A figure moved towards her, scarcely visible in the dark.

'I promised I'd never desert you.' Amiri sat down on the bed beside her and put his arm around her.

Aroha rubbed the sleep from her eyes. 'Amiri! What are you doing here? Get out before anyone sees you!'

Amiri tightened his grip on her shoulder. 'I'm not leaving without you.'

Aroha could feel his muscles tense as he spoke.

'You have to. Hunapo could wake up at any moment—'

　　　David Whittet

Amiri snorted. 'The drunken bastard's out for the count. He won't come round before morning.'

Aroha sat up in her bed. 'Yes, but—'

'I told you I would always find you,' Amiri said. 'The East Wind can go anywhere and find anything. I knew something was wrong when you missed our date. So I started asking questions. Went down to the tavern. Listened to the gossip. And when I heard some kids disrespecting you—'

Aroha bowed her head. She knew Hunapo was still spreading nasty rumours about her being frigid. It hurt that Amiri had heard them.

'Anyway,' Amiri continued, 'I got the truth out of those scumbags. Made them bring me here.'

'Oh, Amiri.' She looked up into his eyes. 'You and I—it's been a beautiful dream. I've loved every minute we've spent together. But that's all it can be. A dream. You've got to go now, Amiri! While you still can.'

Amiri stroked her hair. 'No.'

A cloud passed outside and a shaft of moonlight shone through the window. Aroha tried to hide her face, but she was too late.

'What the hell?' Amiri's eyes narrowed to slits. He'd seen the bruises and swelling on her face. 'Who did this to you? Tautaru? Or was it Hunapo?'

'My father,' Aroha said. 'Please, Amiri, just leave it. Don't make this any harder for me!'

'Bastard! That settles it. You're coming back to Auckland with me!'

Before she could protest, Amiri lifted her off the bed and carried her out over his shoulder.

'Don't look back,' he said.

She didn't. Not until she was safely inside his BMW sports car.

Aroha watched the trees and the telegraph poles flash past in the twilight as they sped away from everything familiar to her. With only the clothes on her back, she was leaving her troubled childhood behind to start a new life in the big city with the man she loved.

Chapter Thirty-One

'It's not how I'd imagined it,' Aroha said, gazing at Kāterina's crystal ball. 'When I was a little girl and you first showed me my future, I was hoping for a knight in shining armour on horseback. I imagined riding off into the sunset, not slinking away in the middle of the night.'

Kāterina grinned. 'I remember. But at least you got away. Tell me, how did you get on in the big smoke?'

'It was a bit overwhelming at first,' Aroha said. 'Mixing with the movers and shakers of the business world. Cocktail parties, dining in the top restaurants, trips to the theatre … you name it, and we lived in a luxury apartment.'

'Sounds perfect,' Kāterina said.

'It was.' Aroha leant back on her stool. 'Or it should have been. But I didn't belong there. I didn't fit in with his circle of friends. I tried to explain it to Amiri. With the telltale tattoo on my chin, everyone knew I was a gang girl.'

'It obviously didn't matter to Amiri,' Kāterina said. 'He wouldn't have introduced you to all his business colleagues if it did. Besides, lots of Māori women in high places have a tā moko.'

Aroha threw her arms in the air. 'Not with a Gang motif, they don't. Amiri kept telling me he knew a plastic surgeon who'd get rid of it if I wanted. In the next breath, he went on about how his best mate, Errol Troy, thought the tattoo looked great. Amiri and Errol. They're both a couple of charmers.'

Kāterina raised an eyebrow. 'I'm with them. Your tā moko is splendid.'

'Really?'

'Yes,' Kāterina insisted. 'Now, tell me more about you and Amiri.'

Aroha scratched her head. 'Amiri did everything he could to help me settle in. I was terrified Tautaru would come looking for me. Every night when we

    David Whittet

went to bed, Amiri told me he'd keep me safe. With that same old line about the East Wind. *Remember, Aroha. I will always protect you. The East Wind will find you wherever you are.*'

'And now you're free of the Gang,' Kāterina said. 'That's wonderful. Isn't it? Why are you looking so miserable?'

'But that's just it,' Aroha said. 'I'll never be free of the Gang. Or Hunapo.'

Kāterina sat upright. 'What do you mean?'

Aroha shivered. 'Like I said, I was frightened Tautaru would track me down. Turns out I should have been more afraid of Hunapo. He just won't let go.'

Kāterina raised her eyebrows. 'He must. Have you started divorce proceedings? You'll need a decent lawyer.'

'Amiri has the top lawyer in the country,' Aroha said. 'For all the good it's done. You don't divorce the Gang. They stick to you like glue.'

Kāterina frowned. 'You've been separated for a couple of years. So legally, you're entitled to a divorce. Amiri's lawyer should know that.'

Aroha shot Kāterina a mean scowl. 'That's a bloody joke. It turns out we were never *legally* married. That wretched ceremony on the marae had no legal status. I knew then it would haunt me for the rest of my days.'

Kāterina stroked Aroha's hand. 'So if you weren't officially married, then you *are* free—of Hunapo and of the Gang.'

'You just don't get it, do you, Kāterina?' Aroha snapped. 'Hunapo still believes he owns me.'

'You could get a restraining order against him,' Kāterina said.

Aroha almost fell off her stool. 'You've got to be kidding. As if Hunapo would take any notice of that. The bastard's been stalking me in Auckland.'

'How did he find you?' Kāterina asked.

'The Gang has spies everywhere,' Aroha said. 'I don't understand why he's so determined to ruin my one chance of happiness. Why can't he just let go?'

Kāterina folded her arms on her lap. 'You've dented his ego. Moving in with a hotshot businessman. Give him time. He's jealous, but he'll come round.'

'It's not as if he hasn't got enough girls to keep him entertained. It was bad enough before I left. Now he's got his own penthouse pad, full of giggling girls.'

'He's an attractive man,' Kāterina said. 'I thought he looked drop-dead gorgeous when I last saw him. But a penthouse pad? How do you know?'

'I caught up with Evie the other week,' Aroha said. 'Her boy Jake was spitting blood when Hunapo got him drunk and stole his girlfriend.'

Kāterina's jaw dropped. 'I know Jake. He's a good boy. Tell me what happened.'

'You really want to know?' Aroha said. 'According to Evie, Hunapo challenged Jake to a drinking game at a wild party. You can guess what happened next …'

'Hey, Jake, how about a game of higher/lower?' Hunapo loved Tautaru's parties. Shuffling the cards, he could get away with *anything*. Cheating his love rivals and making out with their dates. The ultimate double whammy. He'd been flirting with Tammy all evening. Now all he had to do was get her boyfriend blotto.

'You go first, Jake.' Hunapo dealt the first round. 'Oh … bad luck … get that pint down you …'

'That's not fair,' Jake protested, beer sloshing over his face and clothes.

'Perfectly fair,' Hunapo insisted, using the distraction to fix the cards. 'Bummer, you lost again … that's another pint.'

Hunapo poured yet more beer into Jake's mouth. 'It's spirits next round!'

'Stop it, Hunapo!' Tammy protested. 'He's had enough.' She tried to drag Jake away, but he fell onto the table. 'You're stoned.'

'Can't chicken out once the game's started!' Hunapo grinned and upped the forfeits until Jake was absolutely legless.

'Take him home,' Hunapo instructed one of his underlings. 'Poor sod can't hold his booze.'

		David Whittet

'Hunapo made his move on Tammy the moment he got rid of Jake,' Aroha said. 'At least, that's what Evie heard. A few of the women elders were there, but they left once Hunapo started snogging Tammy in front of everyone.'

'Poor Jake,' Kāterina said. 'Poor Evie, too.'

Aroha sighed. 'I can just picture the scene …'

❧

'Get your tongue out of her throat, you dirty bastard,' the girls chanted as Hunapo caressed Tammy's curvaceous breasts and buttocks.

'Stop licking her tonsils!'

'And get your hands off her tits!'

'And her bum!'

'Screaming shits, Hunapo! You're one crazy, twisted son of a bitch!'

Hunapo gave them the finger. He was the ladies' man, the womaniser without equal. Smirking at the shaking heads and envious grins of the other men, he kissed Tammy even more salaciously than before.

Dylan picked up his guitar and strummed a tune. 'This one's for you, Hunapo.' He began to sing, making up the words as he went along.

Playboy of the Gang
Master of the sleaze—

'Master of the gang bang, more like,' Rawiri interrupted, glaring at Hunapo as the gangsters gathered around the barbecue for a singalong.

Everyone cheered and held their bottles in the air as Dylan continued the impromptu song.

He's mad, he's a cad
Full of charm

Gang Girl

Full of shit
He's bad to the bone!

'You ain't no poet, Dylan. That don't even bloody rhyme,' Rawiri jeered.
'I know how it should go.' Kirsty pushed forward and took over the singing.

He's a cad, he's a shit
To the girls, he's a hit.

The men groaned and all the girls joined in a chorus.

God bless Hunapo
Bless his thieving cock!

Hunapo chortled as the gangsters vied with each other to come up with new and even more derogatory verses. He tapped Tammy's bottom in time with the music as Rory ad-libbed a few more lines.

Hunapo's an arse
He got no class.

Rory could hardly get the next line out for laughing.

Takes his girl to the bog
For a quick snog!

Jason fought his way through the throng. He'd just arrived back after taking Jake home and waved a fist at Hunapo. 'Dirty dog! This is for my mate Jake!'
Hunapo winked at him. 'Bring it on.'
Jason cleared his throat, showering Hunapo in spittle.

                    David Whittet

Hand it to the dirty louse

He's got some bloody nowse.

The punk gets you drunk

Drunk as a skunk

And screws the arse off your spouse!

Hunapo took his hands off Tammy's breasts for long enough to give the failed limerick a slow handclap. 'Bloody hell, Jase. That's sick, man. You're an even worse singer than you are a lover!'

Kaine strode over. He didn't applaud. 'Is this the way to treat our future leader?'

'Lighten up, Kaine,' Dylan sighed, still strumming his guitar. 'Is it our fault Hunapo's such a letch?'

Kaine glared at Hunapo. 'And this is no way for the president-elect to behave.'

Hunapo stuck his tongue out at him and then put it back in Tammy's mouth.

Kaine stalked off. Everyone else joined in a reprise, the singing increasingly raucous as everyone downed Tautaru's beer by the crate load.

Hunapo—star bonker

Hunapo—prize plonker!

Dylan laid down his guitar. 'Everyone raise a jar to the Playboy of the Gang!'

'*Playboy of the Gang!*' The gangsters saluted, downing their beer and thrusting their empty bottles in the air.

Jason lunged at Hunapo. 'Come on, everyone! Shove your empties up the bastard's arse!'

'Piss off.' Hunapo gave Jason the finger. 'Come on, Tammy, we're out of here.'

Tautaru's Rottweiler barked as they snuck down the garden path, their bodies still entwined.

'Hunapo!' Tautaru stopped clearing away the barbecue and called after them. 'You slimeball!'

Hunapo looked back and smirked. He didn't wait for the inevitable lecture on how much he had to learn about the Gang. He watched Tautaru feed the leftover meat to his dog, then he disappeared into the night with Tammy.

❧

'It didn't end there,' Aroha said. 'The dirty rat took her to the Rere Falls, and they went skinny-dipping in the moonlight. And that was just the beginning. The cheeky sod claimed Tammy thought he was the Almighty when he screwed her.'

Kāterina raised her hand. 'Enough. I don't need the sordid details.'

'You need to know what the bastard's like,' Aroha insisted. 'Evie said he was boasting about it down at Smash Palace for days …'

❧

'It's the first time I've been starkers outdoors,' Tammy grinned playfully as they splashed around, the seductive gleam in her eyes driving Hunapo wild. 'Sex in the bush! *Frigging unbelievable!*'

She flicked back her long dark hair, exposing her breasts and showering his face with spray.

Unable to contain himself any longer, Hunapo lifted Tammy and held her body tight against his. Tammy wrapped her legs around his buttocks. They waded through the water until they were directly under the falls. The icy chill intensified their desire as it pummelled their skin. Hungry for each other's bodies and precariously balanced on the slippery rocks, they made love beneath the cascading torrent. Rough, raging, mind-blowing sex, with Hunapo thrusting furiously to the rhythm of the pounding deluge, the water streaming over their naked bodies.

'You're an animal, Hunapo!' Tammy declared as they searched for their clothes, which were by now soaking wet on the rocks. 'Screwing you is like bonking a mythical God, filling my insides with a mighty poker'—she gazed up at the stars in wonderment—'or making love to a great Māori warrior and having his spear thrust up my fanny!'

'Don't get all deep on me, girl.' Hunapo pulled on his pants and started to walk home. 'You were a decent shag. Nothing more.'

❦

'They defiled our falls. *Gross!*' Aroha groaned. She wrinkled her nose, wondering if she could ever delete the picture from her mind. 'Of course, he couldn't stop at that. Every party he screwed another mate's girl. Until they all ganged up on him. Jake, Rory, Jason, Anaru—they gave Hunapo the hiding of his life. Left him unconscious.'

Kāterina shrugged. 'Well, perhaps he's learnt his lesson.'

'Hunapo *learn?* That's a joke!' Aroha snorted. 'He was back down the boozer the next night, trying it on again. Nothing will curb that bastard's sex drive.'

Kāterina took the kettle off the stove and made a pot of tea. 'Sounds to me that beneath the swagger, Hunapo's a bit of a wimp. I've heard the gossip. When he gets in a brawl, he doesn't put up much of a fight. I don't think you need to worry. He's not that much of a threat.'

Aroha shook her head. For a hermit, Kāterina's ears were remarkably close to the ground. Had she the faintest idea what she was talking about?

Kāterina poured a cup of tea. 'Well, maybe he'll leave you alone now he's got all these other girls. A penthouse pad, did you say?' She handed Aroha the tea and rubbed her wrinkled forehead. 'He won't hurt you. He was your childhood sweetheart. I remember you coming here in floods of tears because he had dumped you!'

'Hunapo broke my heart back then, and he's destroying me again now!' Aroha pulled back, distancing herself from Kāterina. 'You've no idea what he's capable of. I told you how he found me in Auckland. He kept following me. I tried not to go anywhere alone. But one night we were at this dinner in the

ANZ Building. Amiri was clinching a deal, and I was tired. I told him I'd get a taxi back to the apartment. I could tell someone was following me when I walked down the alley to the taxi rank. I turned around and there was Hunapo, and he had a gun.

'He was on top of me before I could catch my breath. He threw me against the wall and started threatening me.

'"You will *never* escape the Gang! I will never let you go. Wherever you go, I will find you. Wherever you are, I will hunt you down."

'I tried to fight back, but he kept bouncing me on the railing. Then he pointed the gun at me, pushing the barrel into my head and flicking the trigger.

'"Nobody defies me! I'll kill you rather than see you with someone else. Marry that prick … *bang bang!*"'

Beads of sweat appeared on Aroha's forehead as she relived the horror. 'He *will* do it. I could hear it in his voice. I haven't had a moment's peace of mind since that day. I can't eat. I can't sleep. I can't think.'

'I bet Tautaru put him up to it,' Kāterina said. 'Hunapo's always been far too easily led.'

Aroha rocked backwards and forwards on her stool. 'Whatever. He'll still kill me.'

Kāterina placed her hands on Aroha's. 'Hunapo's a drunken wastrel, but his heart's in the right place. He needs time to get used to you being with someone else. It's just an idle threat.'

Aroha jerked away from Kāterina. 'Don't you believe it. And it's not just Hunapo. It's the entire Gang. They all witnessed that wretched ceremony, and they say I've betrayed Hunapo. They still expect me to belong to the monster. How dare they? And to accuse me of bigamy if I marry someone else! That's so unfair. What about all of Hunapo's mistresses?'

Kāterina closed her eyes and muttered a prayer: 'Homai e te Atua te kaha me te whakaaro nui ki a tatou.'

Aroha looked up at Kāterina and shook her head. 'What?'

     David Whittet

'I've asked God for strength and wisdom.'

'Strength?' Aroha lowered her head. 'How can I be strong with the Gang baying for my blood?'

'You're talking like they've hired a hitman.'

'Hunapo would never pay an assassin and deny himself the pleasure of killing me in person. There's a price on my head, all right.'

Kāterina screwed up her face. She reached across and took her crystal ball off its plinth. 'My precious can help us.' She caressed the shiny orb and spoke to it. 'You foretold the coming of the dark stranger from the east. Can you help us now?'

'Kāterina!' Aroha leapt up from her chair. 'I'm not a child any more!' She snatched her jacket and made for the door. 'Anyway, I should go. I've done what I came for. Delivered the binoculars. Even if they are a worthless fake.'

Kāterina hung her head. 'Don't leave like this. Please.'

Aroha was out of the caravan and down the steps. She glanced back over her shoulder at the old woman.

Kāterina held the crystal ball against her face. She suddenly jolted and let out a startled cry. 'E tōku Atua! Oh, my God!'

Aroha tapped her foot on the bottom rung. 'What now?'

'I'm frightened for you … that spark … It struck me when my precious first showed us the stranger from the east. I felt it again now.'

Aroha waved her hand dismissively. 'Why do you always talk in riddles?'

'I had a premonition about Amiri. About his dark side. I wanted to warn you, but you'd gone.'

'For heaven's sake. Can't you take this seriously?' Aroha walked away, down the path. Coming here was a mistake. 'My mind's upside down as it is, without you making it worse.'

Kāterina raced after her. 'I just don't want to see you hurt. How well do you really know Amiri? Maybe it's not Hunapo you have to worry about.'

'I'm not listening to another word.' Aroha turned to confront her. 'Amiri and I—we're soulmates. He's changed my life. Given me a reason to live.'

Kāterina grabbed her arm and stopped her from going any further. 'Perhaps you should let things cool down. Why not postpone the wedding? Get to know Amiri a bit better. Give Hunapo a chance to get used to it.'

'Marrying Amiri is my one chance of happiness. I'm not letting it go for anyone. Hunapo will never give up. I know that even if you don't.'

Kāterina clung on to Aroha's wrist. 'Are you sure?'

'Hunapo can kill us both for all I care. I *am* going to marry Amiri.'

Kāterina shrugged and let go of her arm. 'I just hope he's everything you think he is.' She forced a smile. 'He's definitely spoiling you. I love that jacket.'

Aroha brushed a speck of lint off her lapel. 'It's a Chanel.'

Kāterina sighed. 'I used to wear designer clothes—once. When I was somebody.' Their eyes met. 'Will you say a prayer with me before you go?'

The two women stood face to face. They pressed their noses and foreheads together in a hongi.

Kāterina clasped her hands together and gave a blessing. 'Kia kaha, tāku tamaiti, kia kaha. Be strong, my child, be strong.'

'Amen.' Aroha opened her eyes and stared at Kāterina. 'You will come to my wedding, won't you?'

'Of course I will.'

Aroha began walking down the path. She looked back as Kāterina called after her with more words of encouragement. 'Haerenga haumaru ki te kainga. Farewell, God's strength, safe journey home.'

Aroha paused for a moment and watched Kāterina sit on the caravan steps, still caressing the crystal ball on her lap. What was the old woman thinking? Was there any truth in her ramblings?

With a sigh, Aroha continued the long trek through the forest to retrieve her vehicle from the clearing.

Chapter Thirty-Two

Kāterina sat on the step and stared down the path long after Aroha had disappeared into the distance. More than anything, she'd wanted to help Aroha. But she'd said the wrong thing. Gone on about what she'd seen in the crystal ball, and in doing so had driven Aroha away. Was she completely out of touch with the way young people thought?

Face it, old girl, nobody's interested in you any more. You're a has-been. Kāterina rubbed her hands together, her fingers blue with cold. *Aroha was frightened—she didn't need me going on about Amiri.* Kāterina got up and wandered back into the caravan, still lost in thought. *Why were you hell-bent on interfering with her marriage? If he makes her happy, let it be.*

Kāterina put the crystal ball back on its plinth and prepared for another long night alone in the caravan. She could hardly bring herself to admit it, but she'd grown tired of living as a hermit. The *Gypsy Rose* was in dire need of repair and was absolutely freezing inside.

As a young woman, Kāterina had built up a formidable reputation as an activist, and in her prime, she had advised some veteran Māori leaders. Back then, people listened to her. She had mana. During the fifties and sixties, policymakers turned to her when they needed political influence.

Kāterina tossed the nut roast she had made for supper into the trash. She wasn't hungry. Something Aroha had said that afternoon still played on her mind: *A rare mineral in the rocks at Rere.* So that was why Amiri was in the district—he wanted to develop it commercially. Aroha had said as much. That would plunge them headlong into a blood feud with the Gang.

It's going to be Whatatutu all over again. Kāterina clutched her hands to her chest. *They'll tear Amiri to pieces. The poor bugger has no idea what's coming to him.*

Kāterina curled up in her bunk bed but couldn't sleep. She hadn't known what was coming to her when she led the campaign against oil exploration in the tiny settlement of Whatatutu. That was more than twenty years ago, but it still felt like yesterday. She got up and dusted off one of the old placards she'd saved as a memento of the protest. 'Get your bulldozers out of our town!' it proclaimed.

She sat on the floor, remembering how the juggernaut had charged towards their makeshift barricade. Kāterina had stood on top of the broken tables, chairs and old car parts from the wrecker's yard. She'd pumped her fists in the air and yelled at the developers. 'You're not making money out of our whenua!'

Her followers had waved their homemade banners in a sea of support. As the trucks got closer, the protesters linked their hands in a human chain, chanting at the top of their voices.

'Whatatutu is tapu! We won't let you destroy our land!'

Kāterina had fought back when the police broke up the demonstration. 'They're raping our community!'

'Kāterina Kururangi, isn't it?' the officer had asked. 'Go home before you get yourself into even more trouble.'

Back then, Kāterina had thrived on trouble. She'd fired off letters to the Prime Minister and the Department of Conservation and got her photo on the front page of the *New Zealand Herald*.

The memory was still painful. With a groan, Kāterina pulled herself up off the floor. She rummaged through an old chest. She'd kept another of her placards all these years. There it was: 'My caravan stays here.' That sent another shiver down her spine. It had turned out the oil wasn't directly under Whatatutu. It was further up the valley. Right under her caravan.

It was a winter's evening in the early seventies when Tautaru's predecessor had hammered on the caravan door. His voice raged through the night.

'Get off our land!'

Kāterina had unlatched the door before it fell off its hinges.

'Get off our land!' Maaka repeated the words, his full facial tā moko all the

David Whittet

scarier in the cold moonlight. He turned to the pack of minions behind him. 'Do it.'

One of the men grabbed Kāterina while the rest of the men ransacked the *Gypsy Rose*.

'You get off *my* land,' Kāterina had said, and immediately regretted it when the men smashed her cherished collection of trinkets and treasures. 'Not my oil lamp! Please! And my tapestry—'

Maaka picked up a broken ornament off the floor and waved it in her face. 'I won't tell you again. Get off our land!'

'My grandfather lost his life fighting for this land,' Kāterina said. 'And you expect me to give it up just like that?'

Maaka spat in her face. 'Would you rather we pushed you and what's left of your miserable caravan over the waterfall?'

The men's faces had lit up. 'Can we, boss? That would be choice!'

'Maybe we will,' Maaka said. 'If she won't cooperate.'

A violent crash awoke Kāterina at five the following morning. The *Gypsy Rose* lurched forward. She stumbled out of her bunk, reached for her dressing gown to cover herself up, swaying from side to side as the caravan gained momentum.

'They're going to do it,' she screamed. 'They're going to roll me over the waterfall!'

The *Gypsy Rose* came to an abrupt halt just before it reached the rapids. Her entire body shook as Kāterina climbed out of the caravan. The wheels had stuck in thick mud.

'Get that broken-down piece of shit out of the way,' Maaka ordered his men. 'I want it off our land! Pōkokohua!'

Heaving and panting, the gangsters hauled the caravan out of the bog. Faster and faster, they pushed the *Gypsy Rose* through the Urewera forest, the rickety wheels almost falling off their axles. Kāterina staggered to her feet and chased after them, shrieking as they drove it further into the bush.

'Stop! Bastards! Come back! Aue te mate moku! Woe is me!'

Eventually, the chassis split, and the *Gypsy Rose* crashed into a ditch.

The men rubbed their hands together and disappeared into the forest, laughing amongst themselves. Maaka turned back and waved a fist at her.

'That'll teach you to disobey the Gang! Good riddance and don't you dare come back.'

Kāterina glared at him. 'You'll regret this one day. Karma has a way of catching up with thugs like you.' She picked up her crystal ball and held it high in the air. 'May you pay for your sins, Maaka!'

Maaka gave her the finger and joined his lackeys. But she could tell she'd rattled him.

Kāterina dabbed her eyes when the full extent of the damage hit home. Shattered panels, broken glass, debris everywhere.

She held the crystal ball against her face. 'At least they didn't get you.' With a sigh, she tidied up. 'This will have to be our new home. Out here in the wilderness.'

❧

Almost twenty-five years on and the memory still brought Kāterina out in a cold sweat. She spent the rest of the night going over what Aroha had told her. If they could make money from the minerals at Rere, the Gang would demand the rights. They'd crucify Amiri, and Aroha too—if she stuck with him.

And what about Hunapo? Would he *really* hurt Aroha? Kāterina had believed Hunapo would be the one to end the Gang's reign of terror. He was the *chosen one*. And now he was threatening to kill the cousin he had once held so dear.

Daybreak and Kāterina still struggled to get her head around the situation. She picked some vegetables from her garden and nibbled them for her breakfast. She'd no more appetite than the previous night and fed the leftovers to her horse.

Aroha was like a god-daughter to Kāterina. Ngaio had been like a younger sister, and Kāterina had been present at Aroha's birth. She'd let Ngaio down. No way could she do the same to Aroha.

Pull yourself together. Kāterina sat on her bunk, head in her arms. What was Amiri after? Was he simply another bastard who wanted to plunder their beautiful land for a fast buck? Would he break Aroha's heart, like Hunapo had done?

Kāterina turned once more to her crystal ball. Her soul and her conscience. 'Tell me—am I right about Amiri? Is he just a smart-arsed speculator, here to line his own pocket?' She ran her fingers across the smooth glass and gazed into the sphere. 'Show me everything you know about Amiri!'

Boy from the Wrong Side of the Tracks Signs Multi-Million Dollar Deal. The headline in the *New Zealand Herald* made Amiri's heart sing. He was inordinately proud of his astronomic rise from humble beginnings to one of New Zealand's most successful businessmen. He was stoked when a TVNZ news reporter called him 'the stuff of legend'. Perfect. That snubbed all those doubters and silenced the detractors who'd taken such delight in putting him down. Bugger them. When he turned on the light in his plush new office, he knew the struggle had been worth it. The road to the top hadn't been easy. In fact, it had been a bloody hard slog. He reclined in his state-of-the-art executive chair. It was *so* comfortable and from it he had a view to die for. *I've done it! I've arrived!* He gazed down at Auckland Harbour through the panoramic window and punched the air.

Sipping champagne at a reception at SkyCity, Amiri paused for a moment to think about how often he'd gone to school hungry. His parents had both worked long hours in a factory but still struggled to put food on the table for Amiri and his two younger sisters. The waiter interrupted his reverie with a tray of canapés. The caviar tasted good. *So* good.

School in a low-rent district of Mangere hadn't been much fun either. The institution had a strong hazing tradition, and the seniors subjected the young Amiri to a demeaning initiation ritual, culminating in his being made the slave of an older boy.

Alone in the changing room, Amiri had cursed under his breath as he tore off the ball and chain of his slave's uniform.

The bullying continued throughout his school years.

'Teacher's pet,' his classmates hissed every time he answered a question correctly. Why couldn't anyone understand his desire to succeed?

During break, his tormentors circled him in the playground. *You're not fit to wipe my arse!* they chorused in unison. *You're not fit to wipe my arse!*

'Bastards!' Amiri glared back at the boys. 'Bloody losers, the lot of you!'

Amiri spent more and more time in the security of the school library. Those kids were going nowhere. He fumed under his breath while devouring the textbooks. One day those morons would look up to him. He'd show them.

And he did. Hard work and perseverance won Amiri a coveted scholarship to the world-class Business School at the University of Auckland. Nothing could contain his pride as he strode onto the campus on the first day. This was the opportunity of a lifetime and no way was he going to stuff it up. Graduating with first-class honours, he secured a post as a junior accountant at a merchant bank and surged through the ranks to become an account manager and financial controller. But that was nothing compared to the day he moved into his brand-new office: Amiri Hollis and Associates.

Oh, yes. He'd arrived.

 David Whittet

Chapter Thirty-Three

Thames, Coromandel Peninsula, 1989.

'Any advance on one million? Do I hear one point one million? Thank you, sir.' The auctioneer raised his gavel. 'Going to the gentleman at the front with the purple tie for one million one hundred thousand dollars. Going once, twice—'

Aroha looked nervously at Amiri. The bid was against them. The elegant country mansion on the Coromandel Peninsula was everything she had ever dreamt of, and more. Her mother had shown her pictures of the Coromandel when she was a little girl, and she'd never forgotten it. The estate looked so beautiful in the late afternoon sun at the on-site auction.

Aroha shrugged. Perhaps Amiri had reached his limit.

Just as she resigned herself, Amiri raised his hand. 'One point two million.'

'Thank you, sir. One million two hundred thousand for this exquisite property. Any advance? Do I hear one point three million? No? Going once, twice, three times. Sold!'

Aroha flung her arms around Amiri and kissed him passionately. She didn't care that everyone was looking at her. The man she loved had just bought her a picture-book palace. And best of all, it was remote and far removed from gangland.

She hadn't heard from Hunapo or her father for months. Perhaps Kāterina had been right that everything would blow over. Hunapo must have moved on, doubtless too infatuated with his latest conquest to care about her. Whatever the reason, he was leaving her alone. She could relax and plan her fairy-tale wedding.

Amiri's lawyer, Mr Beresford, wasn't so confident. 'You're taking an awful risk, Mr Hollis. Why not wait a while?'

Amiri shook his head.

Mr Beresford harrumphed. 'Is there nothing I can do to dissuade you from marrying so soon?'

Aroha shivered. She watched Amiri tap his fingers on the lawyer's desk.

'You've got a restraining order on Hunapo, haven't you, Mr Beresford?' Amiri demanded.

'Of course I have. The police have given Hunapo a trespass notice for all your properties.' The lawyer leant back in his chair. 'But be realistic. When did the Māhiti Gang ever take any notice of court orders?'

Amiri stood up, towering over Mr Beresford. 'I *will* marry Aroha next month. And *nothing* you—or anyone else—can do will stop me.'

Mr Beresford straightened his tie. 'Calm down, Mr Hollis. We're on the same side. I just hope you've got adequate security measures in place.'

Aroha reclined on the leather chaise longue in the exquisitely appointed drawing room of their new home, a bridal magazine in her hand. She looked up at Amiri sitting at a desk by the window on the other side of the room, typing a report on his laptop. He'd been so generous. They'd visited all the trendy designers in Auckland before deciding on one of Lavinia Lovat's chic gowns for her wedding dress.

Aroha had nearly fainted when Lavinia told them the price. 'It's beautiful— but can we afford it?'

'Of course we can,' Amiri beamed. 'Your day will be perfect.'

But Aroha noticed he was becoming somewhat less magnanimous with his time. She put down the bridal magazine and sat up on the sofa. He seemed to spend every minute of the day on the telephone or working on his laptop.

She took a deep breath. 'Amiri, darling …'

Amiri looked up from his typing. 'What is it?'

'Must you finish that report tonight? We should get an early night. We've got a big day tomorrow, with the wedding rehearsal at the church.'

		David Whittet

Amiri bowed his head. 'Tomorrow? I'm so sorry, I'm not going to make it. I have to go to Auckland in the morning—'

'You can't!'

'I have to … this deal … If I don't clinch it tomorrow …'

'Cancel it.' Aroha jumped to her feet. 'You must be there. It is our wedding rehearsal!'

'I can't. I'm sorry. It's important.'

Aroha glared at him. 'The rehearsal's more important!'

It was their first real argument. She watched his eyes shift between her and the keyboard. He looked so wounded that she stepped over and put an arm on his shoulder.

'Sometimes I think you care more about your precious business dealings than you do about me.'

Amiri turned to face her. 'Babe, this is for you. This contract—' he tapped the laptop screen with his pencil '—will see us financially sound, set up for life.' He held her hand in his. 'I want to provide for you. Make a secure future for both of us. Keep you safe.' His lip quivered momentarily. 'You do trust me, don't you?'

'Oh, Amiri, yes! Of course, I do!' She kissed him on the cheek. 'Nobody has ever done that for me before.'

❦

'I don't know what I'm going to say to the minister,' Aroha groaned as Amiri climbed aboard the privately chartered aircraft at Whitianga Aerodrome the next morning. 'He's put off his other duties to be free for us.'

'Can't you call him and reschedule? I'll be back tomorrow.'

'Then there'll be another meeting you just *have* to attend.' She kissed him and waved goodbye. 'I know you, Amiri Hollis!'

She watched the aeroplane speed down the runway and wondered what was going through his mind as it took off into the sky. Would he be thinking about her when he signed off on this mega business deal? The cutthroat world of commerce. High-flying executives. It was worlds away from everything she'd known.

Their lives were so different. Or were they? He'd told her about being bullied at school and his struggle to get to the top. Just as she'd fought to escape from the Gang. They had travelled on parallel journeys.

Aroha sighed and returned to her car. A single thought stuck in her head during the drive home through the winding country roads. They *were* soulmates.

David Whittet

Chapter Thirty-Four

Aroha pulled back the curtain as dawn broke over their country estate. 'It's today!' She watched Amiri stroll across the lawn in the immaculately kept gardens. He looked so handsome in his Christian Dior tuxedo. 'The day I have been waiting for all my life.'

She saw him make a call on one of those fancy new phones that upwardly mobile executives regarded as a must-have fashion accessory. Trust Amiri to be doing business on their wedding morning. Could he never stop? She couldn't resist a giggle when he threw his arms in the air and stuffed the mobile phone in his pocket. There was hardly any cellular coverage in rural Coromandel in the early nineties.

'Cover your eyes!' Amiri's sister Fonella pulled Aroha away from the window. 'Haven't you heard it's bad luck to see the groom before the ceremony?'

Aroha averted her gaze. She'd seen Hunapo on the morning of their arranged marriage and look how that turned out.

'We have to get moving,' Fonella continued, a safety pin in her mouth as she adjusted the lace ribbon on Aroha's wedding dress. 'We haven't started on the makeup yet.'

Amiri's other sister, Grace, burst into the room. 'Sis, you've got to help me with the bridesmaid dress.'

Fonella glanced at her watch. 'I've got to get my own dress on too. And it'll take us at least an hour to get to the church.'

Grace slumped on a chair and frowned at Aroha. 'Why did you have to choose a church so far away?'

Aroha had fallen in love with St Andrew's Church, from the moment the Reverend Ranganui Ropata led them inside for their reconvened wedding rehearsal.

'It's absolutely beautiful,' she breathed, tilting her head, her eyes scanning the ornate wooden carvings, the stained-glass windows and the altar. Amiri's business associate Errol Troy had suggested St Andrew's. Nestled in a remote and sleepy coastal community, it was about as far removed from the Gang at it was possible to get.

To Aroha, it was perfect. Magnificent. She gave Amiri's hand a squeeze. 'It couldn't be better.'

Amiri's parents, William and Amelia, joined them for the rehearsal.

'Are you sure you don't mind walking me down the aisle on the big day?' Aroha asked her future father-in-law.

William put his arm around her shoulder. 'It will be an honour.'

She gave him a hug. Amelia did too. It was amazing to be part of such a caring family. Amelia had told her how relieved they felt that their son had chosen such a down-to-earth partner. So much more suitable than all the conceited, self-important businesswomen he had dated previously.

'You will make him happy,' Amelia beamed. She turned to William. 'And she'll be the perfect daughter-in-law.'

Aroha took Amiri's hand as they left St Andrew's after the rehearsal. 'You have taken Mr Beresford's advice, haven't you? And hired a top security company?'

'You'd better ask the best man. He's in charge of that.' Amiri thumped Errol Troy on the back. 'Well, Errol?'

Errol gave them a reassuring smile. 'Don't worry. I've got the best in the business.'

One thing was almost as important to Aroha as the security arrangements. 'Rose petals,' she told Amiri as they climbed into the car to drive home. 'I want rose petals sprinkled on the ground as the guests arrive. You won't forget, will you?'

'Keep still, Aroha,' Fonella complained. 'This isn't easy, you know.'

     David Whittet

Closeted in the vestry, Fonella put the final touches on Aroha's makeup. Aroha kept peeking through the door to watch the guests arrive. A broad grin spread across her face as they stepped over the rose petals and gasped at the bouquets of white flowers adorning the nave.

'Sorry.' Aroha turned back to Fonella. 'I just wanted to make sure your brother got the floral arrangements right. He never remembers the important things.'

Mendelssohn's *Wedding March* rang out on the organ as William took Aroha's arm and they proceeded down the aisle. She glowed as she looked back at Fonella and Grace. Her bridesmaids looked almost as radiant as her in their designer gowns.

The wedding march melody was a familiar piece. Kāterina often played it to her on a musical box when she was a little girl. *One day, Aroha,* she used to tell her. At last, that day had arrived. She caught Kāterina's eye in the congregation and smiled. Most of the other guests were Amiri's family and his business associates. Having at least one of her extended whānau present felt good.

Amiri stood tall at the altar, more handsome than she'd ever seen him before, the blush pink buttonhole enhancing his black tie. Errol Troy stood at his side. As she took her last steps along the aisle, she watched him repeatedly check his pocket for the rings.

William joined Amelia in the front pew. Aroha saw William slip his hand into his blazer pocket for a handkerchief when Amelia blinked back a tear.

'You look stunning. That dress was worth every cent,' Amiri whispered in her ear as the Reverend Ropata began the Order of Service.

'Dearly beloved, we have come together in the presence of God to witness and celebrate the marriage of Amiri and Aroha, and to pray for God's blessing on them now and in their years ahead.'

Aroha glanced back. Amelia and William whispered in each other's ear. Aroha would love to have known what they were saying.

'Marriage is a gift from God, our Creator,' Reverend Ropata continued, 'whose intention it is that husband and wife should be united in heart, body and mind. In their union, they fulfil their love for each other. Marriage provides the stability necessary for family life so that children may be cared for lovingly and grow to full maturity.'

Aroha looked deeply into Amiri's eyes as they prepared to take their vows. She could feel the warmth of their love radiate throughout the church.

The Reverend Ropata beamed at their faces. 'Amiri and Aroha, we are glad to join with you in the celebration of your marriage and to witness your vows, to pray with you and to wish you joy in your life together.'

Aroha's heart missed a beat when the minister reached an anxious moment in the service.

'If any of you here know cause or just impediment why these two people should not be joined together in Holy Matrimony, speak now or forever hold your peace.'

The only sound from the congregation was a gentle rustling of their Order of Service papers.

Aroha could breathe again. So why was her palm sweating? There was nothing to worry about—they had the best security company in the country protecting them. She discreetly dried the perspiration on her dress.

Before the minister could continue with the service, there was a clatter at the back of the church. Aroha felt her muscles tense. She told herself not to be stupid. With so many people, there was bound to be noise. She noticed Amiri flinch. He must have heard it too. She glanced over her shoulder and her jaw dropped. The church door opened, and a masked man made his way to the foot of the aisle.

Hunapo! Her heart stood still and her legs wobbled. She grabbed hold of Amiri to stop herself falling.

Dressed like an executioner in jet black, the hooded man took a couple of steps down the aisle. He stopped and drew a gun.

Marry that prick, bang bang! Hunapo's threat had haunted her since that awful day he'd tracked her down in Auckland. She'd tried to convince herself he wouldn't really go through with it. Kāterina was sure he'd moved on. But here he was, taking aim at her on what should be the happiest day of her life.

How had he found the church? They'd kept it secret. She should have known the Gang had spies everywhere. But how had he slipped through security?

She saw his finger tremble on the trigger. Surely he wouldn't do it. This was the boy who'd promised he'd always be there for her. What had he said? *If you are ever in trouble, I will rescue you.*

Aroha looked at his eyes. He *was* going to fire.

'Hunapo! No! You don't need to do this!' Aroha knew as she said the words that he was about to squeeze the trigger.

Amiri took a step forward, reaching out for the gun. 'Give that to me, Hunapo. Before someone gets hurt.'

'This is the house of God,' Reverend Ropata added. 'Put your weapon down.'

'Please, Hunapo!' Aroha tried to engage his eyes. 'This isn't you! You were my friend—'

Before she could utter another word, the gunman raised his arm, took aim and fired.

Aroha clutched her chest. Blood seeped through her pristine white dress.

Another shot. And a third. The sound of gunfire ricocheted around the church.

The echo faded into the distance. Her head swirled. The stabbing pain in her chest no longer hurt. Her life flashed before her eyes. She tried to hold on to the good bits, but they disappeared in an instant. She was gone.

Chapter Thirty-Five

His eyes were lying. This wasn't happening. Amiri watched the scene play out in slow motion like a bad horror movie. He stood rigid, his heart pounding against his chest as blood spurted from the bullet holes in Aroha's chest. In an instant, her body went limp, her dress sodden with blood. A shower of blood on his face roused him just in time to catch Aroha as she collapsed.

Blood. So much blood. Everywhere.

Amiri tossed Fonella his mobile phone. 'Call an ambulance! What are you waiting for?'

With Reverend Ropata's help, Amiri laid Aroha on the floor in front of the altar. Amiri began the kiss of life while the minister pressed hard on the wounds to stem the pulsating haemorrhage. In seconds, Amiri's immaculate suit and the minister's spotless cassock were as drenched in blood as Aroha's dress.

Amiri glanced over his shoulder in between the mouth-to-mouth resuscitation. He caught sight of the gunman fleeing amidst the pandemonium at the back of the church.

'Don't let the bastard get away!' Amiri glared at the guests, who had taken cover behind the pews, shielding their faces with prayer books. 'Where the hell are the security men?'

Why wasn't Errol taking charge, instead of just standing there like a jerk with his hands over his mouth?

'Go after him, you idiot!' Amiri spat the words in Errol's face, fighting an overpowering urge to give him a kick up the backside. 'Get the guards! They're letting the son of a bitch walk away! I want the bastard strung up—'

'Amiri!' Reverend Ropata tapped Amiri's shoulder. 'Never mind that now. We're going to lose Aroha if you don't concentrate.'

 David Whittet

Amiri cursed himself for letting his temper distract him from saving Aroha. Another two frenzied attempts at CPR. Still not a flicker from Aroha.

Amiri felt his head swelling again. He swung around and blazed at Fonella. 'Where the hell is the ambulance?'

Fonella fumbled with the mobile phone. 'There's no signal.'

'Use the phone in the office,' Reverend Ropata said. 'At the back of the church …'

'Leave it to me.' Kāterina tore through the congregation to the vestry.

'Don't leave me, Aroha! *Please!* You can't leave me!' Amiri panted to keep up with the chest compressions. 'Don't you *dare* leave me!'

The kiss of life—on his wedding day! She was slipping into a profound coma. He could see that. Blood continued to spurt from her wounds. Tears and perspiration poured from his face. The mixture of her blood and his sweat had them both saturated in gore.

'For God's sake, help me,' Amiri shouted at Fonella, his arms buckling underneath him. 'You take over for a minute.' Fonella hesitated, her arms shaking. 'Move, damn you! Don't you want to help her? Pōkokohua!'

Fonella put her palms on Aroha's chest, gasping as she attempted life support. Her chest compressions were erratic and uncoordinated. She began to hyperventilate. 'Aroha! My friend! My best mate! *You can't die!*'

'Christ!' Amiri screamed. 'Didn't you ever learn first aid?'

'I did. On a mannequin.' Fonella gave Aroha's chest another frantic thump. The blood made it so slippery that her hands slid off. 'But this is different.'

'Get a grip,' Amiri bawled. 'She's going to die if we don't get our act together.'

'Die?' Fonella sank into a heap on top of Aroha, rubbing her face in the blood. 'No! She can't die!'

'Here, let me help you.' Kāterina knelt down beside them. 'I can do resus. And don't worry, the ambulance is on its way.'

Amiri shoved her aside. 'Get out of my way, you old witch!'

William stepped forward. 'Steady on, son. You need all the help you can get.'

'You're not helping, carrying on like this,' Amelia added.

'Leave this to me.' Grace pushed passed her parents and took over the CPR.

Amiri sighed in relief. *At least one of my sisters can keep her head in an emergency.* Grace was cool, calm and competent. He looked around to see his mother help Fonella to her feet. Collapsed in Amelia's arms, Fonella sobbed. Amiri bit his lip. His younger sister adored Aroha. Why had he shouted at her like that?

Amiri shuffled towards Fonella and stroked her back. 'I'm sorry.'

Fonella rubbed her bloodshot eyes and looked down at Aroha's apparently lifeless body. 'I wish he'd shot me. Not her.'

Errol burst back into the church. 'Our men are after him—'

'About bloody time.' Amiri glared at him. 'I told you to get the best security outfit in the business.'

'I did.' Errol took a step back. 'They told me the church would be impregnable.'

Amiri snorted. 'Well, it wasn't. The buggers might as well have opened the frigging door and invited the gunman in.'

Turning back towards Aroha, Amiri could see Grace was exhausted. Her compressions had slowed down. He waved a fist at Errol. 'Get over here. We need another pair of hands. Give Grace a break.'

Amiri resumed CPR. Errol squatted beside him on the blood-soaked carpet and placed his hands on Aroha's chest. How had this happened? Two control freaks, cut-throats of industry, both totally out of their depth. Amiri was about to blast Errol for his pitiful attempt to maintain a rhythm when Kāterina raced back into the church, waving her hands in the air.

'They're here!'

The St John Ambulance crew followed Kāterina down the aisle, lugging their life-saving equipment.

'Thank God!' Amiri mopped his brow. Every second waiting for help had felt like a life sentence. Each moment that passed brought Aroha closer to death.

     David Whittet

'We'll take over from here,' the senior paramedic said. 'But well done for keeping her alive until we got here.'

Well done? Has he any idea what I've been through in the last twenty-five minutes?

Julia, the junior member of the ambulance crew, eased Amiri aside. 'You need to stand back, Mr Hollis.'

Amiri had spent his last drop of adrenaline, but he still couldn't let go. 'No, I can't leave her. What are you doing to her?'

'We have to get a tube into her lungs,' the paramedic said. He turned to his assistant. 'Give me a size seven ET tube.'

'Tell me she's going to be okay!' Amiri watched on in horror. What was an ET tube? And what was that thing they were putting in her mouth? A laryngoscope, one of them called it. He glimpsed the tracing on the cardiac monitor they had attached to her. 'What does that mean? It's bad, isn't it? Talk to me, please!'

'Just let us do our job, Mr Hollis. We need to get an IV line in.'

Amiri watched the paramedics struggle to get the needle into Aroha's arm. He heard them muttering about her veins collapsing.

'Don't let her die!' Amiri's eyes darted between the paramedics' anguished faces, the irregular heart tracing, and Aroha's seemingly lifeless body. 'This is our wedding day!'

Julia took Amiri's hand. 'Listen, we're doing everything we possibly can for your wife. But my colleagues need to concentrate if they're going to do their best for her. You mustn't disturb them.'

Amiri glanced up. Her face was so calm, her eyes soothing. 'I know. I'm sorry.'

Still holding his arm, Julia led Amiri out of the church. 'Try to relax. We'll tell you the moment there's any news on Aroha's condition. I promise.'

Amiri nodded. He gazed at the crowd gathered outside the church and wondered if he would ever relax again.

Chapter Thirty-Six

Tautaru's hands tightened around Hunapo's neck. 'Where the hell have you been?'

Hunapo thought he would die. 'Nowhere.'

'Don't bullshit me.' Tautaru dug his fingers deeper. 'Kaine says you've been up in the Coromandel.'

'What if I have?' Hunapo gasped for air. 'Let go of me.'

'I swear I'll kill you if you screw with me.' Without loosening his grip on Hunapo's throat, Tautaru turned to Kaine. 'Tell me again what the bastard said he was going to do.'

'It's no use pretending, Hunapo,' Kaine said. 'You've been slagging Aroha off ever since she met Amiri. Threatening to kill her if she marries him.'

'Yeah, Hunapo.' The other gangsters joined in, imitating Hunapo's swaggering.

'I'll kill the bitch … and that slimeball …'

'She'll be dead meat on her wedding day. I swear it!'

Traitors! Hunapo closed his eyes. He might have known they'd all stick together and grass him up. Damn them!

'You might as well come clean,' Kaine added. 'The old man knows where you were—and what you did.'

'Do you take me for a complete fool?' Tautaru shook Hunapo so hard that he retched. 'We've got spies in the Karangahake mob, and they saw you at the church. With a gun. You tried to kill my daughter.'

Hunapo fought for his breath, certain he would choke on his own vomit. 'You said she wasn't your daughter any more. Not since she shacked up with that rich bastard and turned her back on the Gang. Anyway, I didn't go to kill her. I went to protect her.'

David Whittet

Tautaru snorted. 'Tell that to the cops.' He let go of Hunapo and kicked him in the balls so hard that he fell to the floor. 'You'll have to come up with something better than that.'

Hunapo rolled on the floor holding his groin. Tautaru still sounded off. What the hell was he on about? This was the man who'd told him not to give Aroha any special treatment just because she was his daughter. Two-faced bastard! Didn't he care that Aroha was betraying everything they held dear?

'Trust you to put the Gang at risk.' Tautaru bent down and slapped his face. 'That bastard Rutherford's baying for our blood. The son of a bitch has been trying to shut us down for years.' He gave Hunapo another kick. 'And you've played into the bastard's hands, you bloody idiot!'

District Commander Rutherford! Hunapo winced. And not just from the kick. The very name *Rutherford* made him sweat. The one cop nobody messed with, not even the Gang. They all knew that if anyone could finish the Māhiti Gang, it was Rutherford.

What had he done? Hunapo hadn't meant to hurt Aroha—or gamble with the Gang's future. He'd agonised on the long drive to the Coromandel. Remembered the fun he'd had with Aroha when they were kids. The look on her face when he appeared out of the tree. Or the thrill in her eyes when they careered down the rockslide. Aroha always banged on about saving Hunapo from his father. Now he had to save her from a terrible mistake. He couldn't let her marry that slimy scumbag. She'd be better off—

Hunapo couldn't bring himself to say the word. Not even to himself. He swerved the car to the side of the road. He glanced down at the gun on the passenger seat, gleaming in the sunlight. How could he ever think of using that? He loved Aroha. *Loved her.* His mother used to talk about tough love. And Kiri was right. He had to be strong. Go through with the plan.

He stood outside the church, gun in hand. Organ music blared through the fresh morning air. The wedding march. He peered through the window. There she was. Aroha. Parading down the aisle with that dickhead dressed up in his fancy suit. Hunapo could feel his blood pressure rising. He caught Amiri's smug smile. That was it. With his hand on the trigger, Hunapo burst into the church.

❧

'Get up!' Tautaru spat on Hunapo as he lay on the floor. 'We have to get you out of here before the cops show up.'

Hunapo staggered to his feet. 'They'll be here any minute. They've been chasing me all the way back from the Coromandel.'

Tautaru aimed another blow at Hunapo. 'Then why the hell did you come here?'

Hunapo knew Tautaru's house would be the first place the cops would look, but he'd nowhere else to go. The police pursuit had been hell. His heart had pumped when he saw the flashing blue-and-red lights in his rear-view mirror. A swarm of patrol cars closing in on him on the winding country lanes, with a roadblock coming up. Hunapo only escaped by veering off the road and into a paddock. Thank God for four-wheel-drive vehicles. Would it get him home? He couldn't go back on the highway. Miles of wilderness in front of him. Hunapo had to stay one step ahead of the cops. Hide himself—and the vehicle—in the bush whenever he heard the helicopter buzzing overhead. Even a waterlogged engine from chancing a river crossing couldn't stop him. The truck was a wreck with four flat tyres when Hunapo finally made it to Rere.

Why had he come back to Tautaru's place? The old man was as scary as the police.

No sooner had Hunapo picked himself off the floor than he heard a noise in the yard. Headlights shone through the window. Hunapo felt his body tense. Bugger! The cops had caught up with him.

Tautaru peered through the curtain. 'You can stop shitting yourself. It's only Chase.'

Hunapo collapsed onto a chair. He'd just caught his breath when Chase butted in and waved his fist in Hunapo's face.

       David Whittet

'You're a bastard, Hunapo,' Chase said. 'Aroha's dying. They're taking her to Thames Hospital.'

Tautaru went pale. Hunapo had never seen him look so beaten up before.

'Don't worry, Tautaru,' Kaine said. 'You go to Aroha. I'll take care of things here.'

'What?' Tautaru took a step back, his mouth wide open. 'You think I'd risk showing up at the hospital?'

'She's your daughter,' Kaine said. 'Surely you want to be with her?'

Tautaru hesitated for a moment before replying. 'She's no longer my daughter. Not since she deserted the Gang. Hunapo was right about that.'

While the men shook their heads and glared at Tautaru, Hunapo knew their anger was really meant for him, and he hung his head.

'Don't look so bloody shocked,' Tautaru continued. 'Aroha betrayed us. Bigamy with our enemy. Could she have done any more to disgrace the Gang?' He glanced across the table at Hunapo. 'Aroha is more to blame that Hunapo. None of this would have happened if she hadn't shacked up with that son of a bitch Amiri Hollis.'

Hunapo kept his head down. He could feel the gangsters judging him. No way could he meet their eyes.

Tautaru rose from the table and punched the wall. 'And as usual, it's me who has to pick up the pieces.' He waved a finger at Kaine. 'Get hold of Mathew Bailey. He's in with the cops and the bastard owes me a favour. Take the men. Scare the shit out of the shyster!'

Hunapo groaned. What good was that? It would take more than a bent ex-magistrate to get him out of this mess.

'Damn you, Hunapo,' Tautaru said as the men filed out. 'And damn Aroha too. The pair of you have destroyed the Gang.'

Weren't gangsters allowed crimes of passion? Hunapo wanted to hit back but knew it was useless. Plus, he needed Tautaru's protection.

More noise. Flashing lights in the yard. It wasn't Kaine and the gangsters leaving. This time it was the cops.

'Armed police! Put down your weapons and come out with your hands up.'

'Move it, Hunapo,' Tautaru hissed. 'Get out the back—'

Too late. Hunapo squinted through the kitchen window. Cops everywhere, surrounding the house, and red-and-blue flashing lights illuminating the sky for the second time that day.

The police tannoy blared again. 'I repeat. We're armed. Put down your weapons and come out with your hands up.'

Cowering in the washing room, Hunapo heard Tautaru go to the door.

'It's not you we want, Tautaru. At least not this time. It's Hunapo. We know he's in there.'

It was Rutherford's voice. Hunapo shook and his breathing quickened.

'We can raid the place if you like,' Rutherford continued. 'Who knows what else we might find?'

'Where's your warrant?' Tautaru asked.

'Right here.'

Hunapo knew he was screwed. He might as well just give himself up. But gangsters didn't do that—they fought to the bitter end. Hunapo bolted out of the back door and straight into the line of police.

The familiar words he dreaded: 'You are under arrest for attempted murder. You do not have to say anything, but anything you do say may be taken down in writing ...'

Hunapo wasn't listening. Rutherford grinned as the officers handcuffed him. He must have instructed them to dig the cuffs into his wrists. The pigs drew blood. Hunapo spat in their faces. They pushed his head down as they bundled him into the back of a patrol car. Hunapo glanced back at Tautaru. The old man's eyes were bulging as Rutherford goaded him. Straining his ears, Hunapo caught what Rutherford said to Tautaru.

'When Hunapo goes down, he'll take the rest of you with him. The Gang is history.'

Hunapo glimpsed Tautaru's eyes as the police car drove off. Yes, Tautaru was far scarier than any cop.

 David Whittet

Chapter Thirty-Seven

Amiri cursed himself, staring at the crowd gathered outside the church. Why hadn't he done something about Hunapo before the wedding? The warning signs had all been there. Aroha had told him about Hunapo's obsession with her and his threat to kill her if she married someone else. Now the psycho had done it.

Amiri looked down at his hands, still covered in Aroha's blood. It should be Hunapo's blood. With his connections and inside knowledge, Amiri could have had Hunapo put away for years. Better still, have had someone get rid of the low life once and for all.

Police cars arrived, sirens blaring. Officers surrounded the church, cordoning it off with yellow barrier tape. Amiri kicked the ground, dislodging a headstone. *Police Line: Do not cross.* What good was that? Hunapo had gone. And if he hadn't, Amiri would have torn him limb from limb.

Where was Errol Troy? If he'd done his job properly, the security men would never have allowed Hunapo anywhere near the church. Errol had shirked his duties. This was his fault. No wonder the bugger hadn't dared show his face since the police arrived.

Julia emerged from the church. 'Aroha remains critical, but we've stabilised her, and we'll be transferring her to Thames Hospital.'

Amiri acknowledged her with a nod. He wanted to say something—thank her—but his mouth was parched.

'We'll provide a police escort to the hospital,' one of the officers added. 'We're not expecting any more trouble, but you can never be sure with the Gang.'

Amiri wasn't listening. He'd spotted Errol, chatting with one of the security men as if nothing had happened.

'I left you in charge!' Amiri lunged at his old mate. 'I left you in charge! Where were the guards? They were *your* responsibility!'

'Calm down, bro,' Errol said. 'You need to stay strong for Aroha. Everything's going to be all right. I promise.'

'You don't know that,' Amiri said. 'The paramedics say it's touch and go. If she dies, it'll be your fault.'

'Steady on!' Errol took a step back. 'I care about Aroha too. She's like a sister to me. *A sister!*'

Amiri pushed Errol aside and laid into the security guard. 'We paid you top dollar! Your orders were to guard the church with your lives and not to let *anyone* get inside!'

The guard spluttered, cringing as the blood rubbed off Amiri's hands and onto his neck.

A police officer pulled Amiri away. 'That's enough, Mr Hollis. Leave the policing to us. That kind of behaviour isn't helping your wife.'

Amiri gave the guard a final glare. 'Pōkokohua! I could kill you for this!'

'We'll have no more of that,' the police officer continued. 'We've got roadblocks set up throughout the region. It's just a matter of time till we catch Hunapo.'

Amiri turned his head to see the paramedics transfer Aroha onto a wheeled stretcher.

'Aroha. My angel.' Amiri held her hand while the St John crew loaded her into the ambulance. She looked so pale. How could anyone still be alive after losing so much blood?

'She'll be much better once she gets a transfusion,' Julia said.

Julia continued to comfort him as the ambulance tore through the country roads, siren blaring and lights flashing. He was sure she meant well, but Amiri could read the concern on the paramedics' faces as they continued to work on her during the hour-long journey to Thames. Aroha was deteriorating. They were pouring fluids into her through the intravenous line. Every blip on the cardiac monitor made Amiri's own heart beat faster.

'Darling,' he whispered for the umpteenth time, reaching past the paramedics to touch her. 'Stay with me.'

     David Whittet

Seeing the love of his life so close to death, and witnessing the crew's valiant efforts to save her, forced Amiri to reappraise his values. All his life, he had striven for success. An unswerving determination to reach the top, whatever the cost. Now he was at the pinnacle of his career—and it meant nothing if he lost Aroha.

Julia gave him another encouraging smile. Amiri lowered his head. Within the confined space of the ambulance, the team worked miracles. His life was empty and shallow in comparison. He measured success in terms of deals clinched. Theirs was in terms of lives saved.

When had he last done anything meaningful? Perhaps in the early days, when he had ambitions to change the world. He'd boasted to Aroha about using the health-giving properties of the newly discovered minerals for the good of humanity. But truthfully, it was just to build up his business empire and line his own pocket.

A jolt when the ambulance went over a bump halted Amiri's reflections. He glanced back at the police convoy through the ambulance's back window. Was Hunapo in one of those armoured cars? Was he about to be incarcerated in a dingy cell?

That thought was his one consolation when they arrived at the hospital, where the paramedics rushed Aroha from the ambulance to the emergency department. But why was he wasting his time thinking about Hunapo? Aroha was all that mattered. Was she conscious? Had she any idea what was going on? Did she know he was by her side, holding her hand?

Where am I? What's happening? Aroha was vaguely aware of the ceiling passing by as the hospital staff wheeled her down the corridor on a stretcher. She glimpsed the ominous red signs bearing the single word *Emergency.* Voices echoed through the labyrinthine passages.

'Get an immediate cross-match, she's going to need a massive transfusion. Packed RBCs. At least ten units.'

Dear God! She sensed their panic as the doctors and nursing staff shouted instructions at one another.

'She needs pain relief … draw up the morphine … now.'

A stabbing pain ripped through her chest. Roused by the agony, Aroha raised her head. The nurses were moving her from the wheeled stretcher to the table in the resuscitation room. She glanced around, her glazed eyes struggling to focus on the blurred faces in front of her.

'Is that you, Amiri?' she whispered. 'I want Amiri.'

The effort was too much. Aroha sank back. The voices faded and the pain disappeared.

David Whittet

Chapter Thirty-Eight

'She's in VF!'

From the other side of the swing doors, Amiri froze when he heard the doctor's cry.

Pagers went off everywhere. *Cardiac arrest in ED* resounded over the tannoy.

Amiri held his hands over his mouth as the crash team pushed past him, racing to her bedside. He watched the consultant place the defibrillator paddles on her chest.

'Stand back,' the consultant warned his team as he delivered the shock. All eyes were on the monitor. Nothing. Another shock. Still no pulse on the monitor.

Amiri drew a deep breath as Aroha's heart restarted on the third attempt. Sweating profusely, he staggered back to the waiting room.

'What's happening? Is she all right?' Errol Troy was sitting hunched in the reception area, his fingers fidgeting with his car keys. 'I came as soon as I could.'

Amiri slumped onto the chair next to him. 'She's just arrested.'

'What?' Errol loosened his still bloodstained tie. 'Is she—'

'She's still alive. Just.'

Errol mopped his brow. 'Thank God.'

Amiri leant back and stared at the opposite wall. 'I'm sorry I lost it at the church.' He almost choked on his words. 'I was out of my mind with worry—still am!'

'I understand,' Errol said. 'I'd have been the same.'

Amiri turned his head towards Errol. 'I've never been any good at dealing with situations beyond my control.'

'You can say that again. Always in the driving seat, calling all the shots. That's you.' Errol rummaged in his pocket. 'Here, you should have these.' He handed Amiri the wedding rings.

Amiri rubbed his eyes. 'You're a mate.'

'And you need to look after yourself.' Errol patted him on the back. 'Your wife needs you now more than ever.'

'Dr Cohen will see you now.'

Amiri had drifted into a restless sleep when the nurse came into the family room. Errol had left an hour earlier. Amiri felt like a zombie, struggling to his feet and following the nurse into the trauma physician's office.

'Mr Hollis!' Dr Cohen shook his hand and ushered him to a chair. 'You'll appreciate your wife's not out of the woods yet. Not by any means.'

Amiri nodded. The doctor stared at him over his bifocals. Why didn't he just get on with it?

'She's still in haemorrhagic shock,' Dr Cohen said. 'We need to transfer her to a specialist unit in Auckland. We're waiting for the helicopter to airlift her.'

'Can I go with her?' Amiri asked.

'Of course. We've brought in a surgical team with experience of gunshot wounds to look after her on the flight. And Michael Parry will be waiting in Auckland. He's the best cardiothoracic surgeon in the country.'

A thousand questions ran through Amiri's mind, but there was only one that mattered. 'Is she going to live?'

'You know I can't answer that.' Dr Cohen shook his head and pointed to an X-ray of Aroha's chest on his viewing box. 'She'll need an open thoracotomy to remove the bullets. And that carries a significant degree of risk.'

Open thoracotomy? Degree of risk? Was that medical speak for *she's going to die?* Their eyes met, but Amiri broke it off.

Cohen gathered his case notes together and stood up. 'Parry's a brilliant surgeon. She couldn't be in better hands.'

     David Whittet

The whirr of the rotator blades drowned the noise of the bleeping monitor and the array of equipment in the medivac helicopter. Amiri couldn't make out the medics' voices as they deliberated over her care. That was a relief. They looked every bit as worried as the paramedics had been. Maybe even more so, which must mean she was deteriorating. He had to cover his eyes.

Amiri's head was bursting by the time the helicopter touched down on the rooftop helipad at Auckland Hospital. He'd never seen such frenzied activity. He had to run to keep up when the surgical team rushed Aroha down the passageways and into the elevator.

The helicopter crew briefed Michael Parry and his team. Amiri listened to the handover.

'One of the bullets has lodged right on the pulmonary artery.'

The doctor's blunt statement brought Amiri a fresh wave of panic. Could anything get worse?

'Do you mind if I come into theatre to observe?' one of the medivac crew asked.

'Scrub up. I may need another pair of hands.' Parry pursed his lips and snapped on a fresh pair of latex gloves as they disappeared into the operating theatre suite. 'This is going to be a challenge.'

So this was the great Michael Parry. Even in his green theatre scrubs, he cut a dashing figure. He was about Amiri's height and build and more or less the same age. Amiri guessed Parry had the same single-minded determination to succeed. They had both reached the top of their career ladders.

The sliding doors shut in Amiri's face. He caught a last glimpse of Aroha on the table when the doors opened again to let the anaesthetist through.

The hours passed slowly for Amiri as he paced the corridors outside the operating theatre. Doctors and nurses rushed past him, answering their pagers. He collapsed onto a wooden chair in the deserted waiting area, consuming cup after cup of vending machine coffee. He gagged on the bitter chemical taste. It seemed ludicrous to be missing his usual latte at a time like this.

He felt uncomfortable in his bloodstained Christian Dior tuxedo and wished there'd been a chance to get changed. He fumbled in his pocket and pulled out the wedding rings. He played with them for a minute, then placed Aroha's ring against his lips and kissed it. Fate had denied him the opportunity to put the ring on Aroha's finger. He wondered if he ever would.

Every couple of hours, the doors opened as a theatre nurse came off duty. He could see the exhaustion in their eyes.

'Is she all right? How's the operation going?' Amiri begged one of them.

'As well as can be expected.'

Amiri clung to the nurse's arm. 'What does that mean?'

'You'll have to talk to Mr Parry after the surgery.'

The nurse pulled away and disappeared down the corridor.

The inconsequential chatter of the new staff who arrived to take over was a momentary diversion. More important to Amiri was what was happening on the other side of the sliding doors that reopened to let them into the theatre. Something was wrong. He could feel it in his bones.

Raised voices. Amiri strained to hear what they were saying.

'Damn! Cautery! Quickly, Nurse!' That was Parry's voice. Amiri was sure of it.

Then another voice. 'Blood pressure's dropping. We're losing her.'

It was all Amiri could do not to burst into the operating theatre and see what was going on. Could this really be the end for Aroha?

A bright light beckoned Aroha down an endless celestial tunnel, a benevolent hand leading her towards a new and better world. When Aroha was a little girl, Kāterina had told her about near-death experiences and the afterlife. Now she felt her guardian angel holding her, embracing her, protecting her. Sublime voices echoed in her ears. She was in a beautiful place far removed from the hospital—and from Tautaru, Hunapo and the Gang. The suffering of her short and troubled life was over. She'd found peace in a realm free from violence and bullying.

 David Whittet

Aroha's reverie ended abruptly as the theatre nurse brought her round.

'It's okay, Aroha, you're waking up.'

'What's happening,' Aroha cried, her hands outstretched, desperate to hold on to the divine vision.

'You're in recovery,' the nurse reassured, restraining her arm to prevent the intravenous line from disengaging. 'Your operation is over. You're doing really well.'

The overhead light of the recovery room blinded Aroha, abruptly replacing the splendour of paradise. Those soothing, ethereal sounds turned into the bleeping of her cardiac monitor, and excruciating pain in her chest brought her inner peace to an end.

Aroha groaned. She had glimpsed a life free of the Gang and didn't want to come back to this reality. *Let me stay. Please, God! Let me stay in heaven!*

The staff nurse took Amiri to one side. 'Errol Troy has been on the phone yet again. And the CEO of some international water bottling outfit. Please make sure they don't call again. We need to keep this line open for urgent calls.'

In the week he'd sat at Aroha's bedside in intensive care, Amiri hadn't returned a single business call. Never before had he ignored a deadline. That's how he'd got to the top. Now he couldn't take his hands off Aroha's wrist or his eyes off the array of cardiac monitors.

'She's made terrific progress,' Parry announced on his ward round.

Amiri glanced up and watched him boast to his flock of adulating students.

'As you all know, having worked for the New Zealand Army in Afghanistan, I have extensive experience operating on gunshot wounds. But this was something else. A bullet had lodged between the pulmonary artery and the aorta. A millimetre either way and—' Parry drew his fingers across his throat, relishing the gasps from his entourage. 'Getting it out was a miracle.'

Amiri shuddered and squeezed Aroha's hand even tighter.

Parry turned to acknowledge Amiri's presence. 'She's our star patient, Mr Hollis.' He beamed at Aroha. 'You've done so well. We can let you go home at the end of the week.'

'Home?' Aroha murmured in a scarcely audible whisper. 'I want to go back to that heavenly light—and the beautiful world beyond it.'

Amiri shook his head. What was she on about? *Heavenly light?* She hadn't talked about anything else since she woke up from the anaesthetic. Didn't she want to go home?

    David Whittet

Chapter Thirty-Nine

The reflections of the beautiful Coromandel landscape that flickered past seemed to belong to another world. Had she been here before? Aroha gazed out of the window, searching for answers on the journey home in Amiri's bright red BMW sports car. It all felt vaguely familiar, yet somehow distant and surreal.

'Not much further, darling,' Amiri reassured her as they left the main road. 'You'll be able to rest and recuperate in your own surroundings.'

Amiri had been chattering away throughout the trip, but she wasn't really listening. Only when they drove up the tree-lined drive of their country estate did she start to feel more alive. She gazed at the splendid gardens. Such lovely flowers. Memories of happier times returned. Her eyes fixed on the swing beyond the lawn. When they were first together, Amiri had loved pushing her high in the air on that swing. That was something she'd never forget. Precious recollections of a life she had once hoped would never end. Aroha was a different person now. She no longer believed she would ever be completely free of the Gang.

The jolt when the car came to a standstill outside the front door brought her back to earth, the seat belt digging into her sore chest.

'Home, sweet home,' Amiri beamed, jumping out of the car and rushing around to open the passenger door. 'Here, let me carry you inside.'

Aroha blinked as they crossed the threshold. At least she had Amiri to protect her. And to her surprise, he was proving himself to be a perfect caregiver.

'I'm so glad you're home,' Amiri said, settling Aroha into her favourite reclining chair.

'Me too.'

And she was. Amiri was right, she *could* relax in the security of their magnificent home.

Little things meant so much to Aroha as she grew stronger over the next couple of weeks. After lunch each day, Amiri ground some coffee beans and made her an espresso with his state-of-the-art machine. The aroma of freshly roasted coffee in itself was enough to lift her spirits.

'That was perfect, darling.' Aroha put down her cup. 'Just perfect.'

Amiri smiled. 'So it should be, with the price I paid for that machine.'

Most important of all, Amiri took the time to sit with her during the afternoons. They talked and made plans for their future. Perhaps they'd move overseas once she was strong enough. Leave all the trauma behind.

'Can we really?' Aroha nuzzled her head against his. 'Oh, Amiri! I love you!'

Could this be the new beginning she'd been praying for?

A month on and Aroha convinced herself their lives were looking up. Amiri was different, more relaxed, more understanding. All that changed when Errol Troy paid them a visit.

'Sorry to disturb your cosy tête-à-tête,' Errol announced when he breezed into their conservatory. 'But I need to steal Amiri for a few minutes.'

Aroha groaned as they left for Amiri's study. Did he have to go back to the cut-throat world of commerce? She heard their raised voices. What were they talking about? The rocks at Rere? And the precious minerals? And what was that about the Gang? She'd have gone to the door to listen if her chest wasn't hurting so much.

Errol followed Amiri back into the conservatory, still berating his business partner. 'The bastards are going to beat us to it.'

Amiri glared at Errol. 'Then what are we waiting for?'

Aroha lowered her head. She'd seen that look before, and she didn't like it—the fire was back in Amiri's eyes.

Although Amiri did not leave the house over the next few weeks, Aroha felt strangely alone. He'd given her his undivided attention the past month. Now he spent every waking moment on his laptop or his mobile phone, obsessed with deals and marketing contracts.

'Must you see to that tonight?' Aroha leant over Amiri's shoulder as she finished a cup of cocoa. 'Come to bed.'

'Babe, this can't wait till the morning.' Amiri glanced up from his laptop and spread his arms out towards Aroha. 'I'm doing this for you, to keep us financially secure for the rest of our days.'

He'd made the same promise just before their wedding. She gave him a peck on the cheek and went to bed alone.

Amiri was still on his laptop when they sat down for their afternoon coffee the next day. So much for needing to finish his work last night. Aroha glance around the living room, her eyes settling on the ornate lava lamp Kāterina had given them as a wedding present. An elegantly inscribed card stood beside the mystic lamp on the mantelpiece.

Kia kaha, tāku tamaiti, kia kaha.
Be strong, my child.
With love on this special day,
Your Aunt Kāterina.

'I just adore that lava lamp,' Aroha whispered. 'It's so beautiful.'

Amiri looked up from his laptop. 'It freaks the hell out of me!'

'Amiri, really!' Aroha choked on a mouthful of coffee. 'It was a wedding present from Kāterina!'

'I don't care.' Amiri shook his head and returned to his typing. 'It still freaks the hell out of me! I don't like the look of it.'

'Well, I love it!'

Aroha forced a smile and mopped up the spilt coffee. She got up and took their cups back to the kitchen. Loading the dishwasher, she thought back to those visits to the *Gypsy Rose* as a child. She'd always admired that rusty old oil lamp and Kāterina never tired of regaling her with its history ...

'That lamp's been in our whānau for generations,' Kāterina told the young Aroha. 'It used to belong to Tāmure, a great warrior and defender of our ancestors.' Kāterina fetched a dusty book and showed Aroha a picture of the revered fighter wrestling with a man-eating dragon. 'Have you heard of the dragon Kaiwhare?'

Aroha shook her head.

'In Māori legend,' Kāterina continued, 'Kaiwhare is a taniwha who lived in an underwater cavern south of Piha.'

'A *tani*— what?' Aroha asked.

'I was coming to that,' Kāterina said. 'A taniwha is a dragon that lives deep in the ocean, or sometimes in a river or lake. Often, the taniwha would protect our ancestors. Kaiwhare did at first. But then he started attacking and eating people. That's where Tāmure's story begins.'

Kāterina was a brilliant storyteller and her tales enchanted Aroha from her first trip to the caravan. Aroha snuggled up on the old lady's lap, eager to learn of Tāmure's adventures.

'Tāmure attacked the Kaiwhare with his bare hands, but the dragon got the better of him. Fire and smoke billowed from the beast's huge nostrils almost blinding our hero!'

Aroha rubbed her face. Kāterina's description was so lifelike that she could almost feel the dragon's breath burning her skin.

'With an enormous cry, Tāmure drew his secret weapon—a greenstone with the power to destroy the dragon.' Kāterina pointed to an ornate sculpture of the dragon on the base of the lamp. 'That's Kaiwhare there.'

Aroha's imagination catapulted into overdrive. She pictured the slain dragon, blood flowing like a river from its colossal body.

Kāterina closed the book. 'Tāmure severely wounded the dragon but did not kill it. For the rest of its days, Kaiwhare only ate fish, and thanks to Tāmure, our ancestors remained safe.'

By now, Aroha was so engrossed that she believed she was there, joining in with the excited crowds cheering the triumphant warrior.

Tāmure's courageousness resonated with the young Aroha. Kāterina's yarns had sustained an unhappy childhood. Trudging home through the forest with her mother, Aroha would pretend she was Tāmure's loyal wife, tending to his wounds after the battle. Like Kamaka's binoculars, the lamp became special to Aroha. Kamaka and Tāmure. They were her two favourite stories.

❧

Aroha switched on the dishwasher. It seemed a lifetime since Kāterina had come to the house with her wedding gift. Come to think of it, Amiri hadn't been too pleased back then, pulling a face when Kāterina arrived at the door. He'd looked decidedly uncomfortable when Kāterina had flung her arms around Aroha.

'I know we didn't part on the best of terms,' Kāterina had said, still holding Aroha tight. 'So I wanted to give you something unique for your wedding.' She opened her bag. 'I know how much you loved my oil lamp …'

'Kāterina! You shouldn't have!' Aroha couldn't believe her eyes. Kāterina had brought the beloved lantern into the twentieth century by converting it into the base of a contemporary lava lamp. The sculpture of Tāmure wrestling Kaiwhare and the ornamental Māori engravings blended perfectly with the wax and incandescent bulb of the new top section. 'Thank you so much!' She glanced across to Amiri. 'It's perfect! Isn't it, darling?'

Amiri's muted grunt had told her he was less than impressed with the lovingly restored lamp.

'Kia kaha.' Kāterina had kissed Aroha's cheek when she left. 'It will bring you good luck.'

❧

The dishwasher in progress, Aroha went back to the living room and slumped on the sofa, clutching her aching chest.

Amiri glanced up from his laptop. 'The lamp hasn't brought us much luck so far.' He put the device aside. 'Here, let me get you a fresh coffee.'

He made another espresso and sat next to her on the sofa with his arm over her shoulder. 'I thought you said Kāterina's stories were a load of old bull.'

Aroha sipped her Americano. 'Perhaps not this one.'

She rubbed her forehead. Maybe Tāmure slaying the dragon was just another figment of the old woman's imagination, but she didn't care. And she certainly wouldn't admit it to Amiri.

'We had a lecture from the old girl when I was at business school,' Amiri said with a smirk. 'Kāterina Kururangi. What was it they called her? Oh yes, *a guru for success.* Advisor to the rich and famous. I've never heard such crap. Everyone was laughing at her behind her back.'

'Stop! No more.' Aroha held out her hands, the sudden movement bringing another spasm of pain.

Kāterina could be annoying and full of make-believe, but she had a special place in Aroha's heart. Why couldn't Amiri see that?

Amiri apologised to her over dinner that night. 'I didn't mean to badmouth your great aunt. It's just—I've been feeling a bit tense the last couple of days.'

Aroha sighed. 'You and me both.' She reached across the table and put her hand on his. 'Who would believe what we've been through together?'

'Something tells me it's not over yet.' Amiri got up from the table and paced around the living room.

Aroha felt a sudden churning in her stomach. 'Don't say that.'

'It's probably nothing.' Amiri gazed out of the window. 'I thought I saw someone outside. Are you sure Hunapo's still locked up?'

'Of course he is,' Aroha replied. 'You heard what the police inspector said when he came to take my statement.'

Amiri closed the curtain. 'Well, I hope they throw away the key. Otherwise, I swear I'll take the law into my own hands. I won't see you hurt again.'

		David Whittet

'You worry too much. Come and sit down.' Aroha grasped the side of her chair. The last thing she wanted was for Amiri to turn into a vigilante, but she needed his strong, protective body next to hers. 'Let's try to relax. I can't wait to get back to my book. It's a wonderful story.'

They snuggled up together on the sofa. Aroha fell asleep with the paperback covering her face. The doorbell woke her, and she gave Amiri a poke.

'You get it,' she murmured.

'It'll be Errol,' Amiri said. 'He's got some papers for me to sign.'

Aroha was drifting back to sleep when she caught a snippet of Errol and Amiri's conversation in the hall.

'I don't want to alarm you,' Errol said, 'but someone was snooping around in your garden.'

'I knew it!' Amiri replied.

'I scared the bugger off,' Errol said. 'But he may come back.'

Aroha pushed her book aside. Her knees locked as she got up and stumbled into the hallway. Errol was taking off his coat, and he dumped a heap of files on the table.

'What's going on?' she asked.

'Errol's just confirmed what I suspected,' Amiri said. 'He's out there. It's—'

'It's probably just some hobo sheltering in your greenhouse,' Errol said. 'I'm sorry I mentioned it now.'

'A tramp?' Amiri threw his arms in the air. 'You've got to be kidding! It's Hunapo. Come to kill us in our beds!'

Aroha covered her face. Why couldn't the past leave her alone? Why couldn't Hunapo just let go? Now he wasn't just threatening her, but also the man she loved. Where would it all end?

Errol and Amiri were still talking. Amiri sounded off about getting some mercenaries to guard the house. Aroha shuddered—she didn't want that. She had to pull herself together. It *couldn't* be Hunapo loitering in the garden.

'Leave it, both of you.' Her eyes locked on Amiri. 'I told you, they've put Hunapo away ...'

Chapter Forty

'You've used one too many of your nine lives!' Tautaru slapped Hunapo's face so hard that he fell onto the bench in the police cell. 'Damn you! Bloody idiot! How the hell do you expect me to fix this?'

Hunapo rubbed his smarting cheek. 'I told you. I didn't do it. I'd never hurt Aroha.'

Tautaru gave him another slap. 'Don't start that again. Kaine, the gangsters, everyone. They all heard you mouthing off about killing her.'

'I didn't mean it,' Hunapo said. 'I was just angry. Why don't you believe me?'

Tautaru rolled his eyes. 'Because it's a load of crap.'

The police didn't believe him either. Interview after interview. The same questions and more or less the same answers. Night after night in a cold, dingy, stinking cell. He'd had enough.

Hunapo glanced up at Tautaru. 'Get me out of here. What about Bailey? I thought you said he was in with the cops and he owed you a favour.'

'Already tried,' Tautaru said. 'The bastard's in trouble himself. He's no use to us any more.'

Hunapo shuddered. 'What about Le Squillier?'

Tautaru shook his head. 'He's a bloody moron. We need a real lawyer.'

'Then get one!' Hunapo wrung his hands together. 'I'm in court tomorrow and the police prosecutor is opposing bail.'

'I ought to leave you here to rot.' Tautaru spat in Hunapo's face, hitting him in the eye.

'No, please!'

'Gillespie's the man for this job.' Tautaru gave Hunapo another evil look with his fractured eyes. 'And that son of a bitch doesn't come cheap.'

David Whittet

The following morning, Hunapo washed his face in the tiny basin in his cell and slicked back his hair. He had to look respectable for his court appearance. He'd heard nothing more from Tautaru. Perhaps the old man really had cut him off.

Hunapo waited for the officers to come and collect him. Days in the cell were all the same and he'd lost track of time. But surely he was due in court by now? What was going on?

Eventually, a red-faced custody sergeant unlocked the cell door. 'There's someone here to see you.'

Gillespie was waiting for him in reception. 'Well, that was easy. You're free to go, Hunapo.'

The sergeant handed Hunapo's possessions back to him.

Gillespie grinned. 'Don't be such a poor loser.'

The sergeant glared at both of them. 'You may have won round one. But we haven't finished with you, Hunapo.'

Gillespie drove Hunapo home in his Maserati.

'How did you do it?' Hunapo asked. 'The cops were so damn cocky. I thought they'd stitched me up for good.'

'Simple.' Gillespie put his foot on the accelerator. 'A mate of mine's a ballistics expert. I got him to sign a sworn statement saying the bullets they found in Aroha's chest couldn't possibly have come from your gun. Open and shut case.'

'You're the man, Gillespie. I owe you.' Hunapo gave him the thumbs up. 'And your mate.'

'I wouldn't worry about us,' Gillespie said. 'We were both well paid for our services.'

Hunapo took a deep breath. 'Actually, I don't want to go home. Could you drop me off here, at the car yard?'

Gillespie raised his eyebrows. 'At the wreckers?'

'Yes.' Hunapo hesitated, unsure how much to say. 'My old banger's a write-off. And I need wheels. There's somewhere I have to be.'

'Is there indeed?' Gillespie frowned. 'Should I be worried? Do I need to warn Tautaru?'

Hunapo bit his lip. He *had* said too much. 'No need to bother Tautaru. It's my shit. Not his.'

Gillespie pulled up at the kerb. 'Why do I have the distinct feeling that I'll be back to get you off the hook again before long, Hunapo?'

'You won't.'

Hunapo jumped out of the car before Gillespie could ask any more awkward questions. He strolled into the car yard, trying to look as inconspicuous as possible. Which of those clapped-out vehicles would get him back to the Coromandel?

David Whittet

Chapter Forty-One

Aroha yawned. She'd finished her book and felt bereft. Reading had always been a great escape, and she read widely, from Kāterina's picture books to the trashy novels she'd found stashed away in her mother's dresser.

Looking across the living room, she noticed Amiri was back at his desk, doubtless working on yet another business proposal. That would occupy him for the rest of the night, she thought. Aroha rose to draw the curtains. She paused for a moment and stared into the darkness. Had that tramp returned? With a shudder, she pulled the satin drapes closed.

She was about to wander off to bed when Amiri looked up and beamed at her.

'Why don't we have an early night for a change?' he said.

Had she heard him right? Was she dreaming? No, he was shutting down his laptop. Aroha couldn't remember when he last came to bed before midnight. She ran towards him and they embraced in the middle of the room.

'I love you, Amiri Hollis. Take me to bed!'

'I love you too.' He lifted her in his arms and carried her up the stairs to their bedroom. 'With all my heart and soul.'

Aroha hadn't felt desire like this since before the shooting. She thought her heart would burst with anticipation as he laid her on the bed and helped her undress. Those strong hands, so gentle as they removed her clothes and caressed her skin, carefully avoiding her wounds. She was still sore, and they hadn't been able to make love since she came home from hospital. But tonight she didn't care about the pain. She wanted him and needed to feel him inside her more than ever before.

'Hurry up and come to bed,' she whispered. 'Make love to me like it's the last night of our lives.'

Aroha felt self-conscious lying naked on the bed watching him strip off. She pulled up the sheet to cover the enormous surgical scar on her chest. Unlike hers, his body was perfect. Rugged, sturdy and athletic. She stared at his strapping muscles, watched him flex his arms as he pulled off his shirt. It made her feel safe. Amiri was tough, he could protect her from anything.

'You're a man in a million, Amiri Hollis,' she said. 'Now get yourself in here beside me.'

Amiri pulled back the sheet and climbed on top of her. Aroha instinctively put her hand over her scar.

'Don't look at that. It's so ugly,' she said.

'Baby, you're beautiful. Nothing will change that.'

He stroked her cheek and her hair. That, and the seductive smell of his Versace aftershave, only made her want him more. She sensed he was holding back, not wanting to cause her any more pain, but her hunger for him was urgent. What could she say to encourage him to abandon his self-control? Would he be shocked if she told him what she really wanted?

Aroha didn't have much experience of sex talk. Hunapo had always talked dirty when they made love, and she hated it.

'I know you're trying not to hurt me,' she said. 'But I want you to—' she almost used the F-word but stopped herself '—I want you to take me, go all the way. Don't worry about hurting me. Fill my body. Take me places I've never been before.'

Every nerve ending tingled when he entered her body.

'Harder, harder,' she cried as Amiri thrust into her. 'Oh, God! That feels so good.'

She moaned with pleasure. Everything needed to be perfect—and it was.

His rapid breathing told her he couldn't last much longer. Nor could she. Fireworks rocketed through her head in a dazzling climax. Firecrackers, sparklers, and a brilliant fountain of light from a Roman candle. She could even smell the explosives.

     David Whittet

Her mind was in another realm when a thunderous crash shook not just her brain but the entire house.

'What the hell was that?' Amiri leapt up from the bed and grabbed his dressing gown.

'The earth moved for you too?' Aroha sighed. Why had he left her? It was just another spectacular skyrocket in their heads. 'Come back to bed, darling. We can't stop there. Fill me again!'

'That wasn't in your mind! It was for real!' Amiri fell to the floor when a second Molotov cocktail smashed through the bedroom window. 'Quick! We've got to get out of here!'

Blinded by the fireball, she could vaguely make out Amiri staggering back to his feet. He wrapped a nightgown around her naked body and lifted her off the bed. She wheezed as the room rapidly filled with noxious fumes. The smoke alarm sounded, its piercing noise competing with the deafening roar of the soaring flames. Her heart pounded as Amiri carried her out onto the landing. The fire had spread to the stairway. She closed her eyes. Given its furious speed, she knew the fire would soon consume the entire building.

She felt Amiri's body shake as he put his foot on the top step.

'We're never going to make it,' she cried. 'Look at the flames!'

'We've no choice!' Amiri spluttered. 'There's no other way out … hold on tight …'

Aroha had never heard such panic in his voice. That, more than anything else, made her freak out. Masonry fell all around them as Amiri negotiated the stairs. Aroha put her hand over her mouth, trying to protect herself from the acrid smoke. She felt her hair singeing. Her beautiful, long black hair. The gunshots had destroyed her body. Now the flames were ravaging the last of her good looks.

Amiri's foot slipped, and a timber beam collapsed on top of them. Aroha fell down the stairwell, hitting her head against the bannister.

'Amiri! Help me! I can't move!' Aroha struggled to make herself heard above the roaring cacophony. Her lungs were weak from the surgery and she was choking. She knew she didn't have long before she suffocated. Through the dense clouds of smoke, she could see Amiri crawling down the stairs.

She pulled herself up, gasping for air and waving her arms to attract his attention.

'Over here,' she panted. 'Quick!'

She watched him fight his way through the debris. He was getting closer and closer. Thank God! He was going to rescue her. His hand reached out to her. She tried to get hold of it. Then, with a sudden wrench, the stairway collapsed.

Aroha found herself crushed under a mass of molten wreckage. The entire house was collapsing. She gagged on a vile black tarry mucous in her throat.

'Amiri!' She tried to shift the joist off her chest, but it wouldn't budge. The pain was unspeakable. She only just managed to raise her head. 'Amiri! Where are you? Amiri! *Amiri!*'

Her eyes streamed as she gazed into the smog. Amiri wasn't there—he must be caught on the other side of the rafter. Her heart stood still. He was gone, and she was on her own.

Aroha howled in despair. Nobody would find her now. Even if someone saw the flames and called the fire brigade, they were over six kilometres from the town of Thames, all of it on winding country roads. There were volunteer firefighters at the nearby township of Colville—she'd thought of enlisting herself—but they would never cope with this conflagration. She was going to die. Hunapo had won, the Gang had won.

Unlike her previous near-death experience a couple of months back, there was no bright celestial light beckoning her to a better world. Alone and in pain, the immense heat of the hellish inferno blackened her skin. Delusions intensified as she sank into a coma. She was being dragged down to hell, fighting and screaming. Bizarre thoughts entered her mind. Those Jehovah's Witnesses who called at their door when she was a child. What was it they used to say? Something about being condemned for eternity and doomed to

     David Whittet

endless purgatory. Whatever all that meant, Aroha knew she was beyond help or salvation.

With her dying breath, Aroha lifted her eyes and took a last look around. Someone was coming towards her, battling through the furnace. For a moment, there was hope in her fevered mind. Was it an angel from heaven, come to rescue her from the jaws of hell? Or could it be Amiri returning to save her? Her vision blurred. Was it merely a hallucination? She'd seen a documentary on TV about the effect of oxygen deprivation on the brain.

As the ghostly figure came closer, Aroha sank back into the rubble. The apparition looming over her was not an angel. Nor was it Amiri. It was the devil incarnate, towering over her like Hades. It was Hunapo.

'Get away from me, Hunapo!' she croaked, roused by a last burst of adrenaline. 'I don't want you anywhere near me. I hope you're bloody proud of yourself. This is all your doing.'

'I saw the fire—and came to save you.' Hunapo grabbed her arm. 'Let me help you, or you'll die—'

'I'd rather die here with Amiri than spend another moment with you, Hunapo!' Aroha stammered, her speech fragmented by her heaving for breath. 'Go! Let me die here with the man I love!'

'I'm not leaving you.' Hunapo picked her up and slung her across his shoulders. She was too weak to resist.

She heard distant sirens as Hunapo fought his way through the inferno, ducking to avoid the falling timber and red-hot mortar. Somebody must have raised the alarm. They'd be too late to save her, but at least the police would catch Hunapo.

As the sirens grew closer, Aroha was sure she could hear something else.

'It's Amiri! He's calling me! Put me down!'

Hunapo kept moving. 'No! We have to get out while we still can!'

She had to break free of Hunapo and find Amiri.

'Take that!' Mustering every last ounce of energy, Aroha landed a punch on Hunapo's back. With renewed vigour, she kicked his groin. 'I'm coming, Amiri!'

Toxic smoke stung her eyes, but that was nothing compared to the terror that lay ahead. Trapped under a molten girder, red-hot embers pelted Amiri's body. His flesh melted in front of her eyes. Those once powerful hands disintegrated into nothing. Amiri's face withered, his skin liquefied and poured away from his bones.

She heard him cry out. 'I love you, Aroha!'

A sudden explosion and everything was black.

She'd no idea how long she was out. Jolted back into consciousness, Aroha was horrified to find herself in Hunapo's arms.

'Where's Amiri?' she demanded. 'What's happened to him?'

Hunapo stroked her hair. 'I'm sorry, Aroha. He's gone.'

Aroha stared into the smoke. 'He hasn't.'

Hunapo pulled her back over his shoulder.

'Get off me.' Aroha managed to give Hunapo another thump. 'Amiri's still alive. He must be.'

Another gigantic flame shot down from above, propelling them both to the ground. Hunapo hit his head on a rafter. Aroha rolled away from him. If she kept turning, perhaps she could reach Amiri and expire next to him. She wasn't dying beside Hunapo.

Before she could get to Amiri, she saw figures silhouetted against the fiery carnage. With their full protective gear and breathing apparatus on their backs, the firefighters looked like oversized insects.

'You must find Amiri,' she cried as one of the officers picked her up.

'Don't worry,' the officer said. 'We may have to amputate his leg to get him out, but we'll save him.'

She saw them trying to get Hunapo's foot out from under a fallen beam.

'Not him!' Aroha howled. 'Amiri!' She gestured with her hand. 'Over there!'

The firefighter glanced in the direction she pointed. 'I'm sorry. We can't go back in there.'

'You have to!' Aroha gesticulated madly, flailing her arms in all directions. 'You must save Amiri. Please!'

 David Whittet

'Look!' the firefighter said. More flaming batons collapsed on their heads. 'We have to get you out.'

The entire structure caved in, disintegrating before her eyes.

She continued to harangue the firefighters as they dragged her to safety.

'We have to go back. We have to find Amiri!'

Once they were out of the house, the senior fire officer took Aroha to one side. 'I'm so sorry about your husband. Going back inside would put the crew's lives at risk. I can't do that—'

'You can save him.' Aroha tugged on his arm. 'I know you can.'

'I know what you must be going through. I want you to talk to Maisie. She's our victim support counsellor.'

Maisie handed Aroha a water bottle. 'Have a drink. It'll make you feel better.' She put her arm around Aroha. 'You've inhaled smoke and you're recovering from a serious injury. The ambulance will be here in a minute and we'll get you to hospital.'

'Amiri! My soulmate, my companion, my friend!' Aroha sobbed. 'Please don't leave me! Come back to me! Please!'

Maisie stroked her hand. 'I'll stay with you all the way to the hospital. Now try and take another sip of water.'

'No!' Aroha turned her back on Maisie and confronted the fire crew. 'If you won't go back and save Amiri, I'll go myself!'

'You can't go back in there!' The fire chief grabbed Aroha as she ran towards the blazing house. 'You'll die!'

'Then let me die with Amiri!'

The police arrived at the same time as the ambulance. The senior sergeant took her arm. 'Listen, Aroha. We need to let the paramedics check you over.'

Aroha pulled away. Why wouldn't they understand? 'My husband is in there. Burning to death! And nobody's doing anything about it!'

'It's no use, Aroha,' the sergeant said. 'Your husband is dead.'

Maisie held her other hand, and they took her to the ambulance.

'Believe me, Aroha,' Maisie said. 'If there was anything else we could do for Amiri, the crew would be straight back inside. But there isn't, and we have to look after you.'

The paramedics helped Aroha into the ambulance. Looking over her shoulder, Aroha saw two firemen pull Hunapo out of the wreckage.

'They rescued that scumbag,' Aroha cried. 'Why couldn't they save Amiri?' She flung out her arm and pointed at Hunapo. 'You're a murderer. A cruel, heartless killer!' She spun around to the sergeant. 'Arrest him! He's a murderer! *Go on, arrest him!'*

David Whittet

Part Four

The Prodigal Daughter

Chapter Forty-Two

Waikato Hospital, Hamilton, 1990.

'How can I live?' Aroha flung her arms around Kāterina and refused to let go. 'Hunapo has killed the man I love. The man who was going to take me away from the Gang and give me a new start.'

Kāterina stroked her hair. 'My poor child. Murua ahau!'

Tears rolled down Aroha's cheeks. 'He's dead, Kāterina. Amiri is dead. My friend, my soulmate. He's gone. How can I bear life on my own?'

Kāterina's visit unleashed Aroha's first outpouring of sorrow since the fire. Three months in the burns unit and she'd spent the endless days desperate to cry, scream and rail against the injustice of it all. Perhaps it was the constant sedation, but her emotions remained pent up inside. The doctors kept giving her injections, and the nurses told her to stay calm. Only Kāterina's piercing eyes, with their familiar arched eyebrows, penetrated the depth of her misery.

'Thank God you're here!' Aroha hugged Kāterina so tight that the old lady could hardly breathe. 'You've no idea how much this means to me. Being able to talk to someone who understands.'

'I've been so worried about you,' Kāterina said. 'I should have come sooner, but—'

'You're here now.' Aroha sank back onto the pillow, still grasping Kāterina's hand. 'What am I going to do? Hunapo's telling everyone he's a brave warrior who saved my life. He tried to get in here to torment me, but the hospital's security officers threw him out.' Aroha hung her head. 'I can't even grieve for Amiri in peace. You know his mum and dad blame me for his death?'

'Yes, I know,' Kāterina said. 'The nurse told me.'

Aroha's mind drifted back to the day Amiri's parents barged into the ward, pushing the orderly aside and marching up to her bed.

Amelia had laid straight into Aroha. 'Bloody bitch! I'll never forgive you for this!'

'You murdered my son!' William spat the words in Aroha's face. 'I told him not to get involved with the Gang.'

'Nobody hates the Gang more than I do,' Aroha had protested. 'Amiri's death had nothing to do with me. I *loved* him. I tried to get the firemen to pull him out of the house.'

Amelia pointed a finger in Aroha's face. 'It was your jealous ex-lover who killed him. Amiri's blood is on your hands. He'd still be alive if he hadn't met you.'

William raised a fist. 'I won't rest till the lot of you are behind bars.'

The intensive care sister shot up from the nursing station. 'This is a high dependency unit, and I cannot allow you to disrupt our patients—'

'Come on, Amelia.' William took his wife's hand and gave Aroha a final evil stare. 'I hope you rot in hell!'

Aroha buried herself under the bedclothes.

'Don't take it to heart,' the sister soothed. 'They're grieving and looking for someone to blame.'

'I know,' Aroha whimpered from beneath the sheets. 'It's just … I thought … I hoped they loved me. We were so close before the wedding. I never imagined they'd abandon me.'

Am I to blame? Did I kill the man I love? Am I really that poisonous? Aroha couldn't get William and Amelia's attack out of her mind. The accusations repeated until she thought her head would explode. *How dare they? I would never hurt Amiri.* She pulled the blankets back from her face. *It was Hunapo. Not me. Hunapo killed Amiri.*

'You don't think I was to blame for Amiri's death, do you?' Aroha asked Kāterina.

'No,' Kāterina said. 'I saw how much you loved him.'

Aroha sighed. At least someone was on her side. 'Thank you. That means a lot.'

'One of the nurses told me she brought her daughter in to cheer you up,' Kāterina said.

     David Whittet

'That's right,' Aroha replied. 'Little Emily. She is a sweet girl, but …'

Aroha trailed off, and Kāterina finished the sentence for her. 'She was a bit too much?'

'Yes. I suppose she was.' Aroha closed her eyes. She felt a stab of guilt. The nurse had been kind, and Emily had tried so hard …

'Nobody to keep you company?' the staff nurse had asked when she took Aroha's blood pressure.

Aroha looked away. 'No.'

'We'll see what we can do about that.'

The next day, the nurse arrived at work with her daughter. 'This is Emily. She's come to see you.'

Emily handed Aroha a home-made get-well card she'd crafted at school.

'That's beautiful,' Aroha smiled, squinting at the card with her aching eyes.

Emily was full of life and energy. Aroha struggled to keep up with the bubbly ten-year-old's incessant chatter.

'Emily was exhausting,' Aroha told Kāterina. 'But I always looked forward to her visits. She brought her picture books, which made me think of you. Emily told me her mum and dad read stories to her every night. You were the only one who ever read to me.'

Kāterina squeezed Aroha's hand. 'So she cheered you up a bit?'

'She was good company,' Aroha said. 'I was grateful for that, and I missed her when she stopped coming.'

'What happened?' Kāterina asked.

'She had to go back to school. At least that's what her mother said.' Aroha felt her eyes well up again. 'I think I just gave up after that.'

The orderly arrived with the tea trolley. Aroha groaned—she couldn't face another cup of that dishwater. Random recollections flooded through her subconscious as she watched Kāterina drink her tea.

Aroha had known for some time that she was deteriorating. She'd heard the doctors talking about her as they stood at the end of her bed on their ward round.

'She's given up,' the ward sister told the consultant. 'Wasting away.'

Dr Jenkins, the burns specialist, harrumphed and laid his stethoscope on Aroha's chest. 'Her breathing's shallow, and there's reduced air entry at the bases.' Dr Jenkins removed his stethoscope and gave Aroha a reassuring smile. 'Michael Parry did an admirable job, but the smoke's given your lungs another battering. Don't worry. We'll soon have you feeling better.' He turned to his registrar. 'Get some up-to-date spirometry done. That'll give us an indication of whether the damage is reversible.'

Aroha fought the large doses of morphine that muddled her brain. She could still hear the medical staff discussing her case as they walked away from her bedside.

'A reactive depression is understandable in the circumstances—'

'It's more than that, Dr Jenkins,' the ward sister insisted. 'She's lost the will to live.'

'The psych team put her on Prozac. Isn't it working? You'd better get Dr Vernon to see her again.'

Aroha raised her head, her wounded eyes gazing after them. *Why can't they just let me die? Then I'd be with Amiri.*

A few days later, Anita Bennet, the medical social worker, visited. Aroha remembered her sitting on the edge of her chair at the bedside.

'Is there nobody we can contact?' Anita asked. 'What about your father? Or the man who pulled you out of the fire? Surely you want to see them?'

'Christ, no!' Aroha jolted upright, the force almost dislodging her intravenous line. 'I don't want to see my father. Or Hunapo. Keep them away from me!'

'All right. Calm down.' Anita crossed and uncrossed her legs. 'There must be *someone*.'

Aroha continued to shake her head vehemently, then suddenly stopped. She hauled herself up on the bed and lifted her head. 'Kāterina! Find Kāterina Kururangi! Bring her to me!'

     David Whittet

Kāterina got up and put her empty teacup on the trolley. 'I was going to come and see you, anyway. It wasn't just that social worker.'

Their eyes met. 'I know.' Aroha could see that Kāterina was as close to tears as she was herself. 'I feel a whole lot better for seeing you.'

Kāterina glanced around. She pointed at Aroha's bedside table. 'My old lamp!'

'Yes,' Aroha said. 'The police brought it in when they came to the hospital to take my statement.'

Kāterina picked up the charred brass lamp and polished it with her shawl. 'Dear me. Looks like it only just survived the fire.'

Aroha sighed. 'It was the only thing that did, and it spooked the detective.'

'Why?' Kāterina asked. 'What did he say?'

Kāterina smiled as Aroha recounted the conversation with the detective.

'It's the most extraordinary thing,' he had said. 'It was still shining when we found it amongst the burnt-out rubble. Gave me the willies, I can tell you.'

'It was a wedding present from an exceptional woman,' Aroha had replied. 'It used to belong to Tāmure, a great Māori warrior. At least, that's what my great aunt said.'

'Looks like his lamp is as tough as he was,' the detective had commented, closing his notebook. 'That's all I can say.'

Kāterina held the beloved lantern against her bosom. 'The spirit of the mighty Tāmure *is* indestructible.' She gave the lamp another polish. 'You know, Amiri and Tāmure had a lot in common. They were both fearless fighters. And what about Amiri and Kaiwhare? Amiri was a beast tamed, just like Kaiwhare.'

'Kaiwhare lived,' Aroha said. 'Amiri didn't. And he wasn't a beast.'

'I didn't mean that.' Kāterina lowered her head for a moment then sat bolt upright, her eyes sparkling. 'But don't you see? The lamp was still glowing when the police found it because Tāmure and Kaiwhare's spirits are keeping watch over Amiri's soul.'

Aroha frowned. 'But Amiri hated that lamp. I'm sorry, Kāterina, but he did.'

'I thought he was a bit frosty when I brought it around to your house,' Kāterina said, rubbing her wrinkled forehead. 'Perhaps they were too alike, Amiri, Tāmure and Kaiwhare.'

'Maybe.' Aroha suddenly burst into tears. 'I miss Amiri so much.'

Kāterina took Aroha into her arms. 'I know you do.'

A bell rang through the ward.

'Surely that's not the end of visiting hours?' Kāterina said. 'There's something I need to tell you.'

Aroha dabbed her eyes on her sleeve. 'What is it?'

Kāterina handed Aroha a handkerchief. 'I can't tell you while you're like this.'

Aroha blew her nose. 'Tell me what?'

'I should have told you before—before the wedding.' Kāterina lowered her head and hid her face behind her hands. 'Murua ahau. Forgive me.'

Aroha cried again. 'Not more bad news!'

'It's nothing.' Kāterina lifted her head and smiled. 'Nothing at all. I shouldn't have worried you.'

Kāterina *did* have something important to say. Aroha could see it in her eyes, and in the way her guru, her wānanga, rocked from side to side on her chair.

'Don't cry,' Kāterina continued. 'You concentrate on getting well again. Be strong. For me.'

Aroha grasped the side of the bed. There was no way she could cope with another disaster. The tears came even faster and there was nothing she could do to stop them.

'What's the matter, Aroha?' The ward sister came over and handed Aroha a box of tissues. 'Here, take one of these.'

'Thank you.' Aroha wiped the snot off her face. 'I don't know … it's just …'

'It's all been too much for you, hasn't it? Seeing your great aunt again.' The sister turned to Kāterina. 'Perhaps it's best if you leave her for now. She's vulnerable. Come and see her again another day.'

 David Whittet

Kāterina stood up, her back hunched, and Aroha thought she looked at least ten years older.

'Are you still glad I came?' Kāterina asked.

'I am.' Aroha brushed away the tears. 'I haven't been able to cry until today. And I need to cry for Amiri.' Her eyes met Kāterina's. 'Promise me you'll come back.'

'I will.'

The two women pressed their noses together.

'Kia kaha, Aroha,' Kāterina said. 'I'll pray for you. Kia kaha.'

Chapter Forty-Three

Tautaru pinned Hunapo against the wall. 'Will you never bloody learn? That's twice I've had to bail you out of the clink in a couple of months. Are you trying to get us busted? Whakianga mai!'

Hunapo shook with trepidation from the moment he received the summons to Gang headquarters. He knew Tautaru couldn't wait to get his hands on him. The gruelling twelve-hour interrogation by the police was nothing compared to what confronted him now. Surrounded by a lynch mob of minions, Kaine slapped his face while Tautaru continued to lay into him.

'What the hell were you playing at? Attempted murder. Arson. Murder. And then you get caught. Dickhead!'

Kaine landed him another punch on the head. Chase kicked him in the guts.

Winded by the blows, Hunapo struggled to answer. 'You don't understand. I love Aroha.'

'Didn't stop you sleeping around, did it?' Tautaru spat in his face. 'You've put the whole Gang at risk, you pōkokohua! Why the hell did I make you the vice president?'

Hunapo wanted to say he'd never asked for the vice presidency, but the fire in Tautaru's eyes told him to keep quiet.

Tautaru threw him to the ground. 'You pull your head in, Hunapo. Put one foot out of line again and you're history.'

Punch-drunk from all the blows, Hunapo was vaguely aware of the men moving away. Tautaru was still slagging him off. It was so unfair. As a child, Maahanga had beaten him because of his friendship with Aroha. Now he'd had another pasting from Tautaru because he couldn't let go of her. Neither of them understood his obsession with Aroha. He *had* to have her, and he couldn't let anyone else near her.

David Whittet

Hunapo raised his head to see the men had gathered by the door. Tautaru was still ranting.

'Bloody Hunapo!' Tautaru said. 'The bastard knows I have to stand by him.'

Stand by me? Hunapo spat blood from his mouth. The bashing had broken his teeth. *Kick me when I'm down, more like!*

'Everyone's talking about it, boss,' Chase said. 'This time Hunapo's gone too far. Aroha's one of our own, and that's twice he's tried to kill her. The bastard has no respect for anyone.'

'Boot him out of the Gang!' The men chorused. 'De-patch him! String him up! Cut off his balls!'

Hunapo shook his head, still lying in a pool of blood. *It wasn't like that. I love Aroha.*

'This could be just the break your enemies have been waiting for,' Kaine said. 'We're facing a backlash.'

'And whose fault is that?' Tautaru pulled Kaine aside. 'You're the one who bullshitted me into making Hunapo the Gang's vice president. You and those bloody women.'

Hunapo held his head in his hands as Tautaru continued to harangue Kaine. Had everyone been in on the arranged marriage?

Tautaru poked a finger at Kaine. '"Take Hunapo into your whānau," you said. "Marrying Hunapo and Aroha will unite the Gang and bring back prosperity."'

'It could have done,' Kaine said, 'if only you'd kept Hunapo in line. I told you to make him your puppet. Give him all the unpopular jobs. Make him the scapegoat whenever anything went wrong. You'd have been stronger than ever.'

'Balls!' Tautaru said. 'You tricked me into it. And now that we've told everyone Hunapo's the future of the Gang, we can't cut him loose.'

'I warned you all those public statements were a mistake,' Kaine said. 'But you wouldn't listen. Parading the kid around at parties like a trophy—'

'Shut it, Kaine!' Tautaru said. 'I need to think. I'm the one who has to clean up your mess and turn this around.'

Hunapo groaned. Sod the lot of them. Tautaru, Kaine and the women. What right had they to mess with his life to get what they wanted? Hunapo had never wanted to be the *chosen one*.

Tautaru paced up and down the hall, cursing under his breath. Hunapo watched the old man's cheeks flush and the veins on his neck bulge as they did whenever he was mad. Tautaru suddenly stopped and dragged Kaine out through the back door. When they returned a few minutes later, they were both grinning.

'That's sick, Tautaru,' Kaine said. 'Even by your standards. Now all you have to do is make everyone swallow it!'

Tautaru strode over to Hunapo and gave him a kick. 'Stop snivelling and get up! You're to be at Smash Palace tomorrow lunchtime. Twelve sharp. And for God's sake, have a shower and smarten yourself up.'

Hunapo spent a restless night wondering what the old bugger was up to. *Smarten yourself up. Yeah, right.* There was no way he could hide the bruises from today's thrashing.

When Hunapo arrived at the tavern, the lackeys were there already, hustling the punters in.

'Keep your head down,' Kaine said, grabbing Hunapo's arm. 'Everyone's after your blood. Come on. Tautaru's waiting.'

The mob jeered as Kaine led Hunapo to the front.

'Take that, you sick bastard!'

It wasn't just the gangsters who were mad. The women lunged at him, aiming blows and kicks.

'Traitor!'

'You're a disgrace to the Gang, Hunapo!'

How dare they? These were the women who'd buggered up his life. He was about to raise a fist when Kaine stopped him.

'Enough of that,' Kaine said. 'Tautaru doesn't want any trouble.'

Tautaru stood on a box in front of the crowd. He beckoned Hunapo to stand at his side.

'Screw this up and I'll kill you,' Tautaru hissed in Hunapo's ear. He turned to the people. 'This man is a loyal gangster with the guts to make tough decisions.' Tautaru thumped Hunapo on the back. 'His actions may seem harsh, but nobody is above the Gang. Not even my daughter.'

The women stamped their feet and waved their fists in the air. 'Have you no shame, Tautaru? He tried to murder your daughter!'

Tautaru glared at them. 'Aroha belongs to Hunapo. And she was about to commit bigamy with an enemy of the Gang. Hunapo put his own life at risk to save her from bringing shame on us all.'

The women stamped their feet even louder. 'Bollocks! And you know it!'

Tautaru could hardly make himself heard above the furore. 'Hunapo did this for the Gang—'

'No, I didn't,' Hunapo interrupted. 'I did it because I love Aroha.'

Tautaru dug Hunapo in the ribs. 'Shut the fuck up.' He spun back to face the crowd. 'I repeat, nobody is above the Gang. Hunapo's methods may have been brutal. Foolhardy, even. But may I remind you, he risked his life to rescue Aroha from the fire. Make no mistake, Hunapo is a hero! A brave warrior!'

'Like hell, he is!'

Many of the women stood on the tables, chanting and hurling insults.

'Hunapo out!'

'Tautaru out!'

'Justice for Aroha!'

'Just you wait, Hunapo. You'll get what's coming to you.'

'Get them out of here,' Tautaru said to Kaine. 'Before I have the lot of them shot.'

Kaine signalled to the heavies.

'Okay. Move it.' The men broke up the crowd and ushered them out of the tavern. 'The show's over.'

'You'll respect your Gang vice president if you know what's good for you,' Tautaru shouted after them. 'The prodigal daughter is coming home. Nobody defies the Māhiti Gang!'

Hunapo held his head up high when he followed Tautaru out of the tavern. Tautaru was a miserable bully, but he was still the most powerful man in the community. And Hunapo hadn't expected Tautaru to stand by him the way he did.

'You've got a bloody nerve saying you love Aroha,' a woman sneered as Hunapo walked past. 'You've slept with every whore in the district.'

'Not just whores,' another woman said. 'The bastard shagged my Jackie.'

'And my Amy.'

'Piss off!' Hunapo gave them the finger. With Tautaru's backing, he was untouchable.

❧

A group of half a dozen youths cornered Hunapo in the yard once Tautaru was out of sight.

'Party at my place Saturday night. To celebrate,' Hunapo said. 'There'll be free beer.'

None of them were smiling. What was wrong with them? Hadn't they heard him say *free beer*?

The boys moved closer and formed a circle around him. Hunapo took a step backwards. Why were they being so mean?

Rawiri, an eighteen-year-old skinhead, closed in on him. 'You'll go too far one of these days, Hunapo.'

Hemi gave a loud snort. 'You can do anything, and the old man lets you off.'

'But if we put a foot out of line, we get the bash,' Joe added, pumping his fist. 'It's not right, is it?'

'I've had the bash too. Believe me.' Hunapo lifted his shirt. 'I've got the scars to prove it.'

The boys didn't look impressed. Didn't they realise he was just as much of a bruiser as they were?

Thinking quickly, Hunapo decided he'd have to bluster his way out of the situation. It had always worked in the past. 'But then, what are a few scars? I'm invincible—'

'I wouldn't be so cocksure if I were you,' Rawiri said. 'Your time's running out!'

Hunapo began to sweat. 'What's this all about? We're mates, aren't we?'

'Watch your back!' Rawiri gave him a shove. 'We've got Tautaru's number, and when he's out of the way, there'll be nobody left to protect you.'

'You're joking. Of course you are.' Hunapo pretended to smile. 'You'll never topple Tautaru.'

Rawiri grabbed Hunapo and eyeballed him. 'Tautaru's Tyrants are finished.'

Hunapo blinked. 'Don't let the old man hear you say that. He hates that nickname.'

'Tautaru doesn't scare me. Long live the revolution!' Rawiri pushed Hunapo away and thrust his arm in the air with a victory sign.

The kids chanted in unison as they marched away.

Tautaru's Tyrants are dead! Long live the revolution!

Hunapo fell backwards and landed on an empty beer crate. Was this the rebellion that Tautaru was always on about? So the old man's ramblings weren't just a load of hot air. Those boys were mean—and ready for a fight.

Hunapo remained shaken when he met Tautaru for a lunchtime pint in the tavern the next day. Should he tell the old man what the boys had said? No. That would only send him into another rage.

'Friday we go to the hospital,' Tautaru said, 'and we bring Aroha home.'

'They won't let us in,' Hunapo said. 'I went to see Aroha, but a goon from hospital security threw me out.'

Tautaru took another swig of beer. 'Nobody stops me taking my daughter home.'

'I don't think she'll come back with me,' Hunapo said. 'I don't know why she can't see that I'm her future.'

'That's women for you,' Tautaru thumped Hunapo on the back. 'Wahine kore tuki! She'll come round—she's got no choice.'

Hunapo continued drinking all afternoon, long after Tautaru left on Gang business. He told anyone who'd listen how he saved Aroha from both the fire and a lifetime of misery with a slimy businessman.

'Amiri was full of shit,' Hunapo repeated time after time. 'Shit, shit, shit. And more shit.'

'Man, you're in your cups!' Chase helped him crawl out of the bar. 'Go home and sleep it off.'

Chapter Forty-Four

Aroha cried almost continuously in the days following Kāterina's visit. Her great aunt had given her permission to grieve. Everything came out. The anger, the rage, the bitterness. And the emptiness Aroha felt inside without Amiri.

In between bouts of misery, Aroha wondered about Kāterina's secret. What was she hiding? What could be so terrible that the old woman couldn't just spit it out? Why hadn't Kāterina come back to see her? She'd promised she would.

Aroha decided she'd ask the medical social worker, Anita Bennet, to get in touch with Kāterina. Anita was a master of gentle persuasion. If anyone could convince Kāterina to visit again, it was Anita.

'Kāterina's quite a character, isn't she?' Anita said. 'She's helped you to mourn and let your emotions out. I'll try to find time to go out and see her, but it's difficult with her living out in the forest. In the meantime …' Anita's words petered out.

Aroha could see she was uncomfortable. This normally outgoing social worker crouched awkwardly on the edge of the bed. Surely it couldn't be yet more trouble. Had the doctors found cancer and sent her to break the news?

'What?' Aroha said.

'Dr Jenkins feels you're almost ready to go home,' Anita said.

Aroha heaved a sigh of relief. 'That's good news, isn't it?'

Anita paused. 'Kind of.'

Aroha's breathing quickened. She'd seen that look before. It *was* bad news. 'Something's wrong. Just tell me.'

'I'm sorry, Aroha.' Anita looked away, avoiding eye contact. 'Amiri died intestate.'

'Intestate?' Aroha bit her lip and swallowed hard. 'What does that mean?'

Anita took a deep breath. 'The repercussions are—well, they're far reaching. All your property was solely in Amiri's name. The house, together with all his assets, will be transferred to the Public Trust for disposal and to settle any outstanding debts.'

Aroha gripped the iron sides of her hospital bed. 'You mean I'm homeless?'

'I'm afraid you are.'

Aroha shook her head and stared at Anita. 'But I was his *wife.*'

'Well actually, you *weren't,*' Anita said, 'at least, not in law.'

Aroha sobbed as Anita explained that because the shooting occurred *before* they took their vows and signed the register, the service had no legal standing. 'It's such a pity you didn't complete the marriage after your surgery. As it is, with a relationship of such short duration, you have no claim on Amiri's estate.'

Nowhere to go and nobody to take care of me. Aroha stared into the distance after Anita had left. *What's to become of me?* Aroha wanted to see Kāterina more than ever before. Perhaps she could live with her great aunt.

'No way will the doctors allow that,' Anita said when she returned the next morning. 'Not in that dirty old caravan in the middle of nowhere. Your burns are still healing.'

'So what am I going to do?' Aroha said. 'The caravan would be better than living on the street.'

'I've arranged temporary accommodation at a shelter,' Anita said. 'Just until we can find something more permanent.'

'Temporary accommodation at a shelter?' Aroha screwed her eyes shut. 'What kind of hell is that?'

'It won't be that bad,' Anita said. 'There'll be other women there with similar experiences. You'll make new friends, and I'll come and see you regularly. I'm sure Kāterina will too.'

New friends? Similar experiences? Aroha sank back on her pillow. 'I bet none of them have been through what I've endured the past few months. Or my entire life, come to that.'

        David Whittet

'You'd be surprised,' Anita said. 'Some of my clients have had it rough.'

'Rough?' Aroha shook her head. 'That doesn't begin to describe my life.'

'Maybe not,' Anita said. 'Look, I'm not trying to diminish your suffering, but you'll meet women with some pretty harrowing stories.'

'Such as?'

'Rape victims. Domestic violence. Survivors of child abuse.' Anita reached out and placed a hand on Aroha's. 'You'll find strength in one another's stories.'

'Well, it's not the fresh start I dreamt about. That's for sure.' Aroha sat up and dried her eyes. 'But at least it's away from the Gang.'

What would it be like, sharing experiences with other women who were struggling? Aroha lay awake all night, thinking about it. Perhaps Anita was right. The women could support one another.

Aroha was just drifting off to sleep when a sound disturbed her. Footsteps. She rolled over. It was probably the nurse doing the early morning medicine round. Aroha tried to doze again, but there was something all too familiar about those thudding steps. Her heart raced. She'd know that walk anywhere. Her eyes scanned the ward for an escape route. Too late. Tautaru burst into the ward and marched up to Aroha's bed. Hunapo followed sheepishly behind him.

'Get up and get dressed,' Tautaru said, his thundering voice waking the other patients. 'You're coming home.'

'It's time, Aroha,' Hunapo said, pushing past Tautaru to put his arm on her shoulder. 'Come back with me.'

'Get away from me, both of you.' Aroha pulled herself up to confront them. 'I never want to see you again, Hunapo. You're a murderer!'

Tautaru held a finger to his lips. 'Shut it. No more of that crap.' He glanced around at the stunned patients. 'And definitely not in here.'

Aroha glared at her father. 'Hunapo killed Amiri and you know it!'

Hunapo edged forward again, with a frown on his brow. 'No, Aroha, you've got it wrong.'

'Shut it!' Aroha held her side and sank back on her pillow, exhausted. 'I'm not listening.'

Tautaru stamped his hobnail boot on the floor. 'If you won't go with Hunapo, you'll come to my place first. You'll stay with me until you're ready to go back to your true husband.'

'No, I won't,' Aroha shot back. 'That monster is *not* my husband. He *killed* my husband.'

Aroha pulled away when Tautaru grabbed hold of her arm. She fumbled for her nurse call button with her free hand.

'I'm getting help,' she said.

Hunapo prised the alarm from her fist. 'There's no need for that.'

To Aroha's relief, the ward sister heard the commotion and strode over.

The sister eyeballed Tautaru. 'What do you think you're doing? This is a hospital.'

Tautaru glared back at her. 'I am here to take my daughter home.'

'That's not the arrangement we've made for her,' the sister said. 'I must consult the doctor.' She pointed a finger at Tautaru's jacket. 'And may I remind you, we do not permit gang patches on Health Board properties. I must ask you to leave.'

Tautaru spat on the floor. 'We're going. Come on, Aroha. Get your things together.'

'She is not leaving until I have discussed it with the medical team.' The sister stood between Tautaru and Aroha, her eyes still fixed on his. 'If you continue to disrupt my ward, I will call hospital security.'

Tautaru rubbed his hands together. 'I have my own security outside. Shall I bring them in?'

'You don't scare me,' the sister said.

'Really?' Tautaru grabbed her name badge. 'Amanda Edmonds. I know your old man.'

    David Whittet

'Get off me. I told you, I will not tolerate this behaviour on my ward.'

Tautaru pushed closer, intimidating her with his bulk. 'Your old man owes me money. Perhaps you'd like my men to pay him a visit?'

'Stop it.' Aroha couldn't let her father take it out on the ward sister. Holding her chest, Aroha struggled out of bed and started to gather her few possessions. 'It's all right, Sister Edmonds. I'll go. I don't want any trouble.'

Hunapo tried to help Aroha to pack, but she shoved him away.

She turned to her father. 'I'll go home with you, but I will never go back to Hunapo. *Never!*'

'Are you sure you know what you're doing, Aroha?' Sister Edmonds asked. 'You must sign a "discharge against medical advice" statement.'

Aroha's hand shook when the sister handed her the form.

I'm signing my own death warrant. 'Yes. I'll be all right.'

'I don't think you will be,' Sister Edmonds said, picking up the pen when Aroha dropped it for the second time.

'There you are. She's signed it.' Tautaru frogmarched Aroha out of the ward, giving Sister Edmonds the finger as they left.

Aroha thought she would pass out when Tautaru bundled her into the back of his ute. She heard him talking to Hunapo and, to her relief, Hunapo headed off in his own car.

Tautaru whistled as he reversed the ute and began the long drive back to his place. He'd won. Crushed her spirit and punished her disobedience. Aroha cringed when the ute finally swung into the distressingly familiar backyard. Her dream of escape from the Gang was once again in tatters.

Chapter Forty-Five

Could life back at Tautaru's place possibly be worse than before? The sinking feeling when Aroha set eyes on Manaia, her father's latest live-in lover, told her it would be much, much harder.

A coarse forty-year-old, Manaia was at the house awaiting their arrival. She was a piece of work, cigarette hanging out of her mouth and dressed like an overripe teenager in a tight red miniskirt and fishnet stockings.

'The prodigal daughter has returned,' Tautaru said. 'Keep your eyes on her, Manaia. Make sure she earns her keep and don't take any crap.'

'Don't worry.' Manaia took a drag on her smoke and eyeballed Aroha. 'I'll make sure she pulls her weight.'

Aroha glanced around the kitchen. She'd never seen it so dirty. Layers of grime in the sink. Stacks of unwashed dishes. It would break Ngaio's heart to see her kitchen in such a state. Rewa, too. She had kept the house clean and tidy.

'What happened to Rewa?' Aroha asked.

'That frigid bitch?' Manaia grinned at Tautaru and ran her fingers over his chest. 'Threw her out, didn't you, Totes? Good riddance. You deserve better than her drooping tits and flabby arse.'

Aroha's jaw dropped. How dare she? Rewa wasn't frigid. And anyway, sagging boobs and a less than perfect bum were preferable to looking like mutton dressed up as lamb. But Manaia obviously turned Tautaru on. He was drooling at the mouth. Breasts and buttocks. Were they all her father thought women were good for?

And *Totes!* Aroha would have laughed if she didn't want to cry. If anyone else called her father that, they'd be history.

Tautaru grabbed a beer from the fridge and made for the back door. 'You're in charge, Manaia.' He turned to Aroha. 'And you do as you're told.'

 David Whittet

Manaia lounged on a kitchen chair after he'd gone, her roll-up smudging her gaudy lipstick.

Aroha stood with her mouth still wide open.

'What are you gawping at?' Manaia flicked her ash in Aroha's face. 'The floor needs sweeping. Get on with it.'

'I'm not bloody Cinderella,' Aroha said. 'Do it yourself.'

'And I'm no frigging fairy godmother!' Manaia thrust a broom into Aroha's hand. 'You'll get to work if you know what's good for you.'

Lazy cow. Aroha began to sweep the kitchen floor. Tautaru and Manaia. What a toxic pair. At least when Rewa was with Tautaru, there was someone in the house on her side. *Rewa had a heart. She stood up for me when it counted.* Manaia was just a spiteful tart. Yes, everything was going to be worse than before.

Tautaru came back in to fetch another beer. He sat down at the table and read the newspaper.

Aroha made a start on cooking dinner. If the first couple of days back home were anything to go by, she wouldn't last a week without either going mad or throttling somebody. She had to have it out with her father and the sooner, the better.

Aroha took a deep breath. 'I'm never going back to Hunapo. Get that into your head. He tried to kill me.' Her eyes locked on his. 'Why do you let him get away with it? Don't you care about me?'

'Hunapo's taught you a valuable lesson in life,' Tautaru said. 'A lesson you'll do well to remember.'

'Not that bullshit again,' Aroha shot back. 'You don't believe it any more than I do. Hunapo's a heartless killer. He didn't think twice about shooting me or burning my husband alive!'

'Paru toto! Bloody nonsense!' Tautaru said. 'The cops couldn't pin anything on Hunapo. You know that. And even if it was Hunapo, he had good reason.'

'You may get away with spinning that garbage to your cronies, but not to me!' Aroha said. 'The women didn't believe it either. I heard they gave you a rough ride.'

Tautaru raised a fist. 'I'm warning you.'

'Yes, listen to your father!' Manaia sidled up to Tautaru and glared at Aroha.

'Why pretend?' Aroha shook her head and cut her finger as she peeled potatoes at the kitchen sink. 'Damn!' She flinched and rinsed the laceration under the tap. 'We all know it was only your bent lawyers that got him off!'

'He had to punish you,' Tautaru said. 'You betrayed the Gang. You were a traitor to Hunapo!'

'Yes, Judas!' Manaia added.

'And I'm not staying here either.' Aroha pointed at Manaia. 'Not with her gloating.'

Tautaru put down the newspaper. 'People came from all over to see you and Hunapo married. We've already lost face with you taking off with some bloody arse-licker first chance you got.'

'Yes, *an arse-licker!*' Manaia echoed.

'Shut up, Manaia. You're not a bloody parrot.' Aroha snorted and turned on her father. 'You forced me into that ceremony. I never wanted to be any part of it!'

'Your marriage to Hunapo still matters to the Gang,' Tautaru said. 'You have to stay with him.'

Aroha rolled her eyes. 'No way! I can't believe you expect me to live with the man who killed my husband.'

'Your husband!' Tautaru leant back and laughed. 'The son of a bitch never got to be your husband, did he? Hunapo made it just in time to stop you marrying that piece of tūtae and committing bigamy.'

'*Bigamy?* What balls!' Aroha abandoned chopping the vegetables and wrapped a tea towel around her bleeding hand. 'Hunapo and I weren't even legally married! Call that ridiculous ceremony a wedding? Just some horrid tattoos and wailing women.'

Tautaru got up from the kitchen table and slapped her face. 'You need to learn respect, and fast. Those tattoos are sacred to the Gang. More so than anything in a civil ceremony!' He pointed to the tā moko on Aroha's chin. 'That means you belong to Hunapo forever, bonded by blood. Blood and ink. Gang unions are for life. Nobody can undo them.'

 David Whittet

'What about Hunapo and all his girlfriends?' Aroha threw her hands in the air. 'He's allowed as many girls as he likes, but I'm not—'

Tautaru cut her short. 'You will honour Hunapo. I won't have you shirking your duty.'

'Yes. *Honour. Duty,*' Manaia repeated.

Aroha slammed her hand on the bench. 'You can't make me. I don't owe you anything. I don't owe Hunapo anything either.'

Tautaru gave her another slap. 'You will do whatever I tell you. And that's the last time you answer me back.'

He pushed her against the kitchen sink and charged off, slamming the door behind him.

Manaia lit another cigarette and sneered. 'That told you. Did he hurt you?' She stood up and blew more smoke in Aroha's face. 'You'd better learn how to behave; else you'll be black and blue!'

'Just leave me alone.' Aroha picked up her jacket. 'I'm going for a walk. You can finish making dinner.'

Manaia grabbed Aroha's arm. 'Don't turn your back on me. I'm your boss. Didn't you hear what Totes said?'

'Let go of me,' Aroha said, 'and stop calling my father by that ridiculous name.'

Manaia's voice rose to a screech. 'You're a slut. And you're only back here because your fancy man didn't love you enough to write a will! He left you *nothing!* Because you're *nothing.*'

Aroha pulled herself free. 'So I'm nothing, am I?' She grabbed a carving knife from the drawer and pointed it at Manaia. 'Well, at least I'm not a gangster's whore!'

Manaia staggered against the bench. 'Get away from me!'

Aroha watched Manaia's eyes bulge as the blade approached her throat.

'Totes! *Totes!*' Manaia screamed. 'Come quick! She's gone mad!'

For a dreadful moment, Aroha almost believed she could kill the shameful scrubber. Terrified by an urge totally alien to her nature, Aroha's hand shook. No. She couldn't lower herself to the gangsters' level. Besides, Manaia wasn't worth a murder conviction. Aroha dropped the knife onto the floor and left through the back door.

'You should be locked up,' Manaia called after her, 'and I'll make sure they throw away the key! Where the hell are you, Tautaru?'

Aroha couldn't believe what she'd done. She stared down at her feet as she wandered through the township. What had the Gang reduced her to? Had her father driven her to this? How could she think of harming another human being? Even someone as loathsome as Manaia.

The women elders were filing into the marae. Aroha paused outside. Perhaps she should join them. They'd understand and support her.

No. Aroha was too ashamed to face anyone.

She was about to leave when she heard Lilly's voice coming from the marae. What was Lilly saying? Aroha edged closer and put her ear against the door. The women were talking about her. Something about a *chain reaction*. What on earth was that? And what did it have to do with her?

David Whittet

Chapter Forty-Six

'We started it,' Lilly said. 'We have to put it right.'

Squatting on the wooden floor of the marae, the women huddled together and nodded in support.

Lilly glanced up at Moana, who sat on the podium away from the other elders. Mo was a hard-faced woman, and she didn't show a glimmer of emotion. Lilly sighed. That was typical of Moana.

'We started a chain reaction,' Lilly continued. 'A chain reaction that's destroyed Aroha. We should all be ashamed of ourselves.'

Lilly deeply regretted her part in the women's conspiracy to contrive the marriage between Aroha and Hunapo. She should never have let Moana bully her into harassing Ngaio. Lilly convinced herself it was that fraught confrontation which began the downhill spiral.

'I'm with Lilly,' Evie said. 'This is our fault.'

'I was against Mo's plan from the start, if you remember,' Pania said. 'But would any of you listen to me?'

'Evie and I were against it too,' Lilly said. 'I wish to God we'd stopped it.'

The women chorused their agreement.

'Hear, hear!'

'Me too.'

'Well said, Lilly.'

Moana stood up and faced the women. 'We're all sad for Aroha. Of course we are. But we did what we had to do and we're all better off. We've got money in our pockets, haven't we?'

'Yes, but at what cost?' Lilly couldn't believe what she'd just heard and jumped to her feet. 'You said it would bring everyone back together. But it's split the community apart. Ngaio's gone. Maahanga's gone. Hunapo's driven to a life of crime. We've ruined Aroha's life.'

'That's right, Mo,' Rona said. 'None of us would have agreed to your scheme if we'd known what it would do to Aroha.'

Moana shrugged half-heartedly. 'It worked, didn't it? Perhaps you've forgotten. When Tautaru and Maahanga were fighting, we were all losing money. Once Maahanga buggered off to Wairoa, Tautaru went back to doing what the Gang's good at: making money. And that's put food on the table for our kids.'

'Yes, but …' Lilly's mouth dried up, and she slumped to the floor. 'I'll never understand you, Mo. Don't you care about Aroha? And Ngaio?'

Moana didn't answer. She just glared at the women. Lilly was sure the venom in Moana's eyes was directed solely at her. Had Mo no heart?

Lilly felt a hand on her shoulder. Thank God for Evie.

'Olivia too,' Evie said, stroking Lilly's back. 'Does anyone know what happened to her?'

'I heard Ngaio's at a women's refuge up the coast,' Pania said. 'But as for Olivia—' she mimicked slitting her throat '—well, we all know what happens when you cross Tautaru.'

'You think she's dead?' Lilly said.

Pania nodded.

Lilly closed her eyes. Why hadn't she stood up before, when it really mattered? 'If she is, then we signed her death warrant.'

Everyone was silent. Evie ran her fingers through Lilly's hair.

Eventually, Pania spoke up. 'I knew this would end in disaster. The blood's on your hands, Mo.'

'Collateral damage,' Moana said. 'I don't know why you're all so miserable. You've got money in your pockets again. Thanks to me.'

Collateral damage! 'Take that back, Mo,' Lilly said, 'or I'm leaving the women's group.'

'Count me out too,' Evie said, still embracing Lilly.

 David Whittet

The rest of the women joined in, jeering at Moana.

'Bloody hell, Mo! That's harsh, even by your standards. These are people, not your playthings.'

'You're a bitch, Mo. Look after number one! Is that all you care about?'

Moana drew herself up to full height. 'I call this meeting to a close.' She smoothed down her skirt, jumped off the podium and marched out of the marae.

Pania gave her the finger as she left. The women gazed at each other in complete silence.

Lilly raised her head, her voice croaking. 'The least we can do is to help Aroha get some closure. We should take her to Amiri's tangi. Give her a chance to say goodbye.'

'Surely the funeral was long ago,' Evie said, squeezing Lilly's hand. 'It's months since the fire.'

'Na,' Pania said, raising an eyebrow. 'They couldn't find anything to bury. Didn't you read about it in the paper?'

The women shook their heads.

Pania took a newspaper out of her bag and read out the headline: *'Bizarre Twist to the Amiri Hollis Saga. The family of the controversial business leader plan to hold his funeral at the very church where his bride fell victim to a near-fatal gang shooting during their wedding ceremony.'* She put down the paper. 'But the real story's even juicier. Better than anything you'll read in the *New Zealand Herald*.'

Lilly crossed her arms. *Trust Pania to know. She's a rubberneck without equal.* 'Go on, Pania. Spill. I can see you're dying to tell us.'

Pania rubbed her palms together and told the women how the authorities searched the burnt-out shell for Amiri's body and clues as to the cause of the fire. The fire investigators were sure the fire was deliberate, with flame accelerants being used. Still, they never found the remains of an incendiary device, and the extent of the damage was such that they could not prove arson.

'So that's how Hunapo got off,' Lilly grunted. 'Bastard!'

'More like one of Tautaru's bent lawyers,' one of the elders said.

The women were full of questions.

'So they never found Amiri's body?'

'Can they have a tangi without a body?'

'And why go back to that church? With all those terrible memories?'

Pania raised her arm to silence them and continue her story. 'They found some charred bones. The pathologist said they were Amiri's, and the coroner ruled death by misadventure.'

'How did they know they were Amiri's bones?' Evie asked. 'Surely they could have been anybody's.'

'Some fancy new testing they do now,' Pania said. 'DNA, they call it. Don't ask me how it works, but it was enough for the coroner.'

'So what about the funeral?' Lilly said.

'That's where the story gets really entertaining.' Pania clapped her hands together. 'The vultures were out the minute Amiri died. Everyone claimed he owed them money. Loan sharks with final demands. Legal threats. Everyone determined to get their pound of flesh from the family.'

Serves the buggers right, Lilly thought, grinning to herself. She'd half a mind to make up a claim herself just to spite them. Amiri's family had been so nasty to Aroha.

'So I guess they decided that having the funeral out in the wop wops would keep it under the radar,' Pania concluded. 'I mean, nobody in their right mind would want to go back to that church.'

Lilly sat up and pressed her hands against her cheeks. 'We have to take Aroha to the tangi. Otherwise, she'll never be able to move on.'

'Are you sure?' Evie stared at Lilly and shook her head. 'I don't think Aroha will ever set foot in that church again.'

'She will—if we're with her.' Lilly gazed at the women's shocked faces. 'It might just give her the closure she needs.'

Evie twitched. 'It might send her over the edge.'

'Anyway, it's impossible.' Pania gave a dismissive wave of her hand. 'Tautaru won't let her out of the house. Never mind let her go to the tangi.'

 David Whittet

Evie gave Lilly's hand another squeeze. 'If you're sure it's the right thing to do, I'll take care of Tautaru.' She turned to Pania. 'You say the funeral's next Friday? There's a three-day women's hui in Hamilton that weekend. We tell Tautaru we're taking her to that.'

Pania raised her eyebrows. 'You think the bastard will swallow it?'

❧

Lilly expected an explosion when Evie asked Tautaru if they could take Aroha to the hui. He simply put down his beer bottle and grinned at them.

'Do you take me for a complete idiot? Women's hui indeed. I know what you're up to.'

Tautaru picked the newspaper off the kitchen table and pointed to the headline: *Burnt Business Tycoon's Funeral this Friday in the Coromandel.*

Lilly shrank back. If he knew, why wasn't he shouting his mouth off?

Evie shook. 'We weren't trying to … we didn't mean to … lie to you …'

Evie's voice dribbled to a standstill, drowned by the sound of Aroha and Manaia screaming at each other in the next room.

'Bloody shut up, the pair of you!' Tautaru yelled through the door. He turned back to Evie and Lilly. 'You can take her. At least I'll have a few days' peace from those two bitching.'

Gang Girl 339

Chapter Forty-Seven

St Andrew's Church, Winter 1990.

'Firing squads! *Firing squads!*' Aroha held her hands over her ears as Lilly and Evie helped her through the churchyard.

Aroha glimpsed Amiri's father, William, when they entered the church, and she immediately ducked. *Don't let him see me.* William was talking to a man who didn't sound at all happy. She guessed it was a reporter.

'I understand your son died intestate and left a bunch of unpaid bills,' the man said.

She heard Amelia's voice. 'Our boy would never have owed any money.'

William's voice again. 'No comment. Now, will you please leave us to grieve in peace?'

Aroha raised her head and saw the reporter wagging a finger in William's face. 'There's more to this story than meets the eye and I'm going to sniff it out!'

Turning away to avoid catching William's eye, Aroha began panting as Lilly led her into the church. Evie guided her towards a pew. It was only months since William walked her down the aisle to the strains of Mendelssohn's *Wedding March.* Now a funereal dirge on the organ temporarily blotted out the sound of gunfire in Aroha's mind.

The Reverend Ranganui Ropata came to greet them. 'Oh, Aroha. It's so good to see you again.' He took her hand and squeezed it. 'I've been praying for you.'

Aroha looked up at his white cassock. Pure white. Except it wasn't. Suddenly it turned bright red before her eyes. Covered in blood—her blood.

She felt the bump when she hit the floor. Everything else was a blur. She was vaguely aware of Lilly holding her hand and Reverend Ropata carrying her

     David Whittet

into the vestry. But all she could see was blood. *Everywhere.*

Aroha stirred. She heard the minister give her a blessing. But it was another familiar voice that brought her back to life.

'Aroha! Are you all right?'

'Errol Troy!' Aroha pulled herself up and held onto his arm. 'Thank God you're here.'

Errol helped her stagger to her feet. 'You look dreadful! What's happened? Surely Amiri's family are looking after you?'

Aroha shook her head. 'No. They don't even want me to be here.'

'What?'

'They blame me for—everything.'

'How could they?' Errol headed towards the vestry door. 'I'll talk to them.'

Aroha clutched him even more tightly. 'No, Errol. Please don't. It'll only make things worse.' She turned to Lilly and Evie. 'I want you to take me home.'

Lilly stroked her hand. 'No. You can't run away. You need to see this through.'

'I can't go back in there,' Aroha said.

Evie gave her a hug. 'You've as much right as they have to say goodbye to Amiri.'

Aroha shook. 'I can't face them.'

'Of course you can.' Errol gave her a firm look. 'Take my hand. We're going into the church, and you are going to hold your head up high.'

Aroha's eyes caught Amelia's as Errol led her to a pew.

'Take some deep breaths,' Lilly urged, sitting down next to them. 'You're going to be fine.'

'Am I?' That was easy for Lilly to say. Amelia wasn't glaring at her. Amiri's sisters, Fonella and Grace, were chatting to each other. Were they talking about her? Aroha had been so close to Fonella. Was Grace poisoning Fonella against her like the rest of Amiri's family?

Aroha looked down at her feet. She recognised a voice behind her. It was the reporter who had accosted William outside the church. Now he was boasting to a colleague how he was going to expose Amiri as a fraud.

Aroha groaned. 'You were his business partner,' she whispered in Errol's ear. 'All these claims that Amiri owed money—tell me they're not true?'

'Of course they aren't. He was at the top of his game. I can vouch for that. We'd pulled off some major deals. Now everyone wants a share of the pie.'

'And these wretched reporters, they won't find anything?'

Errol put his arm around Aroha's shoulder. 'No. Stop worrying.'

Reverend Ropata preached about a life cut tragically short by a horrific disaster. Aroha swallowed when Errol got up to deliver a eulogy.

'Don't leave me,' she whispered.

Lilly held her hand. 'Let him go. He's going to put things right.'

Errol spoke of a man of vision, an entrepreneur who was about to bring a life-changing health product to the world when he died. After vowing to carry on his colleague's legacy, Errol described how Amiri had found genuine love with Aroha.

'In all the years I knew Amiri,' Errol said, 'I never saw him as happy as when he met Aroha.'

Aroha shuddered and dug her fingernails into Lilly's hands. She could feel the hatred radiating from Amelia and William.

'I'd like to invite Aroha to say a few words,' Errol concluded.

'No, Errol.'

Aroha hid her face with her hands and slumped her head against Lilly's. How could he do this to her? Didn't he understand how she felt?

A commotion at the front of the church made Aroha lift her head.

'Let go of me, Mum!' It was Fonella, pushing past Amelia. Aroha felt her chest tighten.

Standing in front of the altar, Fonella took a deep breath and addressed the congregation. 'We can all see that Aroha is too distressed to speak. So I would like to say something on her behalf. In Aroha, my dear brother, Amiri, had found his true soulmate. He loved her with all his heart, and he wanted to spend the rest of his life with her.'

            David Whittet

The love in Fonella's eyes brought tears to Aroha's. Fonella's words, together with Errol's, were the kindest she'd heard in a long time. The warm feeling in her heart rapidly disappeared when Amelia jumped to her feet.

'Get back here, Fonella,' Amelia hissed, her eyes bulging in their sockets.

'Butt out, Mum,' Fonella said. 'Amiri would have sacrificed everything for Aroha, and he'd have wanted us to look after her. You know he would.'

Amelia pointed a finger at Aroha. 'She wasn't even his wife.'

Aroha covered her ears. She couldn't bear any more. Her mind went back to that awful interview with the hospital social worker. Amelia was right. Aroha wasn't Amiri's wife. At least—not legally.

'They were husband and wife in the sight of God,' Reverend Ropata declared from the pulpit. 'I saw the love in their eyes at the wedding. What God has joined, let no man put asunder.'

'This is the woman who killed our precious son!' William growled. 'Her gangster boyfriend started the fire and burnt our beloved Amiri alive.'

'Stop it, Dad!' Fonella returned to her seat, tears in her eyes. 'None of that was Aroha's fault! The fire nearly killed her too! She was a victim!'

'Like hell she was!' William said.

'You are in the house of God.' Reverend Ropata glared at Amelia and William. 'Will you please show respect?'

When Reverend Ropata finished the blessing, Aroha wanted nothing more than to get out of the church.

'I need some air,' she gasped, slipping past Errol and running down the aisle to the door.

Fonella caught up and embraced her. 'Don't go.'

Aroha returned the hug. 'Thank you for what you said. But I don't deserve it.'

'You do. You made Amiri happy. He was a different man when he was with you.'

Aroha felt a tug as the two women hugged. Grace was trying to pull them apart.

'Sis!' Grace said to Fonella. 'You're going to get both of us grounded.'

Then came Amelia's booming voice. 'Come here this instant, Fonella.'

'No! Aroha is my friend.' Fonella clung to Aroha with one hand and fought off her mother with the other. 'Amiri wouldn't have wanted this.'

Amelia turned to William. 'Do something, Bill! Don't just stand there! Stop them!'

'Go,' Aroha whispered in Fonella's ear. 'I don't want to get you into trouble.'

To Aroha's relief, Errol took over and stood in front of William and Amelia. 'That's enough. Amiri was my friend, and he deserves better than you two brawling at his funeral.' He took Aroha's arm. 'It's all right. It's over.'

But it wasn't over. Aroha knew that. She still had to get through the burial at the cemetery.

The winter chill and the stark silhouette of the trees added to the melancholic atmosphere in the graveyard. Aroha stood back as the mourners gathered around the freshly dug grave. Lilly and Evie beckoned her to come forward, but she didn't want to be any closer. It wasn't Amiri in that coffin; it was just a few of his burnt bones. She watched a chaffinch perch on a tombstone as Reverend Ropata delivered the prayer of committal.

'Forasmuch as it hath pleased Almighty God, in His great mercy, to take unto himself the soul of our dear brother Amiri here departed. We, therefore, commit his body to the ground; earth to earth, ashes to ashes, dust to dust.'

Aroha took another step backwards. Watching the pallbearers lower the coffin, suddenly everything felt real. Those *were* the mortal remains of the man she loved in that casket.

Errol took her arm and led her to the graveside. 'You need to be part of this, Aroha.'

She could hear Amelia muttering to William.

'Why can't she just leave?' Amelia said. 'She's got some bloody gall, standing there all innocent.' She glared at Aroha. 'You and your boyfriend had it all planned, didn't you? Murderers!'

                    David Whittet

The noise frightened the chaffinch, and it flew away.

Aroha bowed her head. A confrontation like this was exactly what she'd wanted to avoid. Why couldn't Errol have left her to hide in the background?

'Hunapo's not my boyfriend,' Aroha said as calmly as she could. 'Why won't you believe it? I begged him to leave me in the fire. I just wanted to die with Amiri!'

'You expect us to believe that?' William said.

'I believe her,' Fonella said, turning on her parents. 'You should too. Stop being so nasty. Let Amiri rest in peace and allow the woman he loved to grieve for him.'

Bless you, Fonella. Aroha mouthed the words. She lifted her head and their eyes met momentarily.

Reverend Ropata took William and Amelia aside. 'Your daughter is right. Amiri would not have wanted a scene like this. Please remember, we are still on consecrated ground and in the presence of God.'

Amelia grunted at the minister. 'I don't know why you're defending her.'

Lilly pushed forward and tugged on Amelia's arm. 'I know you're grieving, but Aroha is hurting too.'

Aroha looked up at the sky and watched the sun sink behind the tall tōtara trees. The wind made a swishing noise as it blew through the branches. A strange, comforting sound. Was it the voice of Amiri's departing soul?

Reverend Ropata read a closing prayer. Errol gathered a handful of soil and passed it to Aroha to throw onto the coffin. As she took the earth in her palm, Aroha felt her head swimming. The minister's voice became a distant echo in the fog of her mind. She leant forward to sprinkle the soil on Amiri's casket, then collapsed into Lilly's arms.

As she came round, a cold easterly breeze blew across Aroha's face. The East Wind had brought Amiri to her and now it was taking him away. The tall, dark stranger who had arrived shrouded in mystery had left her just as dramatically.

Chapter Forty-Eight

Family hostility. A graveside brawl. Not a hope of saying goodbye. Aroha knew Lilly and Evie had meant well but going back to the church had been a mistake. Closure felt further away than ever, and Aroha wished she'd stayed home.

As the old bus rattled down the country lanes towards Rere, it occurred to Aroha that she didn't have a *home*. She was back at Tautaru's place under duress, and she would *never* call Hunapo's pad home.

Errol Troy had made promises when he saw her off. 'I'm going sort out those shysters at the Public Trust. It's a bloody disgrace, robbing you of your inheritance. Whatever happened to natural justice?' He turned to Lilly and Evie as they followed Aroha onto the bus. 'Look after her. Safe journey!'

Like Lilly and Evie, Errol meant well. Sort out the Public Trust? Get her money and a new home? Aroha knew that was near impossible. And as for his promise to bring down the Gang, Amiri had tried to take them on and had failed. Errol would fail too. So would anyone else.

A group of unwashed farmhands sat behind her and kept kicking the back of her seat. The smell of stale sweat made her feel sick. She held her nose until, to her immense relief, the driver dropped the men off at their workplace.

Both Lilly and Evie had fallen asleep, and Aroha wished she could too. She felt painfully awake as the bus bounced over every single pothole. Her life was going nowhere. She stared out of the window. Each lurch around a winding corner brought her closer to the Gang and endless misery once more. The hope of a better life had died with Amiri.

Lilly stirred. 'Are we nearly there?'

Aroha shook her head. 'We've just passed Ohope.'

'Ohope?' Lilly groaned. 'I thought we were further along than that. My bum's numb already.' She cuddled up closer to Aroha on the uncomfortable bus seat. 'Your mother would've been so proud of you today.'

Aroha looked away. Her mother had been in her thoughts over the past few days. Ngaio had been right about Hunapo from the start. She said Hunapo would ruin her life, and he had. Aroha wondered what Ngaio would have thought of Amiri. Might things have been different if her mother was still around? If Ngaio were here today, perhaps she could have talked to Amelia, mother to mother, and helped her to understand.

Lilly took a deep breath and continued. 'I wish Ngaio could be here for you. I know how much you miss her.' Lilly paused and stroked Aroha's hair. 'Ngaio would have known how to comfort you today.'

'She would have held my hand,' Aroha murmured, her voice scarcely audible over the bus's raucous engine. 'The way she always did.'

'If only we could find her,' Lilly said.

'She's dead.' Aroha blinked back a tear. 'My father killed her. I'm sure of it. Why else would my mother have disappeared without saying goodbye?'

'You don't know that,' Lilly said. 'There could have been another reason.'

Aroha shook her head. 'She wouldn't have left me if she had a choice. Not when I was only twelve.'

The bus swerved, and Evie woke up. 'We're here for you, Aroha,' she said. 'Lilly and I are your friends. We're going to look after you and put things right.'

If only you could. Aroha smiled at them, then closed her eyes. A couple of hours and they'd be back in Rere. She knew Hunapo would be waiting to lay into her the moment she stepped off the bus.

And he was.

'Go away, Hunapo. Can't you see I'm exhausted.'

'Aroha! I've been waiting for you!' Hunapo swayed from side to side as he tried to grab hold of her.

Evie dragged him away. 'Shove off. You're drunk.'

'You're a disgrace, Hunapo.' Lilly put her arm around Aroha and led her down the street.

'I'm not giving up on you, Aroha!' Hunapo yelled after her.

Aroha groaned. 'Will he ever leave me alone?'

'Give him time.' Lilly squeezed her hand. 'Once he finds another girl, you'll never see him.'

Aroha stopped abruptly and shuddered. 'I don't think so. He's obsessed with me. I can't imagine why, but he is. Totally obsessed.' She looked back and watched Hunapo stagger into the tavern. 'He always said he'd kill me rather than see me with someone else.'

'Well, he tried, didn't he?' Lilly said. 'And he failed.'

'Yes,' Aroha said, following Lilly to Tautaru's place. 'But that didn't stop him getting rid of Amiri.'

❦

Aroha was loading the washing machine when Hunapo burst into the kitchen the next morning. She knew what he was going to say before he opened his mouth.

'I don't understand why you're so mean to me!'

'Go away, Hunapo.'

Aroha poured the detergent into the machine and set it going.

Hunapo edged closer to her. 'We've got history. Remember? We used to have such a good time together.'

'That was before you murdered my husband!' Aroha pushed him aside as she continued sorting the laundry. 'You're a monster. Get away from me!'

'You've got it all wrong. I didn't kill the son of a bitch.'

Aroha cut him off. 'You burnt him alive and you're not the least bit sorry.'

'I'm not sorry I saved your life.' Hunapo gave a long, almost inaudible sigh. 'It wasn't me who started the fire. I heard the Gang were after Amiri's blood—and they weren't the only ones. That put you in danger too. I wanted to protect you.'

     David Whittet

Aroha shook her head. 'I'm not listening to any more.'

'The cops know I didn't do it. They let me go.'

'Yeah.' Aroha dumped a pile of clothes on the kitchen table. 'Once my father got one of his crooked lawyers on to them.'

'Kāterina believes me,' Hunapo said.

'She'd believe anything,' Aroha said. 'Her head's in the clouds.'

'You're wrong. It was Kāterina who found out about Amiri's enemies. Just as well she did. If I hadn't been there, you'd both have died.'

'I wish you'd left me to die,' Aroha said. 'Death would be preferable to the hell I'm living now.'

'Don't say that.' Hunapo slumped on a chair. He rolled up his sleeves and stroked the burns on his arms. 'They hurt like hell. But they were worth it. For you.'

Aroha went to fetch the ironing board. She'd cried for the horrific scars his father had given him when they were kids. She wouldn't waste any sympathy on his self-inflicted injuries.

He was still nursing his arms when she came back with the iron. 'Cover them up. You're no bloody hero.'

Tautaru strode into the kitchen and handed Hunapo a beer from the fridge. 'Here. It looks like you need this!'

'I want him to leave,' Aroha said, turning to Tautaru. 'Make him go.'

'Only if you go home with him,' Tautaru said. 'That's where you belong.'

Aroha glared at her father. 'Never!'

'Give her hell, Hunapo!' Tautaru said. 'Until she's back in your bed.'

Tautaru waved a hand in Aroha's face, and he was out of the door.

Hunapo grabbed Aroha's arm. 'Please come back to me. We can put all this behind us. We'll have fun again. Pārekareka!'

That beguiling grin. The wide-eyed smile. Aroha was half afraid she might succumb to it again. *Pull yourself together, girl! Stay strong.* 'Shut up and leave me alone. Let me grieve for Amiri in peace.'

Hunapo's expression soured. He downed his beer from the bottle in one gulp. 'You know that bastard was a sham. You're better off without him.'

'Get out! I never want to see you again!'

David Whittet

Chapter Forty-Nine

'Wake up, Aroha!'

Aroha rubbed the sleep from her eyes. What was Lilly doing in her room in the middle of the night? Why did she look so excited?

Lilly turned on the light. 'We're going on an adventure.'

Aroha sank back on her pillow. 'I've had enough adventures to last me a lifetime.'

'This will be different. I promise.' Lilly pulled back the bedclothes and tugged on Aroha's arm. 'Hurry up. Get some overnight things together. Before Tautaru wakes up.'

Still bleary-eyed, Aroha stared at the clapped-out VW Dormobile parked in the yard.

'Hop in,' Lilly urged. 'Let the adventure begin!'

'We're going in that?' Aroha ran her fingers over the rust and flaking yellow paintwork.

'My old man's lent it to me for a couple of days. I couldn't face another bus ride. My bottom hasn't recovered from the last one.'

Aroha opened the passenger door dubiously, half expecting it to fall off. She was used to her father's run-down vehicles, but none of them were quite as bad as this. 'Just don't expect me to push when we break down.'

'Don't worry. It may look an old banger, but it goes like the clappers!'

Lilly put her foot down on the accelerator, and the old van swung out onto the open road.

'Now will you please tell me what you're up to,' Aroha demanded, clinging onto the grab handle as the vehicle lurched over a pothole.

'We're going to find your mother.'

'*What?* Find Ngaio?' Aroha jolted, almost dislodging the seatbelt. 'You've got to be kidding!'

'*Kidding?*' Lilly gave her a reproachful look. 'I wouldn't joke about your mother. You know me better than that.'

'I do. I just don't see how.' Aroha took a deep breath. 'You're not taking me on a graveyard hunt, are you?'

'Heavens no,' Lilly said. 'I've been tracking Ngaio down for ages. I thought I'd never find her. Then Pania gave me the heads-up that she's living in a women's refuge in Opotiki.'

'What did Pania say? Can you trust her?' Aroha looked down. 'I was sure Ngaio was dead.'

Lilly sighed. 'I know Pania's an awful gossip, but if anyone can help us find Ngaio, it's Pania. And this time, I think she's telling the truth.'

'What makes you so sure?' Aroha said.

'I'd heard her talking to some of the other women about Ngaio. So when we were both rostered to clean the marae last week, I asked Pania straight: "Do you know what happened to Ngaio?"'

'Pania gave me a shifty look. "What's it to you?" she said. "Last I heard, Ngaio was at Te Whare in Opotiki."'

'*Te Whare,*' Aroha whispered the words to herself.

'Always on the lookout for a fresh scandal,' Lilly continued, 'Pania asked me if I was chasing Ngaio because she owed me money. As if, after all these years. When I said no, the cheeky bitch asked me if I needed a women's refuge myself.

'"What's your old man been up to?" she said, digging me in the ribs. "You're a dark horse, Lilly."'

Aroha shook her head. 'Typical Pania. You realise she's probably started spreading rumours about you being in trouble. Anyway, what did you say to her?'

'I told her to naff off,' Lilly said. 'But I'm grateful for the heads-up. I just hope that for once she got it right.'

Aroha lowered her head. 'I still haven't got my head around why Ngaio left without saying goodbye. I don't suppose I'll ever understand.'

'Well, that's what we're here to find out.' The van swerved as Lilly

 David Whittet

momentarily took her hands off the steering wheel to hug Aroha. 'I've wanted to bring you and your mother together for so long. It means so much to me.'

Lilly chattered throughout the two-hour drive through the Waioeka Gorge. Aroha stopped listening. She wasn't interested in the women's bowls league getting into the national championships. Her mind was full of questions. So many unanswered questions.

She stared through the window at the vast mountainous ravine plunging from the horizon above to the abyss below. As the shadows lengthened, Aroha imagined Ngaio making her escape on that dreadful night, struggling across bush, mountain and river. She must have been incredibly frightened, alone and abandoned.

'Nearly there,' Lilly said. 'You've been miles away.'

'Yes.'

As the van pulled out of the valley, Aroha sensed the relief and freedom that her mother must have felt when she reached the far side of the gorge. The canyon was a natural barricade. With such an uncompromising geographic boundary, Tautaru didn't need a *wall* to protect his patch.

❧

'Well, we made it.' Lilly turned off the ignition and patted the dashboard. 'I told you there's still life in this old girl.' She undid her seatbelt. 'Time to find Te Whare.'

Aroha yawned. 'I'm knackered. Can't we leave it till tomorrow?'

'No excuses,' Lilly insisted. 'You need to do this.'

'What will I say to her? Will she even recognise me?'

Lilly opened the van door. 'The sooner we find her, the sooner you'll know.'

Aroha remained crouched in the van while Lilly went to get directions. She glanced up and saw the disparaging looks the locals gave Lilly. Te Whare clearly had a reputation.

Her heart raced when Lilly took her hand and dragged her out of the van.

'Come on,' Lilly said. 'It's just down the street.'

Aroha froze when she saw the imposing building, converted from a former public hall. What if Ngaio didn't want a reminder of her old life with Tautaru? What if it was another disaster like the funeral?

'Kia māia. Be brave,' Lilly reassured her. 'You'll be fine once we're inside.'

Aroha sniffed the distinctly musty odour as Lilly led her into the dingy reception area.

'I could have ended up somewhere like this,' Aroha muttered, her eyes scanning the bleak hallway. 'The social worker was going to send me to a women's refuge when I got out of hospital. But then Tautaru barged in and made a scene.'

A door flung open and the refuge manager, Dawn Jamieson, sprang out of her office. 'Tautaru? Did you say Tautaru? Did he send you? We do not permit gang affiliates on these premises. Not under any circumstances.'

'We're not from Tautaru,' Lilly stuttered, shifting from one foot to the other. 'Well, at least … not exactly.'

A no-nonsense woman in her mid-fifties with steely grey hair, Ms Jamieson stood hands on her hips. 'So you *are* associated with the Gang?'

'No. We're just looking for someone.' Lilly put her arm around Aroha. 'This is my dear friend, Aroha. She lost her mother when she was a little girl. We believe her mother Ngaio may be here.'

Aroha stepped forward. 'My mother came here to get away from Tautaru.'

'You're Ngaio's daughter?' Ms Jamieson eyed them warily. 'You'd better come in.'

Aroha noticed Ms Jamieson draw her eyebrows together as she ushered them into her office. The hard-nosed woman was hiding something. Aroha sank into a chair. Had her mother died? *Please, God. Not more bad news.*

Ms Jamieson sat down behind her desk and fiddled with an earring. 'I'm afraid you've had a wasted journey. You should have called first. Ngaio left us years ago.'

'Do you know where she went?' Lilly asked.

Ms Jamieson shook her head. 'No. Remember, this was ten years ago. I'd just started working here. I was just a junior clerk. As far as I know, she didn't leave a forwarding address. I guess she was afraid the Gang were on to her.'

                    David Whittet

Aroha's eyes filled with tears. She'd psyched herself up for nothing. This was going to be another disaster, just like the tangi. She glanced at Lilly.

'We think Ngaio had a recent miscarriage when she ran away,' Lilly said. 'She'd lost a lot of blood. She must have needed a doctor.'

'Our local GP came to see her a couple of times,' Ms Jamieson said. 'She was still pregnant when she arrived here. And as I remember, very pregnant when she left.'

Aroha gripped the arm of her chair. 'That can't be right. She definitely had a miscarriage. I watched her almost bleed to death in the middle of a forest.'

Ms Jamieson rearranged the ornaments on her desktop. 'I can assure you it's true. Mrs Hudson was our manager back then. I remember how concerned she was for your mother's safety.'

Aroha jumped to her feet and leant over the desk. 'So why did you let her go? I thought refuges were there to make sure women got the help they needed.'

'We did our best for your mother,' Ms Jamieson said, 'but this is not a prison. Our clients are free to leave when they choose.'

Aroha thought her head would explode. 'Did nobody follow up to see if she was all right?'

Ms Jamieson drew back. 'I believe Mrs Hudson checked with the local hospitals. In fact, if memory serves me, she contacted the police and asked them to watch out for your mother.'

Aroha's eyes welled up. 'She probably collapsed and died in a ditch somewhere. Or my father caught up with her and killed her.'

Lilly gently pulled Aroha away. 'I'm sorry. This is my fault. I shouldn't have got your hopes up.' She stood up and shook the manager's hand. 'We'd better get home. I'm sorry we've wasted your time.'

'Wait.' Aroha held up a hand, her mind a blur. They couldn't just leave—not before they'd explored every last possibility. 'I know it was a long time ago, but would any of the women here now have been around when my mother lived here? Could I meet them? She might have told one of them where she was going.'

Ms Jamieson rubbed her chin. 'Some of our clients have been here a good many years. But I doubt any of them would know what happened to Ngaio.'

'I'd like to talk to them all the same,' Aroha said. 'If nothing else, it might bring some closure.'

'I'd have to ask their permission,' Ms Jamieson said. 'But I've no objections.'

Lilly took Aroha's hand. 'Are you sure you're up to this?'

Aroha nodded. 'Certain.'

She felt much less confident when Ms Jamieson led her into the women's sitting room. Her mind was working overtime, trying to piece everything together. Why had Ngaio been so frightened that she kept running away? Aroha shuddered. Perhaps Tautaru wasn't the father.

'Some of you may remember Ngaio,' Ms Jamieson announced. 'I'd like you to meet Aroha, her daughter.'

Aroha took a deep breath and walked up to the women. They welcomed her with open arms, but nobody remembered Ngaio.

'You lost your mother,' a resident said, 'that's so sad.'

Aroha swallowed hard. 'So none of you knew my mother? Or heard what became of her?'

The women shook their heads.

The tea lady came in with her trolley and handed Aroha a cup. 'You should talk to Tūī. She's been here even longer than me. We call her the Matriarch. She might remember your mother.'

Aroha raised her eyebrows. 'Tūī?'

'She hardly ever comes out of her room these days,' the tea lady said. 'She's crippled with arthritis. It's turned her into a hermit. She's worn the same black dress for as long as I can remember, and it's covered in stains.'

Aroha put down the teacup and threw her hands in the air. 'I have to see Tūī!'

'She's an old hag,' another resident warned. 'Don't take anything she says too seriously.'

With Lilly at her side, Aroha's heart beat faster than ever as she climbed the rickety wooden stairs to Tūī's bedroom. Would this frail old lady have the key to finding her mother?

'So you are Aroha,' Tūī rasped with a throaty voice. Her hawkish face bore lines and wrinkles that suggested the passing years had not been kind to her, yet her smile told of a life well lived. 'Let me see you.' She leant forward in her chair, wincing in pain, and touched Aroha's face with her knobbly hand. 'Ngaio told us her Aroha was beautiful. Now I can see she spoke truthfully.'

'Do you know where she is?' Aroha begged.

Tūī sank back, her voice even huskier. 'Ngaio was a sad woman. Scared and sorrowful—always afraid.'

Aroha wiped the tears from her cheeks. 'I want to see her again. You can't imagine how much.'

'Ngaio will be overjoyed to see you too,' Tūī croaked, her dark, solemn eyes focused on Aroha. 'And to see what a fine young woman you have become!'

'Did she ever talk about me?' Aroha asked.

'All the time,' Tūī said. 'I used to hear her crying. Sometimes she wept all night.'

Aroha sighed. 'If only she'd taken me with her when she ran away.'

'She was too scared,' Tūī said. 'I never knew how much she was suffering. Until one day. We were sitting in the lounge. Ngaio suddenly jumped up in a panic.' Tūī caught the drama of the moment with her rasping voice. '"It's today," your mother cried. "I know it's today! Murua ahau!"'

'What was the matter with her?' Aroha asked.

'Everyone thought she'd gone into labour,' Tūī said. 'But it wasn't that at all …'

❋

'Shall I call the midwife?' Mrs Hudson, the manager, flapped. 'I thought you had another month to go.'

Ngaio bowed her head. 'It's not the baby. It's Aroha.'

Mrs Hudson shook her head. 'Aroha?'

'My daughter.' Ngaio rummaged in her pocket for a handkerchief to dry her eyes. 'The daughter I left behind. It's her wedding day and I can't be there for her.'

'That's so sad,' Mrs Hudson said. 'We could have arranged something for you. Taken you there.'

'You don't understand,' Ngaio said. 'She's being forced into a disastrous relationship. It'll ruin her. They'll give her a tattoo, brand her for life. She'll be so frightened and I'm not there to hold her hand. I'm a dreadful mother.'

Tūī got up and put her arm on Ngaio's shoulder. 'I'm sure you're not.'

Ngaio clutched her pregnant belly. 'I am. I tried to give myself an abortion. Every night when I get undressed, I look at the scars I made. I don't deserve to have another child. I'll only let it down.'

'Nonsense.' Tūī reached out with her gnarled hand and placed it on Ngaio's tummy. 'This new baby will bring you luck and bring your daughter back to you. I can feel it in my bones.'

'Fat chance of that,' Ngaio snorted.

'Never give up hope,' Tūī said. 'I wish I could help. You've never told me why you ran away.'

'There's nothing to tell,' Ngaio said. 'I was just escaping from an abusive relationship like everyone else.'

Tūī stroked Ngaio's back. 'Tell me about it. What's your daughter's name?'

'Aroha. She was the only good to come out of that relationship.' Ngaio walked over to the window and stared into the distance. 'And I deserted her. I should be there for her. Today of all days!'

'You said she'd get a tattoo?' Tūī asked.

Ngaio turned back to face her. 'Yes. Like this.' She ran her fingers along the grooves of the tā moko on her chin. 'This is the only wedding present the bastard ever gave me. Marrying Tautaru was the worst mistake of my life. And now the same thing's happening to Aroha.'

Mrs Hudson had been hovering by the door. She suddenly spun around. 'What did you say? Tautaru? You were married to Tautaru?'

                    David Whittet

'The next day she was gone,' Tūī said.

Aroha felt her muscles tense. She couldn't believe what she'd just heard. 'You mean they threw her out of the refuge because they found out she was Tautaru's wife?'

'I didn't say that.' Tūī lifted her eyes to meet Aroha's. 'I think Ngaio worried about putting the other women in danger if the Gang came looking for her.'

'That would be Ngaio,' Lilly said. 'Always thinking about other people.'

Aroha jumped up. 'I don't believe it. The refuge should have protected her. I'm going to have it out with that Jamieson woman.'

Lilly gripped Aroha's arm to stop her. 'Calm down. That won't do any good.'

'Indeed, it won't,' Tūī said. 'What's done cannot be undone. We need to look to the future.'

'What future?' Aroha shot back. 'Do you know what happened to my mother? Did she have the baby?'

Tūī beckoned Aroha to kneel at the foot of her chair. 'Let me see your hands.'

'If you know, just tell me where she is,' Aroha said.

'All in good time, my headstrong one!' Tūī scowled and examined Aroha's hands. 'I need to find out if you're ready to hear the news. You must prepare yourself. Otherwise, I cannot tell you.'

Aroha shook her head. 'You sound just like my great aunt Kāterina. She talks in riddles too.'

'Obviously a wise woman,' Tūī said.

Aroha flinched as Tūī ran her cold, arthritic fingers over her palms. 'It's not bad news, is it? I'm not sure I can take much more.'

'Ngaio has suffered hardship since she left our little haven. I must ensure that you can deal with the news.'

Lilly fiddled with her car keys. 'For heaven's sake, just tell her.'

'Are you ready, Aroha?' Tūī's eyes narrowed. Her forehead wrinkled. 'I believe you are. You must understand that your mother is very sick. She had a difficult labour—'

'So she had the baby?' Aroha interrupted. 'You mean, I have a brother or a sister?'

'She had a little girl,' Tūī said. 'But be warned. She was a sickly child.'

Aroha bit her lip. 'Are you saying the baby didn't survive?'

'She was still with us when last I heard,' Tūī said. 'But Ngaio's stricken with galloping consumption. Her time on this planet is short.'

Lilly raised her eyebrows. 'How can you possibly know all this? Ngaio left the refuge ten years ago, and the other women say you haven't left the building in years.'

Tūī touched her nose. 'I just know. Believe me. I know.'

Aroha felt goosebumps on the back of her neck. 'You *are* just like Kāterina.'

Lilly made for the door. 'Come on, Aroha. She doesn't know anything. We need to get going. I don't want to drive home in the dark.'

Aroha frowned at Lilly. 'Wait. We've come this far. Let's hear her out.'

Staggering to her feet, Tūī grasped Aroha's hand. 'They're living rough. Up the coast at Tokomaru Bay.'

'Do you know whereabouts?' Aroha said.

Tūī nodded. 'Fetch me some paper.'

Aroha rummaged in her handbag and handed her a pencil and a scrap of paper. Struggling with her misshapen fingers, Tūī scribbled the address.

'Heed my warning,' Tūī said. 'Be prepared for a shock when you see your mother. Last I heard, she looked dreadful. Ravaged by disease. The lurgy has nigh on consumed her.'

'I don't care' Aroha cried. 'I just want to see her … and my sister.' She folded the paper and carefully put it in her pocket. 'Thank you, Tūī.'

Tūī kissed Aroha on the cheek. 'You'll need courage—and all the strength you can muster. Now go and find them. And God bless you!'

     David Whittet

Chapter Fifty

Aroha's heart was still racing when they left the refuge. She clutched Lilly's hand. 'I have a little sister! And I didn't even know. Thank you so much for bringing me here.'

Lilly hesitated. 'I'm not sure I should have done so. That old woman didn't know what she was talking about. I don't want to see you hurt again.'

'You won't regret it,' Aroha said. 'Can we set off straight away?'

'No.' They reached the Dormobile and Lilly unlocked the door. 'Tokomaru Bay is three and a half hours away. I'm tired. Let's find a motel for the night, and a fish and chip shop. I'm starving.'

Aroha dumped her rucksack on the motel floor. The musty smell and the day's excitement had reduced her appetite. Still, Lilly got some plates out of a drawer and unwrapped the takeaway.

Lilly dipped a chip in the tomato sauce. 'I still think this trip is going to end in disaster. What makes you think that old witch has any idea what happened to your mother? She admitted she hasn't been out of the refuge in years. Anything she's heard is simply gossip. Nothing more.'

'I know.' Aroha nibbled on a chip. 'Tūī reminds me of my great aunt. She used to predict the most extraordinary things and she always seemed to be right. Did you ever meet Kāterina?'

Lilly tilted her head to one side. 'Kāterina Kururangi? I used to see her on the telly. Telling our Māori leaders how to do their jobs. I thought she was talking a lot of hot air back then. I wouldn't trust anything she says any more than what Tūī has to say.'

'Maybe you're right,' Aroha said. 'But I've nothing to lose and I have to find out.'

Lilly yawned. 'I'm beat. Let's clear up, then I need some shut-eye. Dibs this bed.'

After a shower in the mouldy bathroom, Aroha lay awake, staring at the peeling wallpaper. Was her mother still alive? Could she really have a half-sister? It seemed impossible that a pregnancy could have survived that awful haemorrhage. Perhaps Lilly was right, and it was just the rambling of a demented woman. But one thing was certain. She'd told Lilly she had to know the truth. And she did.

Tired of staring at the ceiling and listening to Lilly's snoring echo off the walls of the pokey motel room, Aroha needed to clear her head. She got up and wandered through the streets of Opotiki, wondering if tomorrow would change her life or just be the latest in a long string of disappointments.

The sun shone through the tattered blinds of the motel room. Aroha went over to the window and gazed out. A bright, fresh morning. That was a good start.

Lilly made some coffee, and they sat at the table.

'You look exhausted,' Aroha said. 'Didn't you sleep well?'

'That bed did my back in,' Lilly said. 'You look tired too.'

Aroha held the mug tight in her hands and took a slurp. 'I am. But excited as well.'

'Don't get your hopes up too much,' Lilly said.

'I won't. It's just …' Aroha searched for the right words but dried up.

'Come on, then.' Lilly walked across to the sink and washed up the mugs. 'We'd better get going. Let's see which of us is right.'

Another long drive with too much time in which to think. Lilly turned on the radio. The blaring music did little to distract Aroha. Every bend in the road and swerve of the vehicle brought her closer to her moment of truth. It was almost twelve years since her mother ran away. So much had changed in that time, and so many precious years lost forever. She'd felt excited yesterday

     David Whittet

when Tūī gave her the address. Today she had a sinking feeling in her stomach. How could she possibly prepare to meet a mother she thought was dead and a sister she never knew existed?

She watched the terrain change as they progressed along the coastal road. Trees and telegraph poles flashed past. Isolated settlements. Run-down baches. The landscape appeared as bleak as Aroha's soul felt barren.

'An hour and a half and we'll be there,' Lilly said when they made a comfort stop at Hicks Bay.

'Lilly,' Aroha said as she grabbed takeaway coffees from the roadside cafe. She hesitated before continuing, 'I'm scared. Maybe this wasn't such a good idea after all.'

'You can't give up now.' Lilly shot her a reassuring grin. 'Besides, you've got me wondering. I want to know if Tūī was talking through her arse or not.'

Aroha looked out over the bay, the blustery waves underlining her uncertainty. She took a deep breath and braced herself as they climbed back into the rusty old van. Another hour and a half. The last leg of the journey seemed to last forever.

It was late afternoon and several potholes later when they finally reached Tokomaru Bay.

'Give me that piece of paper,' Lilly said. 'What was the name of the road?'

'Paikea Street,' Aroha said. Her jaw dropped when they turned the corner into yet another street of ramshackle houses covered in graffiti. 'But shouldn't we find a motel first?'

Lilly pulled the car to the kerb. 'Chin up, girl. The longer you leave it, the more difficult it will be.' She wound down the window and asked an elderly neighbour for directions. 'This is Paikea Street?'

Aroha groaned. 'No. It can't be.' She covered her eyes when the woman pointed to a slum at the end of the street. 'She's got it wrong.'

'I'm afraid not,' Lilly said. She parked the Dormobile next to the collection of wrecked cars that littered the roadside.

Aroha watched a cat playing with a dead mouse on the pathway. 'I can't do this, Lilly.'

'You must.'

Lilly climbed out of the vehicle and beckoned Aroha to follow.

Aroha didn't move from the passenger seat. 'Take me home. Please.'

'You can't give up now.' Lilly opened the passenger door and gripped Aroha's arm. 'Come on.'

Aroha shivered as Lilly led her through the overgrown garden to the front door.

Lilly banged on the door. Not a sound from inside.

Aroha's heart stood still. 'Are you sure this is the right house?'

Lilly nodded. 'Wait here. I'm going to have a look around the back.'

Aroha glanced up at the rotting wooden weatherboards. *Not here. Please, God. Not here.*

Lilly reappeared. 'No sign of life at all. I think we should go in.'

Aroha thought the door would drop off its hinges when Lilly pushed it open.

Aroha gagged when they stepped inside. 'God! What's that smell?'

A rat scuttled down the hallway. Aroha took a step back towards the door, but Lilly pushed her forward.

A groaning noise drew them towards a bedroom. Aroha hovered outside the door, her body shaking.

Lilly stood behind her. 'Go in!'

The door creaked as Aroha pushed it open. The room was dark apart from a small shaft of light breaking through the frayed curtain. It took Aroha's eyes a moment to adjust. She took a step forward. Could that shrunken, wasted woman in the bed really be her mother?

'Mummy! Mummy! Is it you?'

Ngaio stirred. Her eyes looked like tombstones and her face just as grey and lifeless. With a grunt, she lifted her head. 'Aroha? Am I dreaming?'

'No! No, you're not!' Aroha ran to the bed and flung her arms around her mother.

Ngaio pulled up the dirty sheets to cover her soiled nightdress. 'I've waited so long for this day. I never thought it would happen.' Her head dropped back onto the pillow. 'But I didn't want you to see me like this. You see, I can't get up when I need a pee.'

Aroha stroked her mother's face. 'Don't you have … you know, one of those things that you, um—'

'I think you mean a commode,' Lilly said. 'So who's been looking after you, Ngaio?'

Aroha frowned. *It doesn't look like anyone's been looking after her.*

'Hinemoa,' Ngaio breathed. 'Hinemoa's been taking care of me.'

Aroha bit her lip. Was Hinemoa her mother's helper? *Or could she be my half-sister?*

'Hinemoa?' Aroha said. 'Who's she?'

Ngaio raised her head again. 'Of course, you don't know about Hinemoa. It's a long story …' She broke off in a fit of coughing and spat some blood-stained phlegm into a bowl at the side of her bed.

'I'm afraid that story will have to wait,' Lilly said. 'Your mother's tired. I bet she's hungry too. Let her get some rest while we go to the village shop. Then I'll cook her some soup for her supper.'

Aroha gave her mother a kiss. For a moment, it didn't matter that Ngaio was gasping for breath, that she was languishing alone in a filthy dump. Aroha had found her mother.

Chapter Fifty-One

Aroha spoon-fed the nourishing broth to her mother. 'Try to take some more, Mum. It'll do you good. Make you strong again.'

Ngaio had lost so much weight that Aroha wondered when she had last eaten. Who was Hinemoa? If she was Aroha's half-sister, why wasn't she here looking after her mother?

When Ngaio had taken as much of the soup as she could manage, Aroha gave her a bed bath and Lilly changed the sheets.

'Doesn't that feel better?' Aroha said, helping Ngaio into a clean nightdress. 'And tomorrow, Lilly and I are going to clean this place up. We'll start with a new mattress.'

Lilly and Aroha sat quietly on either side of Ngaio throughout the evening. Aroha stroked her mother's cheek and watched her drift in and out of sleep, still gasping for breath.

'Who is Hinemoa?' Aroha whispered, not sure if her mother could hear her. 'Is she my sister?'

Ngaio opened her eyes. She tried to speak but sank into another coughing fit. Aroha rubbed her back as she spat more blood into the bowl.

'Hinemoa's gone away,' Ngaio mumbled, her head falling back onto the pillow. 'She's in with a bad lot.'

Aroha wiped the blood from her mother's face. 'Tell me about her, please.'

'Only if you feel up to it,' Lilly said.

Ngaio gripped Lilly's hand. 'You remember when you came to see me that day, all those years ago? Moana had sent you to talk me into the arranged marriage.'

'Can you ever forgive me?' Lilly said. 'You begged me to stop the wedding, and I didn't listen. If only I had. None of this would have happened.'

'I know it wasn't your fault,' Ngaio said. 'It was Moana.'

'I shouldn't have had any part in it,' Lilly said. 'It still haunts me.'

Aroha glanced from Ngaio to Lilly and back. Both women had tears in their eyes.

'What is it, Mum?' Aroha said.

'I shouldn't have done it,' Ngaio said.

Aroha shook her head. 'Done what?'

Still clinging to Lilly with one hand, Ngaio clutched Aroha with the other. 'I thought sleeping with the enemy would bring you back to me. Not drive us apart.'

'Sleeping with the enemy?' Aroha repeated. 'I don't understand.'

'I think your mother's getting tired,' Lilly said. 'Perhaps we should leave this for tonight.'

'No,' Ngaio said. 'I want you both to hear the truth. Who knows how long I've got left to tell you?'

'If you're sure,' Lilly said.

Ngaio pulled herself up in the bed and tried to make herself comfortable. 'I felt so alone that night after you left, Lilly. I was desperate. The women wouldn't help, and I had to do something. I was so sure that Hunapo was wrong for you, my darling Aroha.'

'You were right,' Aroha said. 'The bastard tried to kill me on my wedding day. Then he murdered my husband. Burnt him alive.'

Ngaio lowered her head. 'I did something I'm ashamed of. But it was the only option left. I turned to your uncle Maahanga.'

Aroha raised an eyebrow. 'Uncle Maahanga?'

'You see …' Ngaio hesitated. 'Maahanga and I … we go back a long way.'

'So it was true?' Aroha said. 'I heard the rumours, but I never believed them.'

'As a girl, Maahanga swept me off my feet. If it wasn't for …' Ngaio broke off and wiped away a tear. 'Never mind all that. I figured Maahanga must have been as mad at Tautaru as I was. I knew what I had to do. I got out my best party dress. Maahanga never could resist me in that little black number. Put on some lippy. When I showed up at his place, the old bugger had the cheek to say I looked like a tart …'

'What the hell are you doing here, dressed up like that?' Maahanga said.

Ngaio pushed her way across the threshold. 'You don't look very pleased to see me. We're old friends, aren't we?'

Maahanga grunted and beckoned her into the kitchen. She watched him limp and clutch his chest. She tried not to look at the bruises on his face as she stepped over the broken furniture and crockery on the floor.

'Tautaru did this to you, didn't he?' Ngaio said. 'Bastard!'

Maahanga nodded. 'That's brotherly love for you. The son of a bitch stole you from me all those years ago, and now he's taken Hunapo.'

Ngaio sat down, half expecting the chair to collapse. 'Any chance of a cup of tea?'

Maahanga switched on the kettle and got out the teapot. Ngaio watched him spill some boiling water on his hand as he filled it, and he swore out loud.

'Here, let me do that,' Ngaio said. 'You need a woman to look after you.' She stood up and fetched the teapot off the shelf. 'And it *would* have been me taking care of you if Tautaru hadn't got in the way. I thought the world of you. You know that.'

Maahanga grunted, and they sat at the kitchen table.

Ngaio poured the tea and took a deep breath. 'Why did we let Tautaru come between us?' She reached across the table and took his hands into hers. 'You were always smarter than Tautaru. You were the clever one.'

Maahanga snorted. 'The clever one, my arse! The bastard's stitched me up!'

Ngaio stroked his hand. 'But Maahanga—'

'But nothing,' Maahanga shot back. 'I know why you're here and you're wasting your time. Drink your tea and go before you get us both into even more trouble.'

Ngaio gazed into his eyes. 'Do you remember the last time I wore this dress? At Mattie's party?'

Maahanga's eyes softened. 'That was a long time ago.'

'Not to me,' Ngaio said. 'Remember how we went down to the beach afterwards and swam in the sea in the moonlight? You told me my eyes shone like emeralds.'

Maahanga managed a half-smile. 'Did I say that? Was I really that full of crap?'

'You were,' Ngaio said. 'And you told me you loved me.'

'I did.' Maahanga paused, his expression suddenly hardening again. 'But it doesn't make any difference. I still can't help you. The women have taken Hunapo away. There's nothing more I can do and there's an end to it.'

Ngaio let go of his hand. 'I never put you down as a victim.'

'You weren't there when Tautaru's men came round. You didn't see what they did to me. The bastards beat the shit out of me! In front of Hunapo!'

'All the more reason to fight!' Ngaio said. 'I can't believe you've just washed your hands of Hunapo.'

Maahanga slammed his hand on the table. 'I fought for Hunapo! Do you really think I just gave up on him? I felt like shit when they took him away.'

Ngaio folded her arms. 'What happened to the ballsy man I used to know and love? The Maahanga of old wouldn't have given up after a hiding. I thought you were a warrior.'

'Piss off,' Maahanga said. 'There are no more warriors in the Gang.'

Ngaio got up from her chair and put her arm around his shoulder. 'Don't let Tautaru get away with it!'

Maahanga threw his arms in the air. 'He already has. I'm screwed. Buggered.' He undid his shirt. 'This what you get for trying to be a hero.'

Ngaio grunted and turned her head away. 'Put it back on. Please. You men and your scars. Why do you have to show them off like trophies?'

'Look, damn you!' Maahanga stripped his top right off, revealing a multitude of lacerations and bruises over his chest and back.

'For heaven's sake cover them up,' Ngaio said. 'I told you, I don't want to see your battle wounds.' She watched the pained expression in his eyes as he put his shirt back on. 'Anyway, I bet they're nothing to what you've given Hunapo. You should be proud to take a beating to defend your son.' She held her breath and stroked the back of Maahanga's neck. 'Listen, between us, we can smash Tautaru.'

'Don't make me laugh!' Maahanga groaned and shook his head. He tried to inch away, but Ngaio had him trapped. 'The bastard's got us right where he wants us!'

'Not if we're smart.' Ngaio caressed his chest seductively, running her fingers across his scars. 'Tautaru is thick. He's made enemies of the wrong people. In fact, I can't understand how he's survived as long as he has.' She rubbed her face against his chest. 'I've been biding my time. Tautaru has no brains, but you and me—'

Maahanga jerked upright. 'You and me nothing! Are you trying to have me killed?'

Ngaio continued to massage his sores. 'Of course not. But I'm not giving up on you either.'

Bracing herself, she burrowed her head under his shirt and kissed his chest. Overpowered by the stench, she inadvertently got some pus on her tongue, which made her gag. She swallowed hard and continued licking his torso, running her long silky hair across his disfigured back.

The glint in his eye and the bulge in his pants told Ngaio that Maahanga hadn't felt an alluring woman's soft touch on his skin in ages. The local gang whores were rough. Her caresses would be irresistible and the experience overpowering.

Ngaio had Maahanga right where she wanted him.

     David Whittet

Chapter Fifty-Two

Aroha lifted her head and met Ngaio's eyes. 'That's why Hunapo ran away, isn't it? He found out you and Maahanga were sleeping together, didn't he?'

Ngaio shrunk back, almost disappearing under the bedclothes.

Aroha sighed. Suddenly everything fell into place. No wonder Hunapo was so damaged. Finding his soon-to-be mother-in-law in bed with his father. That would screw up any young guy.

Aroha pulled the sheet away from Ngaio's face. 'You can't stop there, Mum. You must finish the story. I need to know about Hinemoa. And what about that day in the caravan? When you and Kāterina were fighting and you almost bled to death in the forest on the way home.'

'Everything happened so quickly,' Ngaio said. 'One minute, Maahanga and I were celebrating. We had the numbers to topple Tautaru. The next—'

'You had the numbers?' Aroha interrupted. 'So how come you didn't bring Tautaru down?'

'I worked my butt off for Maahanga,' Ngaio said. 'Drumming up support down in Hawke's Bay. Putting the hard word on men Tautaru had ruined. It was there I first realised something was wrong. It was that time of the month. My body always stuffed things up. Imagine being on the rag while we were on the road campaigning. I couldn't believe it when my monthly didn't come.

'I didn't worry too much at first. They'd been late before when I'd been stressed. But when I started throwing up in the mornings—that's when I panicked. I hadn't slept with Tautaru in ages, so there was no way I could pass it off as his. Imagine what your father would've done if he'd found out I was pregnant by Maahanga. His brother. His sworn enemy.'

Aroha caught her breath. 'He'd have gone crazy. No wonder you were frightened.'

'It was a bloody death warrant,' Ngaio continued. 'He'd have shot me if he'd found out. I knew that.'

'I'm guessing Maahanga wouldn't take any responsibility,' Aroha said.

Ngaio tilted her head back. 'Maahanga was happy enough to see me when I told him we'd got the power to destroy Tautaru. He was all over me then. But not when I told him I was pregnant—'

'And he was the father.' Aroha finished the sentence for her. 'I bet he denied it.'

'He did,' Ngaio said. 'I told him he had to help me. This was his baby. The bastard even accused me of having it off with the men down in Hawke's Bay …'

❧

'You expect me to believe it's mine?' Maahanga growled. 'I saw the way you were flirting with those guys when we were on the road. Flashing your eyes and flaunting your body. How do I know one of them is not the father?'

Ngaio glared at him. 'Maahanga! How could you say that? I've bust my guts for you, getting your supporters to stand up and back you.'

'I didn't ask you to stick your nose in my business,' Maahanga shot back. 'Anyway, you were doing it just as much for yourself as you were for me. And bugger all good it did either of us.'

'Don't be like that.' Ngaio put her arm on his shoulder and stroked his back. 'We could have finished Tautaru. If only one of his spies hadn't got in first and tipped him off.'

'Bullshit!' Maahanga pulled away from her. 'Even Hunapo saw through that in a flash. He told me however many men I had, Tautaru would have more. And he was bloody right!'

'That's not fair,' Ngaio edged forward again, holding out a hand to him. 'Whatever you think about me, this is your child. I haven't slept with anyone else. I promise.'

Maahanga raised a fist. 'Just get out of my life. You flung yourself at me, not the other way around.'

Ngaio snorted. 'I didn't see you put up much resistance.'

'Go!' Maahanga pointed to the door. 'This is all your doing. You've turned my son against me. Made me even more of a laughing stock than I was before, and if you've got yourself up the duff, it's your own bloody fault!'

'The bastard threw me out,' Ngaio said. 'I was on my own. With a time bomb ticking in my belly.'

'So that's why you turned to Kāterina?' Aroha said.

'Not straight away,' Ngaio sighed. 'Kōkā was a last resort. I knew how she felt about abortion. I made an appointment to see my GP. I knew the doctor wouldn't say anything, but I wasn't prepared for the gossips in the waiting room. That busybody Rona would have to be there, asking me all sorts of awkward questions …'

'Ngaio,' Rona said, sitting next to her on the bench. 'We haven't seen you around for ages. What brings you to the doctor? Are you sick? Nothing too serious, I hope. You must get yourself well for the great day in the spring. Everyone's looking forward to seeing Aroha and Hunapo getting hitched.'

'No, it's nothing, Rona.' Ngaio looked down at her feet. 'I'm just here for a check-up.'

Ngaio could feel the receptionists staring at her and nervously held her stomach. Had they guessed why she was there? Surely they wouldn't say anything. Would they?

The practice nurse ushered her into the consulting room. 'Dr Ngata will be in to see you in a moment. In the meantime, would you like me to check your blood pressure?'

Ngaio felt her pulse quicken. 'My blood pressure? Why?'

'Don't look so worried,' the nurse said. 'It's just a routine health check. Now roll up your sleeve.'

'No. I'm sorry. I have to get out.'

Ngaio bolted out of the medical centre. She saw the women in the waiting room exchange glances. Damn them! Word would be all around town before the day was out.

'What were you thinking?' Tautaru demanded when he got home that night. 'Causing a scene at the doctors. Are you sick?'

Ngaio shook her head.

Tautaru glared at her. 'Then you stay away from those quacks. You know I don't approve of anyone else looking at my wife's private parts!'

❧

Ngaio slumped back on her pillow. 'That put the fear of God into me. Why did he say *private parts?* Did he know? Had he worked it out?'

'None of the gangsters like a doctor examining their women,' Lilly said. 'They're all the same. He wouldn't have meant anything more than that.'

'I'm not so sure,' Ngaio said. 'You should have seen the way he looked at me. It made me even more certain that I had to get an abortion.'

'Oh, Mum!' Aroha stroked her mother's hand. 'I wish you'd told me what was going on.'

'You were far too young.'

'At least I wouldn't have been so frightened,' Aroha said. 'And I *was* scared. Even before that awful day in the forest.'

Lilly leant forward and put a hand on Ngaio's shoulder. 'You could have talked to me.'

Ngaio raised her eyes to Lilly. 'I convinced myself you women were all against me. Especially after you—'

'I know.' Lilly lowered her head. 'Damn Moana. Why did I let her bully me into harassing you?'

Ngaio clasped Lilly's hand with her bony fingers. 'That's all water under the bridge. It doesn't matter now.'

 David Whittet

Lilly lowered her head. 'It's just … It breaks my heart to think you went through all that on your own.'

Aroha felt goosebumps on the back of her neck as she watched the two women embrace each other. But she was still impatient to hear the rest of the story—and find out about Hinemoa.

'I didn't understand why you shut me out back then,' Aroha said, encouraging her mother to continue. 'You bit my head off when I suggested that going to see Kāterina might cheer you up. Then the next day we were off to the *Gypsy Rose.*'

'Like I said, Kōkā was my last hope,' Ngaio continued. 'I'd tried the abortion clinics. I had to use a payphone so Tautaru wouldn't hear. I remember fumbling with the coins when the wretched woman on the other end of the phone told me I had to go through my GP or the family planning clinic.'

'Couldn't family planning help?' Lilly asked.

'They probably could have,' Ngaio said. 'But when I called them, I recognised the receptionist's voice. It was Maiki.'

'Maiki?' Lilly said. 'Her husband's best mates with Chase.'

'Exactly. It was bound to get back to Tautaru.' Ngaio gave a long, deep sigh. 'The backstreet abortionists were all I had left.'

Aroha blinked back a tear. 'Oh, Mum.'

'I heard about this doc down in Hawke's Bay,' Ngaio continued. 'He'd been struck off a couple of years back. Found a new career running an abortion clinic.' She squeezed her eyes shut. 'His surgery was on this run-down estate in Hastings. I kept looking over my shoulder, convinced one of Tautaru's men was following me. I remember watching a spider crawl across the ceiling as the doctor felt my tummy …'

'I'd say you're about nine weeks along,' Dr Philip Mullins said as he palpated Ngaio's abdomen. 'So the sooner we get this done, the better.' He gestured for her to get up from the examination table. 'I take it you're in good health?'

Ngaio nodded.

'No medical conditions I need to know about?'

'None.'

Mullins sat down at his desk and handed her a clipboard. 'You need to fill out this consent form.'

Ngaio watched him tap his fingers on the desktop as she struggled with the form, repeatedly crossing out and starting again.

Mullins looked at his watch. 'Just sign there.'

Ngaio scribbled on the dotted line and he snatched the papers back.

Mullins put on his glasses. His face turned white when he saw her signature. 'You're Tautaru's wife?'

Ngaio swallowed hard. 'Yes.'

'Get the hell out of here.' Mullins sprang to his feet and pointed at the door. 'I'm not touching you. Are you trying to get me killed?'

'I don't know how I got home,' Ngaio said. 'I could barely see the road for tears while driving the ute over those winding roads. Sleeping with the enemy had cost me dear. I was sure I'd pay for it with my life.' Reliving the emotion brought on another coughing fit, and she spat more blood into the bucket. Wiping her mouth on the bedsheet, she turned to Aroha. 'When I got back that night, you asked me why we never went to see Kōkā any more. I wanted to say it was because Kōkā wouldn't understand, but instead I just brushed you off. Said I'd been too busy.'

'What made you change your mind?' Aroha asked.

'I agonised about it all night,' Ngaio said. 'I could never sleep back then. I knew all too well that Kōkā believed in the sanctity of human life. Nothing would change that. Hell would freeze over before Kōkā would help with an abortion. But surely she wouldn't turn me away. We'd been through so much together. By the morning I'd decided I had nothing to lose.'

 David Whittet

'I was so happy when you burst into my room that morning and told me we were going to see Kāterina,' Aroha said. 'But I was beyond disappointed when you made me stay outside. I so wanted to talk to Kāterina.'

'You wouldn't have wanted to be inside the caravan that afternoon,' Ngaio said. 'Believe me. It wasn't pretty …'

⚘

'Help me, Kōkā,' Ngaio said, sitting on the edge of her stool in the *Gypsy Rose.* 'When I seduced Maahanga, it was to get Aroha away from Hunapo—not bind them together!'

Kāterina's face gave nothing away. What was the old woman thinking?

Ngaio bit her tongue and continued. 'Don't you see what it means? This child would be related to both of them—Aroha would be a half-sister, and Hunapo a half-brother. Gross! Unthinkable! How sick can you get?'

During the trek through the forest, Ngaio had mentally rehearsed what she was going to say. She couldn't afford to let her emotions get the better of her. But with the explosive atmosphere in the caravan, Ngaio felt her voice rising. The ornaments on the shelf vibrated. Better take it down an octave or two.

'You're my only hope, Kōkā.'

'Of course I'll help you.' Kāterina extended a hand and rested it on Ngaio's knee. 'I've got a friend who's a midwife. We'll hide you away, and once the baby's born, we'll put the child out for adoption. Nobody needs to know.'

'No way,' Ngaio shot back. 'I have to get rid of this abomination. You've got to help me get an abortion. I'm begging you!'

'I can't do that, Ngaio,' Kāterina retracted her arm and tugged at her earlobe. 'We're talking about a precious baby—not a choice.'

Ngaio took a deep breath. *Stay calm.* 'I know you believe that, but *please*— you *must* have an abortionist amongst your Māori medical friends.'

'No. We dedicate ourselves to healing, not killing.' Kāterina again reached out to Ngaio, this time placing a hand on her shoulder. 'Human life is sacred.'

'*Sacred?*' Ngaio pulled away, rocking on her stool. 'There's nothing sacred about a bastard child with Maahanga. It's a parasite growing inside me!'

'*Abomination? Parasite?*' Kāterina clenched her jaw, her face flushed. 'How can you say that? You have a child inside you, a human being with a soul!'

'No, Kōkā,' Ngaio pointed a finger at Kāterina, almost touching her nose. 'This is a death sentence! Don't you understand that? Tautaru will have me killed!'

'Keep your voice down,' Kāterina hissed, turning and glancing out of the caravan window. 'Aroha will hear you.' She continued in a forced whisper. 'Lots of people are desperate to adopt a child. Would you deny them a chance for happiness? My midwife friend will look after you. Don't worry. Tautaru need never know.'

Ngaio shook her head. *How can I make her understand?* 'It won't work. Tautaru has spies everywhere. He's bound to find out.'

Kāterina didn't react. *Keep cool,* Ngaio told herself. *Explain. Give her the facts. That has to change her mind.*

'Just think about it, I'd have to go into hiding once the pregnancy showed.' Ngaio felt the pitch of her voice increasing but couldn't restrain herself. 'And I couldn't come home till after the baby was born. I'd be gone for months. Then there's the wretched arranged marriage coming up in the spring. Don't think for a moment Tautaru would let me miss that. He's dying to rub my nose in it. He'd hunt me down wherever I was and drag me back.'

Kāterina leant back on the bench and hunched her shoulders. 'Not if we do this right.'

'Get real, Kōkā, for God's sake!' Ngaio rolled her eyes. 'If Tautaru finds out I've been sleeping with his brother … *his brother* … his arch enemy, he won't just have me killed, I'll be pilloried, hung, drawn and quartered. There's nothing the bastard wouldn't do to me.' Ngaio shivered. Her body shook. 'Don't worry about an abortion killing the baby. Tautaru would find the infant wherever it was and murder it! The child will be dead either way. Better we get rid of it now than let Tautaru get his grubby hands on the mate paipai!'

'Mate paipai? How can you say that? This is a *child!*'

     David Whittet

'No. It's a mate paipai. A venereal disease.'

'Ngaio!'

Ngaio clasped her hands over her head. *Give me strength.* 'Whatever you believe, surely you can see this is wrong?'

Kāterina leant forward. She reached across to her crystal ball, lifted it off its plinth and gently ran her fingers over it. 'I see a beautiful baby girl. Right here in my crystal ball.'

'Bullshit!' Ngaio felt her blood pressure rise until it pounded inside her head. *'Beautiful girl,* indeed! Can you imagine what this child would do to Aroha and Hunapo? Incest. That's what it is. *Incest.* It would destroy our lives. Are you prepared to sacrifice all of us to your high-minded principles?'

'This isn't incest.' Kāterina continued to caress the ball. 'It's an extended whānau. Lots of Māori families have complicated relationships like this.'

'Not with Tautaru they don't!' Ngaio gazed around the caravan. Her eyes fixed on the tiny closet that doubled as a wardrobe. She leapt up and grabbed one of Kāterina's dresses, tearing it off the coat hanger. 'Well, if you won't help me, then I'll do it myself!'

Ngaio lifted her skirt, pulled down her underwear and shoved the wire hanger inside herself.

Kāterina jumped to her feet, dropping the crystal ball in her haste to stop Ngaio. It rolled around on the threadbare rug as the *Gypsy Rose* rocked in time with Ngaio's rhythmic thrusts.

'Stop!' Kāterina screamed, wrestling Ngaio's hands away from her body. 'You'll kill yourself and the baby …'

'Good! I'll soon be rid of the pakiwhara!'

'Stop calling it a venereal disease. It's a *child!*'

'It's a leech.'

Kāterina caught hold of the coat hanger and dragged it away from Ngaio. 'Pull up your pants. Suppose Aroha walked in.'

Ngaio glared back at her and kicked the crystal ball across the floor. 'I blame you, Kōkā. You and that infernal crystal ball. Damn you both! Filling Aroha's mind with fantasies long before she was old enough to understand what they meant!' She picked up the ball, threatening to throw it out of the window. 'Telling Aroha she would fall for Hunapo! You made this happen, Kōkā. *You!* Damn you to hell!'

'Ngaio, please!' Kāterina slumped back on her bench. 'I only told Aroha what I saw in my crystal ball!'

'You've torn this whānau apart. Always interfering and meddling. You've destroyed us all!'

Ngaio began hitting her stomach violently, working herself into a frenzy of self-flagellation.

Tears ran down Kāterina's face. 'Please, Ngaio! Think what you're doing!'

Ngaio continued lashing her abdomen compulsively. She glared down at her belly, mentally chastising the foetus in her womb. *Take that, you bloodsucker! Kutu! Vermin! Get out of my body!* Blood seeped through her skirt and trickled down her legs. 'Look, it's working! *It's working!*' She thrashed herself even harder. 'Yeah! I've done it! I'm having a miscarriage!'

'Don't do this. Think about Aroha! What'll happen to her if you kill yourself?'

Ngaio lifted her bloodstained fingers from her crotch and held them triumphantly in the air. 'No, Kōkā. I haven't killed myself. I've just saved my life.'

Kāterina grabbed a towel and handed it to her. 'You'll never get home like that. You'll bleed to death. Lie down on the bed. I'll ride into town and fetch a doctor.'

'No. No doctors. I'm leaving.'

'You can't. You'll die!'

'I won't. I'm a survivor.'

Ngaio clutched her battered tummy and hobbled towards the door, tripping over the crystal ball which still lay on the floor. She glanced back at Kāterina, who appeared to have aged twenty years in the past thirty minutes. Their eyes met.

'Please let me help you,' Kāterina said.

'No, Kōkā.' Ngaio bit her lip. 'I'm sorry. I should never have come here.'

Draping a shawl over her clothes to conceal the stream of blood, Ngaio opened the caravan door and called to Aroha. 'Come on. We're going straight home.'

     David Whittet

'I don't remember much after that,' Ngaio said, sinking back in the bed. 'I guess I must have passed out.'

'You did,' Aroha said. 'In the middle of the forest. If Kāterina hadn't come after us with her horse, we'd have both died out there in the middle of nowhere.'

'The next thing I knew, I was soaking in the bath at home, sponging my sore belly,' Ngaio said. 'For the first time in weeks, I could relax. The nightmare was over. I'd got rid of the pregnancy.'

'So you didn't have the baby?' Aroha couldn't hide the disappointment in her voice. 'Tūī said you had a little girl.'

'I still wanted to throw up when I cooked Tautaru's breakfast the next morning.' Ngaio cleared her throat and spat some more phlegm into the bucket. 'And my tummy was still getting bigger. What was I to do? I daren't go to a pharmacy for a pregnancy test. Tautaru's spies were everywhere. Not that I needed a test. It was starting to show. I was sure Tautaru had noticed. I dreaded going to bed. Convinced myself it would be the night he had me shot.'

'When you disappeared, I thought he had killed you,' Aroha said, wiping a tear from her cheek. 'If only I'd known. Why didn't you leave me a note?'

'I couldn't risk you coming after me,' Ngaio said. 'You were vital to Tautaru's game plan. With the arranged marriage coming up, he'd have hunted you down rather than lose face with the Gang. Me—I wasn't important. I told myself Tautaru would be glad to see the back of me. He wouldn't even bother to come after me.' Ngaio pulled herself up in the bed. 'I wasn't going to stand by and wait for him to assassinate me. I'd been too frightened to run away in the past. Now I was too scared to stay.' She raised her eyes to Aroha. 'Leaving you behind was the hardest choice I've ever made. My mind was in such turmoil. You were everything to me—you must believe that. Life without you would be worthless.'

'Oh, Mum.' Aroha wanted to say more, but the words wouldn't come. She just flung her arms around Ngaio.

'It was three in the morning,' Ngaio said. 'I was all packed up to go. I crept into your bedroom. You looked so beautiful in the soft moonlight. I sat down beside you, trying not to cry.'

Aroha's face felt wet as she hugged her mother. Ngaio clearly couldn't hold back the tears as she recounted the story.

'I stroked your forehead while you slept,' Ngaio continued. 'You stirred and opened your eyes for a moment. I wondered if you would ever forgive me. You just rubbed your eyes, snuggled back on your pillow and fell asleep again. I looked at your angelic face. That little dimple on your chin. Would I ever see it again?'

Aroha pulled back. 'It's covered with an ugly tattoo now.'

'I know,' Ngaio said. 'I wasn't there for you when you went through that awful ceremony. Murua ahau!'

'Never mind that now,' Aroha said. 'Do I have a sister or not?'

Ngaio took a sniff of some smelling salts. 'My resolve was weakening. I had to leave then. Otherwise, I never would. I said a prayer. Asked God to protect you. I kissed you until I thought my tears would drown you. Then I tore myself away.'

Aroha fidgeted. It was all heart-wrenching, but would her mother ever tell her about the baby?

Another whiff of the smelling salts and Ngaio continued. 'I'd only reached the end of the drive when I turned back. No way could I leave you alone in such a hostile world. Whatever the risk, I was taking you with me. I snuck back into the house, praying I wouldn't wake your father. Fat chance of that. Before I got to your bedroom, the bastard was bellowing at the top of his voice.

'"What the bloody hell's going on, Ngaio? Get back in here! Wretched woman! Wahine whakarihariha!"

'That sent me into a blind panic. I was sure he was coming for me—with his gun. I bolted out of the house. Believe me, every step that took me further away from you, my beloved daughter, tore my soul apart.' With a gasp, Ngaio lurched forward and clung to Aroha. 'And yes, five months later I gave birth to your sister, Hinemoa.'

          David Whittet

Chapter Fifty-Three

'Tuberculosis? Palliative care?' Aroha put down the phone.

'Bad news?' Lilly asked.

'The doctor says there's no hope of a cure. She's living on borrowed time. Hinemoa didn't call him until the disease had damaged her lungs beyond repair.'

Lilly sighed. 'I'd heard there was TB up the coast. It's housing like this that does it.'

'And lack of decent food,' Aroha added. 'Where's Hinemoa? It's a disgrace, leaving Mum like this.'

Lilly shrugged. 'We just have to make the most of what life Ngaio has left.'

Aroha picked up a shopping basket. 'I'm going to get her some proper kai.'

Another day passed. Still no sign of her half-sister.

'Please don't blame Hinemoa,' Ngaio said as Aroha brought her a plate of steamed fish. 'It's not her fault. She does her best.'

Aroha heaped the fish onto a fork and guided it into her mother's mouth. 'But she's not here, is she?'

Ngaio almost choked on the fish. 'Please …'

Lilly stepped forward. 'Leave it, Aroha. You're upsetting your mother.'

Aroha slumped her shoulders. 'You're right. I'm sorry, Mum. You mustn't worry about anything. Just concentrate on getting better and on finishing your dinner.'

Aroha went through to the kitchen to wash the plate. She heard Lilly and Ngaio talking.

'Thank you for bringing Aroha back to me,' Ngaio said. 'I didn't think I'd ever see her again.'

Aroha peeked through the door. Lilly was perched on the edge of the bed, holding Ngaio's hand.

'I'm so happy I could do something to make amends,' Lilly said, 'to you and to Aroha for what I did or failed to do.'

'Now my life is complete,' Ngaio said. 'Aroha and Hinemoa together at last. The family reunited.'

Together? Reunited? Aroha almost dropped the plate she was drying. Three days she'd been at the house and she still hadn't set eyes on Hinemoa. Thank God Lilly had helped her find Ngaio. If it were left to Hinemoa, their mother would die of starvation.

❋

Two o'clock in the morning. Loud music woke Aroha from a deep sleep. Hinemoa was back.

'You can turn that thing off for a start.' Aroha marched into Hinemoa's bedroom and unplugged her ghetto blaster. 'Where the hell have you been?'

Hinemoa's jaw dropped. 'Who are you? What are you doing in our house?'

'I'm your sister.' Aroha stared at the dishevelled teenager, her hair in knots, her eyes glazed through lack of sleep. At least, Aroha hoped it was merely from insufficient sleep.

Hinemoa gulped. 'Aroha? My long-lost half-sister?'

'Yes.' Aroha sat down next to Hinemoa on the bed.

'Cool,' Hinemoa said. 'Ngaio told me about you. It's going to be wicked having a sister. We're going to have fun.'

'Never mind fun,' Aroha said. 'What about Mum? How could you leave her like that for days on end?'

Hinemoa rolled her eyes. 'Chill out! We've only just met and you're laying into me already.'

'Well, someone needs to give you a good kick up the backside!' Aroha crossed her arms. 'What have you been doing that's so important that you could neglect your own mother? She's lying in a pool of shit and you're out partying.'

Hinemoa slumped on her bed and looked away. 'You've no idea what it's been like for me. I've tried to look after her, but I'm no bloody nurse. Sometimes it's all too much for me and I have to get out.'

Aroha shook her head. 'Why didn't you call the doctor? That was the least you could have done.'

'I wanted to.' Hinemoa sat up and met Aroha's eyes. 'You'll never understand how much I wanted to. I knew something was wrong as soon as she started coughing. But she refused to see the doctor. Said it would get back to Tautaru, and we'd both be dead. She wouldn't let the district nurses in either. What was I to do?'

Aroha edged closer to her sister. 'I'm sorry. I didn't know.'

'I think she was more afraid of the Gang than she was of being sick,' Hinemoa said. 'It hasn't been easy, trying to look after her on my own. We've no friends or whānau up here. And I'm only sixteen.'

Aroha frowned. 'That's still no excuse for leaving her on her own.' She paused and scratched her head. 'If only I'd known. I could have come and helped you.'

'I've done my best for her,' Hinemoa said. 'Honest, sis.'

Something in her sister's soulful brown eyes told Aroha that what she was saying was mostly true.

'Well, I'm here now.' Aroha put her arm around Hinemoa. 'Between us, we're going to make Ngaio's last days as happy as they can be.'

Hinemoa grinned. Aroha had seen that mischievous look before. Of course. She was Hunapo's half-sister, and it seemed she had something of his cocky, good-time attitude.

'Why does the Gang have to mess with everything?' Aroha said after a long pause. 'We're half-sisters and our fathers sworn enemies. They married me off to your half-brother—'

Hinemoa sat bolt upright. 'I have a brother?'

'Yes. Hunapo. Didn't Ngaio tell you?' Aroha smiled. 'I think you two would get along.'

'I can't wait to meet him.'

Aroha stood up. 'We'd better get some sleep. I want to fetch a wheelchair from the community health centre in the morning and take Mum outside to get some sun.' She paused at the bedroom door. 'Tautaru. Maahanga. The Gang. They've done their best to ruin our lives. And Ngaio's. We can't let them succeed.'

Aroha was up at daybreak. After taking Ngaio her breakfast, she walked into the township to meet the district nurses and collect the wheelchair.

'Gently does it.' Aroha beckoned Hinemoa and Lilly to help her lift Ngaio off the bed and into the chair. 'We're taking you to the beach, Mum. The sea air will do you good.'

They stopped at the village store and bought ice creams. Aroha studied Hinemoa's face as they pushed Ngaio along the shore. Her sister had Ngaio's high cheekbones and Maahanga's prominent chin, but it was the eyes and Hunapo's impish grin that defined her the most. Was this a good thing? Hunapo had broken Aroha's heart. She prayed Hinemoa wouldn't do the same.

'It makes me so happy to see my two beautiful daughters together,' Ngaio said. 'I hope you'll always be friends.'

'We will,' Aroha said. She shot Hinemoa a glance. 'Won't we?'

Hinemoa smiled. 'Try keeping us apart.'

The two sisters hugged each other and Ngaio.

Ngaio was short of breath and had another coughing fit when they got home.

'Help me get her back into bed,' Aroha said, wiping the blood-stained mucous off Ngaio's face and clearing the phlegm from her mouth.

'You'd have made a wonderful nurse, sis,' Hinemoa said.

Aroha looked up at her sister. 'I've spent long enough in hospital over the past couple of years. I used to watch the way the nurses looked after their patients. Here, let me show you.'

David Whittet

She handed Hinemoa a cotton bud and helped her to clean the blood from Ngaio's nose.

'Looks like both my daughters are going to be nurses,' Ngaio murmured, resting her head on the pillow and drifting off to sleep.

❧

Lilly cleaned the house from top to bottom over the next few days. Aroha called the local pest control to eradicate the rats. While Hinemoa joined in with the chores and seemed genuinely enthusiastic at first, Aroha noticed her sister was becoming increasingly restless.

'Sis,' Hinemoa said, shuffling from one foot to the other. 'I might push off for a couple of days.'

Aroha gave her a hard stare. 'What?'

'I've met a boy. Ben. He's part of a biking club. He's invited me to go on a rally at the weekend.'

'What about Mum?' Aroha said.

Lilly came in from the yard. 'I think you should stay, Hinemoa. Your mother hasn't got long. She might not be here when you come back.'

Aroha rubbed her eyes. She'd been trying not to think about it, but Hinemoa's plan to take off forced her to face reality. 'Lilly's right. I don't think Mum will last more than the week. She's going out fast.'

'I'm sorry!' Hinemoa burst into tears. 'I'm so selfish. I won't go.'

Aroha embraced her sister and stroked her hair. 'Don't cry. It's not easy watching someone you love die. But Mum needs you to be here, and I do too.'

Lilly grabbed her van's keys. 'I'm going to drive home tonight and fetch Evie. She'll want to be here at the end. So will some of the other women.'

'I need to get word to Kāterina as well,' Aroha said. 'But how? Why does she have to live in the middle of nowhere?'

'I'll ask Jake, Evie's boy,' Lilly said. 'He'll ride into the forest on his motorbike and tell her. This will hit Kāterina hard. Especially after what we've heard from Ngaio these past few days.'

Aroha suddenly felt choked up. She hid her face behind her hands, not wanting Hinemoa to see her break down. Remaining brave for her sister and maintaining her composure had been difficult, but she'd managed. Until now, when, without warning, the injustice of the situation hit her.

'It's going to be hard for me too.' Aroha's legs gave way, and she collapsed onto a chair. 'I've just found my mother again and now she's going to die. How could life be so cruel?'

                    David Whittet

Chapter Fifty-Four

The death rattle grew louder. Aroha knew the end was near. She sponged her mother's face as the rigor broke and rubbed a soothing balm into her dusky blue lips.

'Can you hear me, Mum?' Aroha said. 'There's something I need to tell you. You've given me courage. You were brave. You got away from Tautaru.'

'I wasn't brave,' Ngaio grunted in between gasps for breath. 'I should have taken you with me.'

Aroha gently stroked her mother's cheeks. 'You did what you thought was right at the time, and you've shown me it *is* possible to escape from the Gang. That's just the wake-up call I need.'

Ngaio jerked up on her pillow. 'Don't make the same mistakes as me.'

Aroha took a deep breath. 'I don't know what I'll do or where I'll go, but I'm not going back to those bastards. Tautaru. Hunapo. I'm finished with the lot of them.'

Ngaio grasped Aroha's hand. 'I could never give you the life you deserved. Now I can die in peace, knowing you're free. I'm so proud of you.'

Aroha stared into her mother's eyes. The panting slowed, and she saw a new calm on Ngaio's face.

'Hinemoa! Lilly! Evie! Come quickly!' Aroha shouted. 'It's time to say goodbye.'

Lilly had returned that morning with Evie and a group of the women elders. They gathered around the bedside. Aroha and Hinemoa sat on either side, each holding one of her mother's hands. Lilly and the women stood at the foot of the bed.

'Kia kaha,' Ngaio rasped, struggling to lift her head. 'Stay strong. Be happy. Look after each other. Always.'

Ngaio slipped back. Aroha stroked her tangled hair, tears mixing with her mother's sweat.

Nobody moved. Aroha had no idea how long they all sat there in a deadly hush. Minutes, hours, days even. Time no longer mattered. Eventually, the sound of a door opening broke the silence. Aroha turned her head.

'Kāterina!'

Aroha could see the pain in the old woman's face. Kāterina's eyes were puffy, her face red and blotchy. Aroha beckoned her to the head of the bed.

Kāterina placed her hand on Ngaio's. 'Can you ever forgive me?'

Ngaio opened her eyes for a moment. 'I have two beautiful daughters. But for you, I'd only have one.'

Aroha felt a tightness in her throat as the two women embraced. She glanced across to Hinemoa. Did her half-sister know the whole story?

Ngaio closed her eyes again and took her last breath.

Aroha laid a hand on her chest. The rattling stopped. 'She's gone!'

Her hand trembling, Kāterina drew a cross on Ngaio's forehead. 'She's at peace.'

Aroha and Hinemoa both kissed their mother, then embraced each other.

The women prayed at the bedside for an hour after Ngaio's passing.

Lilly's voice croaked. 'Her pain is over. She is with God.'

'Amen,' Kāterina said. 'Kia mau te rongo, Ngaio. Manaaki Atua koe!'

Evie repeated the prayer in English. 'Be at peace, Ngaio. God bless you!'

Aroha caught Hinemoa's eye. The stony stare spoke more of anger than sorrow. Had her sister worked it out?

Hinemoa left the room when the women began laying out Ngaio's body. Aroha watched Kāterina wash and Evie gently dry the body. Evie smeared kōkōwai over the torso and anointed it with oil.

'Excuse me,' Aroha whispered, 'I need to go after Hinemoa.'

                    David Whittet

'Of course,' Lilly said. 'She must be taking this hard.'

Aroha found her sister crouched on the floor in her bedroom with the radio blaring.

'What is it?' Aroha said. 'Why are you looking at me like that?'

'You knew all along, didn't you?' Hinemoa shot back. 'I saw it in your face when Mum said, "But for you, I'd only have one daughter." She tried to get rid of me, didn't she? You should have told me.'

Aroha turned off the radio and sat down next to her sister. 'I only found out a few days ago. Honestly. I didn't even know you existed until a couple of weeks ago.'

Hinemoa looked down at the floor. 'Ngaio didn't want me. She should've had an abortion. My life's been an endless pile of shit.'

Aroha put her arm around Hinemoa. 'Don't say that. I care about you. We could rent a flat together. Get to know each other.'

'No.' Hinemoa jumped to her feet. 'I'm sorry, sis, but I'm going away with Ben. He understands me—'

'I want to understand you,' Aroha interrupted. 'You can't go. I've only just found you.'

Hinemoa's expression softened. 'I know. But I'm alive when we're on the road with the bikers. I have to go with them.'

Aroha stood up and extended a hand towards her sister. 'At least stay for Mum's tangi. Please.'

'Of course,' Hinemoa said. 'But after that, I'm out of here. Don't be cross with me.'

As more of the women elders journeyed up the coast for Ngaio's funeral, Aroha had something else on her mind. She took Lilly to one side. 'You don't think Tautaru will come, do you? I don't want any trouble.'

They sat down together on the back doorstep.

Lilly scratched her head. 'I don't think so. There's too much unrest on his patch. He won't risk leaving.'

Aroha shrugged. 'I hope you're right. We need a quiet, dignified ceremony for Mum.'

'Besides,' Lilly said, 'he's with Manaia now, and I don't think she'd take kindly to him farewelling Ngaio.'

Aroha snorted. 'Since when did Tautaru take any notice of a woman?'

'I've heard she's got him under her thumb,' Lilly said.

'Bloody hell!' Aroha shook her head. 'Now I've heard everything. Mind you, those two deserve each other.'

'Come on,' Lilly said. 'We'd better get back to work.' They got up from the step and went into the kitchen to help the other women clean the house. 'Too bad the landlord's such a miserable bastard. Ngaio's barely cold in her grave and he wants to re-let the house.'

Evie rinsed her mop in the sink. 'Well, that's a good job done. You can see your reflection in the bathroom floor.' She turned to Aroha and Lilly. 'How about a cup of tea? Let's boil the jug before the electricity's cut off.'

Lilly looked around at the women scrubbing the walls. 'Better make it a big pot. We're all gasping.'

'Evie,' Aroha said, taking a deep breath while they waited for the kettle to boil, 'I saw you talking to Hinemoa yesterday. You seem to get on well with her.'

'My boy Jake met her on a road trip with the biking gang,' Evie said. 'I think he was quite taken with her.'

'I'm worried about her,' Aroha said. 'Those bikers are a bad influence.'

Evie poured the tea. 'She's rough around the edges, your sister. But her heart's in the right place.'

'She's talking about taking off again,' Aroha said. 'Another road trip.'

'Here, this will make you feel better.' Evie handed Aroha a cup of tea. 'Surely she'll stay for the tangi?'

     David Whittet

'She said she would.' Aroha took a sip of the tea. 'Would you talk to her? She might listen to you.'

Evie hesitated. 'I'll try. But I doubt she'll take much notice of me.'

'She's crazy about this boy, Ben,' Aroha said. 'I don't like the sound of him.'

Evie sighed. 'Jake said Ben's a nasty piece of work. I'll do my best to talk some sense into Hine. But no promises.'

Aroha gave Evie a hug, almost knocking over the teapot. 'You're a saint!'

The local minister, Reverend Hohepa, greeted the women as they filed into the small wooden chapel. Aroha breathed a sigh of relief. No sign of Tautaru or any of his minions. Thank God for that. She'd been dreading another disaster like Amiri's funeral. That would have sent her right over the edge. And Hinemoa was by her side. Thank God for that, too.

A peace descended on the congregation as Reverend Hohepa began the service. He spoke of a troubled life now at rest. The minister lifted his arms and raised his eyes heavenwards. Aroha glanced up at the rafters. This was precisely the quiet and dignified ceremony she needed to mourn her mother's passing.

Standing at the graveside after the service, the sea breeze sent a shiver down Aroha's spine. The minister concluded the burial rite and Aroha and Hinemoa both threw flowers on the coffin.

'I love you, Mum,' Aroha cried. 'Rest in peace. You had little enough while you were alive.'

Aroha sensed Hinemoa wanted to add something. But her sister simply flung her arms around Aroha and wept.

The next morning, Aroha watched Hinemoa put on her leather pants and jacket. What could she say? Would anything make her sister change her mind? Evie's talk clearly hadn't made any difference.

'I've spent my entire life trying to get away from the Gang,' Aroha said. 'It breaks my heart to see you throw away your freedom.'

'Cool it, sis,' Hinemoa replied. 'I'm finding myself. Biking's great. It's an adventure.'

Aroha clung to her arm. 'Stick with Ben and his mates and they'll suck you in. You'll never get out.'

Hinemoa shrugged. 'So what? There's nothing to keep me here now.'

Aroha shook her head. 'Like I said, we could share a flat—'

'No.' Hinemoa edged towards the door. 'I have to get away from this place.' She stared back at Aroha. 'Learning that your mother tried to abort you isn't easy.'

'I know that,' Aroha said. 'Let's deal with it together.'

A horn sounded outside. The last chance to save her sister was slipping away.

'That'll be Ben,' Hinemoa said. 'I've got to go.' She grabbed her backpack, then turned back and kissed Aroha on the cheek. 'We have to get on with our lives. You must go back to yours. And please, let me get on with mine.'

'I don't have a life to go back to,' Aroha said.

'Then you need to make one.' Hinemoa hugged her sister one last time. 'Try to be happy for me.'

Another blast on the horn. Hinemoa let go and rushed outside.

Aroha followed her out into the street. 'When will you be back?'

'Weeks, months, years,' Hinemoa called back. 'Who knows? There's no telling once the thrill of the open road takes over.'

The roar of Ben's Harley Davidson reverberated through the street and drowned Hinemoa's voice. Aroha almost choked on the petrol fumes. She couldn't watch Hinemoa ride off with Ben and the rest of the bikers. She covered her eyes and looked away until they disappeared into the distance.

    David Whittet

Kāterina was stacking boxes in the kitchen when Aroha wandered back into the house.

'I've lost her—my sister,' Aroha groaned, slumping against the kitchen bench. 'And I'd only just found her.'

Kāterina patted her hand. 'You're sisters. You'll never lose each other.'

'I'm not so sure.' Aroha dabbed her eyes. 'She might not come back. At least, not for a long time. I may never see her again.'

'Of course you will,' Kāterina reassured her.

Aroha sighed. 'Not if those bikers have anything to do with it.'

'Listen.' Kāterina picked up a stool and perched opposite her. 'I want you to come back with me—'

'To the *Gypsy Rose?*'

Kāterina nodded.

Aroha looked at her dubiously. 'Why?'

'I want to make it up to you,' Kāterina said. 'If I'd handled things differently … understood what Ngaio was going through … perhaps she wouldn't have run away and left you without a mother.'

Aroha leant forward and gave Kāterina a hug. 'That's okay. Ngaio forgave you, and so do I.'

'But you've nowhere to go,' Kāterina said. 'I heard you're not going back to Tautaru, or to Hunapo.'

Aroha shrugged. 'I'll rent a flat somewhere.'

'Are you sure?' Kāterina looked around the run-down kitchen. 'Even a dump like this costs an arm and a leg.'

'I know that.' Aroha drew back. She didn't want to admit it, but Kāterina was right. She'd talked about flatting with Hinemoa, but in her heart Aroha knew it was just a dream. She hadn't the money for a bond and no job to pay the rent. 'Maybe I'll go to a women's refuge. That's what Mum did when she had to get away.'

'I suppose you could. But—' Kāterina took a deep breath. 'Actually, there's something else.'

'What?'

'I want to talk to you about Amiri. I should have told you earlier, but you were too upset.'

Aroha felt every muscle in her body stiffen. 'No!'

'I understand this is hard for you to hear, but there was another side to Amiri. I know what happened in the fire. I've seen it in my crystal ball—'

'Bullshit!' Aroha clenched a fist. 'You know nothing about Amiri—'

'I do. Hear me out. Please.'

'Listen, Kāterina. I'm just beginning to come to terms with losing Amiri. Even if you know something, which I doubt, I don't want to hear it.' Aroha got up and made for the door. She turned back and glared at Kāterina. 'The police, the fire department and the coroner—they've all thrashed out the whole sorry affair of the fire. The last thing I need is you opening up old wounds.'

Aroha stormed off into the yard before Kāterina could reply. What could the old woman possibly know about Amiri?

Lilly and some of the other women were clearing up after a garage sale of Ngaio's remaining possessions.

'We're nearly finished,' Lilly said. 'We'll be off home soon.'

Aroha leant against the 'To Let' sign the landlord had put up by the gate. 'It's all wrong. Mum lived here in squalor all those years. Thanks to you, now the place is spotless.'

Lilly stopped sweeping the backyard. 'I know. The new tenants will be lucky.'

Evie came over. 'Have you decided what you're going to do, Aroha? It's going to be strange going back to Rere without you.'

'Kāterina wants me to go back with her to the caravan, but I don't know.' Aroha broke off and turned to Lilly, staring into her eyes as if looking for a solution. 'She keeps banging on about having something to tell me about Amiri.'

     David Whittet

'Perhaps she just wants some company,' Lilly said. 'It can't be much fun going back to that old caravan on your own.'

'I don't think so,' Aroha said. 'She's lived there long enough.'

'Don't you want to hear what she's got to say about Amiri?' Evie asked. 'Maybe it'll bring you some closure.'

'I doubt it,' Aroha said.

'Maybe there was more to that fire than we know,' Evie said. 'When we were at Amiri's tangi, I overheard—'

Aroha held up her hands. 'Don't talk to me about that ghastly day.'

Lilly put an arm on Aroha's shoulder. 'It was a disaster. I feel bad about taking you. I wouldn't have done if I'd known what was going to happen.'

'It wasn't your fault,' Aroha said.

Lilly met Aroha's eyes. 'What if Kāterina really does know something about Amiri? He was your husband. If it were me, I'd want to know.'

'If she's got something to say, she can do it now.' Aroha returned Lilly's gaze and marched back out into the kitchen.

Kāterina was making sandwiches at the bench. 'They're for the journey home,' she said. 'Are you sure you won't change your mind and come with me?'

'If it's that important,' Aroha insisted, 'you can tell me now.'

'I can't—not *here*.' Kāterina licked a finger and raised it in the air. 'The aura's not right.'

Aroha glared at Kāterina. 'Why do you always have to talk in riddles? Just spit it out.'

Kāterina shook her head. 'You must come back with me to the *Gypsy Rose*. It'll bring you peace.'

'No.' Aroha walked away. 'Whatever it is you think you know about Amiri, you can keep it to yourself.'

That evening Aroha sat on a stone wall overlooking the bay. Lilly, Evie and the other women had just left. Seeing them off had been almost as painful as saying goodbye to Hinemoa. Now Aroha was alone, staring out to sea. The vast expanse of ocean felt cold and empty in the twilight, with the last rays of sunlight disappearing behind the horizon.

Hinemoa had told her she needed to start a new life. Fat chance of that. Every opportunity to break free had been snatched away from her. Kāterina promised her peace—if she listened to more of the old woman's ramblings. Right now, her heart beating in sympathy with the pounding waves seemed to be the only way she'd ever find peace of mind.

It was close to midnight when Aroha returned to the deserted house. The landlord had told her she would have to leave the following day. New tenants were moving in. She packed her things in her backpack in the morning and wandered through the township. Perhaps she'd hitch a lift and see where it took her. The only vehicles to stop were trucks. Not liking the look of the drivers, Aroha backed away and headed out of town on foot. She passed a farmyard and caught sight of Kāterina in the stables mounting her horse, Cleo. Kāterina had mentioned she'd ridden all the way from her caravan on horseback. The old woman was fighting off tears as she set out on her return journey.

Aroha ran towards her. 'Wait! I'm coming with you!'

Every instinct told Aroha to stop. What was she thinking? She'd thrashed it out in her mind so many times over the past twenty-four hours. Going back with Kāterina would be an enormous mistake. So why was she still racing into the paddock?

'Tēnā koe! Thank you!' Kāterina jumped off Cleo and embraced Aroha with a bear hug. 'You won't regret this!'

'Won't I?' Aroha studied her with an even gaze. 'I don't know what this secret of yours is about, but it had better be worth the heartache.'

        David Whittet

Chapter Fifty-Five

'Giddy-up, Cleo! Godspeed to the *Gypsy Rose!*'

Kāterina's shrill command echoed through the farmyard. Cleo trotted down the street, breaking into a canter as Kāterina pushed her hips forward on the saddle.

'Slow down,' Aroha cried. 'I'm going to fall off!'

Kāterina laughed. 'Hold on to me and enjoy the ride.'

The wind blew against their faces as Cleo galloped down the country lanes. When a bunch of motorbikes roared past them, Aroha squinted at the riders' faces. Was one of them Hinemoa?

Leaving the road, Cleo raced over paddocks, splashing the two of them with water as they crossed rivers and streams. The exhilaration of the ride didn't stop Aroha fretting. What did Kāterina have in store for her? Aroha shuddered when they entered the forest. Her mind went back to the last time she had ridden on horseback with Kāterina. Aroha was just fourteen. Her mother was bleeding, and she didn't know what to do. Kāterina had come to their rescue astride Cleo. Ngaio was dying back then. Now she was dead.

'Whoa!' Kāterina pulled back on Cleo's reins when they reached a clearing in the forest. 'Time for a break.'

Kāterina mumbled incantations to herself as she poured the coffee from a rusty old flask.

Aroha picked at a stale sandwich. What was going on in the old woman's head? What could she possibly know about Amiri? 'I've waited long enough,' she said, feeding the butty to some grateful forest birds. 'Tell me now.'

'All in good time. We should get going. It'll be dark soon.'

Aroha rolled her eyes. 'You sound just like Tūī!'

'Who?'

'Tūī. An old woman we met at the women's refuge.'

'Then Tūī was right,' Kāterina said, helping Aroha back on the horse.

'It was Tūī who helped us find Ngaio.' Aroha heaved herself up and tried to get comfortable behind Kāterina. 'You're two of a kind, you and Tūī. She kept saying, "You can't tell anyone anything until they are ready to hear it."'

'We are all passing figures in life's continuum.' Kāterina glanced back at Aroha. 'Lost spirits searching for the eternal truth.' She gripped the reins and squeezed Cleo with her legs. *'Gee-up,* Cleo! Not much further!'

Every muscle in Aroha's body ached by the time she spotted the familiar path to the caravan. Maybe now she would get some answers.

Kāterina dismounted and handed Aroha the caravan key.

'Make yourself at home inside,' Kāterina said. 'Once I've fed Cleo, I'll heat some soup for our supper. Then we can talk.'

Aroha wandered inside. The *Gypsy Rose* hadn't changed since her previous visit. It felt unreal and she took a step back. Her world had turned upside down and, weirdly, Aroha expected everything else to be different too. She sat on the bench, her hands flat on her thighs, waiting for Kāterina. Something caught her eye, tucked behind a stack of dusty old books. She moved across to investigate and pulled out a tattered home-made placard: 'Get your bulldozers out of our town!' And another: 'You're not making money out of our whenua!' Then she found a flier: 'Save Rere. Save the Falls.' That one looked much more recent.

What the hell? Amiri had told her about protesters trying to shut down his business development. She'd seen how the stress had spoilt the last days of his life. Aroha couldn't forgive that. Perhaps, too, if Amiri hadn't had so much on his mind, he'd have written a will.

Grabbing the banners, Aroha charged out of the caravan. Kāterina was warming the soup in a large copper pot on an outdoor gas burner.

'Was it you?' Aroha threw the boards to the ground at Kāterina's feet and waved the flier in her face. 'Amiri was on the verge of a breakthrough when a bunch of protestors ruined everything. Well, I hope you're proud of yourselves.

Amiri said the waters at Rere could help cure sickness. He wanted to bring health to everyone.'

'And you believe that, do you?'

'I do.' Aroha glared at her and screwed up the flier. 'And you and your cronies destroyed his dream.'

'I can explain.' Kāterina handed Aroha a bowl of soup. 'Let's go inside.'

Perched on a stool, Aroha watched Kāterina slurping the broth. *What could justify depriving the world of such a wonderful gift?*

Aroha had no appetite, and she pushed her bowl aside. 'I'm waiting.'

Kāterina swallowed a last mouthful of soup. 'We marched against mining Rere Falls to protect our rights, our mana tangata whenua. To stop them plundering our land!' She sat cross-legged on her bench and covered herself with an old brown rug. 'They were going to demolish the falls and build a huge factory—'

'Bullshit.' Aroha almost fell off her stool. 'Amiri loved the falls. He said they were sacred because they were where we met. He would never harm them.'

Kāterina twitched. 'Listen. Back in the seventies, an oil company wanted to dig up Whatatutu—'

Aroha shook her head. 'I'm not interested in the seventies. I want to know why you undermined Amiri's project.'

'That's what I'm trying to tell you.' Kāterina took a deep breath. 'It was the discovery of oil that put the area on the map. Developers kept coming back. They couldn't get to the oil, but they refused to leave empty-handed. They concocted a cock and bull story about minerals in the rocks at Rere being an aphrodisiac. It would take a marketing expert to make people believe it. Amiri had a growing reputation as a spin doctor, so they brought him in to sell the idea.'

Aroha jumped to her feet. 'How dare you insult Amiri's memory!'

'I'm not.' Kāterina held her hands out in front of her. 'I've long believed in the healing properties of the water at Rere, and I won't let anyone destroy the falls.' She lowered her arms and rubbed her knees and hips. 'I often bathe under them. It works wonders for my aching joints. Some people come from miles away to soak in the water.' She shot Aroha an icy stare. 'But it would never work if it's bottled in a factory and sold in a supermarket.'

Aroha snorted. 'It would. Amiri had it tested.'

'Did he, indeed?' Kāterina shuffled on her bench. 'Well, it wasn't only the smart-arsed business hotshots who cashed in on it. Once the Gang sniffed the money, they drove everyone else out of town. Me included. Why else do you think I'm stuck in this ditch in the middle of nowhere?'

'It doesn't make sense.' Aroha paced up and down the caravan, glaring at Kāterina. 'Besides, I don't know why you have to dredge up all this stuff that's better forgotten.'

Kāterina sighed. 'Hear me out. I've been trying to tell you for so long. I wanted to say something before your wedding, when I brought you the lamp. But Amiri was there, and I couldn't. Then everything happened so quickly. The next time I got to talk to you was when you were in hospital. I wanted to say something then, too.'

'I remember,' Aroha said. 'I wasn't ready for any more bad news.'

Kāterina bowed her head. 'More like I wasn't brave enough to speak up. Murua ahau!'

Aroha watched Kāterina squirm. 'Just tell me. Surely it can't be that terrible.'

'It is.' Kāterina gulped and met Aroha's eyes. 'Why do you think Amiri wanted to marry you—a gang girl? He was a high-flyer. He could have had any girl he wanted.'

Aroha flinched. 'Because he loved me.'

'Because you were useful to him,' Kāterina said. 'There was one last thing in Amiri's way. The Māhiti Gang. And what better way to get over that obstacle than to marry the Gang president's daughter?'

'You're lying! *Lying!*' It was all Aroha could do to stop herself from throttling Kāterina. 'Amiri wasn't like that.'

'Wasn't he?' Kāterina raised an eyebrow. 'I made it my business to find out about Amiri. Asked around. Talked to my old mate Alejandro Guerrero.

 David Whittet

Alejandro was a director of Amiri's company. He told me how Amiri used to dominate board meetings and bully everyone into doing what he wanted.'

Aroha felt herself stiffen. 'So what? Amiri was a man with a vision. He had to fight for what he believed in. No wonder he upset a few rivals on the way.'

'A visionary?' Kāterina shrugged. 'The only thing Amiri cared about was money. Alejandro told me about the boardroom stoush when Amiri announced his plans for Rere. As usual, Amiri was full of himself, boasting about how they'd all make a fortune …'

❦

Amiri rubbed his hands together. 'Gentlemen, let's get ready to make a heap of money!'

Alejandro Guerrero sighed. He'd seen it all before. Amiri in full throttle was even more intimidating than the businessmen back in his native Mexico. What was the incorrigible rogue up to this time?

Towering over the other board members, Amiri continued, his palms flat on the table. 'The media are playing into our hands. All this talk about the magical properties of the water. I trust you all read the article in *Metro?*' He held up a copy of the magazine and waved it in the air. 'I couldn't have written it better myself. Rere's minerals heal the sick, preserve youthfulness, boost fertility, and take your sex life to another level.'

The board members applauded. Not again. Alejandro never understood why they all hung on his every word. It was nothing more than an act.

'I could do with a bottle myself,' Errol Troy said. 'Is there anything Rere water can't do?'

Amiri grinned. 'Not if you believe the press. All voodoo—but highly effective.'

Leon Worthington, the most senior of the directors, scratched his bald head. 'Are we marketing it as an aphrodisiac? That could be risky. Are you sure we can take on Viagra?'

Amiri gave Leon an icy stare. 'This is bigger than Viagra! It'll make Viagra look like a kid's lolly. I tell you, the Rere Falls are a freaking gold mine!'

Alejandro groaned when Amiri jumped up and pointed to the sales projections on the whiteboard. Meaningless numbers. Why couldn't the others see that?

Oliver Nelson, the board's legal counsel, flicked through the papers in front of him and frowned. 'It says here you want a bottling plant right next to the falls. Have you thought that through? What about the protestors? They won't take this lying down.'

'Too bloody right,' Alejandro said. Thank God he wasn't the only one to see through Amiri. 'They've got a ton of support out there.'

Amiri slammed his fist on the table. 'Bottling at the source means more money. We will build the factory at the falls—even if it means flattening the township.'

Oliver shook his head. 'There'll be huge compensation claims!'

'You won't get away with this,' Alejandro said. 'Haven't you heard about the demonstrations?'

Amiri rolled his eyes. 'You mean old Kāterina Kururangi and her band of has-beens? Don't make me laugh!'

How dare he! Alejandro took a deep breath. 'I wouldn't underestimate Miss Kururangi if I were you. She's no fool and she has friends in high places.'

'Not any more,' Amiri muttered.

Alejandro stood up and glared at Amiri. 'Then how come half the neighbourhood turned up for her march?'

'Let's cut the crap,' Oliver said. 'Rere is gangland. The Gang will crucify us if we take their land.'

Alejandro sank back in his chair. Of course, the Māhiti Gang! The most vicious mob in the country. That had to be the end of Amiri's nonsense.

'I don't fancy taking on the Gang,' Leon said with a shudder. 'Remember what they did to those poor sods growing their own cannabis?'

'They won't give us any trouble,' Amiri said. 'I guarantee it.'

 David Whittet

Alejandro pointed a finger at Amiri. 'Haven't you heard of Tautaru?'

Amiri leant back in his chair. 'Yes. I've heard of Tautaru.'

Oliver packed up his board papers and stuffed them in his briefcase. 'Then you'll understand why we can't possibly progress this any further. As your lawyer, I'm telling you, we have to abandon the project and cut our losses.'

'No.' Amiri eyed each of the board members in turn. 'You don't need to worry about the Gang. I've taken care of that. I'm marrying Tautaru's daughter! The president's daughter! The Gang can't touch us now!'

❧

'You're lying!' Aroha sobbed, pushing Kāterina away. 'He loved me. I know he did. We were soulmates.'

'Why does everyone shoot the messenger?' Kāterina sighed. 'It's been the story of my life.'

'Stories *are* your life,' Aroha retorted. 'You're making this up. It's all bullshit like Kamaka and his binoculars.'

Kāterina lowered her head. 'I may have embellished the odd yarn, but never anything serious like this.'

'I still don't believe you.' Aroha dabbed her eyes. 'You weren't there. And I don't remember Amiri having a Mexican in his company.'

'It's the truth. Alejandro Guerrero and I go back a long way. He wouldn't lie to me. I'm merely repeating to you what he said to me.' Kāterina squeezed her eyes shut. 'Standing up to Amiri cost Alejandro dear ...'

❧

Alone in his office, Amiri had his hands around Alejandro's neck.

'Morally reprehensible, is it?' Amiri pushed him against the wall, his fingers digging into Alejandro's throat. 'Don't you ever contradict me again!'

'I just meant … be careful …' Alejandro spluttered. 'We can't afford a blood feud with the Gang … or a land war.'

Amiri released Alejandro and threw him to the ground. 'I've enough dirt on you to see you finished. Crushed and thrown out with the trash!'

❧

'Amiri threatened to ruin him if he didn't keep his mouth shut and do as he was told,' Kāterina said. 'Poor Alejandro. He didn't deserve that.'

'That's it. I'm going.' Aroha waved a fist at Kāterina. 'Is this why you dragged me here? To tell lies about the one man who really cared about me?'

'Wait. There's more.' Kāterina took another deep breath. 'You weren't the target at the wedding. It was Amiri. And Hunapo wasn't the gunman—'

'More lies!' Aroha hit back. 'How can you mention Amiri and Hunapo in the same breath?'

'Listen to me. I was in the vestry making the 111 call. I saw the gunman through the window. He took off his mask, and I got a good look at his face. I don't know who it was, but it definitely wasn't Hunapo!'

Aroha jumped to her feet. 'Crap! I heard my father boasting about bribing a ballistics expert to get Hunapo off.'

'Like you, Tautaru assumed it was Hunapo. He couldn't risk his protégé going to jail. Not after all the boasting and parading of Hunapo as his heir.' Kāterina folded her arms. 'Nobody listened to Hunapo pleading his innocence. Except me.'

'Because you're a storyteller with a vivid imagination.'

'No. Because I saw what happened.' Kāterina inched forward. 'At first, I thought maybe Hunapo had paid a hitman to kill you. The Gang never does its own dirty work. Then I thought back to something you'd said. You told me Hunapo would never pay an assassin. He wouldn't deny himself the pleasure of killing you in person—'

'Bloody right!'

     David Whittet

'That made me think'—Kāterina raised her eyebrows—'and start digging.'

Aroha stiffened. Could there be something in Kāterina's revelations? The old woman's hypnotic eyes took her back to the altar on her wedding day. The scene replayed in her mind. Kāterina was right—she hadn't actually seen the assassin's face. She'd instinctively assumed it was Hunapo. Jumbled up images continued to flicker before her eyes. Was that one of the security guards donning a mask? Yes—and he was loading a gun. Was it real? Or was her mind playing tricks on her?

'Bullshit!' Once the vision disappeared, Aroha stamped her foot and sounded off at Kāterina. 'It was Hunapo.'

Kāterina shook her head. 'Amiri made powerful enemies. The bastard didn't care how many lives he destroyed to get what he wanted. This time he went too far. He got hold of some sleaze on a government minister and used it as a bribe to get consent for a water bottling factory right next to the falls. Then he got greedy. Double-crossed the syndicate. The bullet was meant for Amiri, not you!'

Aroha held her hands over her ears, convinced her head would explode if she heard any more.

Kāterina reached out to Aroha with her hands. 'Trust me. I didn't want to believe all these terrible things about Amiri. But the truth will bring you closure, and peace.'

'Peace? I'll never have peace of mind again as long as I live.'

'You *will.*'

Aroha wiped her face and blew her nose. 'Anyway, it was definitely Hunapo who started the fire. Errol Troy saw him snooping outside that same day—'

'I asked Hunapo to keep watch over you,' Kāterina said.

Aroha almost fell off her stool. *You did what?*

Kāterina flinched. 'I was worried about you. Alejandro Guerrero warned me Amiri's enemies were planning their revenge. You needed someone to protect you.'

'And you chose *Hunapo?*'

'He cared about you,' Kāterina said. 'I saw it in his eyes. He came to see me. Poor kid was in a dreadful state over everything that had happened. He was sitting on the same stool as you are now …'

Hunapo's eyes fixed on Kāterina's. 'Why won't she believe me? I had nothing to do with the shooting.'

Kāterina rubbed her chin. 'I know it wasn't you who shot her. But you threatened to kill her if she married someone else. You were also seen with a gun outside the church on her wedding day.'

'I was there because I loved her.' Hunapo hunched his shoulders and wrapped his legs around the base of the stool. 'I was out of my mind. Couldn't bear to lose her. But you have to believe me—I'd never have done anything to harm her. If I was going to kill anyone, it would have been Amiri. Smug bastard. He was all wrong for her.'

'And you were Mr Right, I suppose.' Kāterina leant forward and put her hands on his. 'Do you still love her?'

Hunapo met her eyes. 'Yes.'

Kāterina frowned. 'What about Maddie? And all those other girls?'

Hunapo lowered his head. 'I threw them out ages ago.'

'Then I want you to look after Aroha,' Kāterina said. 'Keep her safe. She's in danger.'

Kāterina knelt in front of Aroha and put an arm on her shoulder. 'Don't fight the truth. Listen to your heart.'

Aroha shook her head. She didn't know what her heart was saying any more. Her mind was a whirlwind of unanswered questions. 'Why the hell didn't you tell me before? If it's really true, why didn't you go to the police?' She glared at Kāterina. 'You let me go on thinking it was Hunapo. If only you'd spoken up sooner. Who knows? Maybe we could've prevented the fire if we'd been aware.'

        David Whittet

Kāterina returned her gaze. 'Would you have believed me?'

Aroha grunted. She wouldn't have. She still wasn't sure if she could trust the old woman's ramblings, even now.

Suddenly everything was a blur. Aroha felt the walls of the caravan closing in on her. She pressed her hands against her temples like a vice.

Another flashback. The night of the fire. She was looking out of the window moments before she closed the curtains. That masked figure in the shadows with his rucksack. She could see his face now—it wasn't Hunapo.

'This isn't happening,' Aroha cried. 'It's just a bad dream.' She staggered to her feet and paced around the creaking wooden floor of the caravan. 'It can't be true. Amiri loved me! And I loved him—more than life itself. He would never have done this to me!'

'Aroha! Love is blind!'

'Stop. I can't take any more. I can't. *I won't.*' Aroha grabbed her coat. 'I have to get out.'

Kāterina followed her to the door. 'Think about what I've said. Please. Manaaki koe e te Atua, tāku tamaiti! God bless you, my child!'

Chapter Fifty-Six

Aroha walked for days on end, drifting aimlessly through dense bush, living rough and trying to make sense of the nightmare that tore her soul apart. A constant dialogue raged in her head. *I trusted you, Amiri. You said you would take me away from the Gang and give me a new life. You promised to look after me and I believed you.*

Everything was upside down and thinking about it was torture. Could she really have got everything so wrong? Was Amiri her betrayer and Hunapo her saviour? Eventually, she found herself back at the Rere Falls, pulled by a gravitational force she couldn't resist. Aroha couldn't trust people, but she could trust the falls. As a child, they had given her solace and peace of mind. Could the mystic falls now provide the calm that she so desperately needed?

Her life flashed before her as she wandered along the riverbank. The familiar landscape transformed into a teeming montage of agonising images. A glimpse of her first meeting with Amiri under the falls was so acute that it brought a fresh deluge of tears to her sore eyes.

None of the jumbled fragments of her existence made any sense. Another image stopped her dead in her tracks. Her younger self, paddling in the river with Hunapo.

We were so young and innocent—Aroha mentally corrected herself—*well, maybe not exactly innocent. We were hopeful. Optimistic. We said we would always be there for each other, no matter what. Hunapo promised that if I were ever in trouble, he would be there for me, he would save me …*

Suddenly she was back in the fire at their house. Shards of flame and falling masonry crushing her body. *And he did save me! Hunapo was there for me that day! He rescued me!*

David Whittet

Long-suppressed memories suddenly erupted from the dark recesses of her mind. She felt the heat of the flames anew, burning her flesh. Suffocating under the molten debris, she reached out her hand … Amiri was crawling ahead …

'Amiri! Help me!'

But Amiri didn't turn back. She raised her head and saw him scramble away from her through the molten debris.

Surely he had heard her? 'Come back! Please! Amiri!'

Still he didn't look back. Then she heard laughter. Maniacal laughter that competed with the roar of the inferno.

'I'm not dying! I'm not dying for anybody!' Was this the voice of the man who had promised her the world? 'Sorry, Aroha—it's every man for himself …'

A mighty flash suddenly blinded her. An enormous fireball ripped through the carnage. It was chasing Amiri, devouring him with its flaming teeth. Aroha shielded her eyes from the intense heat. When she moved her hands away from her face, Amiri was gone, incinerated by the blazing inferno.

'You left me to die, you bastard!' Aroha stood shaking on the riverbank, waving her fists in the air and screaming at her mental image of Amiri. 'All this pain and all this mess I've suffered is because of *you!*'

She stepped into the river. The icy-cold water on her feet extinguished the fire in her soul. Flaming beams were still crashing all around her, but Hunapo was dragging her through the smoke to safety.

'Hunapo! Hunapo!' She repeated his name constantly as she ran back to the township. She had to find him before it was too late.

Chapter Fifty-Seven

Marika's pure soprano voice rang out through the valley, welcoming the small group of well-wishers to a dawn ceremony in front of the Rere Falls. Aroha looked down at her feet on the muddy riverbank. The last time she'd heard Marika sing was on that dreadful day of her arranged marriage to Hunapo. The memory still brought Aroha out in a sweat, and here she was about to go through it all again. Could she genuinely recommit to Hunapo, the man who had broken her heart so many times and brought her so much pain? Perhaps she should make a run for it while she still had the chance.

Aroha took a few paces downstream, then stopped and listened. Marika's song was worlds away from the one she performed at the arranged marriage.

Today's waiata was a joyful ode to two lost souls.

Dual spirits
Single mind.
Both have crossed
The darkness of time.

The lyrics struck an immediate chord with Aroha and convinced her that this morning's ceremony would be different. Any lingering doubts disappeared when Hunapo arrived, the ornamental sword in his hand and the sparkle on his face matching the shimmering falls. It was all she could do to stop herself crying and ruining her makeup. The women would never forgive her for that. They had been up since three in the morning, making her radiant for the occasion.

The whānau joined hands and made a circle around Aroha and Hunapo. The gangsters stood behind them, their dogs barking wildly at their feet. Marika's

     David Whittet

song was so stirring and the melody so poignant that the men hummed the tune and the women joined in the chorus.

Aroha took a step back when Hunapo unsheathed the ceremonial sword. Her mouth went dry, and she held her breath, waiting for him to prick her thumb, bracing herself for the sharp stab of pain. The crowd clapped as he squeezed a drop of blood from the incision and then cut his own thumb. In this public re-enactment of the ritual which they had performed alone as children, the crowd cheered in unison when he held their thumbs together and again shared blood.

'Bravo! Aroha and Hunapo! Hooray! Hūrē! Hūrē! Hūrē!'

Aroha gazed into Hunapo's eyes and saw in them a new maturity. Was he a brave warrior, willing to risk his life for those he loved, or just a shameless playboy? How could a human being capable of such compassion be the same person as the rat who had so often broken her heart?

She glanced across the river and smiled when she saw a new tree growing where the old rimu once stood. Their tree. Where it all started when that impudent rascal scrambled down the trunk and landed at her feet. The recently planted tree looked sturdy. Aroha prayed their new relationship would be equally robust.

At last, she saw Hunapo for what he was. The man who stood before her was not perfect. He had made mistakes. He was no longer the idol of her childhood dreams. A flawed hero. But he was real, and he was there for her when she needed him most. She couldn't stop looking into his dark, soulful eyes as they greeted their friends and whānau—the eyes that told her he loved her. And only her.

The men staged an impromptu haka while the women performed a poi dance. Aroha gazed at her whānau and the women elders. She beamed at Lilly, who blew her a kiss. Evie, too. And Kāterina. Dear frustrating, inimitable Kāterina. She'd made it despite a flare-up of gout in her knees and ankles. Their eyes locked in shared delight.

As the dancers encouraged the crowd to join in, Aroha caught her father's eye. What was he thinking? After a pause, Tautaru embraced her and they danced together. Father and daughter united at last. Maybe, just maybe, buried under years of resentment and vengeance, her old man had a heart. Aroha sighed when the dance ended and Tautaru returned to his minions. Was that too much to hope for?

She overheard Kāterina tackling Hunapo. 'Don't you dare let her down.'

'I won't.'

'Promise me your days as a playboy are over?'

'Promise.' He met Kāterina's eyes. 'I love her.'

Aroha took in a deep breath. Maybe Tautaru would never redeem himself, but with Hunapo at her side, they had the chance to achieve what they plotted for so long as kids—to change the Gang forever.

The sun rose high above the falls and the celebrations drew to a close. Aroha and Hunapo waded through the rapids until they were directly under the cascading water. Soaked to the skin, with their bodies pummelled by the mighty torrent, they embraced, their eyes still locked in absolute trust.

With a kiss and a hongi, the blood cousins were once more irrevocably bonded.

Epilogue

Two weeks later, Aroha and Hunapo were back at Rere, sitting on a log in front of the waterfall at sunset.

Aroha fidgeted, tapping the wood with her fingers. She glanced over her shoulder at her beloved falls. Tonight they were sublime, bathed in the fading rays of the evening sun.

'Hunapo …' Aroha broke off, avoiding his eyes.

'What is it?' Hunapo said.

'I've something to tell you.' She dried up again. How could she break the news? How would he react?

Hunapo rested his hand on her knee and gave it a gentle stroke.

Aroha felt her muscles tense. She took a deep breath and exhaled slowly. 'I'm carrying Amiri's child.'

Author's Note and Acknowledgements

Aroha was born of the Gang. *Gang Girl* was born of the fifteen years I spent working as a rural doctor at Te Karaka in the Gisborne Region of New Zealand. That Māori community is the heart and soul of my story.

Before I was ready to write the novel, I made an independent film *Amiri & Aroha*. I shall never forget the day I fronted up to a notorious gangster's house hoping for an interview. My heartbeat was even louder than my banging on the door. Eventually, a nine-year-old boy gingerly put his head around the doorframe.

'Is your father at home?' I asked.

'I'll go and ask him,' the boy answered.

A loud voice boomed in the background. 'Is it the cops?'

'No,' the boy replied. 'It's the doctor.'

'The doctor? We didn't call the doctor. Nobody's sick. Are you sure it's not the cops?'

'Positive. It's the same dude that stitched my hand.' He shot me an evil look. 'And it bloody hurt.'

The gangster eventually emerged, his bold, full-facial tattoo radiating an immediate presence. He told me how the Gang forced him to have the tā moko as a teenager. The tattoo was his gang patch. He went on to describe the ceremony and the pain when the bone chisel pierced his flesh. I had my opening scene. When he told me about a gangster's daughter and her lifelong struggle to escape from the Gang, I had my story.

I asked him if he would appear as an extra in the film.

David Whittet

'Me? Act?' He ran his fingers across the grooves of his magnificent tā moko. 'You should ask my mate, Ben. He's a show-off. He'd love that sort of thing.'

His wife came in from the kitchen. 'You can't ask Ben. He's in jail!'

The gangster leapt out of his seat. 'We don't use the J-word in this house! He's temporarily unavailable!'

During my time at Te Karaka, I spent many happy weekends with my family picnicking at the nearby Rere Falls. My children loved to venture behind the cascading curtain of water and glide down the giant rockslide on a boogie board.

As I watched my children play, my mind wandered. Those majestic falls, steeped in Māori legend, *had* to feature in the story. Maybe there were some precious minerals in the rocks below the falls. What if someone wanted to exploit the magical properties of the water at Rere? Turn the iconic waterfalls into a water bottling factory? What if the Gang got involved? The plot began to take shape.

The entire Te Karaka community got behind the project. My sincere thanks go to the cast and crew of *Amiri & Aroha,* who shared the journey with me. Your energy and commitment to the film proved invaluable in breathing life into the story and shaping the character arcs.

I would particularly like to acknowledge Kristel Day, who played Aroha and co-produced the movie with me. Her contribution was immeasurable and together with Walter Walsh, saved the project from languishing indefinitely in development hell. Aptly known as the 'Wiz', Walter breathed a fiery menace into Tautaru. He also acted as my casting director. Walter's immense mana and respect opened so many doors to us throughout the production.

Shayne Biddle, fresh from his success in *The Strength of Water*, took on perhaps the most complex role, infusing Hunapo with a mesmerising screen presence. Complementing Shayne's achievement, Mathew Wikotu's soulful performance as the young Hunapo made the little rascal one of the most engaging characters in the story.

Michael Hollis brought precisely the desired edge to Amiri, the not-quite-so-perfect knight in shining armour.

My old mentor, the late great film director David Lean, gave me this advice: 'You must know what your characters eat for breakfast. It's not that you're going to show them having breakfast, but to portray them accurately, you need to know them in that much detail.' During the shooting of *Amiri & Aroha*, we had many lively discussions about what the protagonists would have for their breakfast. We all agreed that Amiri would be an eggs Benedict man and Aroha more of a muesli and toast girl. There was no doubt in our minds that Hunapo would have eggs and lashings of bacon with black pudding, washed down with a hearty swig of yesterday's beer.

Many people have helped me develop an episodic screenplay into an engrossing novel.

First, I must acknowledge Joyce Cocchi for her tireless enthusiasm and support. Her connection to the story proved legendary, continually challenging my thinking with new insights into character development. Countless times I would heave a sigh of relief after completing a chapter, only to receive an email from Joyce bursting with suggestions for a rewrite. Joyce was invariably right.

Thanks to Nicky Sinclair and Dave Buckeridge for their feedback on my early drafts and Tina Shaw for an initial manuscript assessment that brought fresh insights into the story.

Rebranded as *Gang Girl,* the novel came to life at a masterclass with best-selling Australian author Fiona McIntosh. Her expert guidance on maximising the potential of the opening scene prompted a rewrite of the entire manuscript.

A subsequent in-depth manuscript assessment by Caroline Barron led to another total rewrite and restructuring of the story. Caroline, your contribution was immense.

Sincere thanks to my line and copy editor, Renell Judais, for her meticulous attention to detail and expertise in perfecting the manuscript.

A special shout-out to Renata Curtis, whose stunning cover illustration brilliantly captures the essence of Aroha's spirit. You are an extraordinary talent, Renata, and I am proud to have your work on my cover.

Tēnā koutou. I am eternally grateful to you all.

Above all, heartfelt gratitude to my fantastic family whose engagement was integral to the project. My daughter, Rebecca, played Aroha as a child in the independent film, while my son, Mark, was a legend behind the camera. Both were amongst my most perceptive beta readers. As always, my wife, Siriporn, was the glue behind the scenes, holding everything together.

While *Gang Girl* is a work of fiction, Aroha's struggle reflects that of many extraordinary women I met in the course of my work at Te Karaka. At the heart of the novel, we have a strong woman determined to take charge of her own destiny. In this remote community, many women battle to escape poverty and build a new life for themselves. Their courage is my inspiration and the lifeblood of the story.

Glossary

New Zealand readers will be familiar with many of the Māori words and phrases in the story. For overseas readers and those unfamiliar with the Māori language, the following list defines basic Māori terms. Not included are the Māori words and phrases that are explained within the narrative.

The translation of a Māori word, as with all translations, does not always convey the exact meaning of the original because it lacks the layered cultural and historical context. Many Māori words have more than one meaning. In such cases, the closest definition, within the context of the sentence, is used in this glossary.

Gang life is harsh, and the dialogue inevitably contains some strong language. Māori swear words differ from their European equivalents. Many have a more scatological and less sexual basis. A literal translation of the curses 'kai hamuti', 'pōkokohua', 'pōkōtiwha', 'pūrari paka' and 'whakianga mai' does not convey their intent or their offensive nature. Accordingly, these expletives have been excluded from the Glossary. The vitriol with which the gangsters use these profanities makes their purpose clear. Like the young Aroha, readers may be left uncertain of their exact meaning. They should simply appreciate that they are most unpleasant.

e noho	(phrase) sit down.
e noho rā	(phrase) goodbye—from a person leaving.
haere atu	(phrase) get out.

          David Whittet

haere mai   (phrase) welcome.

haka   (noun) a ceremonial dance or challenge in Māori culture, performed by a group, with vigorous movements, gestures and stamping of the feet and rhythmically shouted accompaniment.

hāngī   (noun) a traditional Māori method of cooking food using heated rocks buried in an earth oven.

hongi   (noun) the pressing of noses in greeting.

hui   (noun) gathering, meeting, assembly.

hūrē   (verb) to say hooray, hurrah, cheer.

iwi   (noun) name given to descendants of kin, tribe, or nation of people related to a specific area.

kai   (noun) food.

kaiāwhina   (noun) assistant, counsel, advocate.

kapa haka   (noun) a Māori performing group.

ka pai   (phrase) fine, good.

ka pai te mahi   (phrase) excellent work.

karakia   (noun) incantation, ritual chant, prayers.

kaumātua   (noun) adult, elder—a person of status within the whānau.

kawakawa   (noun) a native New Zealand tree. The leaves and roots are used as a traditional medicinal plant in Māori medicine.

kia kaha   (phrase) be strong.

kia māia   (phrase) be brave.

kōhine   (noun) girl, female adolescent.

kōkako   (noun) *Callaeas cinerea*—a large, rare forest bird indigenous to New Zealand.

kōkōwai   (noun) red ochre.

korowai   (noun) cloak.

koru   (noun) curled shoot of a fern, a spiral motif.

kōtiro   (noun) girl, daughter.

kutu   (noun) vermin, lice, louse.

māhiti   (noun) cape covered with long white hair of dogs' tails worn over a cloak.

mana   (noun) prestige, authority, influence, status, spiritual power, charisma.

mana tangata whenua   (noun) indigenous rights.

marae   (noun) a communal and sacred meeting ground, a Māori meeting place.

matakite   (noun) diviner, prophet, seer, clairvoyant.

mate paipai	(noun) venereal disease, sexually transmitted disease.
mihi	(noun) speech of greeting, acknowledgement, tribute.
mokopuna	(noun) grandchild, grandchildren.
murua ahau	(phrase) forgive me.
nau mai	(phrase) welcome.
paepae	(noun) orators' bench.
pārekareka	(noun) enjoyment, pleasure, fun.
pikorua	(noun) a twist motif, based on a weave pattern or the fronds of a fern.
poi dancing	(phrase) a dance, usually performed by women holding a weighted ball on a string (the 'poi'), accompanied by singing. The poi is swung in rhythmic movements to accompany the song.
pounamu	(noun) greenstone.
pōwhiri	(noun) the welcome ceremony on a marae.
taiaha	(noun) a long wooden weapon, a fighting staff with one end carved, similar to a spear.
tāku tamaiti	(phrase) my child.
tamariki	(noun) children.

tā moko	(noun) traditional Māori tattooing designs on the face or body done under traditional protocols.
tangata whenua	(noun) people of the land, the indigenous or original people belonging to a place, people born of the area, the local hosts.
tangi	(noun) rites for the dead, a Māori funeral ceremony—shortened form of tangihanga.
taniwha	(noun) monster or spirit form, usually associated with water, which can take many forms, benign or malignant.
tapu	(noun) sacred, forbidden, a religious restriction.
Te Atua	(proper noun) God, a supernatural being or deity.
tēnā koe	(phrase) thank you, hello, greetings. Used as a formal salutation.
tēnā koutou	(phrase) as for tēnā koe, used when there are three or more persons.
tohunga kōkōrangi	(noun) astronomer, an expert in the study of celestial bodies.
toki	(noun) adze, axe, hatchet.
tōku taonga	(phrase) my treasure.
tōtara	(noun) a native tree.

David Whittet

tūī	(noun) a native New Zealand bird.
tūtae	(noun) shit, excrement, faeces.
uhi	(noun) an instrument, usually made of bone, for puncturing the skin, used in Māori tattooing to create the tā moko.
wahine	(noun) woman.
wāhine	(noun, plural) women, wives.
waiata	(noun) song, chant.
waka	(noun) canoe.
wānanga	(noun) wise person, sage, expert, guru, instructor.
whānau	(noun) family, a family group or extended family.
whenua	(noun) land(s), ground, nation.